Unruly
Passions

Unruly Passions

Kate Charles

LITTLE, BROWN AND COMPANY

A *Little, Brown* Book

First published in Great Britain in 1998
by Little, Brown and Company

A CIP catalogue record for this book
is available from the British Library.

ISBN 0 316 64549 4

Typeset in Dante by M Rules
Printed and bound in Great Britain by
Creative Print and Design (Wales), Ebbw Vale

Little, Brown and Company (UK)
Brettenham House
Lancaster Place
London WC2E 7EN

For the Right Reverend Christopher Herbert
with love and thanks

Acknowledgements

This book is quite a departure for me, and I owe a great deal to my friends who read the manuscript and made comments: Suzanne Clackson, Richard Craig, Yvonne Craig, Alison Considine, Deborah Crombie, Christopher Dent, Vanessa Dent, Ann Hinrichs, Jackie Shayler-Webb, Michelle Spring, Marcia Talley, John Tibbs and Lucy Walker. And of course my thanks are due to my agent Carol Heaton and her partner Judith Murray, and my splendid editor Hilary Hale. I am also indebted to various people for their encouragement and specialist knowledge, freely shared: most especially the Rt Revd Christopher Herbert, Bishop of St Albans, who provided first-hand information about the life of an archdeacon.

The Collect for the Fourth Sunday of Easter from *The Alternative Service Book 1980* is copyright © The Central Board of Finance of the Church of England and is reproduced by permission.

Collect for the Fourth Sunday of Easter:

Almighty God,
who can alone bring order
to the unruly wills and passions of sinful men:
give us grace,
> *to love what you command*
> *and to desire what you promise,*
that in all the changes and chances of this world,
our hearts may surely there be fixed
where lasting joys are to be found,
through Jesus Christ our Lord.

Prologue

The two young boys who found the body hadn't been looking for it. Though they were vaguely aware that the police were combing the area for a missing person, fearing foul play, their thoughts were elsewhere on that beautiful June day. They were skiving off school – it was too nice a day to waste, they'd agreed, and they'd headed off towards the river to do a bit of swimming, or perhaps try their luck at catching a fish or two.

The blue car, its windows halfway open, was deep in the woods, down at the end of a dirt track near the river. Though it was midday, it was a very secluded spot, and the boys thought that perhaps a courting couple had discovered their own secret place. They sneaked up on the car, winking at each other. One went on either side of the car, and they prepared to give the couple the scare of their lives.

It didn't work that way. For in the back seat of the car was not an amorous couple but a dead body. There was no doubt that the body was dead, no question of the possibility that the boys had merely caught someone napping. Neither of them had ever seen a corpse before, but they knew that they were looking at death. The place where the knife had gone in was evident if not visible; flies clustered thickly round the stab wound, their buzzing filling the car with an obscene noise. And then there was the smell.

Each boy's face mirrored the horror of the other as they looked first at the body, then across at each other. One of them was screaming; perhaps both of them were. Afterwards they both denied it, of course, and each swaggered about with their friends, boasting that *he* had been the first to see the body, describing it in gruesome detail, joking about his mate's cowardice.

But at that moment it was no joke. The boys fled back through the woods, tripping over the undergrowth and their own feet, seized with a primordial need to escape from the terror of unnatural death.

The story, though, starts some months earlier, before the woods are clothed in the green leaves of summer . . .

Chapter 1

The knife. Rosemary Finch held it up to the light and examined the engraving on the tarnish-blackened handle, then wrapped it carefully in tissue and placed it in a tea chest of similarly wrapped items. She hadn't seen that knife in years; it was certainly too good for everyday use, for the endless cutting-up of cakes and Victoria sponges and flapjack for church teas and parish parties. There were special knives for that purpose, ancient knives with dulled or chipped blades and warped handles. Dozens of them, and they seemed to multiply in the drawer. But this knife was different: a wedding present, from the parish, on the occasion of Rosemary's marriage to their Vicar. Their names and the date of the wedding were engraved on the silver handle. Beribboned, it had been used on that day to cut the wedding cake, then put away. At the time, Rosemary realised, her breath catching in her throat, she and Gervase had probably intended saving it for their children's weddings.

Moving house is usually classified as one of life's great traumas, and when the house being left behind holds the accumulated memories of years, the wrench is even greater. The packing had been going on for days; sometimes it seemed like months to Rosemary, who had found it an emotionally draining process. Each item, each possession, had to be examined and evaluated, its value assessed. Nothing had come into the house by accident, and the meaning behind each thing had to be pondered before it was consigned to the rubbish bin or the jumble sale, or packed up to find a new home with them elsewhere.

And for Gervase, Rosemary thought with a rush of empathy, it was even worse than it was for her. He had been in the house far longer, and it held for him so many memories, not all of them happy. Only he could sort through the contents of his study. He'd been putting it off until the last minute – not that he'd said so, but Rosemary knew him well enough to understand that it was true – and it was bound to be a painful job. The removal men would arrive in the morning; tonight it had to be done, and he was tackling it while she finished up in the kitchen.

The desire to offer her support did battle with the wish not to intrude on his privacy, and overcame it. Abandoning the kitchen, Rosemary crossed the corridor and tapped on the closed door of Gervase's study.

'Yes?' His voice sounded normal. 'Come in.'

Rosemary pushed the door open and leaned in. Gervase was at his desk, facing her, sorting through a stack of old parish magazines. He looked up at her in enquiry, tilting his head down to focus on her over the tops of his half-moon reading glasses, and her heart went out to him in a rush of love. Gervase, with his beautifully ascetic face and his crown of wavy hair. It was silver now, that hair, but just as thick and wavy as it had ever been.

'I wondered how you were doing,' Rosemary said. 'Would you like a cup of tea? I've kept a few mugs out, and of course the kettle will be the very last thing to be packed.'

Gervase smiled. 'Not just yet, my dear. Perhaps a bit later.'

'I'll let you get on, then.' Sensing that he wanted to be left alone, she pulled the door to and stood for a moment in the hallway. The house was quiet – no radio, no television, only the loud tick of the magnificent long-case clock in the corner of the square hall. That clock, the moon now rising on its painted dial, was a relic of Rosemary's childhood. During that childhood it had travelled with her family to a succession of huge old vicarages, turning each one into home as it stood in the hallway, ticking reassuringly through day and night. But when her father died, and her mother moved into a bungalow, the clock had come to Rosemary, bringing with it an echo of her childhood.

This vicarage was nothing like the vicarages of her childhood, of course. It had been built in the sixties, during the era when old vicarages were being sold off wholesale to aspiring middle-class people, to be replaced by new, purpose-built boxes. Victorian vicarages, built in the days when clergymen had tribes of children, were too large for modern clergy families, too expensive to heat, the argument ran, and of course there was something in that. This vicarage *was* warmer than the draughty piles of her childhood, Rosemary acknowledged, but she couldn't help feeling that something had been lost. What memories would her daughter carry with her of this house, where she'd spent all of her life to date?

Daisy. Instinctively Rosemary's ears strained for the sound of Daisy's breathing, but of course she could hear nothing. She crossed the hall, went up the stairs, and pushed on the half-open door of Daisy's room. Daisy hated the dark, and insisted on keeping the door ajar at night, at a precise angle. There was a night-light burning as well, and in its dim glow Rosemary could see her daughter, curled into a foetal ball and sleeping soundly, her arms wrapped round Barry, her teddy. Without knowing that she did so, she smiled and backed out of the door, returning it to its half-open position.

Rosemary went back to the kitchen, intending to resume her packing, but something – something more than procrastination – impelled her to pay a farewell visit to the church. She took the key from its hook, let herself out of the back door and in the dark, guided by instinct and memory, followed the well-travelled path to the large brick edifice which dominated the landscape, and which had likewise dominated her life and that of her family for so many years. A red-brick Victorian church, workmanlike in construction and with no particularly distinguished architectural heritage, it was none the less beautiful in Rosemary's eyes, fitted out as it was in high church trappings, its atmosphere thick with the prayers of a century of worshippers.

There were lights on within, Rosemary could see, and the south porch door was unlocked. Nothing to be alarmed about, she told herself: Gervase had surely locked it earlier, and anyone who was here now had let themselves in with their own key. In the old days, of course, the church had never been locked, day or night, and Gervase preferred it that way. 'It is God's house,' he often said, 'and should be open freely.' But times had changed, and the PCC insisted that sensible precautions had to be taken. The compromise position was that the church should be open during daylight hours, and locked at night.

Rosemary slipped into the church so silently that the woman who was redoing the flowers on the pedestal in front of the rood screen was unaware of her presence for several minutes. She stood at the back and watched Hazel Croom pulling out a few drooping blooms and replacing them with fresh ones, thus ensuring that her arrangement would do for the rest of the week, until she – or the next person on the flower rota – started again from scratch on Saturday.

The white lilies, obligatory for Easter, were still quite fresh, and their heavy perfume was overwhelming, even from a distance. Rosemary breathed deeply, and Hazel Croom turned.

'Rosemary!' She frowned in displeasure. 'You scared the heart out of me, creeping about like that.'

Rosemary came up the aisle towards her. 'I'm sorry,' she apologised. Why, she wondered, did Hazel always make her feel like a recalcitrant schoolgirl? Was it deliberate on Hazel's part – putting her in her place like that – or was it some flaw in her own character? 'The flowers look nice,' she said lamely.

It was at the flowers that Hazel looked, rather than at Rosemary. 'Not bad,' she allowed. 'They'll do till the weekend, at any rate.'

Rosemary's next words were involuntary. 'And we'll be gone.'

'Yes.' Hazel Croom turned to look at her. 'You'll be gone.' It was an accusation, heavy with meaning. 'We shall miss Father Gervase very much.'

The knife twisted. And me? thought Rosemary. What about me? She hated herself for caring, for still craving this woman's approval after all these years, when she knew that she would never have it. And she resented the implication that it was her fault that they were moving, that somehow she was dragging Gervase away against his will. 'And we'll both miss Letherfield, and St Mark's, very much,' she said, knowing that she sounded defensive. 'But I'm afraid that we didn't have any choice.'

'Because of Daisy, you mean?'

Rosemary nodded. 'She's been so unhappy at school. It's been a nightmare, ever since she left the Infants School and moved to the Juniors. Some of the other children have been so cruel. And they just don't have any sort of provision for children with special needs, and no resources – they were insisting that we'd have to send her away to a special school.' Her pain came through in her voice. 'We just didn't know what to do.' She remembered as she said it that Hazel Croom had been one of those who had advocated having Daisy institutionalised, from the time of her birth onwards.

'Yes, well.' Hazel sniffed. 'I'm sure there were . . . other options. There always have been.'

'Daisy is a member of our family,' she said, more sharply than she'd intended, then went on in a more conciliatory voice. 'And the new school is superb. The one in Branlingham.'

'Is it a special school for backward children, then?'

Rosemary flinched; at least Hazel hadn't said 'Mongoloid', though she suspected she'd been thinking it. 'No, it's just the village primary school, but there are several children with special needs. The head teacher is very keen that they should be integrated with other children.'

Hazel pulled out a brown-tinged lily and tossed it into a pail of rejects. 'I'm sure you'll all be very happy,' she said crisply; it was clear that she hoped otherwise.

'The new parish is very nice,' Rosemary said in a hearty voice, sounding to her own ears as though she were trying to convince herself. 'We were so fortunate to find it. The Bishop was so understanding and helpful.'

'I see.'

'It's a lovely mediaeval church,' she went on. 'Not very big, but with some lovely features. And the Vicarage is enormous. The three of us will rattle round in it.'

'I thought there had been some talk of selling the Vicarage,' Hazel probed. 'I'm sure that's what Father Gervase told me.'

'That was the original plan,' explained Rosemary. 'The diocese wanted to sell the old vicarage, and buy a smaller house in the village as a replacement. But there's some pressure group called "Save our Parsonages", dedicated to fighting the sell-off of places like that. They took on the diocese and won, so the Branlingham Vicarage stays. I'm afraid,' she added rue-fully, 'that it's going to be in a terrible state. The old vicar was a bachelor, and only lived in about two rooms. Because they thought they were going to sell it, it hasn't been redecorated at all. And we can't afford to wait to move in, because of the new school term.'

'What a shame,' said Hazel Croom, meaning the opposite. Meaning, if you have the temerity to leave Letherfield, you get what you deserve.

Absently Rosemary stroked the petal of a lily. 'I'm sure it will get done eventually.'

'Don't you know that when you touch lilies, they go brown?' snapped Hazel. To emphasise her point she snatched the lily that Rosemary had just touched out of the arrange-ment, crushed it in her fist, and flung it into the pail. Deliberately she gathered up her paraphernalia. 'I'll finish this tomorrow,' she announced. 'If you're going to stay, you can lock up.'

Hazel had gone. The scent of the crushed lily still pungent in her nose, and the tears still stinging her eyes, Rosemary sat down on the chancel steps. She thought about praying, but knew that her thoughts were in too much of a turmoil to attempt it. Hazel Croom had stirred up so many emotions, so many memories . . . and on this, her last night in Letherfield. When would she see this church again? She knew full well that unwritten church etiquette dictated that they shouldn't return, even for a visit, for several years. Her own parents had always followed that rule to the letter: in Rosemary's child-hood, moving on had meant moving on for good, knowing that there was no chance of revisiting old haunts or renewing old friendships. Gervase, undoubtedly, would feel the same way.

Rosemary's mind went back almost exactly fourteen years,

to the first time she'd ever been in St Mark's. Hazel Croom had been responsible for that; it was something she never let Rosemary forget. 'If it hadn't been for me,' she was fond of saying, 'you wouldn't be here at all.' She closed her eyes and relived that first day.

Rosemary Atkins was a young teacher of English at a secondary school in Long Haddon, a Suffolk market town. Fresh from her vicarage upbringing, with all that that meant, she had naturally enough attached herself to the main parish church in the town centre. Its middle-of-the-road churchmanship was a bit bland, but she attended faithfully.

The deputy head at Rosemary's school was a forceful woman called Hazel Croom. Unmarried and in her early forties, she lived with her parents in Letherfield, a village outside Long Haddon. Unlike most of Rosemary's colleagues, Hazel was a committed church-goer, and to hear her talk, the main upholder of St Mark's in Letherfield. The goings-on at St Mark's were her main topic of conversation in the staff room; everyone, from the head teacher down to the caretaker, was treated to daily stories of her beloved Father Gervase.

Rosemary, as a church-goer herself, was the recipient of even more than the usual quota of St Mark's stories. 'You ought to try it sometime,' Hazel often urged her. 'It's much more interesting than Long Haddon parish church. Father Gervase brings such a wonderful spirit of worship to the place. And of course Laura is such a perfect helpmeet for him. Devotes herself to the parish, she does. Sunday school, flower rota, Mothers' Union, visiting the sick – everything that a vicar's wife should do. Not like that Mrs What's-her-name at Long Haddon parish church,' she sniffed. 'Works in that dentist's surgery. Just not the done thing. I don't know what her husband is thinking, allowing her to have a job like

that. Her place is at his side, working in the parish, and bringing up their children.'

Like water dripping on a stone, Hazel Croom's blandish-
ments worked away at Rosemary. During the Easter school
holiday that year, Rosemary went home to visit her parents,
and when she came back to Long Haddon on the Saturday
night, she resolved to try St Mark's the next morning. Why
not? she told herself. It's only for one Sunday, and Miss Croom
will be pleased.

Besides, it was almost like a soap opera, like listening to *The
Archers*, which she'd done faithfully for as long as she could
remember. Rosemary had heard so much about the sainted
Father Gervase and his perfect family that she was curious to
see these paragons. Then in future when Miss Croom talked
about them, she would be able to picture them properly.

Underestimating the amount of time it would take to get
to Letherfield, Rosemary arrived late, and slipped into a back
pew. She enjoyed the service. With a full complement of
servers, and even incense, it was much more to her taste than
the blandness of Long Haddon parish church – and she
observed the priest with interest. Not quite how she'd pictured Father Gervase, she decided. He was younger and more
callow than she'd expected. An adequate preacher, no more,
with a rather nasal voice.

After the service she found Hazel Croom. Hazel had a bit
of paper in her hand and a frown creasing her forehead.
'What a nuisance,' she was muttering as Rosemary came up
to her. Then she saw her colleague. 'Oh, Miss Atkins! So
you've come to St Mark's at last!'

'Yes, you finally talked me into it.' Rosemary smiled. 'I've
heard so much about Father Gervase that I wanted to see
him for myself.'

Hazel Croom's frown deepened, and the corners of her
mouth went down. 'Oh, it's terrible. Just terrible.'

What?' Rosemary looked at her, puzzled. 'I must admit that I didn't think the sermon was the best I've ever heard, but . . .'

It was Hazel's turn to look bewildered. What are you talking about?'

'Father Gervase's sermon.'

Miss Croom's jaw dropped. 'But *that* wasn't Father Gervase, that was Father Michael, the curate. How could you possibly think that was Father Gervase?'

'Then what . . .'

'But of course, you've been away – you don't know what's happened.' Hazel Croom flourished her piece of paper. 'Didn't you hear the Intercessions? Praying for the repose of the soul of Laura Finch?'

'Oh.' Rosemary stared at her as her mind worked, putting the pieces together. 'Not Father Gervase's wife Laura?'

The other woman nodded solemnly, pressing her lips together.

'But I never knew their last name. I never would have thought . . . What happened?'

'Oh, it was terrible,' reiterated Miss Croom. 'A fortnight ago, it was. You knew she was expecting a baby, a new brother or sister for young Thomas?'

Rosemary nodded; she'd been told, a number of times, that the perfect family was soon to expand.

'It all went wrong. Some sort of blood poisoning, they said. She went into hospital in Long Haddon, feeling poorly, and the next thing she was dead. We buried her last week.'

'Oh . . .' Rosemary let out her breath on a sigh. 'Oh, how dreadful. The poor woman. And poor Father Gervase.'

'That's the point.' Hazel Croom waved her paper again. 'He's beside himself, poor man. Just can't cope with anything. Sits in the Vicarage and cries, and as for young Thomas . . .'

Rosemary's latent maternal instincts surfaced. 'The poor little boy!'

'He's with his grandparents – Laura's parents – at the moment,' Miss Croom informed her. 'I offered to keep him, just for a bit, until Father Gervase is able to cope, but it was felt better that he should go to his grandparents.'

'I'm sure that you're being a great support to Father Gervase,' Rosemary said.

Hazel Croom's lips twisted in a self-satisfied grimace. 'Well, I try to do my bit.' She tapped the paper. 'I've organised a rota for his meals. The women of the parish are taking food in every day.'

'How good of you.'

'Someone has to do it,' Miss Croom said briskly. 'Not that it always goes smoothly. Miss Brown has just told me that she can't manage tomorrow – something about her sister's varicose vein operation. You'd think she could have given me more notice.' She looked up at Rosemary with a calculating expression. 'Of course, *you* could do it.'

'Me? But I don't even *know* Father Gervase.'

'That doesn't matter.' Hazel Croom dismissed the objection with a flick of her wrist. 'You can cook, can't you?'

'Yes, but—'

'I'd do it myself, of course, but tomorrow is Mother's bridge night.' She produced a pen and altered her list, then showed it to Rosemary. 'See, I've put you down for tomorrow night. Monday the twelfth. Some time between seven and half past. Take the food to the Vicarage. Not the *old* vicarage, but the modern one, right next to the church.'

Rosemary gave up. 'What shall I make, then?'

'Oh, it doesn't matter.' Hazel Croom shook her head. 'Father Gervase is a saintly man, not a practical one. He usually eats anything that's put in front of him. But at the moment I don't think he's eating much at all. I've tried to make him eat, but if he doesn't want to . . .'

Returning to her flat, Rosemary perused her cookery book

for something to tempt the palate of a grieving widower. Her vicarage upbringing ensured that she was a competent cook, if not an inspired one; lack of money had always been the limiting factor. Taught well by her mother, she was expert at conjuring up inexpensive meals which could be stretched almost indefinitely to feed as many people as necessary. One extra turned up at the last minute? No problem – add another tin of beans.

But this was different; this was special. Into the night she pored over the book and settled at last on a savoury sausage hotpot, redolent with herbs, and a jam roly-poly. Comfort food.

After school on Monday she nipped round the shops and collected the ingredients. At the butcher's she decided to splurge on his best sausages, rather than the ones she usually had, and when the dish was done she knew it was worth it: it smelled wonderful. If this didn't tempt Father Gervase to eat, nothing would.

Wrapped in newspaper in her basket, the casserole was still hot when Rosemary arrived at St Mark's Vicarage. Her heart thumping with nervousness, she rang the bell.

The man who opened the door wasn't what she'd been expecting, though Rosemary wasn't sure what she *had* been expecting. He looked to be in his late thirties. He was quite tall, and rather thin; he had thick wavy dark hair, parted on the side with a lock drooping over his forehead and worn long – too long – over his ears. His face was elongated in shape and strong-featured, with a sensitive mouth. It was the face and frame, she decided, of a Romantic poet rather than a priest; he should be wearing a cravat and frock-coat rather than that threadbare black clerical shirt. And then she noticed his hands: they were beautiful hands, with long tapering fingers. Definitely the hands of a poet, thought Rosemary, smiling to herself at her fancifulness, her nervousness forgotten. 'Yes?' said Father Gervase, looking at her blankly.

'I've brought your supper,' she said, smiling in what she hoped was a friendly way.

His puzzled look remained. 'Forgive me if I'm being rude, but do I know you?'

Rosemary laughed. 'No, you don't. My name is Rosemary Atkins. I'm . . . new to the parish.' As she said it, she knew that she would not be returning to Long Haddon parish church. 'I work with Miss Croom,' she added.

'Ah.' Father Gervase smiled, and the smile transformed his face. 'I'm beginning to understand.'

'There was something about Miss Brown's sister. Miss Croom asked me to take over,' Rosemary explained. 'Sausage hotpot,' she added, lifting the basket so that the delicious herby scent wafted towards the priest.

'How very kind of you,' Father Gervase said, and though they were stock words – words he'd said a thousand times before, and especially in the past weeks – they were said with an informed sincerity. 'Won't you come in, Miss . . . Mrs . . . Atkins?'

'Miss,' she said. 'Oh, no, I wouldn't want to intrude.'

Father Gervase stepped back and gestured for her to enter. 'It wouldn't be an intrusion at all, it would be a pleasure.'

She couldn't refuse. He took the basket from her and led the way to the kitchen. 'Excuse the mess,' he said in a surprised voice, looking round as if aware of his surroundings for the first time. 'I'm not very good at washing up and that sort of thing.'

That was evident. The kitchen was a disaster area, and Father Gervase had to look for a tiny bit of clear surface to deposit the basket.

'I'm surprised that Miss Croom doesn't do it for you.' The words were out of Rosemary's mouth before she had time to think, and she was immediately sorry she'd said them. They seemed both a betrayal and an impertinence.

But Father Gervase laughed spontaneously, and gave her a conspiratorial look. 'She would, if I would let her in. Not that I haven't had to work hard to keep her out. Miss Croom, and all of the excellent women of the parish. They mean well, of course, and they're very kind, but . . .' His voice trailed off.

'Yes, I understand.' Rosemary felt pleased somehow that he didn't consider her one of them.

'You'll join me for supper?' he urged, taking the casserole from the basket. 'It looks as if there's enough for . . . a whole family.'

'Oh, no. I couldn't possibly,' she said.

'Please. I hate eating alone.' He said it matter-of-factly; it was clear that he meant it and wasn't just being polite.

'Well, then, yes I will,' Rosemary capitulated. 'But only if you'll let me do some washing-up afterwards.'

The meal was a success. Although Father Gervase's appetite wasn't voracious by any means, he ate the sausage hotpot with evident enjoyment, and there wasn't a crumb left of the jam roly-poly.

They talked through the meal, and it stretched out late into the evening. In the back of her mind Rosemary was conscious that she should go, should leave the poor man in peace, but he didn't seem to want her to leave. He offered her coffee, and when it became evident that making it stretched his domestic capacities to the limit, she took over and made it herself, and they drank it at the kitchen table.

Their conversation, while not stilted in the least, was on neutral topics: Rosemary told him of her vicarage childhood, and that led on to the subject of the Church in general. Father Gervase seemed subdued but not melancholy; she sensed that he was trying to avoid the subject of his bereavement, and she had no wish to cause him any pain by mentioning it.

But it was bound to come up. It approached laterally, when

she asked him about his son. 'Miss Croom tells me that you have a little boy,' she said. 'How old is he?'

'Tom is ten next month.' Father Gervase paused. 'A difficult age . . . to lose his mother. And we were so hoping to give him a sister. A little girl . . .' His face creased in pain and he swallowed.

'Oh, I'm so sorry,' Rosemary said impulsively and sincerely.

Her empathy was too much for him. He put his elbows on the table and covered his face with his beautiful poet's hands.

Rosemary had an overpowering urge to take him in her arms, to cradle his head on her breast and to stroke that dark wavy hair. To make it all better, to take his pain away. But of course, being the well-bred vicar's daughter that she was, she did no such thing.

The next day at school, Hazel Croom asked her how she'd got on. 'And what did you think of our Father Gervase, then?'

'Oh, he seemed very nice,' Rosemary said cautiously, sensing that it would be a mistake to admit she'd been in the Vicarage. 'He seemed to appreciate the food.'

'He won't have eaten it, you know,' Miss Croom stated with smug confidence. 'He's completely helpless. Laura always had to stand over him to make sure he ate enough to keep body and soul together. And now that he's on his own, it's hopeless. He needs someone to look after him. He may be a great scholar, and a priest of great spirituality, our Father Gervase, but he hasn't a practical bone in his body.' She paused, considering. 'He should marry again, even though no one can replace dear Laura. Thomas needs a mother, the poor little scrap. And Father Gervase needs a wife.'

Now, fourteen years later, Rosemary Finch sat on the chancel steps remembering all of that. It had been several years after that before she had realised whom Hazel Croom had had in mind for the role of Gervase's new wife. At the time it had simply not occurred to her. Was it because Hazel was so much older than Gervase? In fact, though, Rosemary now realised, Hazel wasn't really more than a few years his senior. Fourteen years ago Gervase had been nearly forty, and Hazel surely had been just the other side of that milestone. She had always *seemed* old to Rosemary, but that was a trick of perception. Hazel Croom was a deputy head, and that position of authority, combined with her naturally domineering personality and her spinsterish air, had made her seem ancient in the eyes of a young woman in her mid twenties.

And of course now that Rosemary understood Hazel's ambitions regarding Gervase, her behaviour had a rational explanation: Hazel's coldness towards her, her subtle and sometimes not-so-subtle undermining of her in the parish over the years, all made sense in that context. Hazel's grievance against her, nurtured in secret, went back far beyond Rosemary's recent sin of being responsible for their imminent departure from St Mark's. That should have made her dislike easier to cope with, but somehow it didn't.

Rosemary had known from the beginning, of course, that Hazel had not approved of her marriage to Gervase, but at the time she had attributed it to Hazel's loyalty to the dead Laura. Hazel and Laura had been friends. Laura had been perfect . . .

Shaking her head to clear it of these thoughts, Rosemary got up from the chancel steps and went to switch off the lights. It didn't matter any more. She and Gervase were leaving St Mark's, leaving to start a new life in a new parish.

The church door closed behind Rosemary with finality, a symbolic closing of a chapter of her life. Unexpectedly her heart lifted: perhaps this move would be a positive one. She would do her best to make it so, for Gervase and herself as well as for Daisy.

Rosemary turned the key in the church door and went

home to tackle the rest of the packing. Her elevated mood didn't last long, though; she passed through the kitchen, intending to check on Gervase, and as she switched on the light in the corridor she caught a glimpse of herself in the hall mirror. There were spots of high colour in her cheeks after her recent run-in with Hazel Croom. Oh, why did she blush so? It put her at such a disadvantage with people like Hazel. She rubbed at the red spots but that only made them redder. Rosemary sighed, dissatisfied as always with her appearance. Her fine, mouse-coloured hair, worn long, hung limply round her face; usually she plaited it but today there hadn't been time for such things. Her fringe was getting too long, bumping the tops of her spectacles; she'd have to trim it soon. And the roundness of her large spectacles only drew attention to the narrowness of her face.

The door of Gervase's study was ajar, so she went in. Gervase was still sitting at his desk, just as she'd left him a short while ago. But having just relived their first meeting, Rosemary looked at her husband differently: not only the colour of his hair had changed, she now realised. He no longer had the face of a poet. Now Gervase Finch had the face of a mediaeval saint, one of the Desert Fathers perhaps, purified by pain. Then Rosemary noticed that instead of a pile of parish magazines, he was looking at a photograph, holding it in his tapering fingers. From where she was standing Rosemary could see that it was a photograph of Laura. Laura had been beautiful.

Gervase raised his head; there were tears in his eyes.

Laura had been beautiful, but Laura was dead. Rosemary was his wife now. She did what she had longed to do fourteen years earlier: she went to Gervase and took him in her arms, cradling his head on her breast and stroking his wavy hair, now silver.

Chapter 2

The phone on the Archdeacon's bedside table rang before the alarm went off. Margaret Phillips was half awake, waiting for the alarm; on this Monday morning it had been set half an hour earlier than absolutely necessary so that she and Hal could make love. The life of the Archdeacon of Saxwell was a busy one, and sometimes that was the only way.

The phone was on Margaret's side of the bed. She groaned and reached for it. 'Hello?'

The voice on the other end sounded distraught. 'Oh, hello. This is Eric Hedges. I'm so sorry to be bothering you this early, but something terrible has happened.'

Margaret sighed. The Archdeacon's day was going to begin earlier than planned, and not in the way she'd hoped.

Breakfast at the Archdeacon's house was usually a rushed affair, especially if Margaret and Hal had lingered in bed until the last minute, as they often did. This morning, as was customary, Hal made toast and put it in the rack while Margaret showered. A fresh pot of tea had just been conveyed into the breakfast room when she appeared, dressed for the day.

The Venerable Margaret Phillips, Archdeacon of Saxwell,

looked severe in her clericals, a force to be reckoned with, as indeed she was. She would not have been promoted to the office of Archdeacon at the age of forty-six – one of the very first women to attain that office in the Church of England – had she not been out of the ordinary. Her gifts were prodigious: she had intelligence, organisational flair, an insightful nature, and a sensible approach to life. And if there was, perhaps, a faint presumption of superiority in her manner, without a suspicion of false modesty, and a hint of bossiness, those too were characteristics of a successful archdeacon. Though there were naturally those who were opposed to a woman as archdeacon, just on principle, almost everyone who knew Margaret agreed, publicly as well as privately, that for once the Church of England had got it right. Margaret Phillips was a natural archdeacon.

And black suited her, her husband Hal thought as she came into the room. While other women priests wore specially made clerical blouses in pastel colours or even flowery prints by Laura Ashley or Liberty, Margaret preferred to stick to traditional black. Somehow the simplicity of the black emphasised her womanly curves better than something fussier and more feminine would have done. And the black, with the white clerical collar, set off her striking colouring. Margaret's still-smooth skin was milky white, her large and prominent eyes were a clear bright blue, and her hair was extraordinary: once it had been black, but now it was true salt-and-pepper, and curled about her head in profusion, electrified, thick and wiry as steel wool. She wore it chin length, rather than cropped short, but tamed it into submission with clips and combs which held it off her face.

Margaret was not a tall woman, but she had a quality about her that commanded attention, and she radiated energy even at this early hour of the morning.

'Cereal?' suggested Hal.

'No time, I'm afraid.' Margaret's voice was low-pitched and pleasing. She sat down and reached for a piece of toast.

Hal poured her a cup of tea. 'What's this all about, then?' He'd still been asleep when the phone had rung and hadn't really taken it in.

'Eric Hedges,' she said crisply, buttering her toast. 'You know, that silly old fusspot at Hardham Magna.'

Margaret had been in her post less than a year, so they were both still getting to know the clergy who fell within her jurisdiction. 'Oh, yes, I remember him,' Hal confirmed. 'Tall and thin. The one who came to see you in hysterics because the mother-and-toddlers group left the church hall looking like a tip.'

'That's the one.' Margaret shook her head at the memory. 'But this time he really does have a legitimate problem, I'm afraid. Someone's broken into the church.'

'Oh, Lord. Anything stolen?' Anticipating her need, Hal handed his wife the marmalade.

She spooned some onto her plate. 'Not much, apparently. A cross and candlesticks from the altar – brass, not very valuable. At least the old fool had the sense to keep the silver locked up. And they took the little wooden box with the post-card and parish magazine money, he said. Probably all of about two pounds fifty.'

'Well, that's all right, then.' His wife taken care of, Hal poured his own tea.

'But that wasn't the worst of it,' Margaret went on. 'They smashed a stained glass window to get in. Rather a nice one, I'm afraid.'

Hal frowned. 'What a nuisance.'

'Apparently it happened during the night. Eric locked up after Evensong, he says, and this morning when he went in to say Morning Prayer, it had happened. He was in a bit of a state, as you can imagine,' she added wryly. 'I have to get over there as soon as I can and try to calm him down.'

'Something you'll do to perfection, I have no doubt,' her husband said with only a hint of irony. Margaret *was* good at such things, and he knew it. If only, a naggingly persistent inner voice sometimes said, Margaret weren't quite *so* perfect, so self-assured, so inevitably right. It wasn't always comfortable being married to a perfect woman.

'And I have meetings the rest of the day,' Margaret went on. 'So I won't be home until probably close to seven.'

Hal buttered a piece of toast. 'What would you like for dinner tonight?'

'It doesn't matter.' Margaret smiled and consciously echoed his words. 'Whatever you make will be wonderful, I have no doubt.' It was such a relief to her that Hal liked to cook, had indeed discovered that he had a real talent for it, and was better at it than she'd ever been. Coming home from a long and difficult day to a delicious meal was a joy. 'Every archdeacon should have a wife,' she added, her generously proportioned mouth widening from a smile to a grin.

Hal grinned back at her, displaying his beautiful white teeth; that grin was one of the most attractive things about this very attractive man and they *both* knew it. 'Very droll, my dear.'

Margaret knew that she needed to go, but she preferred her husband's company to that of Eric Hedges. She poured herself another cup of tea; the Reverend Mr Hedges could wait a few minutes longer. 'And what do you have on today, then?'

'I'm finishing up that job in Stowmarket,' he told her. 'It should take me most of the morning, I reckon. And in the afternoon I have to go to Elmsford to do an estimate for what could potentially be quite a big job. It seems that Valerie Marler wants her house decorated,' he added, watching Margaret's face.

She raised her eyebrows. 'Valerie Marler! *The* Valerie Marler?'

'Of course. You must know that she's the local celebrity in Elmsford.'

'It would be difficult not to know that, as many times as she's had her photo in the local paper,' Margaret said drily, sipping her tea. 'Valerie Marler, bestselling author of upmarket novels for women, cutting the ribbon to open the Elmsford church fête. Or the new supermarket. Or even the new petrol station. Well, I suppose someone's got to do it. And she's certainly more photogenic than most.'

'Is she? I hadn't noticed,' Hal grinned. While it was conceded by the literary establishment, who did not concede such things lightly, that Valerie Marler was a talented writer, no one denied the fact that much of her celebrity owed itself to her beauty. There was an ethereal, elfin quality about her that came across wonderfully well on television, and even in the grainy photos of a local paper.

'Liar.' Margaret smiled back at him over the rim of her teacup.

'You're not worried, are you?' Hal reached across the table and touched her hand. 'Why should I be interested in some anorexic waif when I'm married to the most beautiful and desirable woman in the world?'

'Now I *know* you're lying,' Margaret laughed. 'But what if she throws herself at you, like all of those other women have done?' Her husband's attractiveness, and the fact that he was doing a job that often put him in the homes of lonely women, meant that Hal Phillips regularly received propositions, some subtle and some not at all so. But Margaret knew that as long as he came home and told her about them, even laughed with her about them, she had nothing to worry about.

'I shall gently but firmly tell her no,' Hal assured her. 'Just as I always do.'

'Just as long as you don't tell *me* no as well.' Margaret put her napkin back in its silver ring and got up.

'Not a chance.' Hal stood too. 'Come here.'

She went to her husband and kissed him lingeringly. 'Tonight,' she promised as she pulled away.

'I'll hold you to that, Archdeacon.' Hal watched her go, looking forward to the fulfilment of his wife's promise.

Valerie Marler was up early as well, in her picturesque seventeenth-century thatched cottage. It wasn't really a cottage – it was far too spacious and had too many rooms to qualify, but her public liked the thought of her living in a cottage, and she was happy to indulge them in this fiction. 'Rose Cottage, Elmsford, Suffolk' was her mailing address, and to that address each day the overburdened local postman carried bundles of letters expressing everything from admiration to adulation.

Valerie was a disciplined writer. Though she lived alone at Rose Cottage, she liked to follow a routine, getting up early to write before the distractions of the day began to intrude. Sustained by the carafe of hot black coffee which she kept beside her computer, she could get through at least a thousand words – or fifteen hundred, on a good day – before the post arrived. Then she'd eat a piece of dry toast, washed down with more coffee, while she opened and sorted the post.

She kept a silver letter knife on the kitchen table for the purpose. The table was large, enabling her to create efficient piles of post. There were bills, of course, which Valerie always paid immediately so that she wouldn't have to worry about missing their due dates. There was usually a fairly substantial stack of business correspondence from publishers, from agents, and from organisations that wanted something from her: a signed photo for a charity auction, her presence to do the honours at some ribbon-cutting; these she would reply to before the day was out. One category of post went straight into the bin: those inevitable crank letters, asking for money, frequently, or suggesting that she and the (male) letter writer should meet for activities that were often described in excruciating detail. These epistles made her shudder, as much because of their poor spelling and execrable grammar as for the unsavoury nature of their contents. So into the bin they went, not deserving a reply.

But the largest pile was always the one of letters from her admiring readers, telling her how much they had enjoyed a particular novel, or indeed all of her books. Sometimes those books had changed their lives, inspiring them to strike out on some new endeavour, or getting them through a rough patch when nothing seemed to be going right for them. Valerie Marler loved these letters. No matter how many of them she got, each one was a thrill for her, a fresh voice affirming her worth. She *knew* that she was a good writer, that her books sold in the hundreds of thousands, but the fact that someone – an ordinary person in an ordinary house somewhere in Britain, or in many instances somewhere in America or an even more far-flung locale – had taken the time to sit down and write to her, to pour out their innermost feelings, was a never-ending source of joy. And every one of those letters was answered with care, not with a mere form letter cranked out of her computer. That usually took Valerie the better part of the day, but she never begrudged the time spent on so pleasurable and important a task.

Early on this Monday morning, well before the postman was due, Valerie Marler was at her computer, in her snug book-lined study on the ground floor of Rose Cottage, the room in which the last few of her bestsellers had been written. Last Friday's post had brought a colour proof of the jacket design for the new book, and she'd propped it up next to the computer to inspire her. It didn't matter that the book had only barely been started; publishers needed plenty of lead time for all of these things. This jacket would be displayed in sales reps' catalogues long before Valerie had typed the last full stop, and on posters in the London Underground well before the publication date, nearly a year hence.

The Path Not Chosen was the title: a good one, she thought. Pithy, evocative, and intriguing. She picked up the colour photocopy and examined it. The art department had come up with a new look for her jackets, abandoning the previously successful use of the misty watercolour beneath her name – in large blocky type – and the title, in smaller but equally dignified type. This one was quite different: a monochrome greenish photo of a wood rather than a watercolour and an informal typeface which made her name and the title look as though they had been written by hand. She'd rung her editor and demanded to know why the change had been made. Publishing trends were changing, always changing, Warren had explained. The type of books Valerie Marler wrote, so long at the top of the bestseller lists, were beginning to show a slippage in sales figures. A more contemporary look was what was required, just to keep pace with the times.

But Valerie didn't want to think about sales figures, especially not at this hour of the morning. It was someone else's job to worry about sales figures. She was here to write. And what she was about to write was a pivotal episode, taking place in those woods which were pictured on the book jacket. She'd started the book with all of the obligatory scene-painting, sketching in the background of her heroine Cecily and her family. Cecily lived in a village on the edge of the forest with her husband Oliver, a boring chap with a boring job. Their marriage was not dramatically unhappy, merely boring; Cecily couldn't really put her finger on what was wrong, and Oliver didn't really care. They had two children, both of whom were conveniently away at boarding school so as not to clutter up the plot, but still available to be called in if necessary.

Now Cecily is walking in the woods, thinking about her life and what she might have done differently. She goes round a bend into a glade, and comes face to face with an exceptionally good-looking man, whom she recognises as Toby, her first love, rejected years ago when he was poor and struggling. Now, of course, he is rich and successful, and just as handsome as ever, if not more so.

Valerie tried to picture Toby as he would appear to Cecily. The face that appeared in Valerie's mind was that of her own current lover, Shaun.

Shaun, like most of Valerie's men, was someone she'd met professionally. He was in fact her publicist, assigned by her publishers, the Robin's Egg imprint of the multinational publishing conglomerate GlobeSpan, to promote the books of Valerie Marler. It was only fitting that she should have her own publicist; her books were Robin's Egg's hottest property, securing their niche within the vast GlobeSpan empire. After all, Valerie Marler was one of the most successful practitioners in the genre of women's novels: more respectable than romances though not quite considered literary fiction, they chronicled the lives of upper-middle-class women, and were read almost exclusively by other upper-middle-class women – or those who aspired to be so – who bought them in the millions. Shaun looked after her interests, with the aim of ensuring that everyone in the civilised world would eventually have heard of Valerie Marler. A few months earlier he had begun paying discreet weekend visits to Rose Cottage.

Valerie's fingers hovered over the keyboard, then the words began to come. 'The sun filtered through the over-arching trees, dappling the ground with patches of light. Cecily was so used to being alone in the woods with her own musings that for an instant she thought it was a trick of the light. But no, it was a man walking towards her. He was tall and slender and extremely good-looking. His curly hair was a reddish-gold colour, bright as flame when he walked through a patch of sun, and as he drew nearer she could see the clear sky-blue colour of his eyes, eyes that could belong to only one person. Toby, she thought, her heart doing a flip-flop.

'"Cecily." He spoke her name softly, in the caressing way he had used to say it, the Irish lilt of his voice . . .'

No, that wouldn't do. Irish wouldn't do at all. Valerie stopped, frowning, and reached for her coffee mug.

The phone rang. Startled, Valerie looked at the clock; it was barely half-past six. No one rang at this hour of the morning unless it was an emergency. She lifted the receiver. 'Hello?'

'Hello, darlin',' said Shaun, his Irish lilt intensified somehow on the phone. This annoyed Valerie; Shaun was an educated man, not bog-Irish, but sometimes, particularly on the phone, he sounded it, and she suspected him of putting it on for effect.

'Shaun! What on earth is the matter?'

He chuckled. 'Nothing's the matter, darlin'. I just wanted to tell you how much I enjoyed the weekend. It was grand. And I can't wait to see you again.'

'Why are you ringing me now?' Valerie demanded in a barely civil voice.

'I knew you'd be up. And I wanted—'

She cut across his words coldly. 'I'm working, Shaun. And I've told you *never* to ring me when I'm working. Not ever.' She put the phone down and glared at the offending instrument. Shaun really was beginning to get a bit tiresome. And he wasn't really *that* good looking; her fictional description of him had been a vast exaggeration.

Valerie wasn't even sure that he was all that good at his job. At first she'd thought he was terrific, her perception swayed by his own self-proclaimed opinion of his talents. But just the past week she had been on a tour to promote her latest book, and it had not been the triumph that her previous tours had been, before Shaun's time. In fact there had been one disaster after another: books that hadn't arrived in time, interviewers who hadn't shown up, limousines that had run late. None of it her fault, of course. Shaun was the one who was supposed to see to these things, and the responsibility for the screw-ups was squarely at his doorstep.

But Shaun *had* accomplished one thing recently. He had pulled a few strings, called in a few favours and managed a real coup: Valerie Marler was to be on the cover of *Hello!* magazine, accompanying a long pictorial story focusing on her life at Rose Cottage. In a month's time they would be sending a photographer to Elmsford to take innumerable photos of her seated at the computer in her book-lined study, whipping up a few tasty morsels in the kitchen, and taking her well-earned rest in the sitting room. It was a wonderful opportunity. But a few days earlier Valerie had taken a clear-eyed look round Rose Cottage and decided that it wouldn't do. She'd been there nearly five years, and after the first few months had done no decorating at all. It was beginning to look a bit tired, and at the very least needed a lick of paint. Perhaps she'd be even more ambitious and have some wall-papering done, or some special paint effects in one or two of the rooms – nothing too disruptive to her work or her rou-tine, as she really did need to get on with this book.

Over the weekend she'd asked Shaun to find her a painter and decorator, and Shaun had, as in all things, obliged. She wasn't sure whether he'd used the Yellow Pages, or somehow managed to get a recommendation, but he had arranged it all, and a Mr Phillips was to call this afternoon to have a look and give her an estimate. Not that she cared what it would cost, but she needed to know how long it would take, and she wanted to be sure that Mr Phillips was the sort of man she might feel comfortable about allowing the free run of Rose Cottage. She didn't want some spotty youth who would play loud music on his radio, drink lager with his lunch or make a mess. No, she wanted a nice quiet older man who would get about his business neatly and without intruding on her life. She might make him the occasional cup of tea or coffee, but otherwise she could just forget about him.

The day was going well, after the upsetting intrusion of Shaun's early phone call. Valerie had written her thousand words – that crucial thousand words, in which Toby re-entered Cecily's life – and had breakfasted and sorted her post. After a leisurely bubble-bath, her reward to herself for her labours, she had dressed as she usually did when she was staying at home, in comfortable casual clothes, and had pulled her hair back into a ponytail; if she'd been planning to go out, even just down to the village shop, she would have taken more care with her appearance, but there was no need to put on make-up or smart clothes for the decorator.

She had paid all of the bills from the morning's post, dealt with the business correspondence, by phone where possible, and had boiled an egg for her lunch. Then came the pleasurable part of the day, the part she deliberately saved for last, so that she might look forward to it while dealing with the more tedious matters. Valerie carried the stack of fan letters to her study and began to answer them.

Early in her career, when there weren't so many of them, she had handwritten her replies to her fan mail. But that was no longer practical; she had to use her computer. Shaun had suggested that she might hire a secretary to deal with the volume of letters she received. That was out of the question, and Valerie had told him so; clearly he didn't understand how important it was to her, this ritual, this direct contact with those whose lives she had touched.

Some of them asked for a signed photo. She had a huge stack of them at the ready. It was a good photo, taken by Jerry Bauer, the internationally known specialist in author photos for book jackets. He had captured the elfin quality of her beauty to perfection: her silver-blond hair floated round her face like a gossamer cloud, her shapely lips were softly parted, and her widely spaced blue eyes looked out with candour.

Valerie picked up the first letter. It was on the top of the pile because she'd been unsure whether it belonged here or in the bin, but she'd decided to give Derek the benefit of the doubt. Derek, the letter told her in the scrawl and with the spelling of one who didn't spend much time with a pen in his hand, was sixteen years old and thought she was the most beautiful woman in the world. His mum liked her books, and told him he should read one, but he wasn't much of a one for reading and would rather look at her photo. Would she send him one? Valerie took a photo from the stack and inscribed it: 'To Derek with love from Valerie Marler'. She didn't want to think about what Derek would be doing with the photo.

Most of the others were more straightforward, and she tackled them with enthusiasm, losing track of the time. When the doorbell rang she looked up, startled, at the clock. Of course – it was time for Mr Phillips to call.

Valerie got up and went to answer the bell.

The white-overalled man on the other side of the door was neither a loutish youth nor a tidy old man. He was somewhere in between – in his forties, she judged – and one of the most attractive men that Valerie, who surrounded herself with attractive men, had ever seen. He wasn't tall, but an active life had kept his compact, muscular body trim. His hair was short but thick, a deep honey-gold colour, and he had extraordinary eyes of dark, brownish hazel in a tanned face; that unseasonal tan, Valerie surmised in the split-second she had to think about it, was probably the result of working out-doors. Then he smiled at her, and involuntarily Valerie caught her breath. It was a devastating smile: it revealed beautiful straight teeth, blindingly white against the tan, and the crinkles that formed at the corners of his eyes only increased the effect.

What a waste, thought Valerie in another split-second, that such a gorgeous man should be a mere painter and decorator, and thus beyond the pale. Valerie was aware that some women enjoyed 'a bit of rough trade', but she was far too fastidious for that. She, in common with the heroines of her novels, only slept with men of her own class. The difference was that Valerie went to bed with them readily, while her worthy upper-middle-class heroines agonised about it for at least a hundred pages before succumbing; otherwise there would have been no story.

He looked into her eyes in a way that in any other tradesman she would have considered insolent, but all that Valerie Marler could think of, absurdly, was the fact that she'd never seen eyes quite that colour before: how would she describe them?

Then he spoke. 'Miss Marler? I'm Hal Phillips. I believe you're expecting me?' His voice was not the rustic Suffolk drawl she'd anticipated; it was pure Oxbridge, cultured and beautifully modulated.

Valerie Marler's lips parted and her eyes widened, staring at him.

He seemed to understand, and the devastating grin returned. 'Perhaps you *weren't* expecting me,' he said drily.

With an effort she recovered. 'Mr Phillips, of course. Do come in.'

Valerie showed him all over Rose Cottage, from the flag-stoned entry hall to her white-carpeted bedroom. He took measurements and made notes on a pad of paper as she admired his strong, square-fingered hands; there was a gold band on the left one, she noticed. When he'd finished she offered him a cup of coffee, and he accepted. She drank one with him at the kitchen table.

Later, when he'd gone, she lingered at the table, drinking another cup of coffee. Hal Phillips, she said to herself, looking into the murky black coffee and seeing only those white teeth against a tanned face.

Valerie tried to remember what they'd talked about, but uncharacteristically for her she couldn't recall many details of the conversation. She'd done most of the talking, she thought, explaining to him about the *Hello!* cover story. He'd been polite, and seemed interested, but her efforts to draw him out, to discover who he was and why he was working as a decorator, hadn't been very successful. It wasn't that he'd refused to answer her questions; he just seemed to evade them somehow, and now she had no more secure sense of who Hal Phillips was than she'd had when she'd opened the door and seen him for the first time.

And what did he think of *her*? He had said, in a joking way, that she didn't look like her photos. She'd been suddenly self-conscious, then, about her appearance: the casual clothes and the hair pulled back from her face. Oh, why hadn't she at least put on some make-up?

Remembering, finally, that she had been interrupted in her routine of answering her fan mail, Valerie put the coffee cups in the dishwasher and returned to her study. She sat at the computer and looked at the half-written letter on the screen, her mind not at all on the words of gracious acknowledgement.

Valerie closed the file and called up the one she'd been working on early that morning. She scrolled to the passage where Cecily and Toby met in the depths of the woods, highlighted a large section of the text, and hit the delete key. Toby, in his Shaun-like incarnation, disappeared.

Her fingers paused over the keys for a moment, then Valerie began to write.

'The sun filtered through the over-arching trees, dappling the ground with patches of light. Cecily was so used to being alone in the woods with her own musings that for an instant she thought it was a trick of the light. But no, it was a man walking towards her. Though he was not tall, he was muscular and well built, and extremely good-looking. His sleek, short hair was the colour of dark honey, sparking with golden highlights when he walked through a patch of sun, and as he drew nearer she could see the colour of his eyes.'

Here Valerie paused, considering for a moment, then went on. 'Those eyes were distinctive, an unusual hazel colour, brown with mossy-green undertones, the exact colour of the ancient Barbour jacket he wore, and they could belong to only one person. Toby, she thought, her heart doing a flip-flop. He smiled at her then, that devastating smile – white teeth against tanned face – which had never failed to melt her insides, and she felt her heart rising to her throat.

'"Cecily." He spoke her name softly, in the caressing way he had used to say it, his cultured voice drawing out the syllables."'

Valerie Marler reread what she'd written, nodded and smiled at the screen.

Chapter 3

The next morning, Valerie Marler rose at her usual time and went back to her computer. Things were going well: Cecily and Toby's meeting was about to have repercussions for both of them, and Valerie couldn't wait to get on with it.

Originally she had thought that Toby, his heart still belonging to Cecily, would not have married. But now she decided that Toby should have a wife. It would complicate things still further, and make the story more interesting.

What sort of woman would Toby's wife be? Perhaps he had married above him, a grand, snooty sort of woman with a pedigree stretching back to the Conquest and an unlimited chequebook to match. That could be the source of Toby's wealth: he had married money, rather than earning it by the sweat of his brow. That would make it more difficult to ditch his wife for Cecily.

Valerie decided to call her Pandora, the Honourable Pandora, daughter of an earl. She would be unpleasant, manipulative, and not at all inclined to let Toby get away. While Cecily's husband Oliver was just plain boring, Pandora would be far worse than that, and a worthy adversary.

The time whizzed by; Valerie was surprised to find, when

she glanced at the clock, that she'd done more than her oblig-
atory two hours. She saved the file, picked up the cold mug of
coffee that she'd poured and never drunk, and went to the
kitchen to make a fresh pot.

On the way she collected the morning paper, as the post
had not yet arrived. While the water boiled for the coffee,
she opened the paper to the arts pages; she had recently done
an interview – arranged by Shaun, of course – with a journalist from this paper, and was expecting to see it written up.
Yes – there was the Jerry Bauer photo, surrounded by several
columns of interview.

She'd felt that the interview had gone well, so it was with a
sense of dislocated shock that she read the words on the page.
The journalist, a woman who had seemed sensitive and interested in what she had to say, had twisted Valerie's words so
that she sounded vacuous and conceited. The article dripped
with vitriol and spite.

Shaun's fault, yet again, Valerie raged. Why on earth had
he agreed to this woman's request for an interview? He
should have done his homework better, should have protected
her from this dreadful attack.

And there was worse to come. In a sidebar next to the
interview was a review of her new book, and the reviewer
had not liked it. 'Valerie Marler seems to have lost her deft
touch with characterisation,' the review declared. 'To call her
characters wooden would be an insult to wood. And her sex
scenes verge on the ludicrous.'

Valerie had never before received a negative review, and
couldn't believe how much it hurt. Consciously she pushed
the feelings aside, told herself that it didn't matter. It was the
reviewer's problem, not hers: she had missed the point of the
book, hadn't seen what she was trying to do. She was a cretin
who didn't deserve her plum job as book reviewer for a
national paper. Valerie would not let it bother her.

With relief she heard the click of the letterbox as the post fell onto the mat. Deliberately she folded the paper and put it in the waste bin, then went to fetch the post.

She sorted through it quickly. Hal Phillips had suggested that he might put some figures on paper and send them to her, to arrive in the morning post, then call round later to discuss them.

Valerie knew it was the right envelope even before she opened it. The address on the front was bold and black, masculine, written with a felt-tipped pen: just the sort of writing she would expect, and very different from that which characterised her female readership.

She slit the envelope, drew out the paper, and scanned it eagerly, not because she was interested in its contents – she could afford to pay whatever it would cost, and would do so gladly – but in the hopes that his writing would reveal to her something about Hal Phillips. The numbers were written in the same distinctive hand, bold, yet neat and precise.

She looked at the heading of the notepaper. It had been professionally printed as business stationery. 'Hal Phillips', she read, 'Painting and Decorating, The Archdeaconry, Saxwell, Suffolk'. Below there were numbers for phone, fax and mobile phone.

This was instructive. Saxwell she knew: it was the nearest market town, only about six miles away.

But what about The Archdeaconry? That didn't make sense. Hal Phillips was a painter, not an archdeacon. Then she realised that it was probably an ancient designation, like The Old Vicarage in Elmsford. No vicar had lived there for years, but the old name carried with it a certain cachet which made it worth retaining.

Valerie took the paper with her as she went into her bathroom and drew a bath. The tub was an old-fashioned claw-footed one, long and deep; Valerie adjusted the water temperature carefully and added a generous dollop of expensive aromatherapy bath oil – purple, the sensual one. Hanging her dressing gown on the back of the door, she stepped into the steaming bath and luxuriated in the scented warmth of the water. In her hand she still had the piece of paper, held carefully above the water. As she leaned back in the bath she stared at it, studied it, as if in looking at it long enough she would be able to fathom the man.

After her bath she went into her bedroom and dressed carefully. Today there would be no casual clothes, no unbecoming hair-style. She chose a pair of black leggings, pencil-slim, which showed off her slender, shapely legs and her flat stomach, and topped them with a loose silk tunic in a rich turquoise colour, complementing her eyes. Skilfully she applied a curling iron to her hair, surrounding her face with a tumbled mass of silver-blond curls, then spent time on her make-up, enhancing the effect of the turquoise shirt with a very subtle touch of eye shadow and emphasising her cheekbones with the merest hint of blusher. She didn't want to look as if she'd taken any particular care with her appearance; the effect was to be natural, as if she were just allowing her own beauty to shine through.

When she'd finished Valerie surveyed herself critically in the mirror. Yes, just right, she decided. Casual, unstudied, yet elegant. She was ready.

At the Vicarage in Branlingham, the day was starting in quite a different way. It would be Daisy Finch's first day at her new school.

While Gervase went to the church to say the Morning Office, Rosemary prepared her daughter for the big day. She helped Daisy to dress in the pretty new frock that her own mother had sent to her granddaughter as an Easter present:

wide pink-and-white candy stripes, like a stick of rock. Pink was Daisy's favourite colour, and she loved her new dress.

'Will the other girls have a dress as pretty as this?' she chirped. Her speech, though slightly difficult to understand to an untrained ear, was perfectly comprehensible to her mother; Rosemary, trained as a teacher, had in fact worked with her since her infancy, so that she spoke much more clearly than many children with Down's syndrome.

'Oh, I shouldn't think so, my darling. This is a very special dress,' Rosemary assured her, doing the buttons up the back.

'Granny sent it to me.'

'Yes, she did. And I've told Granny how much you like it.' Thank goodness for Granny, Rosemary thought. Daisy was her only grandchild, and she adored her. Though Rosemary's mother was not well off, on her clergy widow's pension, she lived frugally and enjoyed spending money on little treats for her granddaughter. It was a great help to Rosemary, who found it difficult to stretch Gervase's clergy stipend to do more than cover the basics of existence. And money would be even tighter now, as they had this huge house to heat. They would just have to shut rooms off and hope for an early hot summer.

Rosemary knelt down to brush Daisy's hair; it was a darker brown than her own, but just as fine and straight, falling to her shoulders, and she too had a fringe. Daisy had also inherited Rosemary's near-sightedness, and had worn spectacles from the age of four. They gave her an owlish air, magnifying the already enormous and moist dark eyes of a Down's syndrome child. 'Can I have the pink ribbons?' she asked.

'Yes, of course.' Her mother tied them into her hair, then leaned back to survey the result. 'You look beautiful,' she said gravely.

Daisy pirouetted in front of her, smiling in delight. She was a happy child, and an affectionate one. 'I love you,

Mummy,' she announced, flinging herself into Rosemary's arms and giving her a moist kiss.

Rosemary held her close, in a fierce maternal embrace. 'And I love you, my darling Daisy,' she said.

She *did* love Daisy, profoundly, which didn't mean that it was always easy being the mother of a handicapped child. The unpleasant business at the old school had been as painful for Rosemary as it had been for her daughter. And it wasn't likely to be the last time that such things happened.

Only occasionally now did Rosemary recall the distress she and Gervase had felt when they'd realised that their much-wanted and adored baby was not perfect, that she had been born with Down's syndrome, albeit in a relatively mild form. They had come to terms with it, of course. Daisy was sweet-natured and not often difficult, and with Rosemary's careful oversight and tutelage she had developed much better than might have been expected. But at moments like this, hugging her daughter, Rosemary lived with the knowledge that Daisy would not experience a so-called 'normal' life, would never marry and have children of her own. That she herself would not be a grandmother. And then there was the hard, statistical fact about Down's syndrome: that those afflicted with it were unlikely to live out a full lifespan. That was the ache that never went away.

But Daisy, just in being herself, had brought so much joy into their lives. So Rosemary went on hugging her, until Daisy became restless and squirmed out of her arms.

Once again Valerie Marler and Hal Phillips were sitting together in her kitchen, drinking coffee. Once again she tried to draw him out, to learn more about him, but he continued to prove elusive.

'Are you originally from round here?' she asked.

'No, I'm not,' he replied. 'But what about you, Miss Marler? How long have you been here in Elmsford?'

Valerie frowned. 'Nearly five years.'

'Yes, you did tell me that yesterday,' he recalled, misinterpreting her frown.

'I moved here after my marriage broke up,' she told him suddenly; really, he was very easy to talk to, and seemed interested in what she had to say. Not like most men, who only liked to talk about themselves. But then she hadn't really thought that Hal Phillips was like most men.

'I didn't know you'd been married.'

'Only for about four years.' She knew he was too polite to ask what had happened, so she told him. 'We split up because of my career. When I wrote my first book, he thought it was just a little hobby, something to take my mind off changing nappies. And when I sold it to Robin's Egg for a great deal of money, he just couldn't handle it.'

'You have children, then?' he deduced.

Valerie nodded, swallowing hard. 'Two. Ben is eight and Jenny is seven. They're with their father,' she added. 'In Australia.' It wasn't something she ever talked about; she didn't even allow herself to think about it very often. There were no pictures of the children in the house, nothing to remind her. It was too painful. And most people just weren't interested; she didn't think that Shaun even knew that she had children. Really, Hal Phillips was a most extraordinary man, to get her to tell him such things.

On their second cup of coffee, he asked Valerie if she was happy about his quote for the work.

'Yes, of course – it's fine,' she assured him. 'When do you think you might make a start, then?'

'Tomorrow, if you like,' he said. 'I don't have anything else urgent on at the moment. I can pick up the paint this afternoon and start first thing in the morning.'

'And how long do you think it might take?'

'For the basic painting – what I've quoted for – not much more than a fortnight,' Hal said. 'Three weeks at the outside.'

'Oh,' Valerie said, trying to keep her voice neutral. 'That's not long.'

Hal grinned. 'I'm a fast worker. But I thought that was what you wanted.'

She stared down into her coffee cup, not daring to look at him for fear of betraying what that smile did to her insides. Why did this man make her feel like a silly schoolgirl? Then she registered his words. Did they mean what they seemed to mean? Surely . . .

'If you decide that you want something special in the bedroom, of course it would take a bit longer,' he was saying.

The bedroom. Something special in the bedroom. Oh, he *was* a fast worker. Just like other men, like Shaun and so many others; she was obscurely disappointed, even as her heart beat faster.

'You mentioned wallpaper,' Hal went on. 'Personally, I don't think you really need it. A nice warm colourwash would do the job just as well.'

Wallpaper? Colourwash? Valerie looked up at him, startled, and he gave her an innocent smile. 'Wallpaper?' she echoed.

'You did mention it yesterday,' he reminded her. 'Why, what did you think I meant?'

So he was just being coy. She could deal with that; quite a few men were shy at first, overawed by her beauty and her fame. Perhaps he was even afraid of rejection. All he needed was a bit of encouragement. 'When most men talk about something special in the bedroom, they're not talking about wallpaper,' Valerie said in a throaty voice. She leaned across the table and stroked the pale golden hairs on the back of his hand. 'But I don't mind. You're not like other men.'

Gently but firmly Hal withdrew his hand. 'I *was* talking about wallpaper. I'm sorry if I gave you the wrong idea.' To take the sting from his words – words quite similar to those he'd used on a number of such occasions – he smiled his most charming smile. 'This is my job, Miss Marler, and I don't believe in mixing business with pleasure.'

It was over a week since they'd moved to Branlingham, and Rosemary was still unpacking. The unpacking wasn't as emotionally draining as the packing had been, but somehow it seemed to take longer. Each item, already scrutinised and evaluated at the other end, now had to find a home. And it was difficult to do with Daisy about; today, with her at school, was the first opportunity that Rosemary had to get on with it and make real progress.

All the while, though, she felt as though her mother were watching over her shoulder, and that slowed her down. Rosemary's mother had been, in her time and for her time, the quintessential vicar's wife: the perfect support for her husband in his various parishes, always the one who taught Sunday School and organised the church fête and arranged the flowers. And she ran her household with the same efficiency that characterised her parish work, keeping the Vicarage immaculate and feeding her family tasty and nutritious meals without any fuss. She was efficient with a sewing machine, of course, making all of her own clothes and Rosemary's as well; every time they moved she would remake miles and miles of curtains to fit the windows of yet another vast and draughty vicarage. She knitted, she mended, she washed and ironed, and somehow she always seemed to be on top of things, and have unlimited time for her husband and daughter as well. Hazel Croom would have approved of Rosemary's mother.

Rosemary had been a late and only child of the marriage,

born long after both of her parents had given up hope of having a child. She had grown up cherished, secure in the knowledge of her parents' love.

And yet, somehow, she had never felt worthy of all that love. She was all too aware that she lacked her mother's domestic skills and her efficiency. In the kitchen Rosemary was an adequate cook, but she was all thumbs with a needle, and she loathed housework. At moments like this, remembering the way that her mother had dealt with the frequent moves from vicarage to vicarage, she felt her own shortcomings most keenly. It all seemed too much.

Quite unusually, Gervase was at home. In all the years of their married life, Rosemary could think of only a handful of times when the two of them had been alone in the house together for more than a few hours. For the first years there had been Tom, and then Daisy had arrived, both of them needing vast amounts of attention if for different reasons. Motherhood had occupied Rosemary, even as the Church had dominated Gervase's life, and between the demands of the two, their time alone together had always been limited to the evening hours, when the children were in bed and the endless parish commitments over for the day.

But at the moment Gervase was in limbo. His induction as Vicar of St Stephen's, Branlingham had not yet taken place – it was fixed for two days hence, on the Thursday – so he as yet had no official standing within the parish. Without his church and parish duties he scarcely knew what to do with himself; Rosemary had urged him to use the time to work on the book he'd been writing for years, a re-evaluation of the life and theology of Henry Parry Liddon. Dr Liddon had been an influential figure in the Oxford Movement, a stirring preacher and the biographer of Dr Pusey, but his own reputation had dimmed and he was now little known, even amongst scholars of the period; no book about him had been published since

1905. Gervase, who felt aggrieved on his behalf, sought to change all that; he had originally intended his book to be ready for publication on the centenary of Dr Liddon's death, in 1990, but he had missed that deadline years ago and seemed no nearer finishing it now than he had then. There were times when Rosemary suspected that he didn't really *want* to finish the book, that the writing of it had some sort of life of its own, without which he would feel that his own life had no focus.

Gervase had accepted Rosemary's suggestion, and had spent much of the past week in his study while she got on with the unpacking. This morning she decided to work in the drawing room, filling the shelves in the alcoves with her collection of novels. It was a large collection, as she was a voracious reader, but apart from a few nice volumes which had been given to her as gifts, by and large they were shabby paperbacks, other people's cast-offs, bought for a few pence each at church fêtes and jumble sales. It was one advantage of being the Vicar's wife, Rosemary thought wryly as she surveyed her books: she always had the first choice of the donations for the bookstall. That was a great blessing. The public library in Long Haddon had been a reasonable one, but with Daisy to worry about she'd had scant opportunity to visit it in the past few years.

The CD player, her prized possession, had been unpacked and set up within the first day or two; now she could work to the accompaniment of one of her favourite CDs. Compact discs were expensive, so her collection of those was small but much loved and much played. She favoured choral music recorded by cathedral choirs, and never tired of listening to the pure sound of boys' voices, underpinned by the men's harmonies. This morning the music soothed her, taking her mind off her mother's hovering spirit as well as her inevitable worries about Daisy: how was she getting on at the new school? Would the other children accept her? It seemed so wonderful, but would she be happy there?

When the long-case clock – once again in a setting befitting its age and size – chimed one, Rosemary broke off her labours and went to the kitchen to make lunch. She had some sandwich things on hand, and a tin of soup, so she put the soup on to heat while she made a few rounds of sandwiches. There was a bit of the Sunday joint of pork left; that went into some of the sandwiches, along with the leftover applesauce, and the rest were cheese and pickle. She arranged them on a plate and called Gervase to lunch. The tiny table from their last kitchen was dwarfed in the expanses of this huge Victorian one, but this was one room that was habitable in its current state. The dining room, its paint and plaster peeling, most certainly was not. The previous vicar, a bachelor who had gone over to Rome when a female archdeacon was appointed, had lived in the kitchen, the study, and one of the bedrooms; those three rooms were shabby but passable, and the rest of the house was a disaster. They'd put Daisy in the best bedroom, in spite of its sombre masculinity, and were making do with the rest of it until something could be done.

Gervase came into the kitchen, flexing his hand to ease its stiffness; eschewing such things as computers and even typewriters, he wrote by hand, with a heavy antique fountain pen.

'How is Dr Liddon, then?' Rosemary asked cheerfully. The progress she'd made during the morning, and the spirit-elevating music, had at last put her in a positive frame of mind, in spite of all that was left to do.

'Very well, for a man who's been dead for over a hundred years, anyway.' Gervase sat down and selected a pork sandwich while Rosemary ladled the soup into two bowls. 'Did you know that in 1867 he went to Russia with Lewis Carroll? Charles Dodgson, that is?'

'I think you might have mentioned it before.'

'Quite likely,' he agreed. 'I do think it's extraordinary, though.'

Rosemary nodded. 'Fascinating.' She wasn't being patronising; Gervase's enthusiasm was genuinely infectious, and he was – perhaps alone of his generation – enthusiastic about Henry Parry Liddon.

He took a bite of his sandwich and shook his head to clear it of the nineteenth century. 'Any post?' he asked.

'A few bills,' Rosemary said with a sigh. 'Reconnection charges for the gas and the electric and the water and the telephone. It's a real nuisance that they've all come at once, on top of the costs for the removal people.'

'We'll manage,' said Gervase. 'And the diocese will reimburse us for the removal.'

Yes, they'd manage, if she juggled the housekeeping, and left one or two of the bills unpaid until the red notices appeared – assuming that the diocese had paid up by then.

'And there was this as well.' Rosemary got up from the table and retrieved a folded leaflet, which she put down next to his soup bowl. She wasn't sure why she was showing it to him; he wouldn't be interested. And even if he was, they couldn't afford it.

'Music in Country Churches,' he read. 'A concert?'

'Yes, in Dennington Church. It's a beautiful church, you know.' She wasn't very successful in keeping her enthusiasm out of her voice. 'And the concert sounds wonderful – choral music by Tallis and Byrd and Gibbons, and a viol consort as well.'

Gervase scanned the leaflet, then lifted his head and looked searchingly at his wife. 'You'd like to go?'

'Oh, I'd love to!' she said spontaneously, then added in a sober tone, 'But of course we can't afford it.'

Gervase smiled. 'I think we could manage. I didn't tell you this – I was saving it for a surprise – but one or two of the parishioners at St Mark's slipped me a bit of cash as a leaving present.'

Rosemary didn't dare to hope that it could really happen. 'Shouldn't that money go to pay the bills, then?'

'Certainly not! It wasn't meant for that.' Gervase pulled out his diary and consulted it. 'It's just before your birthday, isn't it? We could call it an early birthday treat for you, if you'd like. Why don't you go ahead and order the tickets, my dear? I'll put it in my diary right now.'

'But what about Daisy?' They rarely went out, and never without their daughter.

He waved away the objection. 'I'm sure that someone from the parish will look after her for a few hours.'

Rosemary got up again and hugged his shoulders joyously. It really would be a wonderful concert, a rare treat, and it gave her something to look forward to for the next few weeks.

The phone rang, and without even thinking about it she went out in the hall to answer it. Whether Gervase was there or not, it was part of her unpaid job as a vicar's wife to act as a call screener for him.

He looked up as she returned. 'Anything important?'

Rosemary hesitated. 'It was Christine,' she said reluctantly.

Her husband frowned, as she knew he would. Gervase, who had not an unkind bone in his body nor an enemy in the world, and who liked everyone as a matter of course, did not like Rosemary's friend Christine. His objections to her were on his wife's behalf rather than his own: he felt that Christine used Rosemary, and took advantage of her generous nature. When she was being perfectly honest with herself, Rosemary admitted that he was right, though she wasn't about to tell him so. Christine, for all of her faults, was her friend, and in fact her only friend in Letherfield. 'What did Christine want?' he asked, with a cynicism in his tone that was uncharacteristic except where Christine was concerned.

'She wants to come by tomorrow afternoon and see me – see *us*. See how we've settled in and so forth. I've invited her to lunch.'

Gervase raised his eyebrows. 'Well, I shan't be here tomorrow afternoon. I have to drive over to Saxwell to see the Archdeacon, to talk about the induction service.'

Seizing the opportunity to change the subject, Rosemary asked, 'Are you *sure* that I don't have to worry about the catering for that?'

'Quite sure,' Gervase stated. I've spoken to the churchwardens, and they promised me that the Mothers' Union had it all in hand. They didn't think that you should have to take any of it on.'

There were few parish occasions when the vicar's wife was let off the hook like that, and Rosemary felt both relieved and guilty. Apart from her shortcomings as a housekeeper, she knew that she was not the ideal vicar's wife, stalwart of every parish function. For the first few years of her marriage she had tried conscientiously to live up to the examples set by her own mother and by the dead Laura, but had always fallen short of what she perceived to be the standards that the two of them had set. And then Daisy had come along. Daisy's disability had given Rosemary the excuse she hadn't even realised she'd been looking for, to withdraw from various parish activities, to redefine her role on her own terms. She knew it was cowardly of her, but that didn't stop her from using her daughter: she couldn't compete with Laura or her mother, so she was no longer going to try.

'Hal, you're appalling! You didn't *really* use that hoary old chestnut again!' Margaret's voice was amused but scandalised. '"Mixing business and pleasure." Honestly, Hal! Talk about cliché!'

It was late that night. Margaret and Hal Phillips were in bed.

'Well, what was I supposed to do?' he defended himself. 'She threw herself at me. I could have used the other cliché about being a happily married man, but I didn't think that was any of her business.'

'And I suppose you're going to tell me that you didn't flirt with her or lead her on,' Margaret teased.

'No, of course not.' He switched on the bedside lamp so his wife could see the sincerity of his expression. 'You know I don't do that. I never do.'

'And still these women throw themselves at you.' Margaret sighed dramatically. 'Oh, the curse of a handsome face.'

'It's not funny,' he insisted. 'What am I supposed to do?'

'Well, you *will* work at a job that puts you into contact with women, alone with them in their houses day after day,' she pointed out. 'Lonely women, sex-starved women. I suppose it's an occupational hazard, handsome face or not.'

'An occupational hazard,' Hal repeated, liking the sound of it. 'I'll remember that the next time.'

'And of course there will be a next time.' Margaret raised herself on one elbow and looked at him, smiling. 'When you decided to leave the rat race and chuck it all in, why didn't you just go to work as a petrol station attendant, or something like that? Some job that didn't constantly surround you with lonely women?'

'And waste this handsome face?' he said provocatively.

'Oh, Hal, you're impossible.' The Archdeacon of Saxwell did something that those in her pastoral care would have found hard to believe, knowing her only in her serious professional incarnation: she thumped her husband with her pillow. He responded to the challenge by tickling her in a spot that always got results, and the evening ended most satisfactorily for both of them.

*

Through the afternoon and evening Valerie Marler had managed to keep herself busy, following her routine. She sorted her post, paid the bills and answered the fan letters, using that routine to keep all sorts of unwelcome thoughts at bay. The upsetting incident of the newspaper was as firmly buried in her psyche as the newspaper itself was beneath the coffee grounds in her bin, and she put Hal Phillips firmly out of her mind. She prepared and ate her evening meal, read a little, and carried out her night-time ablutions.

But later, alone in her bed, she could avoid her own thoughts no longer. Strangely enough, it wasn't Hal Phillips who dominated those thoughts initially, but her children, her babies. She had managed for so long to avoid thinking about them, and now he had reminded her, dredged them up from the recesses of her mind where they had been so carefully filed away. Under 'C' for children. Or perhaps 'M' for motherhood.

She'd wanted to be the perfect mother. But she'd been so young, and motherhood wasn't at all what she'd expected. She hadn't had siblings; she'd scarcely ever held a baby before. Then two babies in as many years: endless dirty nappies and greedy mouths, screaming to be fed. Valerie had discovered, to her horror, that she didn't really like babies very much. Edward had been a much better father than she'd been a mother.

Her writing had been her escape valve, the only way she'd managed to keep a grip on any sort of reality. All of those stories which she'd always created in her head, finally translated onto the page. She'd discovered what a gift she had for it, and how much pleasure it gave her.

It had cost her her marriage.

And she'd let him take her babies from her. She had let him.

At the time it had seemed the only way for her to keep her sanity. She hadn't fought for them at all.

Valerie couldn't bear to think about her children. They were part of her past. She would concentrate instead on the present, on Hal Phillips, that fascinating and utterly attractive man.

She screwed her eyes shut and conjured up his face: those eyes, that smile. For a moment the pleasure of that recollection was enough to distract her from her pain, but then she remembered what had happened, and her eyes stung with angry tears as she replayed the humiliating scene in her mind. He had rejected her. *He* had rejected *her.* Gently, but he had rejected her.

Men did not reject Valerie Marler. She was beautiful, she was rich, she was famous. Men didn't reject her, not ever. She was the one who did the rejecting, if any rejecting was to be done.

Oh, God, he had rejected and humiliated her. But who did he think he was? How dare he behave in that insolent way, when she had done him the honour of noticing him? After all, he was merely a painter and decorator, when it came down to it. So what if he had a devastating smile? So what if he had beautiful eyes? So what if he had a posh voice? He was a decorator, a tradesman. How dare he have the cheek to treat her like that?

She would ring him and tell him not to come back tomorrow. Too bad if he'd already bought the paint for the job. She couldn't bear to have him in the house with her for the next fortnight, after the way he'd treated her. Valerie sat up in bed, snapped on the light, and reached for the bedside phone. She would ring him right now.

She'd left the piece of paper with the quote on the bedside table. Her hand hesitated over the receiver. Perhaps she wouldn't ring him now – it was late. Well, what of it? Angrily she punched the numbers, and heard the remote buzz of the phone on the other end. It rang three times, then a sleepy voice answered. A woman's voice.

Valerie slammed the receiver down.

She would ring him in the morning and tell him not to come. She would get another decorator instead.

But wouldn't that be letting him get the better of her? Wouldn't that be admitting to him that he had upset her by his behaviour?

Wouldn't it be better to let him come? Yes, let him come. Then she could treat him with icy politeness, could put him in his place. A tradesman, that's all he was. She would show him how tradesmen ought to be treated. Let him come.

Chapter 4

Daisy's first day at Branlingham Primary School had been a great success. She had come home bubbling over with excitement, and the next morning she was still talking.

She had, it would seem, made a friend, and one with a name that might trip up any young tongue, but Daisy enunciated it clearly. 'Samantha Sawbridge is my best friend,' she told her parents at breakfast. 'My very best friend. I asked Samantha Sawbridge if she would be my best friend, and she said yes.'

'How nice, darling.' Rosemary was delighted that it had all gone so well and that Daisy was happy. She thought back to her own school days, and her friend Barbara. She'd been a few years older than Daisy when she'd met Barbara, and they'd become best friends instantly. They'd stayed best friends through those difficult years of adolescence, and when, inevitably, Rosemary's family had moved, they'd kept in touch through frequent letters, managing to get together during school holidays. They'd made plans to go to the same university, but things didn't work out quite as they'd thought: during their first term Barbara acquired a boyfriend and her priorities changed. Now, recalled Rosemary sadly, they had lost touch completely. She wondered where Barbara was now and what she was doing.

Daisy's voice recalled her to the present. 'And do you know what Samantha Sawbridge said?'

'What did she say, darling?' She caressed her daughter's head in passing as she went round the table to refill Gervase's coffee cup.

'She said that my name was pretty. She said that it was a flower and a bird. Daisy Finch. A flower and a bird.'

'And so it is,' Gervase confirmed, smiling, as he reached for his cup. 'Samantha Sawbridge sounds a clever girl.'

'Oh, she is, and pretty too.' Her voice was admiring and without envy. 'She has yellow hair.' Daisy touched her own dark hair. 'Can I have the pink ribbons again today, Mummy?'

'Yes, of course.'

'Samantha Sawbridge liked my pink ribbons. She's my best friend. My very best friend. My very, very, very, very, very best friend.'

'That's wonderful, darling.' Rosemary caught her husband's eye over Daisy's head, and they exchanged one of those wordless communications at which married couples become so practised when there are children in the house. We've made the right decision, it said. No matter how difficult an upheaval the move has been, and no matter what lies ahead in the new parish, we've made the right decision.

Branlingham Primary School was a short distance from the Vicarage, a five-minute walk through the village. Daisy walked at her mother's side with eager steps, holding her hand and talking away. Really, thought Rosemary, after only one day at the new school, Daisy was like a different child. It was such an enormous, blessed relief. Going to the old school had been a nightmare and an ordeal, day after day, Daisy dragging her feet and occasionally bursting into tears. Now she couldn't wait to get to the school gates.

As they approached, Daisy gave an excited cry and dropped her mother's hand. 'Samantha Sawbridge!' she said, running up to a tiny blond girl who was approaching from the other direction.

Rosemary followed. By the time she arrived, the two little girls were already chattering away to each other. 'Mummy, this is Samantha Sawbridge. My best friend,' Daisy announced proudly. Samantha was a beautiful child, petite and dainty, with enormous blue eyes and masses of long yellow hair, that extraordinary gilt colour that never lasts past childhood.

'How nice to meet you, Samantha,' said Rosemary.

'Hello.' The little girl gave her an enchanting smile. 'Can Daisy please come home from school with me today?'

Rosemary frowned. 'Oh, I don't know about that.'

'Samantha has been talking of nothing but Daisy since yesterday,' said a woman with a pram, whom Rosemary hadn't noticed. 'It would be lovely if you'd let her come home with us.'

Daisy had tears in her eyes. 'Please, Mummy. Samantha has a kitten. I want to see him. And she said I could play with her baby brother.'

'Well . . .' She looked appealingly at the other woman. 'I'm just not sure. She's never done anything like that before.'

'She'll be fine,' the other woman assured her.

'Please?' added Samantha.

Sensing she was outnumbered, Rosemary capitulated. 'All right, then.'

With whoops of pleasure the two girls joined hands and went through the school gates, their heads together, and not a backwards glance from either.

'Well.' Rosemary stood staring, amazed, remembering the scenes she'd endured on an almost daily basis, her own heart wrenched as Daisy cried and begged her not to leave her.

When the girls had disappeared from view she turned to

the other woman. 'I'm Rosemary Finch,' she said, belatedly. 'But I suppose you guessed that.'

'Indeed so. And I'm Annie Sawbridge.' The woman had a strong Scottish accent. She smiled warmly and put out her hand to shake Rosemary's.

Looking at her, Rosemary found it difficult to believe that she was the mother of the exquisite Samantha. She was small, like her daughter, but there the similarity ended; Annie Sawbridge was as dark as Samantha was fair, with a jolly round face and laughing brown eyes under a mop of short brown curls. 'Oh, I know. I'm nothing like Samantha,' Annie said wryly. 'She takes after my husband, not me. Fortunate child. Wee Jamie,' she added, indicating the baby in the pram, 'is going to look more like me, poor bairn.'

Rosemary bent over the pram and smiled at the baby. 'Your daughter is beautiful.'

'Isn't she?' agreed Annie cheerfully. 'And the amazing thing is, she's as sweet and good-natured as she is bonny.'

'I can tell.' Rosemary shook her head. 'Girls who looked like that at *my* school were always horrid. They always *knew* how pretty they were, and made up for it by being unpleasant to girls like me.'

Annie laughed. 'Oh, I know exactly what you mean. But you don't have to worry about Samantha. She'll look after your wee Daisy, all right.'

Daisy safely – and happily – delivered to school, Rosemary set her mind to deciding what to make for lunch. Gervase announced that he would be going out before lunch, so it would be just the two of them, Rosemary and Christine. It wasn't as if it were a big deal; Christine had dropped in on her for lunch so many times in the past, both announced and unannounced. But somehow she felt that Christine's first visit to Branlingham was rather special, and deserved something a bit out of the ordinary.

Christine always liked a curry. Sunday's pork was gone, of course, so Rosemary explored a shelf in the pantry that she reserved for gifts from parishioners, many of whom liked to treat the Vicar's family to little dainties, and found a tin of chicken. Chicken curry, then, with rice and some of Hazel Croom's nice homemade apple chutney.

Her friend arrived just on time, driving up in her familiar red car; Rosemary saw her coming and had the door open before Christine could ring the bell.

'Rosemary!' Christine kissed her on both cheeks. 'What an amazing house! It looks as though you have hundreds of rooms!'

'It's a bit bigger than we need,' Rosemary admitted. 'And unfortunately most of it needs a lot doing to it before it will be fit to live in.'

'So you said.' Her friend stepped inside the shabby, gloomy Gothic Revival entrance hall and looked round with frank curiosity. 'Oh, it's enormous. Can I have a tour?'

'Of course, if you'd like. Though we haven't finished unpacking yet . . .' Rosemary had been afraid of this. She couldn't help mentally contrasting it with Christine's own house, a modern semi-detached on the outskirts of Letherfield, built around the same time as the new vicarage. Christine kept its small rooms immaculate, putting Rosemary to shame. Perhaps Roger and the two girls were better trained at keeping things tidy than Daisy and Gervase, Rosemary rationalised. Or maybe Christine was just a better house-keeper than she was. Either way, a visit to Christine's neat-as-a-pin house had always made Rosemary feel inferior and vaguely depressed. And to make matters worse, Christine did all this while holding down a full-time job, while Rosemary was only the Vicar's wife.

Without waiting for her hostess to lead, Christine started up the massive dark-painted staircase. 'How many bedrooms do you have, then?'

'It depends on what you count as bedrooms. But I think there are ten.' Rosemary followed her up the stairs. Christine stopped outside the first door at the top. Rosemary caught her up and opened it for her. 'This is Daisy's room,' she said unnecessarily. It was inhabited by a great crowd of colourful stuffed animals, some of them arranged on the bed and others sitting on the floor or on the chest of drawers.

'Hmm. Nice. It has potential.'

Rosemary supposed that it did; all it needed, really, was a coat of cheery paint to cover the masculine brown, unlike many of the other rooms with their crumbling plaster.

'Let's see the other rooms, then,' Christine said.

'There's not much to see, really,' Rosemary demurred. 'None of them are very nice.'

Christine opened a door into an unfurnished room, dank and cheerless. 'I see what you mean.'

'Our bedroom is here, but it isn't much better.' Rosemary opened another door to show her. 'And that's about all there is to see upstairs. The rest are just empty rooms.'

'Don't you have a guest room, then?'

'Not yet,' Rosemary admitted. 'We haven't needed one. There will be one, of course, when things are sorted a bit.'

Christine laughed in a teasing way. 'You must, for when I come to stay.'

'Oh. Yes, of course.' It hadn't occurred to Rosemary that her friend would ever require overnight accommodation; after all, Letherfield was less than an hour's drive away.

As she led the way downstairs to view the rooms there, Rosemary asked over her shoulder, 'So you have the day off today, then?'

'Yes, that's right.' This was not an unusual occurrence;

Christine was a nurse at the hospital in Long Haddon, working shifts, and often had various parts of the day or even whole days free. 'I've been on nights,' she added.

So overworked accountant Roger would have to put the girls to bed, Rosemary thought. At least Christine would be able to collect them from school. Uncharitably, she wondered who would collect them when their mother was back on the day shift, now that Rosemary was no longer available to do it. Immediately she hated herself for the thought; it was Gervase's fault, always disapproving of Christine.

Christine's Polly was the same age as Daisy, and Gemma was two years younger. Their mothers had met at a play group, when the older girls were quite small, and had become friends. Though Christine Bryant was not a church-goer, that was an advantage rather than a drawback: Rosemary was desperately lonely for a friend but had always been warned by her mother against forming close friendships within the parish. And Christine, for her part, found an educated woman like Rosemary to be a cut above the other women in the village. An added benefit to the friendship, at least on one side, had become evident when Christine went back to work after Gemma's birth: Rosemary was always available, and always quite willing, to act as a free baby-sitter, to collect Polly from nursery school, latterly from school, and keep her at the Vicarage until Christine finished her shift. Christine even managed to feel virtuous about this – after all, a child like Daisy, who was to all intents and purposes an only child as well as being handicapped, would surely benefit from contact with a child like Polly.

The downstairs tour accomplished, the women ended up in the kitchen. 'I almost forgot – I got so carried away with wanting to see the house,' said Christine, proffering a book. 'I brought you a pressie. You haven't read it, have you?'

Rosemary took it from her and examined the cover. It was

the latest Valerie Marler paperback, only slightly scuffed from Christine's careful reading of it. 'No,' she said, delighted. 'And I've been wanting to. Is it any good? This is the one that takes place in Italy, isn't it?' The watercolour on the cover showed a sun-baked Tuscan hillside.

'That's right. After her divorce she goes to Tuscany with her sister and falls in love with the unsuitable young man who turns out to be the son of a count. I thought it was terribly good.'

'What's she called this time?' Rosemary asked, smiling. It was a joke between them that Valerie Marler's heroines were in fact always the same person, with only the name changed.

Christine laughed. 'Portia.'

'Yes, she would be.'

'And the Italian is called Roberto,' Christine added.

'Of course. Anyway, thanks so much for that. I can't wait to read it.'

While Rosemary stirred the rice, waiting for it to be done, she watched Christine, who was prowling restlessly round the kitchen. It was the first time she'd looked at her properly since she'd arrived, and Rosemary realised that there was something different about her friend. Something subtle, but definitely something different.

It was her hair. Christine's chestnut hair had always been worn in a well-cut but sensible bob; now it looked softer and lighter round her face, with artful wisps carefully arranged to give an impression of artlessness. And perhaps her make-up was different as well; Rosemary couldn't remember that her cheeks had ever looked quite that pink before. 'You've had something done to your hair,' she ventured.

'You noticed.' Christine put a hand to her hair. 'I suppose you would. *Roger* hasn't noticed, but then he wouldn't,' she added, scornfully, then went on. 'Lowlights. And a good cut. I've found a new hairdresser.'

Without thinking, Rosemary put a hand to her own hair;

she hadn't got round yet to trimming her overgrown fringe. She could feel that Christine was surveying her critically. 'I could get you an appointment with her, if you'd like,' Christine suggested. 'You'd look totally different with a good haircut. You really could make something of yourself, you know.'

Rosemary shrugged off the implied criticism; she was used to Christine's manner and knew that it was well meant. 'Good haircuts cost money,' she said matter-of-factly and without bitterness.

'But there's no reason why you shouldn't get a job now, with Daisy in school. A part-time job. Earn a bit of cash for yourself. Meet new people.' Christine's eyes sparkled as she warmed to her theme. 'Live a little bit, Rosemary. Have an affair.'

'An affair?' Rosemary stared at her, baffled, the spoon suspended in mid-stir. 'Why on earth would I want to do that?'

Christine's voice was passionate. 'To prove that you're still alive, that you can still feel, that you're not stuck in a boring marriage when you're not yet forty with nothing else ever to look forward to—'

'But I'm *not* stuck in a boring marriage,' Rosemary protested. 'I *love* Gervase, and I love Daisy, and I'm very happy with my life.'

It didn't slow Christine down, and she paced even more frantically. 'You say that, but you don't know what you're missing out on. I don't suppose there's anyone very exciting in your congregation, but surely there are other options, other men about. I mean, you've just moved. Your house needs lots doing to it. Isn't there some dishy young plumber or hunky electrician in Branlingham that you fancy?'

Rosemary could feel herself blushing furiously. The very idea . . . Why would Christine even think such a thing? And then it came to her, and she dropped the spoon with a clatter. 'Christine! You're having an affair, aren't you?' she blurted.

It all came out, in a rush, before the curry made it to the table, and was elaborated on at length during their lunch. Christine was indeed having an affair.

She had never made a secret, to Rosemary, of the fact that she found her husband boring. Roger, as she had so often told her friend, was interested in only two things: accountancy and watching sport on television. He worked long hours at his job, and when he was home he collapsed in front of the telly. At the end of the evening he barely had enough energy to propel himself to the bedroom, let alone do anything exciting once he got there. And even when he made the effort, it was nothing to write home about. All of this Rosemary knew; she'd been told it over and over again by an increasingly frustrated Christine.

So now Christine had done something about it.

Rosemary was responsible for it in a funny way, or so Christine claimed. Her move to Branlingham had prompted in Christine a restlessness to move as well, out of Letherfield and perhaps into Long Haddon, where more was going on and there were bound to be more interesting people.

And there were. She hadn't even needed to move to Long Haddon to find Nick Morrison. He was working in the estate agency there, and happened to be the one deputised to help Christine in her search for a house.

Keen to be of assistance, he gave her personal service.

The affair had been carried out, as Christine told Rosemary in some detail, in a series of empty houses. She was confining her house search to those with vacant possession, and that meant that Nick had the keys. Each day they would meet at a different house. It had been going on for nearly a fortnight now, she told Rosemary, and while it was wildly exciting – she'd never felt so alive – there were also aspects of it which, she admitted, offended the fastidious Christine. There were of course no beds in these houses, so the floor had to do. And worse than the lack of comfort on bare boards was the lack of hygiene on carpets – most of the carpets were smelly and dirty, or else they wouldn't have been left behind.

But the joy of it! The excitement! Nick's young body, his eagerness for her – Rosemary heard about it all, with nothing left out.

Christine talked through the meal, her eyes glittering with excitement and her face flushed. She didn't seem to notice what she was eating, and in fact the relentless flow of the narrative meant that she didn't eat much – Christine, whose appetite had always been so keen, and who specially loved curry. It was as if she *needed* to tell Rosemary, and tell her everything. There was certainly no one else she could tell this overwhelming, this all-consuming secret.

Rosemary, for her part, hoped that she was being a good listener, and was not betraying the shock she felt, though she doubted that Christine would have noticed. She *knew* that people had affairs – people in Valerie Marler's novels did all the time – but it was not something that had ever impinged on her own world in such a way. Thinking about it afterwards, as she inevitably did, Rosemary decided that the shock was due not so much to the *fact* of the affair, but to its precipitate speed. All of this had happened in less than a fortnight.

'But what about Roger?' Rosemary said finally, feeling that she should at least bring him into it.

'Roger?' Christine looked at her blankly. 'What about him? What does it have to do with him?'

Rosemary pointed out the obvious. 'He's your husband.'

'He doesn't matter.' Christine waved a dismissive hand. 'It has nothing to do with him.'

Then the doorbell rang, and Christine's hand went to her throat. 'Oh. It's him,' she said breathlessly.

'Roger?' Rosemary asked, baffled.

'No, of course not! Nick!' Christine's face went even pinker and her lips parted, gulping in shallow breaths of excitement.

'I told him to meet me here. I knew you wouldn't mind.'

Feeling like a character in a play of which she hadn't read the script, Rosemary went to the door, Christine at her heels.

The man at the door was undoubtedly Nick Morrison. Estate agents were as unmistakably identifiable a breed as Mormons, Rosemary reflected in that split second of recognition, and not all that different from Mormons, either: all long-sleeved white shirts, short haircuts and synthetic smiles. The uninitiated might be hard put to tell one breed from the other, except that estate agents tended to wear far more exotic ties than Mormons. This one was sporting a multihued number, wide and garish, of a sort that no Mormon would be caught dead in.

Nick was young. He had slicked-back dark hair, sleek like a seal's. His synthetic smile was for Rosemary's benefit, but it was over her shoulder, at Christine, that he was looking. Rapid introductions were made, with awkwardness on all sides; Rosemary found it difficult to meet Nick's eyes when she'd just had described to her, in intimate detail, what he looked like without his clothes. Without that white shirt and that lurid tie . . .

'Would you like some coffee?' she offered brightly. 'Or a cup of tea?'

Valerie Marler had never been one for female friends; she was a man's woman, subconsciously viewing all women as potential rivals. In the ordinary course of things she had no use for women, and surrounded herself with men: her agent, her editor and her publicist were all men, as were her doctor, her solicitor and her accountant. One woman, though, was instrumental in her life: her cleaning lady, Sybil Rashe. Their relationship might even have been described as an odd sort of friendship, had Valerie's innate snobbery permitted the use of that word, across the boundaries of age and class and wealth and social standing. Perhaps, in fact, because Mrs Rashe was in no way a rival, and could not possibly be construed as such, Valerie had permitted a certain amount of intimacy with her to develop.

Mrs Rashe 'did' for Valerie one afternoon a week, on a Wednesday. She would have been delighted to have come to Rose Cottage more often, but Valerie disliked any interruption to her working routine, and as she lived on her own and was by nature a tidy individual, once a week was enough for Mrs Rashe to keep things under control. Her husband Frank was a farm labourer, and they lived in a tied cottage on the edge of Elmsford. Although Sybil Rashe had a few other cleaning jobs that occupied her on the other days of the week, it was Valerie Marler whom she considered her chief 'client', and from whom she derived much of her prestige in the village. She was much given to talking in a proprietorial way about 'my Miss Valerie', not only to Frank but to her chums. It was through Mrs Rashe, in fact, that the village of Elmsford gained much of its knowledge about its most famous resident. She prided herself on her discretion, of course; she would never have let slip anything that Miss Valerie might have considered privileged information. But the minutiae of life at Rose Cottage were grist for her mill, day in and day out.

Her afternoons at Rose Cottage had a certain rhythm. She would arrive just before Miss Valerie's lunch, and have a quick whisk round the study with Hoover and duster while Miss Valerie ate. Then, when Miss Valerie retreated to the study to deal with her correspondence, Mrs Rashe would start in Miss Valerie's bedroom and work her way down through the house, ending up in the kitchen. There, after giving the quarry-tiled floor a good going over and wiping the work surfaces, she would fill the kettle, put it on the Aga and wait for Miss Valerie to join her.

This, then, would be the highlight of her week: she and Miss Valerie settled down at the kitchen table for a nice companionable cup of tea and a natter.

Miss Valerie didn't much like to talk about herself, though of course she occasionally let titbits slip which Mrs Rashe could ponder and share with her chums, if appropriate. So Sybil Rashe did most of the talking. Valerie was by now intimately acquainted with the Rashe family, their interests, life-styles and proclivities, though she'd never met them. She knew all about Frank and his tendency to have one pint too many down at the pub on a Saturday night. She knew, too, everything there was to know about the three Rashe children, now grown. Brenda, the eldest, had made a mess of her marriage – though thank goodness there were no kiddies to complicate things – and was now divorced and living above a video shop in Ipswich with its proprietor, whom Mrs Rashe believed to be some sort of Indian or other foreigner, though she hadn't met him, and didn't want to, thank you very much. Kim, the younger girl, was even more of a disappointment: she was living in a caravan with some worthless layabout who'd never held down a job in his life; they were both on the dole, to Mrs Rashe's great shame. The only one of the Rashes who had made anything of himself was Terry, the boy in the middle. He lived in Branlingham, a few miles away from Elmsford, and was the caretaker at Branlingham Primary School. But he too had blotted his copybook by marrying a woman who rejoiced in the name of Delilah, and was, according to her mother-in-law, 'no better than she should be'. Mrs Rashe was convinced that her only grandchild, little Zack ('and who ever heard of a name like that, anyhow?'), was not her grandson at all, but the result of some torrid liaison between Delilah and the barman at the George and Dragon in Branlingham.

All of these things, and much more, Valerie had gleaned during her many cups of tea with Sybil Rashe. As a novelist, this rich glimpse of human life interested her, though of course her fictional world was peopled with characters as far removed from the Rashe family as Tuscany – or even Sloane

Square – was from a video shop in Ipswich. But her creative imagination did not waste such material; Mrs Rashe would have been astonished if she had known that in Valerie's last-but-one book, Brenda, she of the failed marriage and messy divorce, had been recast and reincarnated as Portia, finding romance with her Italian lover Roberto.

Now, on this Wednesday afternoon as they sat together drinking tea, the contrast between the two women – in appearance as in every other way – could not have been greater: Sybil Rashe, of an indeterminate age, a small and stringy woman with wisps of grey hair framing a wrinkled and weather-beaten face, dressed in her overall, and Valerie Marler, lovely and coolly elegant. In fact, observed Mrs Rashe, Miss Valerie was even more elegant than usual today, wearing silk instead of her customary casual garb.

Mrs Rashe was curious about the man who was painting the front room. 'Don't you think, Miss Valerie, that we should offer him a cup of tea?' she suggested.

Valerie shrugged her silk-clad shoulders. 'You may take him one if you like, Mrs Rashe. Though I believe he's brought his own flask.'

'I think I will,' Sybil Rashe declared. 'He's worth having another look at, that one, though my Frank wouldn't like to hear me say it. A real good-looker, that Mr Phillips is.'

'Is he?' Valerie said in an uninterested voice, examining her fingernails.

Mrs Rashe chortled. 'Oh, Miss Valerie! If you don't think so, you want your eyes testing! He's a fine figure of a man, all right.'

As Mrs Rashe scuttled off with the tea, Valerie took several deep breaths. Hal Phillips had arrived, as promised, first thing that morning. She had carried out her resolution to treat him with icy politeness, and he for his part acted as if nothing had passed between them, maintaining an attitude towards her of impersonal courtesy. He'd started to work in the front room, well out of her way, and worked quietly and efficiently. But through the morning Valerie had been acutely aware of his presence in the house, and had found it difficult to concentrate on her own work. She had managed, through force of will, to keep herself from going in frequently to check on his progress or to offer him refreshments. In fact, listening to the latest exploits of Terry and Delilah, she had almost managed to put him out of her mind altogether. But now Mrs Rashe had focused her attention on him once more.

Valerie closed her eyes and saw his face. Oh, God, if only he weren't so good-looking. Overnight she'd convinced herself that she'd exaggerated his attractiveness in her mind; he was, after all, only a tradesman. But in the morning, the sight of him on her doorstep, smiling that smile, was like a physical blow, taking her breath away. She just couldn't let him see the effect he had on her. Icy politeness was the only way.

Rosemary was troubled and disturbed by the afternoon's events. Christine and Nick hadn't stayed very long, but it was long enough to make her thoroughly uncomfortable. By entertaining the lovers together in her house, even just drinking tea and making eyes at each other, Rosemary felt that she had become an unwilling accomplice to their affair. Gervase was right, she finally admitted to herself: Christine was a user. The motivation behind her visit to Branlingham was all too clear, and it had nothing to do with friendship.

Should she tell Gervase about it? She knew that her mild-mannered husband, who never got angry about anything, would be extremely displeased. Quite apart from his moral outrage at Christine's adulterous behaviour, which would be considerable, he would be incensed on a personal level, to have his wife's hospitality abused in such a way.

But what good would it do to tell him? He couldn't undo

what had happened; he could only get himself upset about it.

And Christine, for all of her faults, was her friend. The things that Christine had told her were confidences, not to be betrayed, even to Gervase.

But Gervase was her husband. Didn't she owe him the greater loyalty?

Back and forth Rosemary went in her mind, through the afternoon and as Daisy was safely delivered home by Annie Sawbridge. Daisy was in a state of high excitement, thrilled by her new friendship and enchanted with Samantha's kitten.

'His name is Jack,' she announced. 'He's black and white. He let me stroke him and hold him.'

'That's nice, darling,' Rosemary responded absently, her thoughts elsewhere.

'Can I have a kitten, Mummy?'

Rosemary was not used to denying Daisy anything she wanted, but the idea of being responsible for another living creature – for she, of course, would be the one who would be responsible – was more than she could cope with at the moment. 'Not just now, darling. Perhaps one day,' she said.

'Jack was nicer to play with than Samantha's baby brother,' Daisy stated frankly. 'The baby doesn't do anything but sleep.'

Profoundly relieved that Daisy wasn't demanding a baby brother, Rosemary let her chatter on about the kitten. She was still talking when Gervase came home.

'How was your meeting?' Rosemary asked.

'Oh, it was fine. Everything seems on track for tomorrow evening. The Archdeacon is a nice woman – you would like her.'

Rosemary's mind wasn't on the Archdeacon any more than it was on the kitten. 'That's nice.'

'And how was your lunch?' Gervase enquired, raising his eyebrows. 'How is Christine?'

Rosemary took a deep breath before she replied; she wasn't

sure what she was going to say until she opened her mouth and it came out. 'Oh, it was fine,' she said with deliberate nonchalance. 'Christine is just the same as ever.'

That, at least, was true: Christine *was* just the same as ever, only more so.

One of the ways in which Hal Phillips maintained his trim figure was with a weekly squash match at a gym in Saxwell. He played regularly on a Wednesday evening. His partner on most occasions was Mike Odum, a policeman who was a few years younger than Hal and good-looking in a clean-cut sort of way. Hal liked playing against Mike Odum; they were evenly matched, and equally competitive about the sport, both of which factors made for a more interesting game.

After their match, the two of them would repair to the pub next door, where the loser would buy a round of drinks. Mike was a bit of a gossip, entertaining Hal each week with stories about the lives and loves of the local constabulary.

This week he seemed particularly full of good stories. 'Have you ever thought about writing scripts for *The Bill*?' Hal joked, in a good mood after beating Mike in a closely fought match, three games to two.

The policeman shook his head and sighed theatrically. 'If I wrote what really goes on, no one would believe me. But it's a thought. I could sure use the money, mate.'

Hal sipped his drink, preparing himself for another episode featuring Mike's own part in the ongoing soap opera. Mike was strapped for cash, maintaining a wife and family while he carried on an expensive affair. He was frank with Hal about this, perhaps because Hal, as someone with no connection at all to the police force, was the only person he could really talk to: his mistress was a fellow police officer, and the affair was, astonishingly enough, a well-kept secret at work.

So Mike quite enjoyed the weekly opportunity to moan about his financial position, while bragging about his lover's attractions.

These were many and great, according to Mike, who called her his 'little tiger'. 'You'd never know to see her at work what she's like when we're alone. All prim and proper she is, in her uniform. But in her flat – cor.' He rolled his eyes and fortified himself with a sip of his drink at the heat generated by the memory. 'She wears one of those Lycra body things.' Here he put his drink down and described her shape with an expressive gesture requiring both hands. 'And a leather mini-skirt. Believe me, I do mean mini,' he added, again illustrating with his hands. 'And when she gets her kit off – oh, Hal. The woman is unbelievable.'

Hal had heard it before, and was certain he would hear it again. 'And your wife doesn't suspect a thing?'

'Not her.' The policeman shook his head, rubbing his hand over his short-cropped bristly hair. 'Mind you, I've been lucky so far. I always tell her I'm on duty when I'm having an evening in with my little tiger, and she's never had occasion to check up on me.' He moved his glass on the counter top, swirling damp circles in its wake. 'Tell me, Hal. A chap like you, meeting women all the time in your work. You must have had plenty of affairs?'

'Never,' Hal replied promptly. He doubted very much whether Mike Odum knew that he was married to the Archdeacon, or indeed whether that consideration would have made any difference in Mike's assessment.

'Well, you should. I can recommend it. Does your ego no end of good. Not to mention other parts.' He raised his glass. 'The parts that even this can't reach.'

Hal laughed. 'No thank you, my friend. Believe me, one woman is all I can handle.'

Chapter 5

Early on Thursday, the morning of the day that would end
with Gervase Finch's induction as priest of the parish of St
Stephen's, Branlingham, Archdeacon Margaret Phillips once
again had an unwelcome phone call. Another village church
within her jurisdiction had been burgled, though this time no
break-in had been involved. The culprit or culprits had not
had to bother breaking in: the church had been left unlocked,
and they'd had to do no more than turn the heavy iron ring
on the massive wooden door and help themselves to the treasures within. Fortunately the burglars were not, it would
seem, practised ecclesiastical thieves; they'd taken the silver-
topped churchwardens' staves, which had been left fastened to
the pews, and a pair of cheap mass-produced silver candlesticks from the altar, but they'd ignored the immensely
valuable and irreplaceable mediaeval eagle lectern. Thank
God, thought Margaret as she set off for the scene of the
crime, for the ignorance of the burglars.

Meanwhile her husband was setting off in his van in the
opposite direction, towards Elmsford and Rose Cottage.
Though it was nearly the end of April, the day was chill;
spring had been a long time coming this year, and the flowers

were well behind schedule. But the sun was shining, and Hal Phillips, by nature a sanguine man, found his spirits elevated by the sunshine. He began whistling an elaborate psalm chant, rejoicing in the knowledge that he didn't have to spend such a lovely day shut in an office.

It had not always been thus. Hal was a man who had known worldly success in great measure. As soon as he'd been awarded his Cambridge engineering degree, he had begun his own computer company, in the very infancy of the microprocessor revolution in computing. The company had started small but had rapidly grown, producing a huge turnover and vast profits for its sole owner.

Not that it had been without effort. Hal Phillips had worked all the hours that God gave, and then some, to build his company into a successful money-making machine and to keep it on the cutting edge of new technology. And there had been a cost; his marriage had been under stress, inevitably, and his son Alexander had grown up scarcely knowing his father. Hal's health had been affected as well, though he refused to give in to it. His back played up periodically, he developed a spare tyre round his middle, and he endured blinding migraine headaches. Then, not yet forty, he had suffered a massive heart attack.

He had survived it, though for a time it had been touch-and-go. And that had been the turning point for him. Through sheer determination he had fought his way back to health and vigour, and had decided that from that moment on his life would be different. He sold his company, which made him a very rich man indeed. He could have retired to enjoy the rest of his life as a man of leisure, pottering about the house and garden or chasing a little ball round the golf course.

But he turned his energies in another direction. Early in his life he'd discovered an aptitude for painting and wallpapering; he'd helped out with a few such jobs to earn a bit of money during school and university holidays, and when he and Margaret were newly married he had enormously enjoyed the fixing up of their tiny first flat, accomplished together amidst much laughter and love. Latterly, of course, there had been no time for such things; when they'd moved to their vast country house in a village outside of Cambridge, bought with the profits of his labours, they'd hired professional decorators. Even then, at the height of his success, Hal had at the back of his mind regretted the fact that he couldn't do it himself.

So when the time came for a radical change in his life, Hal knew what he wanted to do. Opting out of the high-pressured rat race, he was determined to set himself up as a painter and decorator. He'd been at it for several years now, and couldn't imagine doing anything else.

It wasn't easy work, but it was rewarding. He loved being the instrument of transformation, turning a dingy room into a thing of beauty which would give pleasure to its inhabitants. He loved, as well, the sheer physicality of the work. He felt healthier than he ever had in his life: there were no more migraines, no more back pains, no more spare tyre, and his heart was in fine shape. He was trim, he was fit.

And he met such interesting people. Unfortunately, due to the nature of the job, most of them were women.

Hal Phillips knew that women found him attractive; it was not something he could have failed to notice. He did not consider himself a vain man, or take any particular pride in his looks, realising that it was due to an accident of nature and not of his own doing. What he *was* proud of, with a pride verging on smugness, was his ability to resist their charms.

Valerie Marler's charms were greater than most, he acknowledged to himself as he drove towards Rose Cottage. Even if such waif-like beauty was not to his personal taste, she was a lovely woman. But Hal wasn't interested; he wasn't even tempted. He was no Mike Odum. He was invulnerable.

His marriage was strong; he loved his wife. Margaret, that paragon of sometimes irritating perfection, was the only woman for him.

And fortunately, like all of the others before her, Valerie Marler seemed able to take 'no' for an answer.

Like Hal Phillips, Gervase Finch had a life founded on certainties.

On that Thursday morning, even before Hal left for Rose Cottage, Gervase's day had begun, as he spent a very long time on his knees in prayer in the mediaeval church of St Stephen. He felt that he needed to prepare himself, spiritually, for the service that evening. During that service he would be installed – literally, led to the incumbent's stall in the chancel – by the Archdeacon, but before that he would be inducted into the parish, taking charge of the building. This taking charge would be enacted symbolically, as the Archdeacon accompanied him to the church door; there he would signify his stewardship of the building by locking and unlocking the door. And before that, even, he would be 'collated' by the Bishop. Rosemary always laughed at the word, declaring that it sounded like something to be done to parish magazines rather than priests, but it was indeed a solemn moment as the Bishop handed over the 'cure of souls' to the new incumbent.

Gervase Finch could scarcely remember a time in his life when he hadn't wanted to be a priest. He had grown up with the certainty that it was his calling, and he hadn't wavered from that. The only change had been in the direction of his churchmanship: his childhood and school days had been spent in an Evangelical atmosphere, and it wasn't until he went up to Oxford that he was gripped and swept away by Anglo-Catholicism. In the home of the Oxford Movement of over a century before – at St Mary Mag's, at Pusey House, at St Barnabas, Jericho – he had fallen in love with the sacramental approach to faith, and had taken its ceremonial externals to his heart as part and parcel of that faith. His conviction of the life he was to lead had intensified, and it was to Mirfield that he went to train for his vocation.

He would have liked to have been a Mirfield Father, a monk remaining in West Yorkshire to take part in the monastic life of the Community of the Resurrection, or going out as a missionary to their other base in South Africa. It had been his intention, from the first. But he had discovered, to his chagrin and humiliation, that he was not cut out for the celibate life. The longings and urgings of his body were too strong, filling his mind with impure thoughts and distracting him from his life of prayer.

Agonised, he had brought himself, finally and with great embarrassment, to discuss the problem with his wise old confessor and spiritual director. Casual sex was not an option: what was he to do? The old monk had smiled at him with sympathy and understanding. 'You know what St Paul says, my son: "It is better to marry than to burn." It is clear that celibacy is not for you. You must marry.'

And so he had. Leaving Mirfield with regret, he had gone south as a curate and had very quickly married Laura, the young daughter of the Vicar of the church where he served his title. The Vicar had encouraged the match, throwing his curate and his daughter together at every opportunity, and was delighted when his matchmaking led to marriage, thus 'keeping things in the family'.

The marriage had not been a success, in spite of outward appearances. Laura, though undeniably beautiful, had turned out to be a cold person, both in the emotional and the physical senses, and the very relief for which Gervase had married was ironically not very often available, and then only with shows of reluctance. But he had coped, they had kept up appearances for the parish, and they had both taken delight in their son Thomas, Laura smothering the boy with the love she'd seemed unable to give his father.

Laura's late pregnancy had been an accident, unwanted by her and for which she blamed Gervase. When it had resulted in her death, he had been overwhelmed and engulfed by guilt: guilt that he had not loved her enough, and guilt that her death was his fault.

And then God had given him Rosemary and a second chance at happiness. Happiness it had been, undreamt-of happiness, in abundant measure. Rosemary was different from Laura in every way. Though she was inexperienced she was eager; the physical side of their marriage brought delights he'd never before imagined possible, and had certainly not come close to with the frigid Laura. And emotionally she was nurturing, caring: the perfect vicar's wife, and the perfect wife for him. Her unassuming nature, her sweet, artless face – everything about her was infinitely superior, infinitely more congenial to him, than Laura's chilly beauty. Gervase adored her with every fibre of his being, and thanked God every day for the enormous, unbelievable blessing of her presence at his side in life.

Never a talkative or demonstrative man, he wasn't very good at telling her how much he loved her. But surely she knew. She must know how happy she made him, and how much he needed her, how he couldn't imagine life without her.

And she'd given him Daisy, who brought so much love and delight into both of their lives. Those who pitied them for having a handicapped child had no idea what a joy and a privilege it was; after the initial period of shock and adjustment, he wouldn't have traded Daisy for a 'normal' child for all the world.

Truly, he had much to be thankful for.

Gervase had not really wanted to move away from Letherfield, he acknowledged to God that morning as he knelt in the empty church.

His childhood had been spent in an army family, moving frequently from place to place, and he'd hated that. So when he'd taken up the incumbency at Letherfield, all those years ago, he had determined to stay. He had no ambitions to rise within the Church; all he wanted was to settle down and be of service to his parish and his God.

That he had done, with much success. He was a good priest of the old-fashioned sort; his gifts were pastoral and spiritual. He was a caring man, and a man of prayer, and his parish loved him. He would happily have stayed in Letherfield for the rest of his life, and the parishioners would have been equally happy with that arrangement. But Daisy's needs had intervened, and he had not hesitated to do what was necessary to ensure her happiness. Perhaps, he now said to God, it had been meant; perhaps he had some great purpose to achieve here in Branlingham. He asked God's help in facing whatever was ahead, and pledged himself to His service, and the service of His people in this place. That night he would make a public declaration of the same; this morning it was between him and God.

Valerie Marler was not having a good morning. Her writing was not going well, for a start; it was one of those days when the characters were being awkward and the plot seemed bogged down in trivialities. She couldn't see the way forward for Cecily and Toby, or decide how they should cope with the problem of the possessive Pandora. (She liked the alliteration of that and decided to put it as dialogue into Toby's mouth at some point.) Pandora was a formidable woman, not to be trifled with, and while that added a desirable element of conflict to the plot, it did require some careful handling.

In most of her books, the characters agonised for quite a few pages before succumbing to their passion, all in the interest of dramatic tension. But this time, for some reason,

Valerie didn't want them to wait. Whether they were ready or not, she was ready for them to go to bed together. Abandoning the waffling conversation they were having – something about Pandora's plans for the garden – she struck out in a different direction. Toby suddenly swept Cecily into his arms, his lips hungrily reaching for hers, and before they knew it . . .

But wait a minute. They weren't in a very convenient place for this to happen. They were walking in the woods, and it was raining.

Never mind; she'd fix that later.

Valerie's fingers flew over the keys. She usually wrote very discreetly when it came to sex: her readers liked to be titillated, but they didn't want anything very graphic. Part of her success was due to the broad-based appeal of her books; there must be nothing in them that would offend someone's maiden aunt. So her books always promised more than they delivered: a few passionate kisses and the closing of the bedroom door behind the lovers was her style. But this time she was inspired, and Cecily and Toby were uninhibited in their enjoyment of each other.

It was wonderful. By the time she finished the passage, Valerie was breathing hard and her own body was tense with excitement. She'd never felt that way before with Portia and Roberto, or Francesca and Jeremy, or any of the other lovers who inhabited her books.

Then she read through what she'd written, and knew that it would never do. Her editor would have his red pencil through it straightaway, mindful of all those maiden aunts, and she'd be back to the discreetly closing bedroom door. But she couldn't bear, just yet, to wipe it out, nor could she bear to go back to their inane conversation about Pandora's garden. So she saved it on disk, and, for the first time she could remember, left her study before her allotted time was up.

She made herself a piece of toast and paced the kitchen as she ate it. Or tried to eat it: the texture of the dry toast seemed suddenly hateful to her, and she was unable to swallow it. She wanted to eat something luscious – a ripe peach, dribbling its juice down her chin, or a spoonful of creamy rich ice cream, coating her tongue with butterfat. Instead she put the toast in the bin and poured herself a cup of black coffee. The coffee tasted bitter; she tipped it down the sink.

The post arrived early. Valerie fetched it and prepared for her daily sorting routine. But the first envelope she opened contained a letter that pointed out, in an obnoxiously pedantic way, one or two errors of geography she'd made in the Tuscan book. Didn't she realise, her correspondent queried, that if you took that particular road, it wouldn't take you to where Portia had ended up? And in that town where she'd strolled arm-in-arm with Roberto, the campanile was in fact on the north side of the square, and couldn't possibly be seen from the corner where they were standing.

Valerie threw the letter down in disgust. Didn't people have anything better to do? She couldn't face the rest of the post; what she needed was a nice hot bubble bath, always an anodyne remedy for her.

Emerging from her bath a while later, refreshed but no more settled, she towelled herself dry, splashed on some fragrant body oil, slipped into a slinky silken dressing gown, and surveyed her wardrobe. None of her clothes seemed right. Why had she ever bought anything in that poisonous lime-green colour, or that hideous orange? Of course they had been the fashion, but they did nothing at all for her, with her fair colouring.

New clothes. It was spring; before long, with any luck, it would be warm. She needed new clothes. That meant a trip to London soon.

Valerie took her time, pushing hangers along the rail of

the wardrobe and pulling out garment after garment in a vain hunt for something to wear. She was still at it when the door-bell rang. Tying the sash of her dressing gown more securely, but otherwise making no concession to modesty, she went downstairs to answer it.

'Good morning, Miss Marler.' Hal Phillips, damn him, smiled at her with that devastating but infuriatingly imper-sonal smile. His eyes registered nothing; he didn't even seem to be looking at her, let alone appreciating the view. 'I'll get on with the front room. It's coming along nicely.'

She stood in his way, and didn't move; he had to brush past her to get to the front room. Valerie shivered with excitement at his touch and followed him, watching as he used a screw-driver to remove the lid from the paint tin, then poured the viscous, sticky liquid into the tray. Before he could go up the ladder with his tray and roller, Valerie moved close to him and put a hand on his arm, feeling its warmth through the white overall. 'Would you like some coffee?' she asked in a voice at least a register deeper than normal. 'Or is there anything else I can do for you?'

'Oh, no thank you,' he replied politely. 'I'll just get on with this, Miss Marler.'

As he climbed the ladder, she fled back to the sanctuary of her bedroom, her cheeks flaming with embarrassment and anger. Oh, how could she let him humiliate her like this?

Valerie flung off the dressing gown and stood naked in front of her full-length cheval mirror. Surely she wasn't really repulsive and undesirable? Other men, many other men, had admired her body, had lusted for it and begged her for her favours. Almost always she had obliged them, whether she enjoyed it or not. It was worth everything that followed to see the looks on their faces, the undisguised admiration and desire as they watched her undress. The white skin, the flat stomach, the narrow but shapely hips, the high, firm breasts:

some men had actually had tears in their eyes at the sight as she stood before them revealed in all her glory. And Hal Phillips wouldn't even *look*, damn the man. What would he do if she walked downstairs and appeared before him like this? Would he gaze somewhere over her shoulder and ask her if she approved of the colour she'd chosen for the front room walls? She had a horrible feeling that that was exactly what he would do.

She could understand it, and forgive it, if he were gay. One or two men she'd come across in the publishing world had been gay, and it had been clear from the beginning that she would be wasting her time with them. She could accept that. But Hal Phillips wasn't gay; he was married. He wore a wedding ring.

Many of the men in her life were married, and wives had never impinged much upon Valerie Marler's consciousness or conscience. If a woman couldn't keep her husband's interest, it was her own fault and not Valerie's. But now she found herself wondering about Mrs Hal Phillips. What sort of woman was she? Was she perhaps younger, more beautiful, than Valerie herself? A new second wife, perhaps, youthful and delectable? That, while galling to contemplate, might explain his lack of interest.

While she pondered the question, imagining the wife as she might be, Valerie got dressed at last. Spurning her more elegant wardrobe, she put on the casual clothes she often wore while working at home and not expecting to see anyone: a pair of faded jeans and a sweatshirt. She didn't usually bother with make-up when dressed like this, but never failed to slather her face with moisturiser to keep it from drying out.

She had to shake the bottle of moisturiser to get the last drops out. How had she managed to let it get this low without getting a new bottle? If she rang Shaun today, he could pop into Harrods and pick some up to bring to her at the weekend.

But could she wait till then? Perhaps she should get some locally. Not this brand, probably, but something that would tide her over until the weekend. The village shop in Elmsford wasn't a very promising possibility, but there was a Boots in Saxwell.

Suddenly Valerie was seized with the need to get out of the house, to escape from the prospect of a morning alone with Hal Phillips, so maddeningly attractive and so infuriatingly aloof. She couldn't bear to be there another minute. Without changing her clothes or even putting on any make-up, she ran down the stairs, grabbed her handbag and keys, and called out in the direction of the front room the information that she was leaving and would be back later.

She would go to Saxwell.

Valerie didn't shop locally very often. Her clothes, of course, came from London, and most of her food did as well, delivered weekly from Harrods' food hall and Fortnum & Mason. She supplemented the deliveries with occasional purchases of staples and emergency fare from the Elmsford village shop, but she rarely went into the larger town of Saxwell, some six miles away.

She stopped for petrol on the Saxwell road. It wasn't a garage she'd ever used before, to her knowledge, but the attendant gazed appreciatively at the red Porsche, then followed it with a searching look at its owner. 'Ah, you must be that Miss Marler as writes them books,' he deduced in his broad Suffolk accent. 'I've heard about you, like. No one else round here drives a car like this.' She was pleased to see that his admiration for the driver, even dressed as she was, more than matched his appreciation of the car; he leered at her as she signed the credit card voucher. He might be just a country bumpkin, but at least he was one with good taste, she told herself as she pulled out and headed into Saxwell.

An ancient market town, Saxwell had been named, aeons ago, for the Saxon well at its centre. But its Saxon past was long forgotten in the modern world of commerce; Saxwell looked like any other market town of its sort, the old narrow streets of the town centre lined with the garish plastic shopfronts of typical high street shops and thronged with too many cars and too many shoppers, especially on market day.

Regretting the impulse that had brought her here, Valerie found herself enmeshed in a complicated one-way system. The first time round she missed the sign for the pay-and-display car park and had to circle through the whole town again, praying that she would negotiate it with the Porsche intact.

But luck was with her when she finally made it into the pay-and-display; though it was full, another car was pulling out just as she arrived, and she slid the Porsche neatly into the vacant spot.

Valerie found the Boots in the High Street, sandwiched between Barclay's Bank and a chain travel agency. She went straight to the cosmetics department, perused the choices, selected the most expensive moisturiser on offer, and queued to pay. As she handed a twenty-pound note to the girl at the till, she asked casually, 'Do you happen to know where a house called The Archdeaconry is?'

The girl held the note up towards the fluorescent ceiling lights and squinted at it. 'Don't know,' she confessed cheerfully. 'Never heard of it.'

But the woman behind Valerie in the queue was more helpful. 'It's out the Bury Road,' she offered. 'Maybe a mile from here, dearie. On the left.'

'Thank you very much,' said Valerie, smiling her gratitude and receiving an uninterested smile in return.

There was something wrong. She hadn't been recognised, Valerie realised belatedly as she made her way back to the car park. Neither the girl at the till nor the woman in the queue had known who she was. The attendant at the petrol station had recognised her, but it was her car rather than her person that had triggered that recognition. In sweatshirt and jeans, in the middle of Saxwell, she could be any attractive young woman out shopping. It was an odd feeling; Valerie had always enjoyed the admiration that came with being a public figure, but suddenly she was exhilarated with the freedom of anonymity. There were so many possibilities, so many things she could do . . .

On impulse, to test her new-found anonymity, Valerie diverted her steps and went into a chain bookshop. Her own latest paperback bestseller occupied a dump-bin near the door, and her photo was not only on the back of the cover but also smiled out from the top of the dump-bin. She picked up a copy and took it to the till.

The girl at the till gave her a cheerful grin. 'Ooh, Valerie Marler – my favourite,' she enthused.

'Yes?' Valerie's smile was tentative; perhaps she *had* been spotted.

'I've read them all,' the girl went on, 'but I think this is my favourite. That Roberto is so-o-o sexy.'

'I'm glad you liked it,' said Valerie, anticipating a request for an autograph.

The girl winked as she took her money. 'But I won't spoil it for you if you haven't read it. She lives round here – did you know that? Only a few miles away, at any rate. Our local celebrity, like.'

'Is that so?' With a small shock Valerie received her change.

'Mind you, I've never seen her,' the girl admitted, flipping the book over to admire the photo as she slid it into a bag. 'Dead beautiful, she must be.'

Valerie resumed her progress, reclaimed the Porsche, re-entered the one-way system, and circled round the town centre till she found the Bury Road. Oblivious to the annoyed driver behind her, she drove slowly, scanning the houses on the left side.

She almost went past it, but her eye caught the lettering on the gatepost. The Archdeaconry stood apart from the houses on either side, a substantial double-fronted detached residence with a semi-circular gravel drive at the front.

Valerie's heart beat a bit faster. She turned left down the first side street, then left again and twice more so that she could drive past another time, even more slowly. The Archdeaconry. Hal Phillips's house.

She'd seen a corner shop down the side street. Some unformed instinct made her drive past it and pull into another street a bit farther on, where no one would see her getting out of the Porsche.

Valerie flipped down the visor and checked herself in the mirror. No, those people in the town hadn't been blind; without make-up and with her hair pulled back like that she didn't look like Valerie Marler. If her luck held, she wouldn't be recognised. She wasn't sure why that mattered, but it did.

A bell tinkled as she entered the shop; there were no other customers. Valerie looked round for something to buy. The shop seemed to be primarily a newsagent's, with the inevitable confectionery as well as various other assorted useful items. She grabbed a decorating magazine and a bar of chocolate and took them to the till.

There were two women behind the counter. The younger one, who reached for Valerie's purchases, had a square, heavy face with a severe underbite and a large jaw; the other one, rearranging chocolate bars on a display, had an older version of the same face and was clearly her mother.

Valerie reached into her handbag for money and tried to think of a conversational gambit. 'There are some lovely houses round here,' she began.

Houses didn't interest the girl. 'I suppose,' she responded in a bored tone.

'The Archdeaconry is especially nice,' Valerie persevered.

The older woman leaned over and joined in. 'The Archdeacon is one of our customers,' she said proudly. 'Comes in every day to pick up a paper.'

'Oh!' Valerie was startled and disorientated; she had explained the house's name away in her own mind as an ancient designation and had not reckoned on an archdeacon being involved in any way. What could Hal Phillips possibly have to do with an archdeacon? 'The Archdeacon?' she echoed.

'Ever such a nice lady,' the woman stated. 'No airs and graces at all. And no holier-than-thou. Just a regular person, like you or me.'

Valerie's sense of disorientation increased, and her bafflement must have shown on her face. 'Lady?'

The woman laughed. 'So you didn't know that we've got a lady Archdeacon? One of the very first in the country, she tells me.' Her voice was as full of pride as if she'd had something to do with the appointment herself. 'A good customer, the Archdeacon. And a nice lady at that, Mrs Phillips.'

Mrs Phillips. Valerie licked her lips nervously, trying to readjust her thinking as the pieces rearranged themselves and fell into place. 'Does she . . . have a husband, then?'

'Oooh, him,' the girl interjected, her heavy face coming alive. 'He's dishy, that one.'

Her mother gave her a make-believe clout. 'You watch it, girl. He's old enough to be your dad. *And* he's married to the Archdeacon, so don't you go making eyes at him.'

Married to the Archdeacon. Valerie couldn't take it in. Hal Phillips – that gorgeous man – married to a parson.

Without thinking much about it, she went round the

corner in the opposite direction from her car, and strolled past The Archdeaconry, walking slowly, staring at the house to imprint its every detail on her mind. She went as far as the next crossing, then turned and sauntered back.

She was approaching The Archdeaconry from the other direction, not quite there yet, when a car pulled into the circular drive. It was an ordinary-looking dark blue car, and as Valerie reached the drive she had a clear view of the person getting out.

A woman. A middle-aged woman, dressed neatly and severely in black: black shoes and tights, knee-length black skirt, black cardigan, black shirt, relieved only by the white band of the collar.

A magpie, thought Valerie, all black and white. Even her hair was black and white.

The woman didn't look her way, but gathered a sheaf of papers from the passenger seat, locked the car carefully, and let herself into the house with her keys.

The Archdeacon. Hal Phillips's wife.

In her shock, Valerie stood still for a moment, staring at where the woman had been. Then she walked up and down the road a few more times, her mind in turmoil, hoping that perhaps the woman might come out again.

How could he? she thought. How could he be married to that hideous old woman, that magpie? A dried-up old crone. It just didn't make sense. If his wife had been young and beautiful, she could have perhaps understood, if not forgiven, his rebuffing of her own advances, but that old woman . . . What could she possibly have to offer to a man like Hal Phillips?

Rosemary found the service that evening profoundly moving, far more so than she had expected. Although she had been to similar services involving various churches in the Long Haddon deanery, this one was different and special: this was now her home, and Gervase was the central character in the ceremonies that were enacted in the ancient stone church. The tiny church was full to the bursting point; joining the numerous clergy and diocesan officials, the new parishioners were out in force, and a coach-load had come from Letherfield to swell the congregation, to support their beloved Father Gervase, and to cast a critical eye over his new surroundings.

From her vantage point in the front row, Daisy at her side, Rosemary watched, rapt, as it all unfolded. With solemnity and joy, Gervase accepted the responsibility for the spiritual nurture of all within the parish, and then took symbolic possession of the building itself, moving from the crossing to the west door in procession.

It was the Archdeacon who put Gervase's hands on the door and inducted him into the benefice. She stood by as he tolled the church bell to declare his induction publicly, then in the choir stalls took his hand and placed him in his own incumbent's stall.

Gervase had met with the Archdeacon on several occasions, but this was the first time that Rosemary had seen her, and she was impressed. Though Margaret Phillips barely came up to Gervase's shoulder, she exuded confidence and competence; watching her, so clearly in control, Rosemary conceived an idea which she resolved to carry out during the reception that would follow.

The reception, catered by the Mothers' Union, was held in the village hall. Having no responsibilities for the catering, Rosemary was free to circulate among the other guests. She'd never felt comfortable in crowds, but she'd had years of practice at it; it was part of her job as a vicar's wife to mingle, and she didn't shirk her duty. Gervase didn't have to tell her that it was especially important for her to greet and welcome those who had travelled from Letherfield. She did her best to speak to each one.

Hazel Croom cornered her for a time, intent on complaining about what had been happening during the interregnum at St Mark's, and angling for an invitation to come back to the Vicarage after the reception.

Rosemary evaded this unwelcome hint before it became a more concrete suggestion by saying, apologetically, 'I do wish we were in a position to entertain you and the others from Letherfield ourselves, but the house is in no fit state for visitors. Perhaps when things have settled down a bit, you might come over one day and have tea with us.'

'That would be very nice,' Hazel replied crisply, managing to imply by her tone that it was inadequate, but the best one might hope from Rosemary. Her eyes looked over Rosemary's shoulder, following Gervase as he worked his way round the hall, hand-in-hand with Daisy, to greet everyone who had come.

From the beginning of the reception, the Archdeacon and the Bishop were surrounded by a phalanx of clergy. Eventually, though, Margaret managed to slip away from the crowd and made her way to Rosemary.

'I'm sorry we haven't had a chance to meet till now,' she said, extending her hand. 'I'm Margaret Phillips, the Archdeacon. And you must be Rosemary. I know it's a bit late, but welcome to Branlingham.'

Rosemary smiled shyly, feeling her cheeks reddening as she accepted the firm handshake. 'Thank you, Archdeacon.'

'Please, call me Margaret,' the other woman insisted, then went on, 'I trust you're settling in well? Everything is satisfactory?'

It was now or never, Rosemary told herself, taking a deep breath. 'Actually . . . Margaret, the Vicarage is in rather dire condition. I don't know whether Gervase has mentioned it.'

Margaret looked surprised. 'No, I don't think so.' She took a sudden decision. 'Why don't you show me? Now?'

This was exactly what Rosemary had hoped for. The two

women slipped away from the party and walked the short distance to the Vicarage.

'But this is appalling!' Margaret said at once, taking in the peeling paintwork and the crumbling plaster. 'You can't be expected to live in conditions like this!'

'I was afraid that Gervase might not have told you. I did ask him to mention it, but he's not very . . . worldly.'

Margaret shook her head. 'Men,' she stated flatly. 'I asked the churchwardens, before you moved in, if the house needed any work, and they told me it could do with a lick of paint. That was the understatement of the century.' With her finger she flicked a bit of loose plaster; it turned to dust and trickled to the floor. 'I'm so sorry, Rosemary. No one should have to live in conditions like this. It was my responsibility, and I shouldn't have trusted the word of anyone else.'

Now that Rosemary had got this far, she became apologetic. 'It wasn't your fault. I know that there wasn't much time to do anything before we moved in.'

'Well, something shall be done now,' Margaret said in an authoritative voice. 'As soon as possible – if not tomorrow, then first thing next week. I'll send someone in to do the plastering, to make all the walls good.'

'And the decorating?' Rosemary said without much hope, imagining a working party from the parish invading her house for weeks.

'Oh, that as well.' Margaret smiled to herself, as if at a private joke. 'I know a decorator who gives the diocese a very good discount.'

Rosemary let out her breath in a sigh of relief. 'That's all right, then.'

'Don't worry about a thing,' Margaret assured her. 'It will all be taken care of, and as speedily as possible. You have my word.'

Chapter 6

Margaret Phillips was not just good at her job; she loved it as well. Most of what she did involved fairly detailed and potentially boring administrative work. Even that she loved, bringing to it her methodical and disciplined mind and taking from it the satisfaction of creating order from chaos.

Sometimes the pleasures were more concrete, as on Friday morning. Arranging the necessary repairs to the Branlingham Vicarage was, in a sense, a routine task, but for Margaret it was informed with the satisfaction that came with knowing how much of a difference it would make to Rosemary Finch and her family. She had liked Rosemary, and it pleased her to think that she had it in her power to bring her a bit of happiness.

Margaret had not always been so sanguine about her life. There had been a time, and not so long ago, when she'd been desperately unhappy.

Though she'd come to it relatively late, the Church was in fact her first career. Before that she had devoted her life to supporting Hal in his business, as a stay-at-home wife, mother and hostess. They'd married immediately after coming down from Cambridge, and Alexander had arrived soon after, keeping her busy for the first few years. When her son was old enough to go to school she might have worked, but her history degree, without teaching qualifications, had not equipped her to do much in the way of a proper job, and there was no financial incentive to find one; by then Hal's business was spectacularly successful and money was available in abundance.

And Hal had liked her to stay at home. He'd enjoyed showing off his beautiful wife, the mother of his intelligent and charming son, to his business associates. He'd liked coming home to their exquisite country house – when he came home at all, that was – to find her waiting for him, dressed in expensive clothes and putting a hot meal on the table.

She'd done it all, and had done it well. But she'd hated virtually every minute of it. While others would have given much for that sort of idle and pampered life-style, cushioned as it was by unlimited wealth, Margaret had found it stifling and miserable, without intellectual stimulation of any kind. She'd never liked to cook, and she'd never been interested in clothes; the black 'uniform' of the archdeacon was far more to her liking than the wardrobe of designer garments with which she had once adorned herself.

And of course during those years she'd rarely seen Hal, who had been obsessed with his business to the virtual exclusion of all else. Their marriage, founded on so much love, had foundered on the rocks of his success. Though it appeared perfect and idyllic to the outside world, Margaret knew it to be hollow at the heart, a mere sham. They went through the motions, observed the rituals of a shared home and a shared bed, while all of Hal's thoughts and energies were directed elsewhere. Margaret was certain that he wasn't having affairs: he scarcely had time for *her*, let alone for other women. She'd never stopped loving Hal, but her anger with him had built up over the years, overwhelming her with unhappiness. Their rows had been intense but infrequent; after all, it wasn't possible to row with someone who wasn't there. Often she'd thought of leaving him, though, and might have done so if it hadn't been for Alexander.

Her son was the only thing that had kept her sane. Margaret would have liked more children, but persistent gynaecological problems had prevented it, so she poured all of her energies into the raising of Alexander. She loved him unreservedly, and begrudged him nothing; Alexander reciprocated with loyalty and love.

The first wrench had come when Alexander had gone away to boarding school. His absence had exposed the emptiness at the heart of Margaret's existence, and she had despaired. Outwardly serene and in control of her life, inwardly she had stared into the void. But somehow she had coped, and carried on.

And then had come that terrible year, the year that had changed everything. It had all seemed to happen at once: Margaret had had to have a hysterectomy, there'd been the dreadful business with Alexander, and then Hal's heart attack.

Hal had almost died. Not yet forty, and she had almost lost him. Margaret's quiet despair had escalated into frenzy as Hal's brush with death threw into relief her love for him while perversely it increased her anger with him. How dared he do that to her? After all she'd suffered for him, how dared he kill himself with overwork?

She'd sat by his bedside in hospital while he hovered between life and death, holding his hand, loving him, hating him, overwhelmed with anger and guilt. No one to turn to, no one to talk to about the emotions that were tearing her apart inside.

And then a man had come along: a gentle, sweet-faced man in a black cassock. The hospital chaplain had taken Margaret aside and had listened to her. For hours on end he listened as she poured out the years' worth of bottled-up rage and misery. He didn't lecture her or censure her; he didn't mouth pious platitudes about God's will. He merely listened to her, with a compassion that went beyond sympathy to the deepest sort of empathy, his own eyes filled with tears as he accepted the vicarious burden of her pain.

Margaret had never been a church-goer. She'd grown up in a household that placed immense value on education and achievement but none at all on the things of the spirit. She'd been brought up to regard religion as little more than superstition, a crutch for people who had nothing better to do. Her exposure to clergymen had been limited, chiefly, to Hal's father, a rather remote figure whom she knew not at all well. Nothing in her life had prepared her for the selfless caring she received from the hospital chaplain; it was a revelation.

And ultimately, of course, it had led her to where she was now. Her conversion hadn't happened overnight; it had been gradual, growing out of that initial contact with a man of true faith and spirituality. She had begun reading the Bible, had started going to church, and in spite of the very evident lack of perfection among many of the churchgoers she'd encountered in those early days, there was something there that held her and drew her in more deeply, until one day she realised that it was the mainstay of her life. She'd felt strongly called to priesthood, at a time when that option was nothing more than a hopeful dream for women. So she'd taken the path then available: two years at theological college, ordination as a deacon, and a curacy. By the time she was ready to move on, the Church of England had caught up with her aspirations, and she was able to be priested.

Now her life bore no resemblance at all to that of the frustrated stay-at-home wife she had once been. The job was demanding and occasionally exhausting, but she was more than up to the challenge of it; she was happy and fulfilled in her work. Her marriage, too, had been transformed by the upheavals they'd both undergone. They had exchanged roles, and Margaret felt that it suited them both down to the ground. Hal enjoyed cooking and pottering about the house as she had never done, and he seemed a different person now that the pressure was off. Margaret knew that *she* was a different person as well, a better and infinitely happier one. The love between them, tested so painfully, had come through it all stronger than ever. Last year they'd celebrated their silver wedding, but there were moments when she felt more like a newlywed, rediscovering her husband after so many years.

She thought of her husband now as she prepared to sort out the problem of the Branlingham Vicarage. He should, he'd told her, be finished at Valerie Marler's in another week or so; that would be just about right.

As a thoroughly modern archdeacon, Margaret had all of the tools of up-to-date technology at her disposal. She opened her computerised database and found the name of a plasterer who'd done some other work for the diocese, then picked up the phone and rang him. He was interested; he was available. With any luck he'd be able to get to Branlingham that afternoon.

If only everything in life were that easy, Margaret Phillips reflected as she went on to the next task at hand.

Valerie Marler was at her computer that morning as well. After a slow start, rewriting the scene wherein Toby had swept Cecily into his arms – it was, after all, too soon for that, and she now realised it – she conceived a new and exciting idea: Pandora should die. Not too soon, not just yet, but she should die. Perhaps it would be by vehicular means, a car out of control striking her down on a zebra crossing. Or perhaps she could be stung by a bee in her blasted garden, and die of an allergic reaction. Or drown in her swimming pool.

Killing her off wasn't as easy as it sounded, Valerie recognised. People *did* die, all of the time, but healthy young women in the prime of life didn't just pop their clogs because they were inconvenient. It wasn't like Victorian times, when a writer could give someone an interesting cough one day, and the next day write them into early oblivion with consumption. These days it just didn't happen like that, and a sudden, unexplained death could come across as contrived.

Unless, Valerie thought suddenly, Toby or Cecily murdered her. Toby. Or Cecily. Or more likely both of them together. A conspiracy to murder.

It wasn't the sort of book she'd ever written before, but that didn't mean she couldn't do it now. In her youth she'd read everything that Agatha Christie ever wrote; she was familiar with the conventions of the genre. Her loyal readers would go along with her no matter what she did, and her publishers would surely follow. It could be accomplished in a subtle way, so that it would be considered 'ground-breaking'.

Oh, it could work very well. Valerie's mind churned with ideas she couldn't wait to get down. If they weren't in it together, then Toby could suspect Cecily and she, in turn, could suspect Toby; that would add an interesting dimension to the plot, and serve as a useful device to keep them from getting together too soon. Or if they *were* in it together, the very act would poison their budding relationship and drive them apart. But where would that leave Valerie? They had to get together in the end, one way or another.

The minutes flew by, and when her allotted time was up, Valerie kept on working.

Shaun Kelly was also at his desk that morning, looking at a printout of the sales figures for Valerie Marler's latest book. They were, he admitted to himself, a bit disappointing. Val's editor had been making frightened noises, saying that public tastes were changing. But it was early days yet; the new hard-cover, and the paperback of the last-but-one book, had only been out for a few weeks. There was plenty of time for an upturn, and it would surely happen. Wasn't that why he was here? And hadn't he always done well by her in the past? Shaun felt that a great deal of the credit for her success was down to him. Yes, of course Val wrote the things, but the women of the world would not have bought them in the quantities they'd always done in the past if he had not been doing his job and doing it well.

Yes, the sales figures would surely show an upturn within the next month. After all, he had arranged the *Hello!* shoot, and that in itself would be a great sales boost. And the next book would be even more successful, he promised himself. Publication of *The Path Not Chosen* was nearly a year away, but already he was making plans: lining up slots for her on radio and television talk shows, chatting up literary editors, and exploring the possibilities of a first US tour. That would be smashing; he closed his eyes and pictured it. Val taking the country by storm, swanning round Manhattan in a limousine, the toast of the town. Appearing on every national talk show. Partied and fêted by movers and shakers. And then a triumphant progress across the country, finishing in California. Hollywood, where they would be begging her for screenplay rights.

And he would be at her side. He, Shaun Kelly. At her side in the limos and at the parties, and in her bed at night. All of those rich, high-powered Americans would want her, would lust after her elfin beauty, but he would know that she was all his.

She was the best thing that had ever happened to him.

Mind you, Shaun had always known that he had it in him to be successful. Growing up in Luton, one of a huge tribe of children, he had mentally detached himself from his surroundings and lived a secret life in his head. He had dreamed his dreams, had seen a future for himself that was far removed from Luton, from the street of narrow terraced houses that had then prescribed his physical world.

As soon as he could get away, he reinvented himself. Shaun left Luton behind him for ever, literally and figuratively. He forgot his family, put them out of his mind, and they in turn forgot about him; after all, he was just one of many. The new background he concocted for himself was much more romantic and glamorous than the back streets of Luton: the green fields of Ireland which had spawned his distant ancestors now became his adopted birthplace, and he cultivated the broad brogue that went with it. He drank Guinness; he larded his conversation with references to the Ould Country. With complete lack of shame he implied, and let it be assumed, that he had attended Trinity College, Dublin, and there was even a hint of some youthful indiscretion, perhaps some ill-judged but exciting Republican involvement, to add a dash of mystery to the romantic persona he had created.

His first few jobs had not been all that glamorous, in spite of all that. But he had worked his way up to where he was today: Valerie Marler's personal publicist, responsible for her worldwide fame.

And Valerie Marler's lover. Effortlessly his thoughts moved on from triumphal tours of America to reflections of a more intimate, and more immediate, nature: Val's beautiful body, white as alabaster but warm and yielding, and tonight it would be his. Shaun Kelly could hardly wait.

Rosemary Finch's morning was more tranquil. Delivering Daisy to school, once again she met Annie Sawbridge at the school gates. Annie invited her to come home with her for a cup of coffee, and she accepted gladly.

The Sawbridges lived in a new house on the edge of

Branlingham, equipped with the latest in gadgetry and furnished in a sleek, modern style. It was unlike anything in Rosemary's experience, used as she was to living with parish cast-offs for the whole of her life. She admired it without envy, as one might admire something in a foreign country, recognising its worth without necessarily wanting it for oneself.

The kitchen she found especially interesting, all fitted out with labour-saving appliances and as clinical-looking as a hospital, with shiny white fitted units, white tiled walls and a white floor. Annie brewed the coffee from freshly ground beans in a built-in coffee-making machine, then carried it through to an enormous front room with exposed roof beams, where they sat on minimalist modern furniture, drinking coffee while Jack the kitten played round their feet and baby Jamie slept in his carry-cot.

Annie, a cheerful and uncomplicated woman, was a born talker, and Rosemary was quite content to let her talk. She heard all about how the Sawbridges had moved 'doon sooth' a few years earlier: 'It serves me right for marrying a Sassenach,' Annie admitted with a philosophical grin. Colin Sawbridge worked in London, Rosemary learned, but Annie, while resigned to leaving Scotland for the heathen south, had drawn the line at living in the city, so they'd settled in Suffolk, within commuting distance of London, and had had the house in Branlingham built for them.

The baby began to fuss; Annie pulled up her jumper and fed him unselfconsciously, and when he was sated, she offered the bundle to Rosemary. 'Would you like to hold wee Jamie, then?'

Rosemary took him from her and cradled him in her arms, looking down into his tiny face with decidedly mixed feelings. The weight of the little body against her breast brought her strong maternal instincts to the surface, mingled with the knowledge that she would never have another child of her own. She was too old; the doctors said it was too risky, with one Down's syndrome child already, and besides, raising Daisy took all the energy and resources she had. Another child was out of the question.

A boy, a son, would have been nice.

Laura had given Gervase a son. Rosemary thought about Thomas as she stroked the peach-fuzz cheek with her finger. She hadn't known Tom when he was this size; perhaps things would have turned out differently if she had.

She had tried her hardest with Tom, but it just hadn't worked. He had never accepted her, had in fact actively resented and even despised her, and had done everything in his power to undermine her. She'd hoped to be a mother to the little boy, but he hadn't wanted that. His grief at his mother's death had been extravagant and real; he was determined that no one would take her place.

The battle between them, which started even before she'd married Gervase, was carried out in private. Tom was sly enough to keep his detestation of the usurping stepmother from his father, and, for Rosemary's part, she wanted to spare Gervase the knowledge of the pain his son so deliberately inflicted upon her. 'I hate you. You're not my mother,' he would say to her whenever they crossed swords over some innocuous matter. On one occasion he'd added, his eyes – so like Gervase's eyes – glittering with malice, 'And my father doesn't love you either. He only married you because he needed someone to look after him.'

He'd only needed to say it once. The words had embedded themselves like slivers of ice in Rosemary's heart, and there they'd stayed, reinforcing a fear she had not until then dared to articulate to herself but that had been there all along. And although Tom, with the cruel but unerring instinct of childhood, had put his finger on the nub of her insecurity, there was more to it than Tom could understand. Gervase needed her – needed someone – to look after him on a day-to-day basis, to take care of the details of life that he found too cumbersome to deal with. That was what Tom had meant, and she knew that it was true. But she had also realised, very early on in their relationship, that Gervase had a strong sex drive, and needed what a wife could provide him in that department as well. After all, why else would he have married her, when he'd known such happiness with the beautiful Laura? And of course she couldn't ask Gervase; she didn't want to know the answer, didn't want to force him to admit the truth.

'I'd better go,' Rosemary said at last, handing Jamie back to his mother. There was still unpacking to be done at home, she explained.

But when Rosemary got back to the empty vicarage – Gervase had now embarked on his parish duties, and wouldn't be back all day – she didn't start unpacking. After a brief struggle with her conscience, she succumbed to one of her guilty pleasures: she made herself a cup of tea, put a favourite CD in the machine, and curled up on the sofa with her new Valerie Marler paperback. Before she knew it, her own insecurities and shortcomings, and even her shabby surroundings, had faded into the background, and she was wandering the hills of Tuscany with Portia and Roberto. It was bliss.

Valerie, when on her own, didn't eat very much, but she was quite capable of cooking when she had to. Friday afternoons, once her correspondence had been dealt with, were now generally given over to preparing something rather special for Shaun's supper.

Shaun liked his food, and since he'd started spending his weekends at Rose Cottage, Valerie had enjoyed cooking for him. Today she was feeling a bit guilty about Shaun; she'd scarcely spoken to him all week, or even thought of him. So she resolved to make a special effort, to make it up to him. She'd decided on *coq au vin*, so she prepared the chicken and the vegetables, planning to get the casserole ready to pop into a slow oven well before Shaun arrived.

But she found it difficult to concentrate, even on so simple a task as peeling carrots. From the dining room came the distracting sound of Hal Phillips's cheerful whistle. It was enough to drive her mad.

Valerie had tried to stay out of the dining room, but that whistle was a constant reminder of his nearness. In spite of her resolutions, she found herself moving towards the whistle, vegetable peeler in hand.

Hal Phillips was up on a ladder deploying a paint roller; he stopped whistling and looked down as she entered the room. 'It's coming along nicely,' he said, smiling.

'I was wondering if I'll be able to use the dining room this weekend,' she said in something approaching a normal voice.

'I'm almost finished,' he reassured her. 'You'll be able to eat in here tonight, if you don't mind the smell of paint.'

Valerie swallowed, knowing that the smell of paint would always remind her of Hal Phillips. 'I don't mind.'

'I'll open a few windows when I've finished, so it shouldn't be too bad.' He nodded towards the peeler in her hand and added, 'Something special tonight, then?'

Her heart leapt involuntarily, even as she told herself that no *double entendre* had been intended. 'Just . . . a friend.'

'Right.' He leaned down and moved the roller back and forth rhythmically in the paint tray.

'You won't join me for a cup of tea?' she found herself asking.

Hal shook his head. 'I won't, thank you, Miss Marler. I'd better get on with this.'

She went back into the kitchen as the whistling resumed.

Automatically she put the kettle on the Aga, though she didn't really want tea, and went to the fridge for the milk. The bottle was nearly empty, and there didn't seem to be another.

Without thinking about it, Valerie closed the fridge door and called, 'I'm just about out of milk. I'm going out to get some.'

She might have gone to the village shop, of course, but before she realised it Valerie found that the Porsche was on the road headed towards Saxwell. She put the window down and breathed in the cool air, blanking her mind of what she was doing.

In Saxwell, Valerie bypassed the town centre and headed out the Bury Road. She slowed down as she passed The Archdeaconry, causing the driver behind her to brake and lean on his horn angrily, but there was no car in the drive or any other sign of human habitation.

Valerie parked the Porsche down the same side road she'd used the day before, and retraced her steps to the corner shop. This time the heavy-faced girl was on her own; she looked at Valerie with a glimmer of recognition as she put the carton of milk on the counter by the till. 'You were in here yesterday, weren't you?'

'That's right,' Valerie admitted.

'New in the neighbourhood, are you, then?'

Valerie gave a vague wave of her hand. 'Not exactly.'

'You were asking me about Mr Phillips,' the girl recalled. 'The Archdeacon's husband, you know.'

'Was I?'

The girl grinned as she punched numbers into the till. 'Remember, I told you that he was dishy.'

'So you did.'

'Mum doesn't like me talking about him,' she confided. 'I reckon she fancies him herself, you know. He *is* awfully fanciable.'

Reaching into her handbag to extract her purse, Valerie asked nonchalantly, 'He comes in here, then?'

'Oh, yes, now and again. Not often enough for me.' She gave a roguish wink.

Valerie couldn't think of any way to prolong the exchange without betraying undue interest, so she took her change and her milk, nodding to the girl as she left.

Instead of returning to her car, she walked round the corner and strolled past The Archdeaconry. The dark car was back in the drive, so the Magpie must be at home. Valerie felt conspicuous; she couldn't continue to walk up and down the road without some nosy neighbour noticing and ringing Homewatch. She didn't look like a housebreaker or a confidence trickster, but these days people were so suspicious.

There was a telephone box on the other side of the road, at a slight angle to The Archdeaconry but with a reasonably good view of the drive and the front door. Valerie crossed the road and took up a position in the phone box, holding the receiver to her ear just in case anyone was watching. She remained for nearly half an hour, and as she was about to give up and go home, the door opened and the Magpie came out and got in her car. Valerie wished that she were in her own car; it would be interesting to follow the Magpie and see where she went. Instead she watched till the car was out of sight, then put the phone back on the hook and returned to the Porsche, with one last stroll past The Archdeaconry.

By the time Shaun arrived that evening, all was in readiness. The casserole was in the oven, the champagne was on ice, and Valerie, deliberately, had changed into the sort of slinky outfit that Shaun liked. True to his word, Hal Phillips had finished the dining room and tidied up after himself; apart from the faint smell of paint, one wouldn't have known he'd been there. Valerie laid the table well before Shaun's arrival, but waited until she heard his car to light the candles.

The secrecy of their affair was something that appealed to Shaun; he enjoyed arriving under cover of darkness, secreting his car in her garage, and letting himself into the house with his own key. Though both of them were free agents, with no spouses to answer to, there was a whiff of the illicit about the way they conducted their affair, giving it an added *frisson* of excitement. One day, Shaun was convinced, he would possess Valerie Marler publicly, but for now it pleased him that no one else knew of their relationship.

Valerie had arranged herself picturesquely on the sofa, waiting for him. 'Hello, Val me darlin',' he said softly, bending to kiss her.

She frowned. 'I've told you not to call me that.' The stage-Oirish voice grated; she'd never liked being called 'Val', and now it was made worse by the fact that it reminded her of 'Hal'. This was not, she apprehended, a good start to the evening.

But things were quickly back on an even keel, following the established pattern of their weekends together. They sipped their champagne and chatted about the events of the week; for Shaun these were much the same as usual, but in Valerie's case it was a highly edited version of the truth that she presented to him.

Shaun looked round the front room with appreciation. 'I see that the chappie I found for you has finished in here. He's done a good job.' The Irish accent had been abandoned.

'Yes,' Valerie agreed in a neutral tone. 'He's very efficient. He's done the dining room as well.'

The evening took its usual course. When the champagne bottle was empty they moved into the dining room. Shaun enjoyed the *coq au vin* while Valerie picked at her portion, her appetite poor. They finished up the bottle of burgundy and moved on to port with the cheese.

Valerie cleared the table in preparation for the sweet course; as she put the plates into the dishwasher Shaun followed her into the kitchen and came up behind her, wrapping his arms round her and sliding his hands over the slippery silk of her tunic. 'We haven't had the pudding yet,' Valerie said, trying to keep the irritation out of her voice. 'It's chocolate mousse – your favourite.'

'Bugger the pudding,' Shaun murmured, nibbling at her ear. 'Let's go upstairs. You're my favourite pudding, sweetheart.'

She pulled away from him. 'Please, Shaun. Not yet. I want my pudding and my coffee.'

Shaun stood back and gave her a long, searching look; she was not usually so coy or reluctant, and now she was refusing to meet his eyes. She bit her lip and looked down, and Shaun was seized with a sudden intuition. 'There isn't anyone else, is there, Val? You haven't been two-timing me?'

'I told you not to call me that.' Valerie raised her eyes and gazed at him defiantly. Why had she ever found him attractive? she wondered in a detached way. His eyes were too close together, and she'd never liked that gingery sort of hair. In fact, looking at him now, she realised that he was rather repellent in appearance as well as in personality.

'Because I wouldn't like that,' he went on, as though she hadn't spoken. He reached out and circled her neck with his hands, entwining his fingers in her hair and stroking the base of her throat with his thumbs. 'Old Shaun wouldn't like that at all. He's a jealous sort of bloke, is old Shaun. He couldn't bear to think of his Val with another man.'

Valerie swallowed, feeling the pressure of his thumbs. 'There isn't anyone else,' she whispered.

The Irish accent returned, deliberate and exaggerated.

''Tis glad I am to hear it.' He pulled her towards him, kissing her roughly, forcing her lips apart with his tongue, and after a while his hands left her neck and dropped down to unbutton her tunic.

She submitted to his embraces and let him make love to her. But Valerie remained detached. Shaun was like a child, she realised, a spoilt child, who was not nearly as charming as he thought he was. And he was capable of behaving reasonably as long as he got his own way, but could turn nasty when thwarted. She kept her eyes closed, and the face she saw behind her eyelids was not the face of Shaun Kelly. It was the smiling face of Hal Phillips.

Chapter 7

Rosemary wasn't used to being looked after, so it had come as a pleasant surprise to find that the Archdeacon was as good as her word. The plasterer, a kindly and voluble old gent, had arrived as promised, and had worked wonders on the crumbling walls of the Vicarage. Now everything was in readiness for the decorator, who was due to begin this morning. Used to workmen who didn't show up when expected, she was none the less inclined to believe in the powers of the Archdeacon to get the decorator there on time.

She gave Gervase and Daisy breakfast, and then took Daisy to school. As they walked the short distance to the school gates, Rosemary noted with delight that there was a new warmth to the sun that hadn't been there the day before; perhaps spring, so long delayed, was finally about to put in an appearance. The flowers, unable to be held back any longer, were already blooming in profusion, and now the buds on the hawthorn hedges were swelling, seeming about to burst forth into white may blossom. She could smell the earth, and the unmistakable spring-like scent of green things wafted in the air. Tempted to linger and dawdle on her way back, Rosemary looked at her watch and remembered the decorator, and increased her pace. By the time she got home she felt over-warm in her jacket, and only partly because she'd hurried; perhaps by afternoon, when she went to collect Daisy, she wouldn't even need a cardigan. Rosemary realised, now that spring was seemingly on the way, how much she'd missed its early promise, and its late flowering was all the more wel-come for being so long delayed.

Gervase had gone off to do some hospital visits. Rosemary took her jacket off and hung it up; a cup of tea seemed in order, and she'd just put the kettle on when the doorbell chimed.

The man at the door was dressed in an immaculate white overall, and had a nice smile. 'Mrs Finch? I'm Hal Phillips,' he said. 'You're expecting me?'

'The Archdeacon said you'd be coming this morning,' Rosemary responded, wondering why the name sounded vaguely familiar. 'And she seems to be a woman of her word.'

His smile broadened into a grin. 'Oh, I'd agree with that. Absolutely. It would be more than my life is worth not to follow the Archdeacon's orders to the letter.'

'The kettle's just boiled. Would you like a cup of tea?'

'Yes, please,' he said promptly. Hal looked round with a professional eye at the vast dark expanses of the hall as he fol-lowed her through to the kitchen. It was a wonderful house, he thought enthusiastically, with great possibilities. How for-tunate that the diocese hadn't sold it.

'I've brought some colour charts, Mrs Finch. I'll start on the trim – I've plenty of preparation to do – but you can at least begin to think about colours.' He spread the charts out on the kitchen table as she poured boiling water into the teapot.

'Oh.' Rosemary looked at him, flustered. 'I hadn't realised it would be up to me.'

'But of course, Mrs Finch.' He smiled reassuringly. 'You

and your family are the ones who have to live here. Or should
I say, have the privilege of living here. It's a splendid house.'

'Well, then . . . magnolia?' she ventured. The Vicarage at
Letherfield had been painted magnolia, top to bottom.

Hal Phillips stared at her as if she'd uttered blasphemy, and
his expletive mingled shock with contempt. 'Magnolia!'

Rosemary felt herself blushing, despising herself for it. 'I
don't know. I thought . . . I mean, why not magnolia?'

'Because magnolia is boring,' he said instantly and with
conviction. 'Boring, boring, boring. *Everyone* has magnolia,
and it's boring.' He noted her flaming cheeks, felt guilty
that he'd caused such a reaction, and attempted to soften
his words. 'This house deserves better than that. It's a wonderful house, Mrs Finch. It has such character. It's *not* a
boring house.' And you're not a boring person, he wanted
to add, surprised at himself that he was already sure of that
fact.

'Then . . . what?' She looked at him appealingly. 'I'm not
very good at things like this. You must help me, Mr Phillips.'

If virtually any other woman had said those words, Hal
Phillips would have seen it as a flirtatious ploy: the 'helpless
woman' scenario. But there was nothing in the least flirtatious about Rosemary Finch's level gaze and self-deprecating
smile. She meant what she said; there was no coy subtext.
He opened his mouth, and the words that came out were
not the ones he'd intended. 'Please, Mrs Finch. Call me Hal.'

'Hal.' She tried it out, liking the straightforwardness of the
name. 'Is that short for something? Henry, or Harold?'

'No, it's just Hal.' He grinned. 'My mother saw a produc-
tion of *Henry IV Part One* a few weeks before I was born. She
fell in love with Prince Hal, so Hal it was.'

She poured the tea. 'I always like to think of my name as
being Shakespearean as well. You know, "There's Rosemary,
that's for remembrance." Ophelia.' Somehow there didn't

seem anything odd in discussing Shakespeare with the man who had come to decorate her house.

'Rosemary.' He hadn't known that was her name; Margaret had only spoken of her as Mrs Finch. It suited her, he decided.

'But it probably wasn't Shakespearean at all,' she added. 'I've never asked my mother, because I'd rather not know that it was probably something as prosaic as a big rosemary bush in the garden of my parents' vicarage that gave her the idea.'

'You grew up in a vicarage?' Hal asked, somehow not surprised.

'Yes, quite a few of them in fact, one after another. My father didn't seem to stay very long in one place. Do you take sugar?'

'No, thank you, just as it is.' He sipped his tea and went on. '*My* father is a clergyman as well.'

'So you're vicarage too.' Perhaps, thought Rosemary, that explained the instant sense of familiarity with a man she'd never met before.

'Well, not exactly,' Hal admitted. 'Only for the first few years of my life, at any rate. Then my father left parish work and became a cathedral canon, at Malbury Cathedral. Most of my childhood was spent in a cathedral close, not a vicarage.'

Rosemary would have liked living in a cathedral close: all that wonderful music, she thought. 'That must have been nice.'

'It was.' Why, wondered Hal, was he telling her this? 'All that wonderful music.'

Her face was transformed by a smile of delight. 'You like cathedral music?'

'I love it. I was a chorister for years, till my voice broke.'

Rosemary rushed out of the kitchen, returning a few seconds later with a stack of compact discs. She put them down on the table in front of Hal. 'Here's my collection,' she told him. 'It's my favourite sort of music in the world.'

He flipped through the stack. 'This one is nice – I have a copy of it myself. But I haven't heard this one.'

'Oh, it's a wonderful one, one of my favourites,' she enthused. 'I'll play it for you, if you like.'

'I'd love to hear it.'

They took their tea into the drawing room, where Rosemary put the CD into the player. They sat in companionable silence for some minutes, sipping tea and listening to the clear boys' voices soaring to the high mediaeval vaulting of the cathedral. Eventually, though, when the long-case clock in the hall chimed the hour, Hal looked at the time. 'I really ought to get on with my work,' he said with real regret. 'I've been here nearly an hour and haven't accomplished a thing.'

'Why don't you start in this room?' Rosemary suggested. 'Then you can listen to the music while you work.'

'An excellent idea,' he approved.

Hal made several trips to his van, bringing in dust sheets, tins of paint, and various equipment. Rosemary stayed on the sofa and watched him as he prepared the skirting boards and window architraves to receive a coat of gloss paint. When the disc finished she changed it for another, and remained to listen to it.

After a while Hal spoke over the music. He raised the subject of colour again, but this time he did it more tactfully. 'This room could take a really strong colour – a deep green, or a terracotta,' he observed.

Rosemary looked dubious. 'If you say so.'

'Houses like this were built for strong colours,' he assured her. 'I mean, look at pictures of William Morris's house, or Wightwick Manor. The Gothic Revival was all about a return to the mediaeval, to those deep primary colours of the mediaeval church. Look at the colours in those windows.' He indicated the stained glass panels that ran across the tops of the windows in the room. 'Rich reds, dark blues, deep greens, intense golds. Think in terms of those colours for this room. It would look stunning.'

'But wouldn't it be awfully dark?' The vicarages of Rosemary's childhood had all been dark and gloomy; the magnolia of Letherfield Vicarage had seemed a welcome change to her.

Hal shook his head. 'Not necessarily. It's an enormous room, with a high ceiling. It could take it.' He looked round with an appraising eye and continued, 'I'd recommend wallpaper for this room, rather than paint. You could get a subtler, richer effect with paper.'

'Oh, but that would be expensive,' Rosemary protested.

'You don't need to worry about that,' he said dismissively. 'The diocese is paying.'

'Surely it wouldn't authorise spending any more money than necessary. I mean, money is such an issue these days. The Archdeacon—'

Hal grinned. 'Leave the Archdeacon to me.'

'You know her? Well, yes, I suppose she sent you, but . . .'

'As a matter of fact I know the Archdeacon rather well,' he said, straight-faced but with a smile tugging at the corner of his mouth; this was a game he enjoyed playing, and had done so a number of times before. 'I've been married to her for twenty-five years.'

'Oh!' Rosemary flushed as the pieces fell into place in her mind. 'Oh, the name – of course. I should have realised.'

'No reason why you should have done.'

She bit her lip and picked at some frayed threads on the arm of the sofa. 'Oh, I *am* sorry. You must think me awfully dim.'

'No, of course not,' he tried to reassure her. Once again Hal was conscious of having distressed her in some way, of having tapped some well of insecurity, and he regretted that he hadn't been more sensitive. She was an unusual woman, this Rosemary Finch, not like any woman he'd ever encountered before, and certainly not like self-confident Margaret. In some ways he felt as if he'd known her for years; their conversation was so easy, so effortless and lively. But there was something enigmatic about her as well: the essence of her personality eluded him, and intrigued him.

Valerie was finding it difficult to concentrate on her writing, exciting though the book had become. She'd just had another endless-seeming weekend with Shaun, who was proving impossible to get rid of. He seemed unable to take a hint, as so many others had done before him, and withdraw gracefully from her life.

And how she wanted him out of her life, or at least her private life. He had managed to convince her that she still needed his professional services, but his private ones had become abhorrent to her. It was all she could do to keep from shuddering when he touched her.

It was the trouble, Valerie reflected, with mixing business and pleasure. She'd always managed it before, but the other men hadn't been like Shaun; they'd been less selfish, perhaps, not as tenacious in clinging on to her. Shaun seemed, for some reason, to look on her as his permanent property, rather than as a temporary partner in a light-hearted relationship, someone to pass the time with until the next one came along.

For Valerie, if not for Shaun, someone else *had* come along. Hal Phillips dominated her waking thoughts as he monopolised her dreams. She thought of him endlessly, lingering in her mind over his smile, his eyes, his voice. When she wasn't fantasising about him making love to her, she was running over in her mind like a videotape the various conversations they'd had, scouring them for hidden meanings or for anything that could be construed as holding out the tiniest morsel of hope for her.

Now, she remembered an early exchange between them.

He'd been the one, she recalled, who had come up with that old cliché about mixing business and pleasure. Cliché it may have been, but it was certainly true when it came to Shaun; how she wished she'd never got involved with him.

And then, with a blinding jolt that passed almost like a surge of electricity through Valerie's body, she saw new meaning in Hal Phillips's words. Mixing business with pleasure. He'd been working for her at the time he said it, and of course from his point of view that was a sensible precaution. She could see that now, in the light of her problems with Shaun.

But he wasn't working for her now. He'd finished at the end of the previous week. She'd contrived various little jobs to keep him on for three full weeks, but eventually she'd run out of rooms to be decorated, and he had departed for the last time on Friday.

He wasn't working for her any more. That changed everything, she now realised. Now he was free to get involved with her, as he had undoubtedly wanted to do from the very beginning. Only his professionalism had prevented it.

Valerie smiled to herself. It all made sense: of course he had fancied her from the start, but he'd just been holding back until after the job was finished. Now he was free to approach her, to make his feelings known. He would ring her, of course he would, and soon. He would propose, perhaps, that he might drop by Rose Cottage for a drink, and things would take their course from there. She might even, now that she had the upper hand, play a bit hard to get: she might suggest next week instead of this week, or feign reluctance, just so he wouldn't take her compliance for granted.

It would happen soon, today or the next day. Probably today. He wouldn't find her sitting eagerly by the phone, though; it wouldn't do for him to know that she was waiting for his call. She would carry on and follow her routine.

That routine, immutable for so long, had changed over the past few weeks. Now, after the writing and after dealing with her post, Valerie's routine included a trip to Saxwell.

The reasons she contrived for the trips varied from day to day. But whatever else she did in Saxwell – buying something in a high street shop, for instance, or even doing a bit of research at the public library – the visit always ended with a drive up the Bury Road. Some days she parked the Porsche round the corner and walked past The Archdeaconry, attempting to look nonchalant even as she watched the house closely. Other days she only drove past, slowing down and hoping for a glimpse of something, of someone.

On several occasions she'd seen the Magpie coming or going. The Magpie didn't seem to have a regular pattern or routine, which annoyed Valerie greatly. How could she live her life like that, without any kind of structure? What sort of woman was she?

Now, as she drove towards Saxwell with a light heart, it all seemed so clear to Valerie. Hal couldn't possibly love the Magpie. After all, he'd only said that he didn't believe in mixing business with pleasure; he hadn't used those other clichés which appeared so often in books (though not of course her own). He hadn't said 'I'm a happily married man' or 'I love my wife'. He hadn't mentioned his wife at all; if he hadn't been wearing a wedding ring, Valerie wouldn't have even known he had a wife. Therefore she was an irrelevance, not even to be considered as an obstruction to Valerie's own future with Hal.

Her future with Hal. Now that she was sure of the outcome, she could allow herself to think those words.

Their future together. It would be wonderful, of that she was sure. From their first meeting, she had known that he wasn't like other men. Their relationship, which had taken time to come to fruition, would be different as well from

those she'd had with all the others. It wouldn't just be a physical thing, a pleasurable union of bodies – though that too
would be of a different magnitude from anything she'd
known before, intensely pleasurable to both of them – but it
would be a true meeting of minds, a transcendent union, a
joining of souls. They were indeed soul-mates: she'd known it
from the first, as one always knows these things. He had
known it too, of course, which was why he had so scrupu-
lously avoided giving in to it too soon. She respected him for
his integrity; it made her love him even more.

Love. It was the first time that Valerie had articulated the
word to herself in relation to Hal. Now she acknowledged it to
herself: she loved him, as she had never loved any of the others.
Not that she'd ever even pretended to love them; she'd known,
and they'd known, that it wasn't for love that they'd come
together. But with Hal it was different. It was the real thing.

They would make each other so happy; they would share
such delights. She could give him everything that the Magpie
couldn't, and he would erase for her the memory of all those
other men, and of her unhappy marriage. It would be for
ever; it would last. He would be at her side through life, her
consort, supporting her in her career and enriching every
moment with love and joy. Happily ever after.

They might even have a child. A little boy who looked like
Hal, a little girl who looked like her, or even the other way
round. Or a blend: a child of either sex combining her looks
with Hal's would be beautiful indeed. And this time she *would*
be a perfect mother, having learned from her previous mistakes and with Hal at her side to support her. A second chance
at motherhood, with Hal's child.

With those blissful thoughts playing through her mind,
Valerie didn't even bother with an excuse to go into Saxwell
town centre. She headed straight for the Bury Road, automatically slowing down as she approached The Archdeaconry.

Something happened that hadn't happened on any of her previous trips: just before Valerie reached The Archdeaconry, the bonnet of the Magpie's car emerged from the drive and pulled out in front of the Porsche.

Valerie didn't have to debate with herself about what to do next. Keeping a discreet distance behind, she followed the dark car out of Saxwell and into the country. It wasn't a straightforward route, but involved several rather narrow lanes between hedgerows just beginning to turn white with may; Valerie wished that she were driving something less conspicuous than the Porsche. What if the Magpie looked into the mirror and realised she was being followed?

Well, what of it? Valerie told herself defiantly. What difference would it make? The Magpie's marriage was history, as far as she was concerned. Why should she care if the Magpie saw her? All the same, she wished that she weren't driving the Porsche. These narrow country lanes were barely big enough for one car; what if she were to meet someone coming in the other direction, and scraped the side of her car in the hedgerows?

But turning back now was out of the question, even if she'd wanted to.

At Branlingham Vicarage, Hal worked on to the accompaniment of choral music on CD. The time seemed to pass quickly. Rosemary Finch had remained through most of the morning and talked to him as he worked; usually Hal preferred working in solitude, but when she'd suggested, guiltily, that she ought to leave him alone, he'd found himself assuring her that he didn't mind at all. After her embarrassment over discovering that he was married to the Archdeacon, Rosemary had backed off from talking about anything personal, but the conversation had flowed effortlessly none the less, mostly about music and books. Eventually, between CDs, she offered him a tour of the house, and he accepted with eagerness. As they moved from room to room his enthusiasm for the job at hand grew; there was such enormous potential there. With the sort of loving attention he could provide, the house would be a showpiece for the diocese. How fortunate that it had been saved.

They were coming back down the staircase from the tour when the long-case clock struck the maximum number of times. Rosemary stared at the clock, aghast. 'Is it really midday? Where has the morning gone?'

Hal was about to joke that he, at least, had accomplished something, but stopped himself in time; it was just the sort of remark that would upset her. Instead he consulted his watch. 'Yes, it's noon all right.'

'My husband is coming home for lunch, so I'd better get busy.' She hesitated, giving Hal an uncertain look. 'Would you like to join us? It will only be soup and bread, but you'd be welcome.'

He was touched, and wanted to accept, but knew that it wouldn't be proper. 'No, thank you, I've brought my sandwiches.'

'If you're sure.'

Rosemary went off to the kitchen then, and Hal returned to the drawing room to resume work. Later she brought her husband in to introduce him.

Gervase Finch wasn't at all what Hal had been expecting: he was some years older than his wife, for one thing. Tall, thin and ascetic-looking, he had a kindly, if somewhat abstracted, manner.

'Mr Phillips is the Archdeacon's husband,' Rosemary explained.

'Oh, yes?' Gervase peered at him, as if trying to puzzle out what the Archdeacon's husband was doing in his drawing room, wearing a white overall and wielding a paintbrush.

'He's the decorator,' Rosemary amplified.

Hal grinned. 'Shameless nepotism.' Then, lest they take that at face value, he went on, 'And I work cheap.' In fact he didn't charge the diocese anything for work like this; he didn't need the money, and he enjoyed knowing he was doing something for the Church.

After his sandwiches Hal returned to work. He heard Gervase go, and half expected Rosemary to come back into the drawing room and resume their conversation, but she didn't return. Later she popped her head round the door to tell him that she was going out. 'I hope you don't mind being left alone in the house,' she said. 'It will only be for a few minutes. I need to collect my daughter from school.'

Hal knew that the Finches had a daughter; he'd seen the room upstairs with the stuffed animals on the bed, and Rosemary had identified it as 'Daisy's room'. He knew nothing else about Daisy, though the stuffed animals were a rough clue to her age.

And so when Rosemary brought the little girl in to meet him, he was surprised to see, behind her spectacles, the characteristic slanted eyes of a Down's syndrome child .

'This is Daisy,' Rosemary said, watching his face for his reaction. 'Say hello to Mr Phillips, Daisy.'

'Hello,' said the girl, bestowing an open and friendly smile. Apart from the eyes, and a slight slackness round the mouth, she was very like her mother, with her straight, silky hair and her spectacles. This resemblance, with its cruel variation, moved Hal deeply; he hoped that his face didn't betray him.

He dropped his paintbrush and crouched down to her level. 'Hello, Daisy,' he greeted her with grave courtesy. 'It's nice to meet you.' He extended his hand.

Delighted, she put her tiny hand into his large one and shook it, as she had seen her parents do with other grown-ups.

'I've seen your room,' Hal said to her. 'With all of your lovely animals. It's very nice just as it is, of course, but I'm going to paint it for you. Would you like to choose the colour?'

'Oh, yes!' Daisy beamed. 'Pink! I want pink. Pink is my favourite colour.'

Hal retrieved his colour charts and spread them out for her. 'There are lots of pinks. You choose.'

She scanned the charts and stabbed her finger down on the most garish hue, a bright bubble-gum pink. 'That one.'

'Don't you think this one would be nicer, darling?' her mother interposed, indicating a more subtle shade.

'No. This one.' Daisy's voice was adamant.

'It's Daisy's room, and she must have what she wants,' Hal stated. 'I think that's a lovely colour, Daisy.'

The girl smiled, enchanted, at her ally. 'Will you paint my room soon?'

'As soon as I've finished this room,' he promised. 'That is,' he added, looking up at Rosemary, 'if your mummy agrees.'

'Yes, of course.' Her voice sounded odd. 'Daisy, darling, why don't you go up to your room now? I'll be along in a moment to help you change your clothes, but I need to have a word with Mr Phillips.'

'All right, Mummy. Can I give Mr Phillips a kiss?'

Rosemary hesitated for an instant. 'If you like, darling, and if he doesn't mind.'

'I would be delighted,' Hal said with a smile.

Daisy threw her arms round his neck and planted a wet kiss on his cheek. 'You're my friend,' she said, then skipped out of the room.

'I don't know what to say,' Rosemary began when she'd gone.

Hal straightened up to her level. 'I hope you don't mind too much.'

'Mind? Mind what?'

'That we overruled you on the colour. And that I promised to do her room next.'

She stared at him for a moment, and then gave him a radiant smile. It was a smile worth waiting for, Hal decided. 'But of course I don't mind! Mr Phillips . . . Hal,' she amended awkwardly, 'how can I thank you for treating her like a real person? It was so very . . . kind . . . of you.'

'But she *is* a real person,' he pointed out, puzzled.

'You'd be surprised how few people think so,' Rosemary said, her voice taking on a bitterly passionate edge. 'People treat her like something subhuman. They talk over her head, *about* her, rather than *to* her. And when they *do* talk to her, they patronise her. It drives me mad.'

'But she's lovely,' Hal stated sincerely.

There were tears in Rosemary's eyes, and her cheeks were flushed. 'Thank you . . . Hal,' she said, then went after her daughter.

What an unusual woman, Hal thought as he drove his van back towards Saxwell late in the afternoon. She displayed such an odd combination of ingenuous honesty and enigmatic shyness. She wasn't beautiful, not by any stretch of the imagination, but there was a certain quality about her, an inner beauty that somehow came to the surface every now and then and transformed her rather plain face into something arresting.

He rolled the window down. Spring had come to Suffolk very suddenly, and the air was warm. The winter had been a protracted one, the cold weather lasting well into May, and now everything had exploded at once, as though spring could be contained no longer. Spring flowers that usually bloomed sequentially had all come out together, crowding each other for space and providing a feast for the eye, and the may hedges had gone, in virtually a matter of hours, since he'd been this way in the morning, from tentative bud to foamy white blossom. Hal drank it all in, glad to be alive.

Margaret was late coming home that evening. She'd been from one end of her jurisdiction to the other, taking a funeral while the parish priest was on holiday, then traversing the countryside to a deanery synod meeting some miles away. She hadn't minded the drive; the day had been a beautiful one, spring-like at last. But she hadn't had time to eat, and was both tired and hungry.

Hal, knowing that she'd be late, had made a pot of chilli and left it to simmer on the back burner. Margaret sniffed the welcoming spicy aroma as she came in, and saw, passing through the house, that he'd laid the table in the dining room rather than in the breakfast room. There were candles on the table, and a good bottle of claret uncorked on the sideboard. Every archdeacon should have a wife, she said to herself, not for the first time.

She found Hal in the kitchen, tossing the salad. 'You look tired, my love,' he said with concern in his voice.

'I'm knackered.' Margaret came to him and gave him a kiss. 'And starving. But the chilli smells wonderful.'

'It's ready whenever you are.' He led her into the dining room, brought the food through, and lit the candles.

'So,' Margaret teased as he poured the wine, 'what have you done, then? Smashed up the van? Bought yourself some expensive new gadget? You can tell me.'

Hal gave her a baffled look. 'What are you talking about?'

'Guilt, my dear.' She smiled, indicating the candles, the wine, and the table laid with the good silver. 'Isn't that what a candlelit dinner, out of the blue like this, is supposed to mean? That you're feeling guilty about something and are trying to make it up to me, or soften me up for the bad news?'

'Perhaps it just means that I love you.' His voice was light.

'That's all right, then.' She really was, she thought, very lucky to have a husband like Hal. After a few bites of the chilli, which was as delicious as it smelled, she asked him, 'How was your day, then?'

'Oh, fine.'

Margaret remembered that he'd been going to Branlingham Vicarage. 'How did you get on with Rosemary Finch?'

'I found her very pleasant,' Hal responded neutrally.

'She didn't throw herself at you, then?' Margaret teased, smiling. She said it in jest, more as a jibe at Hal's awareness of his own charms than anything else; Rosemary Finch hadn't seemed to her, in their brief meeting, the sort of woman to throw herself at any man, even one as attractive as Hal.

He didn't smile in return, and he didn't sound amused. 'No, she didn't. Not every woman does, you know.'

Margaret knew when to back off. She ate in silence for a moment, then deliberately changed the subject. 'I had a strange experience today,' she said. 'I could swear that I was being followed.'

'Followed?'

'In the car. By a red Porsche. I suppose it was just my imagination, but it was behind me for miles, down some pretty narrow country roads. Just a coincidence, I suppose – the driver must have been going to the same place that I was.'

'A red Porsche,' Hal repeated to himself, and Margaret knew it wasn't just her imagination that he looked as uneasy as she felt.

Chapter 8

A funeral. The Magpie had been conducting a funeral. Valerie shuddered involuntarily at the memory of it, lifting her fingers from the keyboard of her computer. It was difficult to take seriously the activities of Cecily and Toby when there was death – real death – in the world.

Horrible – it had been horrible. Obscene, almost, that intrusion of death into the most beautiful day of the year. Flowers so bright their colours almost hurt the eyes, the trees flaunting the lacy pale green of their new leaves, and everywhere the may, adorning the hedges and trees like sea-foam. In the midst of it, like a wound, that slash of earth, brown and gaping.

Valerie had parked the Porsche a safe distance away, up a country lane, and had walked back to the church where the Magpie's journey had ended. She wasn't sure what she'd expected to find, but it hadn't been this: the Magpie, more like her namesake bird than ever in black cassock, white surplice and black stole, standing by the side of an open grave, surrounded by weeping mourners.

She'd hovered in the trees at the edge of the churchyard, wanting to leave yet somehow unable to make her legs carry

her away. Valerie had stayed very still as the coffin was low-
ered into the ground, as the Magpie intoned the words 'Dust
to dust, ashes to ashes' and the clods of earth hit the coffin lid,
echoing hollowly through the churchyard. Then she'd turned
and fled, back to the Porsche, where she'd sat for an age, shivering and weeping at the horror of it.

Valerie hated funerals. As a child she'd been taken to her
granny's funeral, not knowing what to expect; her strong,
instinctive revulsion to the proceedings had ended in a scene,
as she'd screamed hysterically at the graveside. She could
remember it now as if it were yesterday: they'd told her that
Granny was in that box, and she couldn't understand why
they were putting it in the ground and throwing dirt on it. So
she'd screamed her protest and her horror, shrilly and without
pause.

Her father had been furious. He'd shaken her, and eventually even slapped her to make her stop, but the shrieks had
gone on, seemingly out of her control. She wanted to please
him, she wanted to stop, but the screaming had a life of its
own, filling her ears, filling her head.

She'd never been able to please her father, even when she'd
tried. And she'd never stopped trying, though she knew, deep
down, that by having been born a girl she had forfeited all
chance of gaining his approval. He'd never said so, but she'd
known it: he'd wanted a son, and he'd got her instead. There
was nothing she could do about it; neither could she stop
trying to make him love her. All through her childhood, and
even later, everything she did – the hard work at school, the
regimented life-style – was calculated to win her father's
approval, but she had never succeeded in eliciting even the
tiniest hint of approbation from him.

And now it was too late. Her father's funeral had been the
last she'd been to, and it had been fully as horrifying as the
first. She'd been grown up by then, better in control of her

outward actions, but the screaming had gone on inside her head, unabated by the years. It was too late: now she would never be able to gain his approval.

So Valerie had sat in her Porsche, the symbol of her success in worldly terms, weeping for the father who would never know that his daughter, who should have been a son, was famous and admired.

Now Valerie rested her elbows on her desk and put her head in her hands. She must get a grip, she told herself. That funeral had had nothing to do with her; it was no one she knew, no one whose life had touched hers in any way. *She* was still alive, and she had everything to live for.

Hal hadn't rung, but he would. Probably today. He had most likely even tried to phone while she was out. After all, it would be difficult for him to ring in the evening, with the Magpie at home.

Valerie realised that she'd been so upset over the funeral that she hadn't even checked her answering service. Abandoning any pretence of writing, she picked up the receiver and dialled the access number. 'One message,' said the tinny digital voice. 'Hear it?'

That would be it. Eagerly Valerie tapped the '1' in assent.

'Message received at three forty-three p.m. yesterday,' the voice informed her in its odd artificial cadence. 'Play it?' Again Valerie pressed the key.

'Hello, Val darlin',' drawled Shaun's voice.

Without waiting to hear what he had to say, Valerie put the receiver down.

'You're in a good mood this morning,' Gervase observed at breakfast, smiling at his wife.

Rosemary looked out of the window. 'It looks like it's going to be another beautiful day,' she said. 'I love the spring.'

'Me too,' Daisy chirped. 'I love the flowers. Can we go on a picnic, Mummy? Can we?'

'You have to go to school,' Gervase interposed.

'No, she doesn't.' Rosemary reminded him that this was a so-called 'Baker Day' when the school would be closed for in-service teacher training; she'd mentioned it the night before but he clearly hadn't taken it on board.

'I don't have to go to school today,' echoed Daisy excitedly, bouncing up and down on her chair. 'Can we go on a picnic?'

Gervase caught his wife's eye. 'A picnic sounds a capital idea,' he agreed.

'A picnic! A picnic!' Daisy chanted. 'Daddy, will you come too?'

He got out his diary and consulted it. 'I don't see why not. Someone is coming to see me this morning, but I should be finished in plenty of time.'

'That would be lovely,' Rosemary said, smiling at him as she began to clear the table. What could be nicer than a picnic with her family on a beautiful spring day?

Gervase spent the morning in his study with a parishioner, while Rosemary organised the picnic, boiling eggs for the sandwiches and making sure they had everything they needed. She loved going on picnics; it was a ritual associated with her childhood, and she'd transmitted her love of that ritual to Daisy. Of course the weather seldom co-operated, and when it did there were always ants, or something else went wrong, but that was all part of it.

Rosemary had expected to have Daisy under foot, 'helping' with the picnic preparations, but to her surprise Daisy disappeared into the drawing room and spent the morning chatting to Hal Phillips as he worked. Mid-morning Rosemary took him a mug of coffee, intending to rescue him from her chatterbox daughter, only to discover that he didn't want rescuing.

'We're fine,' he assured her, taking the coffee. 'Daisy is telling me all about Samantha's kitten.'

'Jack,' Daisy affirmed. 'I want a kitten too, but Mummy says wait and see.'

Hal winked at Rosemary. 'Wise Mummy. Kittens grow into cats, you know.'

'Are you sure you wouldn't rather have Daisy helping *me*?' Rosemary offered again. 'I don't want her to distract you.'

He shook his head. 'She's not distracting me.'

'We're having a conversation,' Daisy stated solemnly.

Rosemary suppressed a smile. It was the first time she'd heard Daisy use that word, and she suspected that it was inappropriate under the circumstances: it didn't seem likely that Hal Phillips would be able to get a word in edgeways, with Daisy in full flow. 'Well, I hope that Mr Phillips will let me know when he's had enough of your . . . conversation,' she said, glancing at him over Daisy's head.

Daisy's rejoinder was confident. 'He won't.'

An hour later all was at the ready: the hamper was packed and the picnic rug had been found, after a frantic search, in a tea chest in the attic.

But just as Rosemary was about to announce to her family that they could leave at any time, the phone rang. The call was for Gervase; she put it through to his study.

'I have to go out,' he said a few minutes later, coming into the kitchen. 'An emergency, I'm afraid.'

Rosemary felt a twinge of disappointment, but knew better than to ask whether it couldn't wait until after lunch; as a good vicar's wife, she was accustomed to last-minute changes of plan, no matter how inconvenient or unwelcome. 'At least take a sandwich with you,' she suggested with philosophical acceptance, delving into the picnic hamper and producing one for him.

'Thank you, my dear.' He took it from her.

'But Daddy!' Daisy wailed. 'Our picnic! You said you would come!'

'I'm sorry, darling. But this is important.'

She had tears in her eyes. *'Our picnic* is important.'

'But, darling . . .' Rosemary interjected.

Hal Phillips chose that moment to come into the kitchen with his empty coffee mug. Daisy flung herself at him. 'Daddy says he can't come on our picnic!' she announced dramatically.

'What's all this?' His voice was gentle and he stroked her hair.

'Daddy can't come.' Her tears stopped abruptly and she looked up at him, smiling as an idea formed. 'You come instead,' she demanded. 'Come on our picnic with us.'

'No, I couldn't,' he tried to explain, glancing at Gervase for help.

'Go on,' Gervase urged. 'Please – as a favour to me. I'd be very grateful, Mr Phillips.'

He looked at Rosemary; she shrugged. 'It will make Daisy happy.'

'Well, all right then,' he capitulated, and was rewarded with a radiant smile from Daisy.

'I've been thinking about where to go,' said Rosemary. She had the rug, Hal carried the hamper, and Daisy skipped ahead of them, ecstatic.

Hal didn't know Branlingham very well. 'Near the church, perhaps?'

'Over here! Over here!' shrieked Daisy, who could hardly wait for the picnic to begin. She ran to the summit of a small rise near the edge of the churchyard; it was crowned by a single tree, and she threw herself down under it.

'Looks good to me,' said Hal, who was beginning already to feel the weight of the hamper. 'What have you got *in* this thing?'

'Oh, just the usual.' Rosemary unfurled the rug. 'Egg may-onnaise sandwiches, of course – it wouldn't be a picnic without them. Plates and cutlery. Crisps, tomatoes, fruit, ginger cake, a couple of flasks: orange squash for now, and tea for later.'

'Ginger cake,' Daisy repeated with anticipation. 'Oh, yes. Yes, yes, yes.'

'Another necessity,' explained Rosemary. 'Surely you must have your own picnic traditions like that.'

Hal shook his head ruefully. 'I'm afraid not. I've not been on many picnics, and I'm counting on Daisy to show me how it's done.'

The girl stared at him in disbelief. 'Not been on many picnics? I'll help you, then,' she declared.

Throughout the repast she chattered to him, and he was quite happy to listen. Rosemary distributed the food, smiling at the non-stop flow of information and opinion.

'And Mummy's ginger cake is the best of all,' Daisy sighed at the end, replete.

'I should say so.' Hal licked his fingers. 'We've eaten it all, without even leaving any crumbs for the ants.'

Daisy giggled. 'Poor ants.'

'Tea?' Rosemary interposed, pulling out the second flask.

'Oh, yes.'

Daisy's eyelids drooped, and while her mother poured out the tea she curled up on the rug.

'I believe she's asleep already,' observed Hal, accepting a steaming mug.

Rosemary smiled fondly at her daughter. 'Peace and quiet at last.'

He leaned back against the tree trunk and surveyed the countryside. 'What a wonderful day – you'd never believe, would you, that two days ago it still seemed like winter? And what a wonderful way to enjoy it.'

'I love picnics,' said Rosemary, closing her eyes.

'I can see why. This is the life.'

'But surely,' she realised with a guilty start, her eyes flying open, 'you need to be getting back to work. I don't think that the diocese would appreciate it, paying you to sit on a hillside and eat ginger cake when there's decorating to be done. Or are you being paid by the job, rather than by the hour?'

'Neither.' He smiled enigmatically, deciding how much to say, then went on. 'Actually, I don't usually tell anyone this, but I don't charge the diocese at all for jobs like this. I enjoy doing it, and it saves them money. I feel as if I'm doing my bit.'

'Oh, how generous of you!'

He was sorry he'd told her; it sounded to his ears as if he'd been fishing for praise. 'Not at all,' he backtracked, and repeated, 'I enjoy it.'

Rosemary looked away from him. 'If it's not a dreadfully impertinent question, how did the Archdeacon's husband come to be decorating houses? I mean, it *is* a bit unusual.'

'It's unusual for archdeacons to *have* husbands,' he pointed out, grinning.

She smiled. 'Yes, I suppose so, when you put it like that.'

'But that's not answering your question.' Hal sipped his tea. 'Do you really want to know?'

'Only if you want to tell me.'

He *did* want to tell her, he discovered. 'It's a long story,' he warned.

'Start at the beginning.' Rosemary pulled her legs up and hugged her knees, ready to listen.

The beginning. 'I suppose it began when I met Margaret,' Hal said. 'Freshers week at Cambridge. We've been together ever since.' He was silent for a moment, remembering Margaret as she had been then, picturing her in his mind: untamed black curls springing wildly from her head, framing a white face alive with a fierce intensity. She'd been wearing a black T-shirt, braless; he wasn't sure to this day whether it was that arresting face or her magnificent breasts that had first captivated him. Fresh from his sheltered upbringing – clergy family, cathedral close and single-sex school, he'd been a bit naïve; from that first day he'd been bowled over by her, entranced and enchanted. She was his first love, his only love.

He went on, then, to tell Rosemary of the intervening years: the years when his business had seemed more important than anything else, when he'd neglected his family – Margaret and Alexander – in pursuit of worldly success. He didn't spare himself in the telling; it seemed important to be totally honest. 'I was a terrible husband,' he said frankly. 'A terrible father. It's a wonder she didn't divorce me. I wouldn't have blamed her if she had done.'

'No. Surely it wasn't that bad,' Rosemary protested.

'Oh, it was. Worse, probably. All I can say in my defence is that it happened gradually, and I didn't realise what was happening.'

'And . . . the Archdeacon?' she asked, awkward about using her name in a familiar way, though she was discussing her intimate emotional history. 'How did she feel about it?'

'Well, she wasn't the Archdeacon then, of course. Margaret wasn't even a churchgoer, let alone an archdeacon.' Hal shook his head. 'But to answer your question: she was miserable, desperately unhappy. I know that now. As I said, it's a wonder she didn't divorce me.' He told her, then, about the turning point for both of them, for their marriage: his brush with death, Margaret's discovery of the Church, his change of careers. 'And that's how I ended up decorating houses,' he concluded. 'Not the expected thing for an archdeacon's husband, I'll admit, but it suits me down to the ground.'

Rosemary played with the fringe on the side of the rug. 'And being an archdeacon seems to suit . . . your wife.'

'Oh, absolutely. She's brilliant at it.' He smiled to himself, struck by a humorous thought which he decided not to share: if Margaret's inclinations had been different, and she had gone into politics instead of the Church, she would be Prime Minister by now, following in the footsteps of that other formidable Margaret.

Daisy, sound asleep, stirred slightly as a butterfly alighted for a moment on her face, which was sticky with squash and ginger cake. Hal looked at her and smiled. 'My biggest regret . . .' he said, then stopped.

'Yes?' Rosemary urged after a moment. 'Your biggest regret?'

Hal gazed off into the distance. 'My biggest regret is that we didn't have a daughter. You're so lucky to have Daisy.'

'You'd be surprised how many people don't think so.' Rosemary's voice was quiet but passionate, verging on bitterness. 'How many people pity us. Well-meaning people, I suppose, who tell us that she should have been institutionalised from birth. Or even that it would have been better for us if she'd never been born.'

Hal turned his head to look at her. 'Oh, no. That's daft. Just think what you would have missed.'

'Exactly.' Her eyes met his. 'You *do* understand, I can see that. She's been such a blessing to us, such a joy.' Then, conscious of her own intensity, Rosemary smiled and tried to lighten the tone of the conversation. 'Well, Hal, you may not have a daughter,' she said, 'but one day you'll probably have a granddaughter. That's just as good, isn't it? Even better, some people say. All of the fun without all of the work.'

'No,' he said quietly. 'I won't have a granddaughter.'

She was confused by the sad gravity of his tone. 'But you have a son. Alexander . . .'

'Alexander is gay,' Hal stated matter-of-factly.

'Oh.' Surprised, Rosemary wasn't sure how to respond; she didn't want to offend him by making any assumptions.

'And how do you feel about that?' she asked cautiously, after a moment.

Hal focused on the sleeping girl as he spoke. 'I've come to terms with it. It's not the life one would choose for one's child, of course, but he seems very happy. He has a lovely partner – they've been together . . . oh, I suppose about five or six years now, since his early days at university.'

'But it took some time to come to terms with it?' Rosemary suggested, taking her cue from his words.

'Oh, yes. It's not,' he said quickly, 'that I have any objection to homosexuality, in theory. At least not for *other* people. I had several gay friends at university, and it never occurred to me to be bothered by it. But my own son, my *only* son . . . It was difficult to accept. I . . . well, I felt guilty about it,' he admitted.

'Guilty? In what way?'

His voice was quiet. 'That it was my fault somehow. You've heard all of the clichés – absent and ineffectual father, dominant mother. Well, I couldn't have been a more absent father during Alexander's formative years. I really did blame myself.'

'But that's nonsense,' she said.

Hal smiled wryly. 'Yes, I know that now. And as I say, he's very happy, so I'm happy for him.'

'And his mother?' Rosemary asked, empathising with the other woman. 'How does she feel about it?'

'Margaret.' He looked off into the distance for a moment, reflecting. 'Margaret was devastated. She took it far worse than I did, even. When we found out. This was,' he added in explanation, 'several years ago. That same horrible year when I had my heart attack. Not too much before that, in fact. It all seemed to happen together. And it almost killed Margaret, I think.'

'The poor woman,' Rosemary said softly.

Hal tried to explain. 'He was still at school. Only a child, really, at least in his mother's eyes. She adores Alexander –

they've always been very close. So you can imagine how
guilty *she* felt.'

Rosemary could imagine. 'How did you find out?'

'He told us.' Hal closed his eyes and remembered that day
at Sunday lunch: Alexander almost defiant as he uttered the
words, Margaret's white face whiter than ever, the chicken,
uneaten, congealing in its own grease. 'I'll never forget it – it's
one of those moments that's etched on my brain for ever. He
announced it, flat out.'

'But didn't you think,' Rosemary suggested, 'that he'd grow
out of it? I mean, they say that lots of boys go through a
phase at school. He might just have been going through a
phase.'

'It's funny.' Hal's mouth twisted in a sort of smile. 'That
never occurred to us. He seemed so sure, and we were sure as
well, as soon as the words were out of his mouth. It seemed
so obvious, once he'd said it. As if we should have known all
along, and we felt so foolish that we hadn't seen it – I suppose
it was because we didn't *want* to see it. But we never had a
moment's doubt that it was true.'

Rosemary picked up her forgotten mug of tea and swirled
the cold dregs round in the bottom. 'Has Margaret come to
terms with it now as well?'

'Oh, yes.' He nodded. 'It took her longer than it took me, I
think, but she's absolutely fine about it now. She and
Alexander are as close as ever. And she absolutely loves Luke –
that's his partner. She thinks of him as a member of the
family. So it's all turned out all right.'

But not without an incredible amount of pain, Rosemary
sensed. She was moved, and touched, that he had shared this
with her. Somehow she knew that he was not the sort of
person who confided his innermost thoughts easily or glibly –
much like herself, in fact. The empathy between them was
almost palpable; she wanted to offer him something in return.

'Well, you think I'm lucky to have Daisy, and I think you're lucky to have such a good relationship with your son,' she said, looking into the dregs of the tea. 'I have a stepson about the same age as Alexander, and we've never got on.'

Hal was surprised. 'A stepson? I didn't realise that your husband had been married before.'

'Oh, yes. His first wife . . . died.'

It was Hal's turn to feel his way through a potential minefield; the bleakness in Rosemary's voice suggested that there was an emotionally explosive story behind those bald words. He asked the most neutral question he could think of. 'How long ago was this?'

'Fourteen years ago. I never knew Laura. I didn't meet Gervase till after she died,' she said tersely.

He decided to get back to the stepson; after all, that was where the conversation had begun. 'So your stepson must have been quite young when his mother died.'

'Nearly ten. A terrible age to lose his mother. They were very close.' She glanced at her sleeping daughter, adding softly, 'I don't blame him for hating me.'

'But that didn't make it any easier for you, I'd imagine,' Hal said. 'Even if you understood.'

Rosemary turned to him, moved by his insightfulness. 'It was hell,' she stated. 'He didn't just hate me in silence. He took every opportunity to tell me how much he hated me. How vastly inferior I was to his mother in every way.'

This was getting close to the heart of it, Hal realised intuitively; he could almost see the pit of insecurity yawning at Rosemary's feet. 'But surely your husband stood up for you,' he said.

'He didn't do it in front of Gervase. And I didn't tell him. How could I?' Rosemary's voice shook with raw emotion. Raw still, Hal noted; this was not something she'd worked through, as he had worked through his conflicted feelings about Alexander's homosexuality. 'I didn't want to hurt him. And how could I have given Gervase the opportunity to . . . confirm . . . how much better Laura was?'

'But you said that you'd never met Laura,' he pointed out.

Rosemary had just about enough self-control left to check that Daisy was still sleeping; these were things that Daisy did not need to hear. 'But I've seen photos of her. I've talked to people who knew her. Laura was beautiful. She was kind, and good. Everyone loved her. Everyone in the parish. Gervase adored her. Her death devastated him.'

'That may all be true. But Rosemary,' Hal said earnestly, 'Gervase married *you*. He fell in love with you, and he married you.'

'Gervase needed me. He needs me.' Her voice was flat. 'You've seen him, seen what he's like. He needs a wife.'

No wonder the woman was insecure, Hal thought, appalled. Hers was nothing more than a marriage of convenience, and the convenience was all on the side of Gervase. What had she got out of the marriage, apart from Daisy? 'I'm sure he loves you,' he said in what he hoped was a reassuring voice.

'And I'm sure he needs me.' Rosemary blinked rapidly to forestall tears; Hal's evident pity was too much for her. 'But I didn't mean to tell you all this,' she added in a different tone. 'We're here to enjoy the beautiful spring day, not to talk about my marriage.'

Something in her voice penetrated through the layers of sleep; Daisy stirred and sat up. 'What's the matter, Mummy? Why do you look sad?'

'I'm not sad, darling.' She forced a smile. 'Have you had a nice sleep?'

Daisy yawned hugely. 'I'm thirsty, Mummy. Is there any more squash?'

'Just a bit, I think.' She reached for the flask and refilled

Daisy's cup. 'And then we really ought to be getting back home. We've kept Mr Phillips from his work for long enough.'

'Don't hurry on my account, Sleeping Beauty.' Hal grinned at Daisy. 'I'm having a wonderful time. Much better than work any day.'

Daisy giggled at the nomenclature. 'I didn't mean to fall asleep.'

'I could use another drink myself,' he declared. 'Is there any more tea in that flask?'

'It's gone cold, I'm afraid,' Rosemary apologised. 'I left the cap off.'

'Never mind,' Daisy said. 'You can share my squash with me.' She held out her cup.

As her daughter launched into another round of chatter in which Hal seemed a willing accomplice, Rosemary leaned back against the tree trunk. Why *had* she told him? she wondered. She had just shared with him things that she'd never told another soul: not Christine, not her mother, not Gervase. She'd only known Hal Phillips for a little over twenty-four hours, yet she'd entrusted him with her most private thoughts, her deepest insecurities. It was extraordinary, that feeling of having known him for ever, of being able to trust him completely.

She looked out over the surrounding landscape. There was a copse of trees not far away, and for a moment she thought that she'd caught some movement among the trees out of the corner of her eye. Some animal, perhaps; surely they weren't being watched by human eyes. But they were on high ground, exposed, visible to anyone who might be lurking about or passing through. Rosemary shivered, suddenly, and wrapped her arms round herself.

That evening Valerie did something that she hadn't done since she was an insecure teenager: she sat on the sofa and stared at the telephone, willing it to ring.

Hal would ring her tonight; she was sure of it. It was his perfect opportunity to do so, because the Magpie was away. Valerie knew that she was away; that afternoon she'd followed a taxi from The Archdeaconry to Saxwell station, and had seen the Magpie getting out of the taxi, carrying an overnight bag. She'd managed to find a space in the short-term car park, and had caught up with the Magpie on the platform, in time to see her board a train to London.

The Magpie hadn't seen her, of course. But Valerie recalled that as she'd disembarked from the taxi, she'd glanced at the Porsche and frowned.

The Porsche *was* a very conspicuous car, Valerie realised. It would be most unfortunate if the Magpie were to feel that she was being followed; it might make her suspect something.

And there would of course be something to suspect soon: Valerie's affair with Hal.

It would be a good idea to get another car, she decided suddenly – something neutral that would blend into traffic. Dark blue. A Polo or an Escort or a Metro, a few years old. The sort of car that thousands of people drove, and no one noticed. The sort of car that Valerie, who *liked* to be noticed, had always scorned.

She thought about the logistics of buying a car; it would have to be done in a way that didn't draw any attention to her. The idea excited her. It wouldn't be easy, but she could do it. She'd have to take the money out of the bank in cash, and she'd have to buy the car in a town some distance away.

She could take a taxi into Saxwell, go to the bank for the money, then catch a bus to Bury St Edmunds.

Valerie reached for the Yellow Pages and flipped through till she found the section on 'car dealers'. Yes, there were several listed in Bury. She jotted the addresses down on a scrap of paper. She would go tomorrow afternoon.

But tomorrow, she recalled, was a Wednesday, and Mrs

Rashe would be coming. That wouldn't do; Mrs Rashe would want to know where she was going, and the arrival of the new car would certainly not escape her attention. No, the car had to be bought and safely hidden in the garage by the time Mrs Rashe arrived. Valerie would have to leave first thing in the morning.

Oh, if only Hal would ring. Valerie stroked the receiver of the phone as she thought of him, and how good it would be when they finally got together. Why was he wasting this opportunity? His wife was away. They could be together tonight, if only he would ring. She would abandon her plan to be coy and hard to get; she would invite him here. They could have a drink, then they could go upstairs. What was he waiting for? Why didn't he ring?

Perhaps he was too shy, still in awe of her beauty and her fame. Perhaps he just needed a bit of encouragement. Perhaps it was, after all, up to her to make the first move.

Without giving herself time to think about it, Valerie picked up the receiver and dialled the number, which she'd already committed to memory.

On his own and still comfortably full from the picnic lunch, Hal had not bothered to cook an evening meal. He'd eaten some leftover fruit salad, then opened a bottle of wine, poured himself a glass, and took it through to the drawing room and sipped it while he relaxed with the newspaper. He was used to Margaret's absence in the evenings, but this evening felt different somehow because she would not be returning home at all. Hal could please himself: he could stay up late reading a book or listening to music or watching television, or he could have an early night.

He decided that an evening of mindless entertainment was in order, and checked the television listings in the newspaper. An old movie, preferably one in black and white, would be nice, Hal thought. He was in luck. *Brief Encounter* was on, a movie he hadn't seen in years. That should be good for a laugh.

Hal went to the kitchen to replenish his wine glass, fetched the cordless phone in case Margaret rang to check in with him, then went upstairs. Having the large house that went with Margaret's status as Archdeacon, and without children at home to fill it, they had the luxury of a room dedicated to the rarely watched television. It was a small, cosy room, furnished comfortably. Hal settled down on the leather sofa, took his shoes off, and switched on the set with the remote control.

Instantly he was transported back in time more than fifty years to a country he scarcely recognised, an England of picturesque railway stations and moral certainty. Rock-jawed Trevor Howard met doe-eyed Celia Johnson, and, accompanied by the juddering Rachmaninoff soundtrack, they found themselves falling in love. It was powerful stuff.

Hal, for his part, found himself unexpectedly gripped by it. Celia Johnson was no beauty – she could even be described as plain – but there was something about her that aroused the protective instinct. And something, he discovered without being able to put his finger on it, that reminded him of Rosemary Finch. Perhaps it was the expressiveness of the face, coupled with the buttoned-up reticence. Or maybe it was something about the eyes, huge and vulnerable.

The bleat of the phone jolted him from his reflections. Margaret, he thought, putting it to his ear as he turned down the volume on the television with the remote control in his other hand. 'Hello,' he said genially.

'Hello, Hal,' said a voice on the other end, in a throaty whisper. 'I've been thinking about you.'

Not Margaret. Definitely not Margaret. For an instant he wondered if it could be Rosemary Finch, then dismissed that thought as even more absurd.

Hal paused. 'Who is this?'

'Oh, Hal. You know who it is. Still playing hard to get, are you?' The voice sounded amused, confident.

The penny dropped. 'Miss Marler?'

'Clever boy.' She laughed in a Lauren Bacall way. 'Oh, Hal. I've been waiting for you to ring. Don't you think it's time to stop playing games? I mean, I'm alone, and you're alone. Why don't you come round? I have a bottle of champagne on ice.'

'I don't think that would be a good idea,' he said neutrally, as he tried to work out how she knew that he was alone.

'I can come to you, then. Or would you rather make it tomorrow? How long will your wife be away?'

'I don't think so. Good night, Miss Marler.' He clicked the phone off, staring at it without seeing it. His voice had sounded calm, but he was badly shaken. How did Valerie Marler know that Margaret was away? As far as he was aware, he had never even mentioned his wife to her. Of course he wore a wedding ring. But she seemed to have specific knowledge not only of Margaret's existence but also of her movements.

Hal remembered, then, what Margaret had said the night before about being followed by a red Porsche. At the time he hadn't put much stock in it; he'd had other things on his mind. But Margaret was not given to flights of fancy.

On the screen, Celia Johnson looked up at Trevor Howard with appealing helplessness, her mouth moving soundlessly. Chilled, Hal punched a button and the would-be lovers faded into oblivion.

A few seconds later the phone rang again. He was almost afraid to answer it, but decided that if it were Valerie Marler again, he would confront her about following his wife.

This time, though, it was Margaret. 'Just checking up on you,' she teased him.

'You know that last night you mentioned a red Porsche,' he said abruptly. 'Did you by any chance see it again today?'

Margaret paused, remembering. 'As a matter of fact, I thought I did. I wasn't aware of it following me this time, but I noticed it just as I got out of the taxi. But I decided I must be imagining things. Why do you ask?'

'Oh, nothing.' Hal changed the subject; there was no reason for *both* of them to worry. 'Did you have a good dinner, my love?'

They chatted for a few minutes, but Hal wasn't concentrating on the conversation. All he could think about was Valerie Marler, and the fact that she had been following Margaret. What on earth was the woman up to?

Chapter 9

Gervase customarily went to St Stephen's the first thing in the morning, before breakfast, to say the Morning Office in solitary splendour. It was a time he enjoyed, if such a word is appropriate: alone with God, and surrounded by the ancient beauty of mediaeval stone, as light streamed in through the east window above the altar. Even on a dull day, with no sun, there was a quality of light and spaciousness emanating from the very stones in the chancel. Much as he had loved St Mark's for so many years, Gervase now loved St Stephen's, as something precious and beautiful that had been entrusted to his charge, and gave thanks daily for the privilege of serving there.

On Wednesday morning he'd gone off as usual, while Rosemary tackled the task of getting Daisy ready for school. The girl was still over-excited from the day before, and torn between her eagerness to be reunited with Samantha Sawbridge and her reluctance to miss Hal Phillips. She danced up and down as her mother tied ribbons in her hair. 'He'll still be here when you get home,' Rosemary assured her. 'Hold still for a second, darling.'

Intent on the task at hand, Rosemary didn't hear the door,

and was startled when Gervase appeared outside Daisy's bed-room. Quickly she perceived that he was in a state of great agitation. 'Gervase! What is it?'

Gervase gasped for breath. 'The church,' he managed to say. 'St Stephen's. It's been broken into.'

'Oh!'

Tersely, in a voice quite unlike his usual measured tones, he told her the rest: how on his arrival he had known at once that something was amiss, and how he'd found the lock on the vestry door shattered and the door kicked in. Apart from that rather crude way of gaining entry, no lasting damage had been done to the building, but the wall-mounted box in which money was collected for parish magazines and post-cards had been smashed and rifled. Even worse, much worse, the silver candlesticks and crucifix were missing from the high altar. 'I just don't understand how anyone could do it,' he choked, tears in his eyes. 'And how could I have let it happen?'

'It's terrible,' Rosemary agreed. 'But it's not your fault, Gervase. You mustn't blame yourself.'

'I should have locked the silver in the safe,' he stated bleakly. 'I *knew* that churches round here have been broken into lately – the Archdeacon told me so. I should have taken more care. But I just didn't think it would happen here. Not at St Stephen's.'

Knowing him as she did, Rosemary realised that he was taking the violation personally, as well as the responsibility, and her practicality asserted itself. 'You must ring the Archdeacon,' she said.

'This early?' He looked at his watch. 'It's only just gone eight o'clock.'

Rosemary nodded. 'I'm sure she's used to it.' Abandoning Daisy for a few moments, she led him downstairs to his study and found the number for him.

The call was answered by Hal Phillips, who informed him that the Archdeacon was not at home.

'She's gone to London, for a meeting with the Chancellor,' Gervase repeated to Rosemary when he'd put the phone down. 'She won't be back until some time tonight.' He looked at her appealingly. 'What should I do now? I don't know what to do.'

Her instincts were to take him in her arms and comfort him, but she knew that he would probably disintegrate completely if she did. 'You could ring the Rural Dean,' she suggested briskly. 'And the churchwardens. And the insurance company. And of course,' she added, 'you must ring the police.'

'The police,' Gervase echoed. He put his head in his hands.

'What are you meant to be doing today?'

He found his diary and handed it to Rosemary silently; she found the page and scanned the entries. 'Nothing you can't get out of, if necessary,' she judged. 'You'll probably have to cancel your appointments and stay by the phone.' Making the phone calls would give him something to do, and it wasn't likely that he'd be able to concentrate on carrying out his normal duties in any case.

The implications of Gervase being at home all day didn't fully dawn on Rosemary until she was on the way to school with Daisy, half listening to the girl's chatter. Christine! she thought suddenly. She would have to do something about Christine.

She'd been putting off seeing Christine again, after that excruciating lunch-time visit; Rosemary just wasn't up to hearing any further gruesome details about Christine's affair. But Christine had rung last week and suggested another luncheon get-together, and today was the day that had been set. This latest development – the break-in at St Stephen's – would give Rosemary an excuse to get out of it. After all, the last thing Gervase needed today was seeing Christine and having to be polite to her.

Annie Sawbridge, with baby Jamie in his pram, was just departing from the school gates as Rosemary and Daisy arrived. 'Do you have time for a wee cup of coffee?' she invited, as she sometimes did when they met at the gates.

'A quick one, perhaps,' Rosemary agreed, conscious that she needed to get home to Gervase. 'If you wouldn't mind me using your phone for a short call that I need to make.'

'Of course I don't mind.'

Annie left her alone with the phone while she went to make the coffee. Rosemary wasn't sure that Christine would be at home: she might be taking her girls to school.

But Christine answered the phone on the second ring. 'Hello?' Her sleepy voice proclaimed that she was still in bed.

'Christine, this is Rosemary. Sorry to disturb you so early.'

Christine's yawn could be heard down the phone. 'I'm still on nights – I just got to bed a couple of hours ago.'

'Oh, I'm sorry,' Rosemary repeated.

'What's up? Besides me, now.'

Quickly Rosemary explained that it wouldn't be convenient for Christine to come for lunch, with Gervase at home. She heard herself apologising for this, though Christine had invited herself in the first place.

'Oh,' said Christine in a cross voice. 'Can't you get rid of him, then?'

She pressed her lips together to hold back a sharp retort. 'No, I can't.' And I wouldn't want to if I could, she added to herself.

'Well, I must say, Rosemary, it's not very good of you to let me down like this. I won't pretend I'm not disappointed.' Then, as if realising that she was pushing her luck, she went on in a more conciliatory tone. 'But of course I understand.

I'll give you a ring in a few days and see if we can arrange a day next week.'

Rosemary was still simmering with resentment when Annie came through with mugs of coffee on a tray. She made an effort to rearrange her face in a smile.

'Actually, I'm glad that I have you here,' Annie said, handing her a steaming mug. 'I wanted a wee word with you about Samantha's birthday party.'

'Samantha's birthday party?' Rosemary echoed blankly.

Annie laughed. 'Don't worry, it's not something you should know about already. But I wanted to mention it to you before I send out the invitations.'

'You're inviting Daisy?'

'Yes, of course – she's Samantha's best friend.' Annie sat down with her own mug. 'I just wanted to make sure you were happy about the arrangements.'

Rosemary took a sip of coffee. 'Tell me about it.'

'Well, Samantha wants to have it at Kinderland,' Annie stated.

'What on earth is Kinderland?'

Again Annie laughed. 'Oh, it's the "in" place for parties these days. One of Samantha's wee friends had her birthday party there a few months ago, and now nothing else will do for Samantha. You know how these bairns are.'

'But what *is* it? *Where* is it?'

'It's in Saxwell,' Annie explained. 'Not far from the town centre. And as for *what* it is, I can hardly tell you.' She sketched an enormous shape with her hands. 'A huge warehouse sort of place. Full of climbing equipment and slides and ball pools.'

Rosemary was still at a loss. 'Ball pools?'

'Oh, you know. They come down a long slide into a mass of coloured rubber balls. Anyhow, the way it works is that they all spend about ninety minutes running about playing on everything, and when they've worn themselves out they go into a room and stuff themselves with pizza and birthday cake.'

'It sounds awfully dangerous,' Rosemary frowned. 'Daisy's not the most co-ordinated child. She might hurt herself.'

'They can't hurt themselves,' Annie assured her. 'Everything is padded.'

Picturing Daisy charging round, over-excited and hyper-active, Rosemary still felt uneasy, and sounded unconvinced. 'I don't know.'

'And of course Samantha would look out for wee Daisy,' Annie added. 'She'd make sure she was all right. And I'll be there, too, to keep an eye on things.'

'Well . . .'

'I'll tell you what,' Annie suggested briskly. 'One day soon I'll take you there, to look the place over. I'm sure you'll be satisfied that nothing could happen to your Daisy.'

Valerie went through with her plans for the morning. As she rode the bus to Bury St Edmunds – out the Bury Road past The Archdeaconry – dressed in what she now regarded as her 'disguise', the phone call of the night before played and replayed in her mind.

It hadn't gone as she had hoped. Hal had put her off yet again. At least he hadn't said that he didn't want to come, only that he didn't think it was a good idea. Why wasn't it a good idea? And she thought she had detected a different note in his voice this time. Fear. It had sounded like fear, she realised suddenly.

Then it came to her: he was afraid of his wife. Afraid of the Magpie, and no wonder. She was a pretty terrifying crea-ture, in her black and white get-up. He was probably afraid of what she would do if she found out that her husband was having an affair. Perhaps he was even worried about what the

Magpie might do to Valerie, and was trying to protect her from that.

And God came into it too, Valerie recognised. The Magpie was a parson, a priest. She would have scruples about adultery, and about divorce. Hal might even share those scruples.

Things were more complicated than she'd realised at first, Valerie now saw. It wasn't going to be a straightforward matter, taking Hal away from his wife. If neither one of them believed in divorce . . .

And if divorce wasn't an option, there was only one other way. The Magpie would have to die.

Once the thought had entered her mind, Valerie knew that she wouldn't be able to dislodge it. It was fated that she and Hal should be together; therefore the Magpie must die.

But as she knew, from her involvement with Toby and his inconvenient wife Pandora, that wasn't as easy as it sounded. The Magpie was old, but she wasn't *that* old – middle-aged at best. She could expect to live for quite a few more years – more years than Valerie and Hal could wait.

Unless . . .

Hal Phillips's van was in the Vicarage drive, and a police car was just pulling up behind it as Rosemary arrived home from Annie Sawbridge's. She hurried to greet the man who unfolded himself from the front seat of the cramped panda car: he was tall, as tall as Gervase, with a shock of floppy hair which he smoothed back from his forehead as he emerged.

'Detective Inspector Elliott,' he introduced himself, reaching for his warrant card. 'Saxwell CID. And you're Mrs . . .'

'Mrs Finch,' Rosemary supplied. 'The Vicar's wife.'

He nodded. 'Sorry I couldn't get here sooner, Mrs Finch. The morning traffic coming from Saxwell is something shocking.'

'Yes, of course.' She led him towards the front door. 'I'll take you to my husband. Unless you want to go to the church first?'

'I think I'd better talk to Reverend Finch first,' he agreed, then hesitated at the door. 'Is that what I should call him? Reverend Finch?'

Rosemary smiled; it was often a vexed issue with people whose acquaintance with the Church began and ended with *The Vicar of Dibley*. 'He prefers "Father" as a title,' she answered truthfully. 'Father Gervase, or Father Finch. Or just plain "Vicar" will do.'

When the introductions were made a moment later, the policeman settled on the latter as the easiest to deal with. 'It's good to meet you, Vicar. Sorry about the circumstances.' He shook his head. 'This seems to be a new trend round here, churches being broken into and so forth. This is the second one this week, and it's only Wednesday.'

The phone began ringing as Valerie put her key in the front door of Rose Cottage. Hal! her heart sang. He'd thought about it, and he'd changed his mind. Her hands shook with excitement; she fumbled with the lock. Successful at last, she flung the door open and seized the phone. 'Hello?' she gasped breathlessly.

'Hello, darlin'.'

'Shaun.' Valerie couldn't keep the disappointment out of her voice.

'Who else, darlin'? Or were you expecting the Prince of Wales?'

'Don't be silly,' she snapped. 'What do you want?'

He was reproachful. 'You haven't been returning my calls. I've been leaving messages for the last three days. Where have you been?'

Valerie bit back a rude reply; on a professional level she

was still afraid to alienate Shaun, much as she'd like to get him out of her private life. 'I've been busy,' she said vaguely.

'Well, we need to talk about the *Hello!* shoot. I'll be coming down, of course, to supervise, but—'

'Oh, Lord. When is it?'

Shaun laughed. 'Tomorrow, of course. You hadn't forgotten?'

She had, but wasn't about to admit it. 'No, of course not. I just didn't recall what time they were planning to get here.'

'Early. About eight. It will take them all day,' Shaun explained. 'And I just wondered if . . . well, I thought it might be more convenient if I came down tonight,' he added with a sly chuckle. 'So I wouldn't have to get such an early start in the morning. And . . . well, you know.'

'No,' she said. No, she just couldn't face it. Shaun at the weekend was bad enough, but to have him in her bed midweek was more than she could bear. 'No, I'm busy tonight. And I'm busy *now*, Shaun. I'll see you in the morning.' Firmly she put the phone down, and ignored it when it rang again.

Valerie *was* busy. It was nearly time for Mrs Rashe to arrive, and the post hadn't even been sorted yet. She went through to the kitchen, where she'd left it heaped on the table, unopened.

As she applied the silver letter knife to each envelope, deftly sorting them into piles, her thoughts were not on the task at hand, nor was she thinking of Shaun or *Hello!* magazine: Valerie was mentally reliving her morning's car-buying adventure.

It had been successful, and had gone largely according to plan. There had been just one hiccup, one moment of panic. She had assumed that a cash transaction would be straightforward, and that her anonymity could be preserved. But the man at the garage had wanted her name and address for his records. Valerie, looking at her watch and thinking about how long she had before Mrs Rashe's arrival at Rose Cottage, had been caught off her guard and had said the first thing that came into her head: her name was Kim Rashe, she'd told him, and she lived at Grange Cottage, Elmsford. That was the address of Frank and Sybil Rashe rather than their daughter's caravan abode, but it was close enough, Valerie reckoned; he wasn't going to be checking up on it. Telephone number? he asked. 'I'm not on the phone,' she'd told him, thinking quickly.

Then he'd produced the registration papers, and her panic had multiplied; she was going to have to lie, and it would cause all sorts of complications. But he'd merely handed her the top copy and told her to send it in to the DVLC herself. The tax disc didn't expire for another ten months; there would be plenty of time to worry about all of that later.

And now the car, a suitably anonymous-looking dark blue Metro some five years old, was ensconced in the garage next to its more glamorous companion. It was the spot where Shaun usually parked his car to keep it from the eyes of prying villagers. But tomorrow's visit from Shaun would be a professional one, completely above board, so he could just park his car in the drive like everyone else. And at the weekend – well, she'd just have to think about that later as well.

Valerie hadn't finished with the post when she heard the unmistakable clatter of Mrs Rashe letting herself in with her own key. In a moment the other woman came through to the kitchen.

'Oh – Miss Valerie! I wasn't expecting you to be in here. I thought I'd put the kettle on and make myself a cup of tea before your lunch.' Her eagle eyes took in the unopened post. 'But you're not finished in here yet, I see.'

Putting a hand to her forehead, Valerie spoke in a thin, pained voice. 'I'm sorry to be in your way, Mrs Rashe. But I've had the most frightful headache this morning, and I'm way behind myself. As you see, I haven't even finished sorting my post.'

'Oh, you poor lamb,' clucked Sybil Rashe in instant sympathy. 'Sit down. Let me make you a cup of tea.'

Valerie obeyed, letting the other woman take over. 'Thank you. That's very kind.'

Mrs Rashe filled the kettle noisily and plopped it on the Aga. 'Bad timing, with those magazine folks coming tomorrow,' she declared. 'Got to get everything spick and span.'

'I'm sure that you have everything under control, Mrs Rashe,' said Valerie with a weak smile.

'That's as may be. But we've got to get you feeling better as well, Miss Valerie. It wouldn't do for you to be poorly. I hope you're not sickening for something.' Sybil Rashe scrutinised Valerie with a penetrating stare, her eyes narrowed.

'It's just a headache.' She rubbed her temples. 'But a bad one.'

'Sweet tea, that will do the trick,' stated Mrs Rashe, getting out the sugar bowl. 'Nothing like a good cup of tea, I always say. For whatever ails you.'

Valerie hated sweet tea, but she submitted meekly to Mrs Rashe's ministrations and sipped the tea when it came. 'Thank you so much. You're very kind.'

'And how about some lunch, Miss Valerie? I don't suppose you've had any breakfast, and you ought to get something in your stomach. A bowl of soup?' she suggested.

'I don't want to trouble you, or take you from your work.'

Sybil Rashe shook her head. 'No trouble at all. It won't take me a tick to open a tin of soup.' She surveyed the contents of Valerie's store cupboard. 'Or would you prefer a nice soft-boiled egg?'

'Soup, please.' Valerie found herself enjoying her role as the invalid. 'Tomato, perhaps?'

'Whatever you like, Miss Valerie.' The other woman selected a red tin.

At Mrs Rashe's insistence, Valerie went to bed after her lunch, leaving her post unanswered. She didn't sleep; she wasn't tired, and her mind kept returning to the thoughts of the morning.

The Magpie's death.

Valerie hated funerals, but that was one she would attend with pleasure. Seeing that coffin going into the earth, knowing that nothing now stood between her and Hal . . .

But how? How was the Magpie going to die? That was the question.

Later in the afternoon Valerie professed herself much better, and went back to the kitchen for the customary ritual of tea with Mrs Rashe. The other woman had been through the house like a whirlwind, deploying Hoover, mop and duster with fierce intensity, and now was ready to relax over a soothing cuppa.

'You're feeling better, then? Didn't I tell you that sweet tea and a nice nap would sort you out?' Sybil Rashe declaimed in a complacent voice as she once again filled the kettle. Really, she thought, it was a wonder that Miss Valerie survived when she wasn't there to make sure she looked after herself.

Valerie sat down at the kitchen table. 'Thank you, Mrs Rashe. You were quite right,' she said meekly.

Waiting for the kettle to boil, the woman in the overall surveyed her handiwork. The floor was spotless, the Aga gleamed, and the sink virtually dazzled the eye. 'Rose Cottage looks a treat, though I say it myself.'

'You've done a marvellous job, Mrs Rashe. But of course you always do.'

'You know I'd be willing to come more often, Miss Valerie. Say twice a week?' This exchange, too, was part of the ritual, though Sybil Rashe entertained a sneaking hope that one day Miss Valerie would take her up on the offer.

Valerie made her expected response. 'But you do more in one afternoon than anyone else would manage in two days.'

It was true, and Sybil Rashe knew it. She warmed the tea-pot with a drop of almost-boiling water from the kettle, tipping it into the sink with great care lest the sink's pristine beauty be spoiled by water spots, and giving it a wipe for good measure. 'I could come back in the morning, before those magazine folk get here,' she offered. 'Make sure every-thing is just right. I could even stay about while they're here. Just in case.' Her daughter Brenda, an avid reader of *Hello!*, wouldn't half be impressed if she could give her an eyewit-ness account of the photo shoot.

'I'll be very careful tonight,' Valerie assured her. It would be bad enough to have Shaun underfoot tomorrow, let alone Mrs Rashe hovering round the proceedings, telling people to mind where they put down their coffee cups.

She accepted the rejection with equanimity – it had been worth a try – and settled down at the table with the freshly made tea.

It was time for the next part of the weekly ritual. 'And how is your family, Mrs Rashe?' Valerie asked dutifully.

'Well.' She took a deep breath. 'It was my Frank's birthday at the weekend.'

'Oh, yes. You'd said. You were going to have a family party.'

She was prepared. From the pocket of her overall, Sybil Rashe produced a thick packet of photos.

'Photos – how nice,' Valerie said in a bright voice.

'Well, Miss Valerie, you always did say you'd like to see what they all looked like. As you know, we've never been much of a family for snapshots – too much trouble trying to use up a whole film, then taking them into Boots and all. But our Kim has a new camera – one of those fancy instant ones, so you don't even have to wait to have them developed.'

Valerie was curious in spite of herself. 'Let's have a look, then.'

'Here's my Frank and me.' She handed it to her. They were an oddly matched couple: a bear of a man, with a gut that proclaimed his fondness for the odd pint, and his tiny stringy wife. His face was as red and smooth as hers was leathery and wrinkled. Probably neither one was as old as they looked.

'How nice.'

Sybil Rashe felt that some commentary was called for. 'He's a good man, my Frank,' she said fondly. 'He has his faults, but he's a good man.' She put the next one down on the table. 'And here's our Brenda.'

Brenda took after her mother, Valerie could see: she had the same small frame, but she possessed a certain elegance which her mother had probably never even thought of aspiring to. Her hair was blond and precisely styled; her small-featured face, with or without its careful make-up and plucked eyebrows, might even have been described as pretty. She wore her clothes well, too, though they clearly were cheap chain-store knock-offs of the season's current fashions. 'What about her chap?' Valerie asked, now truly curious. 'Do you have one of him?'

Mrs Rashe gave a disdainful sniff. 'He didn't come. Frank won't have him in the house. Frank won't even eat curry,' she added. 'Calls it "foreign muck". I must admit I don't mind a bit of curry myself.'

Frank sounded like a real charmer, thought Valerie.

'And here's our Terry,' Sybil Rashe went on, handing her the next photo.

Terry, too, favoured the female parent in size; in masculine form that translated to weedy. His eyes, though, were like Frank's: small and fractionally too close together. Like Frank, too, he had a thatch of brown hair.

In the next photo, Terry was holding a small boy with bright carroty orange hair and a solemn expression. 'Zack,' confirmed Sybil Rashe, pronouncing the name as though it were in inverted commas. 'I never can get on with that name.'

'What about Delilah?' Valerie put out her hand for the next photo. 'Do you have one of her?'

'Oh, Miss High-and-Mighty didn't come,' the woman in question's mother-in-law said with undisguised disdain, clutching the remaining photos to her thin chest. 'Had better things to do, if you please. Or so she said. Off with some other man, I shouldn't wonder.'

'Does Delilah have ginger hair?' Valerie couldn't help asking, though she suspected that she knew the answer.

'Not her,' Mrs Rashe sniffed. 'Jet black, her hair is. But the barman at the George and Dragon, his hair is just that colour,' she added with a meaningful nod, tapping the side of her nose.

A succession of other snapshots followed, doled out one by one: the family members in various permutations, Frank opening a brightly wrapped parcel, Frank and his birthday cake. But apart from the absent partners, someone else was missing; Valerie realised that she was curious to see Kim, the young woman whose identity she'd borrowed. 'Don't you have any of Kim?' she prompted.

'Our Kim was taking the photos,' Mrs Rashe reminded her. 'And she doesn't much like having her photo taken. But she let me take one of her. And that useless Kev,' she added dismissively.

The photo was out of focus, but it was quite clear that Kim, of all the Rashe children, favoured her father in build. She was a big girl, large-breasted and wide-hipped, with a thatch of brassy bottle-blond hair, the dark roots visible.

Kim was sitting on Kev's lap, and though he was obscured by her bulk, it looked as though he was a match for her in size. They both wore jeans, none too clean, and Kev was sporting a black leather jacket.

Valerie smiled to herself; the incongruity of her identification with this girl was most amusing. Fortunately Kim's mother's attention was on the photo rather than on her employer. 'Look at that ring,' she said, pointing.

Indeed, the focus of the photo was in the foreground, as Kim stretched her hand out towards the camera with a proud grin; on her left hand she wore a ring with an enormous stone.

'A ring?' Valerie echoed, bemused. 'Is she engaged, then?'

Sybil Rashe twisted her head to look at her with reproach. 'Of course she is. I told you at least a fortnight ago. Kev's bought her a ring, and they're getting married.'

'Yes, of course.' Valerie nodded, though she had no recollection of any such conversation. 'Have they set a date?'

'Not yet. Still trying to talk her way round her dad, to get him to pay for it.' Mrs Rashe tossed her head. 'Kim says that he spent a packet on Brenda's wedding, and he has to do the same for her. Mind you, our Kim always has been able to wind her dad round her little finger. But I say that if Kev can afford a ring like *that*, he can afford to pay for his own wedding. And them living together like they were already married and all. Things weren't done like that in my day.'

'I thought that Kev was on the dole,' Valerie wondered aloud.

Mrs Rashe was in full flow. '*And* they're planning to get married in church, if you please. A white wedding, no less! We've always been Chapel, not Church, as you know, and our Kim hasn't even set foot in the chapel in donkey's years, let alone any church. And I shouldn't think that Kev has *ever* seen the inside of a church before. But nothing will do but that they have to get married in church – looks better in the photos, Kim says. They've even been to see the Vicar. Can you imagine?' She turned to Valerie, expecting a response, but she was disappointed. Valerie's face was a blank; she was no longer listening. The mention of the church and the Vicar had reminded her, vividly, of the Magpie. Not of a wedding, but of a funeral.

Gervase, though soothed by DI Elliott's professional manner, was still in shock. Keeping busy on the phone had helped to prevent him from brooding about the sense of personal violation he felt; Rosemary kept him well supplied with cups of tea, and made soothing noises at regular intervals.

'The Archdeacon still isn't answering her phone,' he said just before four o'clock, as Rosemary delivered a cup of tea to his study. 'Could you ask her husband if he knows when she's expected home?' He nodded towards the drawing room, where Hal Phillips had been working all day. 'And perhaps you might offer him a cup of tea, my dear.'

Rosemary, for reasons she didn't really understand – and felt were better left unexamined – had stayed out of the drawing room while Hal was working. She'd greeted him in the morning, and had seen that he had everything he needed; after that she had kept away from the drawing room. But at Gervase's suggestion she acquiesced, taking through a cup of tea.

She found Hal up a ladder, painting the ceiling with a roller. He grinned down at her with delight, dropped the roller in its tray, and climbed down. 'Tea, how splendid.' He looked at his watch. 'It's later than I thought. Time for Choral Evensong. Were you going to listen?'

Rosemary switched on the radio. 'It's one of my favourite times of the week,' she admitted. 'Four o'clock on a Wednesday afternoon. I usually make myself a cup of tea and put my feet up, if Daisy will let me get away with it.'

'Where *is* Daisy?' Hal wanted to know. 'Shouldn't she be home by now?'

'When I went to collect her, she begged me to be allowed to go to Samantha's house to play,' Rosemary explained.

Hal shook his head and grinned. 'The fickle little minx. She leads me on, tells me I'm her friend, then goes off to play with someone else.' He quirked an eyebrow at Rosemary.

She smiled back at him. 'Gervase wondered if you know when the Archdeacon might be at home.'

'No idea. It could be any time from now till late this evening. She usually rings to let me know what her plans are – or more specifically, whether she'll be wanting me to cook her an evening meal.' He glanced over towards his mobile phone, resting on a table where he could reach it quickly. 'But she hasn't rung yet.'

It hadn't occurred to Rosemary that Hal might do the cooking in his household, but of course it made sense that he should. How nice for the Archdeacon, she thought involuntarily.

As if on command, Hal's mobile phone bleated. Rosemary jumped; Hal reached for it and pushed the button to connect. 'Hello?'

'Hello, Hal,' responded the voice at the other end; it wasn't Margaret. 'I was just thinking about you, and wondering how you were.'

Hal took a deep breath, then said quietly, 'Please don't ring me again.' He punched the disconnect button and returned the phone to the table.

'Not the Archdeacon?' Rosemary surmised, puzzled.

Had Rosemary Finch been a different woman, or a different sort of woman, Hal might have made a joke of it. If Margaret had been there instead, he might have shrugged and said, 'One of my legion of admirers'. But for some reason he didn't want Rosemary to know about Valerie Marler. 'No, not Margaret,' said Hal firmly. 'Wrong number. Now.' He fiddled with the radio to improve the reception as the precentor in some distant cathedral intoned, 'Oh, Lord, open thou our lips.'

'Are you going to join me for Choral Evensong, then?' he asked. 'Though I suppose you ought to be the one doing the inviting, as it's your radio and your house.' Again he grinned at her.

'An offer I can't refuse,' she smiled back.

Hal's squash game wasn't as good as usual that night, and he was beaten rather soundly by Mike Odum, three games to one.

Afterwards, in the locker room, Mike was voluble in his triumph. 'You're getting lazy, mate,' he announced. 'Out of shape. You're obviously not getting the same sort of exercise that I am, if you know what I mean.' Fresh from the showers, he dropped his towel unconcernedly on the floor and began getting dressed.

'And who ever said that a policeman's lot is not a happy one?' Hal said lightly, towelling his damp hair. He wasn't in the mood to listen to lascivious descriptions of Mike's little tiger and the quality of the exercise she provided. It was time to change the subject, he decided. Heretofore the two men's conversation about Mike's police work had been limited to gossip, mostly of a personal nature, but Hal saw no reason why he shouldn't move the boundaries a bit. 'Speaking of policemen, I saw one of your lot today.'

Mike, ever on the prowl for good gossip, looked interested. 'Oh, yes? Who was he, then?'

'We weren't introduced,' admitted Hal. 'He came to Branlingham Vicarage, where I'm working. The church there was broken into last night, and this chap was investigating.'

'Tall chap, floppy hair?' Mike hazarded, rubbing his own bristly head.

Hal nodded in confirmation. 'That's right.'

'Pete Elliott,' the policeman announced. 'DI Elliott, that is. We've had quite a few of these church break-ins lately, and he's been dealing with most of them.'

'DI Elliott.' Hal tried to remember what he'd been told about Pete Elliott; since Mike's co-workers were only names to Hal, sometimes he had trouble remembering which was which. 'Remind me about him.'

Mike shrugged dismissively but with a tolerant smile. 'He's the one who falls in love every other week or so with a different woman. And hasn't got a snowball's chance with any of them, poor bloke.'

'Why not?'

'Well, he's no oil painting, is he?' Mike had the grace to grin in a self-deprecating way, glancing over Hal's shoulder into the mirror. 'Not that I am either, mind you. But Pete still lives at home with his mum.'

'I don't see why that should make a difference,' Hal protested.

'But you don't know Pete.' Mike tied his shoelaces as he tried to explain. 'The thing is, he doesn't fall for the mousy little secretaries, or women he might have a chance with. No, he falls big time for the glamour babes, the sort who wouldn't give him the time of day. The more unattainable the better, it seems.'

'Does that include your little tiger?' Hal teased.

Mike gave an amused laugh. 'She'd have him for breakfast. I think he's a bit afraid of her, to tell you the truth.'

Hal was beginning to remember what he'd been told about Pete Elliott. 'And he tells everyone about his hopeless passions, you said?'

'Yes, that's the other thing about Pete,' Mike confirmed, unzipping his sports bag and stuffing in his sweaty clothes. 'He wears his heart on his sleeve. He just can't resist telling absolutely everyone about the latest babe. But the thing is, it's all very chaste, all very hearts-and-flowers. If by some miracle he got one of his babes alone, and she was willing, I don't think he'd know what to do with her.'

'Sounds pretty harmless to me.' Hal studied himself in the mirror, giving his hair a last swipe with his comb and checking to make sure that the parting was straight.

Mike tucked his racquet under his arm. 'But I wouldn't want to give you the wrong idea about Pete. He may be a bit of a wally when it comes to women, but he's a damned good policeman. And if anyone can catch whoever's been breaking into those churches, Pete Elliott can.'

Chapter 10

Valerie's new car, the anonymous blue Metro, made her feel both invisible and invincible. Several days passed; the team from *Hello!* came and went. She managed to put Shaun off for the weekend by telling him that she was expecting other guests. He was suspicious – why hadn't she mentioned this before? and who were they? – but at least he didn't come. Freed from the constraint of his presence, Valerie spent most of the weekend in the blue Metro, driving round Saxwell.

She had a great craving to see Hal, even briefly and from a distance; it had been over a week since she'd seen him, and she needed to reassure herself that he was indeed as attractive and desirable as she remembered. And so on Saturday afternoon she took the familiar turning into the Bury Road. Parking the Metro round the corner from The Archdeaconry, she took up her position in the phone box across the road. The white van was in the drive, so Hal must be at home.

That proved to be an erroneous assumption. When she'd been there for some time – involved in her own thoughts, she'd lost track of how long – the Magpie's dark sedan pulled into the drive and they both got out: Hal and the Magpie. Hal and his wife. It was the first time Valerie had seen them together, and she was surprised at how much it hurt. Yes, Hal was as gorgeous as she'd remembered; he turned to say something to the Magpie, flashing that heart-stopping grin, and Valerie caught her breath with the pain of it. As the front door closed behind them she found that she was still holding her breath; she expelled it slowly and unclenched her hands. Her nails had left little half-moon indentations in the palms.

She'd accomplished her mission; she'd seen Hal. It would have to do. But as she was preparing to leave the phone box, the front door of The Archdeaconry opened again and the Magpie came back out, this time on her own. She got into her car and drove away.

Her hands shaking with excitement, Valerie fished in her pocket for her phone card. Hoping for just such an opportunity, she'd bought one at the petrol station that morning when she'd filled up the car. She slotted it in and punched Hal's number.

He answered after two rings. 'Hello?'

Oh, that voice. That polite, posh voice, with its hint of humour and its promise of passion. Valerie opened her mouth and found she couldn't speak.

'Hello?' Hal repeated. 'Is anyone there?'

Valerie clutched the receiver, picturing him standing by the phone, puzzlement on his face. She tried again to speak; nothing came out but a noise from the back of her throat, a strangled croak.

'Hello? Is someone there? Are you all right?'

After a moment she heard a click as he hung up. The phone card popped out of its slot. Valerie shoved it back in and dialled again.

This time the number was engaged. He was probably ringing '1471' to find out who had rung him, she guessed. Well, that wouldn't help him, as it was a pay phone. After a moment she tried again. She was successful in getting through, but she made no effort to speak; it was enough just to hear his voice.

And as long as he was on the phone with her, whether they were talking or not, he was in some way engaged with her. Not with the Magpie, not doing anything else, but focused on *her*. She would stay here, pushing the card in and dialling his number, until her phone card ran out, or until he stopped answering. All afternoon, if need be.

On Sunday morning Valerie was back at her post. She wasn't entirely surprised to see Hal and the Magpie coming out of the house together; she'd expected that they'd probably be going to church. Indeed, the Magpie was dressed as usual in her ugly black and white, and Hal . . . Hal was wearing a suit and tie. It was the first time that Valerie had seen him in a suit, and he looked wonderful, even better than the day before, when he'd been wearing casual trousers and an open-necked shirt. Her heart thudded.

She had toyed with the idea of trying to follow them to church – after all, it was a public place, and she had as much right to be there as anyone – but knew that she'd feel uncomfortable in that environment. The thought of sitting through a sermon, especially a sermon by the Magpie, wasn't even to be contemplated. The sight of Hal was almost enough to make her change her mind. She could sit somewhere behind and to the side of him, where she'd have a good view, and watch him through the service.

But it was too late; they climbed into the Magpie's car and were gone before Valerie had a chance to get to her car.

Her idea was that in their absence she might get a closer look at The Archdeaconry. It seemed a perfect time to do it: for once she was sure that both of them were out of the house, and were likely to be away for at least a couple of hours. And there wasn't much traffic in the Bury Road on a

Sunday morning. People were still enjoying a lie-in, not driving about or looking out of their windows at their neighbours' houses.

Casually Valerie strolled across the road and up the drive, trying not to appear furtive.

She'd had ample opportunity to study the front of The Archdeaconry from her vantage point in the phone box. An impressive house it was, double-fronted, with mature clematis and wisteria in full bloom, flinging themselves exuberantly round the door and up the red brick walls. But closer to she was able to see into the windows. To the right of the central door was a room that appeared to be a study, lined with bookshelves and furnished with a large desk and several chairs. The Magpie's, she decided dismissively. The room on the other side seemed to be a drawing room. The curtains at the window were heavy and expensive-looking, and Valerie could see two lushly upholstered sofas and matching chairs.

On the right-hand side of the house was a gate leading into the back garden. Valerie tried it and found it unlocked. Delighted with her luck, she went round the side of the house and into the garden.

The garden itself was lovely, in a deliberately overgrown sort of way; someone in this house knew something about gardening, and enjoyed doing it, Valerie deduced. Either that or they had a gardener. She strolled up to a lilac tree, heavy with purple blossom, and inhaled its delicious perfume as her eyes scanned the back of the house.

Ah. Someone had left a window open at the ground floor level. Careless Magpie, Valerie gloated censoriously to herself. Someone could break into your house if you did things like that.

Without giving herself time to think, Valerie moved to the open window. But before she launched herself through it, she paused for a moment. She wasn't worried about being seen from the outside: the back of the house was not overlooked. What, though, if someone were inside? Someone she didn't know about, like a live-in housekeeper or even a child? The thought that Hal and the Magpie might have children had never crossed Valerie's mind till now, but there could be a teenager at home, shut in a bedroom listening to rock music and never venturing forth.

She would just have to risk it. This was her best chance; the window was open and the church-goers were bound to be away for at least an hour, probably more.

Climbing through a window with no one to give her a boost from behind was more difficult than Valerie had imagined. But she struggled her way in and found herself in a sort of mud room or scullery, behind the kitchen. There was no mud, just a couple of pairs of welly boots lined up neatly on the clean quarry tiles of the floor, and an assortment of coats hanging on pegs. An old Barbour jacket, just the colour of Hal's eyes, attracted her attention, but she passed through the room without pause; it wouldn't do to waste too much time lingering in the mud room, when the whole house was waiting for her.

The kitchen was large and well equipped; it was clearly the domain of one who liked to cook. There was a shelf of well-thumbed and even food-stained cookery books, and a large quantity of spice jars arrayed in racks. Microwave, food processor, electric kettle, built-in cooker, ceramic hob, dishwasher, large fridge-freezer. No Aga for the Magpie, then, thought Valerie, with a feeling of smug superiority.

And no dirty breakfast dishes in the sink, either, which was a point in the Magpie's favour. Valerie opened the dishwasher; the cups, cutlery and plates were neatly rinsed and tidily slotted within, waiting to be washed.

She opened a few cupboards at random, and found the breakfast cereal: cornflakes, muesli, Weetabix. Were those

Hal's choices for breakfast? Then she moved to the fridge, approaching it with interest. It was well stocked with the usual sorts of things: skimmed milk, Flora, jars of condiments, a bottle of mineral water. Vegetables in the vegetable drawer, a lemon, various cheeses, a bowl of fruit salad covered with cling film. What about the meat for their Sunday lunch? She went to the cooker and discovered the chicken within, the timer set; the vegetables for lunch were prepared and waiting on the hob. Someone – the Magpie, surely – had been busy already that morning.

She'd spent enough time in the kitchen, and moved on towards the front of the house. There was a large breakfast room beyond the kitchen, and a formal dining room on the other side of the central hall. Valerie deduced that they ate most of their meals in the breakfast room; it had a cheery, lived-in feel, while the dining room was almost excessively formal, with dark walls and heavy velvet curtains and antique mahogany furniture. It was all done with exquisite taste, she acknowledged. Hal's taste, of course – he would have done all of the decorating himself, surely.

Valerie went down the hall to the drawing room. Again, it was most beautifully furnished and decorated. She admired the carved marble fireplace surround and the sumptuous oriental rug which covered most of the polished floorboards. Not only taste but a great deal of money was involved here; she was intrigued. Did the Magpie have a moneyed background, then, like the fictional Pandora? Or was the money on Hal's side? And in either case, why on earth was he spending his days decorating other people's houses? Like so many things about Hal, the answers were fascinatingly elusive.

Across the hall, the Magpie's study was much as Valerie had imagined: shelves and shelves of books, all of them boring tomes of theology. She cast a cursory eye over them, then looked at the rest of the room. Filing cabinet, tidy desk, computer and printer. Nothing here to detain her. Except for the framed photo on the desk: it was Hal, of course, along with someone else. She picked it up and studied it. A casual snapshot, it appeared, of a slightly younger Hal, carefree in an open-necked shirt, grinning at the camera. It captured the essence of him to perfection; Valerie felt her chest constrict in pain. She shifted her attention to the other person in the photo. It was a young man, perhaps in his late teens, who could only be Hal's son, so like Hal was he. The same eyes, the same smile; the only thing he'd taken from the Magpie was his hair, black and curly rather than smooth and golden. Hal and his son; for some reason it brought Valerie to the verge of tears. The urge to put the photo in her pocket was overwhelming, but common sense prevailed. She replaced it on the desk and turned to go.

As she left, though, her eye was caught by a thick red book on a shelf near the door: *Crockford's Clerical Directory*. That might tell her something interesting. She pulled it down and flipped to the 'P's. Phillips – there was a page-and-a-half's worth of people called Phillips, and she didn't even know the Magpie's Christian name. And it all seemed to be in code. But the word 'Saxwell' jumped off the page at her, and she focused on the entry. 'Phillips, Ven. Margaret Jane.' So she was called Margaret. That was fitting: Margaret, Maggie, Magpie. She would always be the Magpie to Valerie. The date with the 'b' must be the year of her birth – it would make her forty-seven this year. That was about right, Valerie reckoned. Middle-aged. Past it.

She was hoping that it might say something about Hal, but amongst the jumble of code – d, p, C, V, Adn, dates, place names – there didn't even seem to be any indication of marital status. Disappointed, Valerie shut the book and returned it to the shelf.

Valerie crept up the stairs, looking at her watch. She still had plenty of time, so she decided to save the main bedroom until last. It was probably, she guessed, one of the two large rooms at the front of the house; she moved towards the back instead.

The house was silent; no tell-tale sound of rock music seeped from under any of the closed doors. But she opened the first door with caution, ready to run for it if by chance it was occupied.

Clearly this was the son's room, and just as clearly he wasn't in residence. His things were there, a few books on the shelves, sporting trophies, framed photos and certificates on the wall, but the room was far too tidy for even the neatest of inhabitants and, when Valerie peered into the wardrobe, she found that it contained only a few spare pillows and blankets.

A quick look at the things on the wall told her that his name was Alexander Phillips, and that he was a keen rower. His face, with its painfully familiar cheeky grin, was easily found in the photos of his Cambridge college's rowing eight, and the earlier school photos showed that face in younger versions.

Valerie couldn't bear to look at Alexander Phillips. She left his room and tried the next one along the corridor: a bathroom, and one that wasn't in daily use. No clutter of toothbrushes and toothpaste round the basin, and a pair of pristine hand towels on the towel rail.

The next room was more interesting; it was some sort of den or family room. Unlike the formally furnished drawing room, it was cosy, comfortable, though there was nothing of the shabby about it. A television and video recorder occupied one corner, and there was a stereo and a collection of compact discs as well. Here, too, were a number of bookcases with the books that didn't fit into the professional collection in the Magpie's study: novels, classics, biographies, popular history, travel. Valerie scanned the shelves eagerly, hoping that she might find one or more of her own books there, but she was disappointed. She should have known that the Magpie didn't have very good taste – except when it came to men, Valerie acknowledged.

Next to the den she found a small room – not more than a box room, really – furnished as an office, and her pulse quickened. It must be Hal's office! A tall grey filing cabinet stood in the corner, presumably containing details of his various jobs. Valerie pulled out the second drawer, labelled 'L–Z', and flipped through till she found a file marked 'Marler'.

She wasn't sure what she'd expected to find in the file, but there was nothing more than a copy of his estimate for the job and a copy of the receipt, marked 'paid' in his distinctive hand. Disappointed, she replaced it and pushed the drawer back in, turning to the desk. It was a small desk, without room for much apart from the computer and the printer. But there was a framed photo on that desk as well, and Valerie picked it up.

The Magpie, of course. That was bad enough, but it was the Magpie in her wedding dress. Impossibly young, rapturously happy, undeniably beautiful. Black and white: a slip of a white dress, a cloud of black hair under a mist of white veil. Valerie wanted to smash it, to bring it down on the desk again and again until the glass was shattered in a million pieces, and then to tear the photo to bits, to obliterate that face that smiled out at her with such radiant hope and joy.

Instead she left the room. There were two doors remaining at the front of the house; Valerie pushed one of them open and knew instinctively that she was looking into the marital bedroom, so she went to the other one instead.

This one was furnished tastefully but impersonally as a guest bedroom, with a random stack of tempting books on the bedside table and – Valerie found when she checked – an empty wardrobe. Not much here to command her attention, so she moved on.

Valerie had deduced that, the main bathroom being unused, there must be an ensuite attached to the master bedroom. She passed quickly through the bedroom and opened a side door, proving herself right.

This bathroom *was* in use on a daily basis. Here were the toothbrushes, the thick bath towels, and the dressing gowns hanging on twin hooks on the back of the door. Two dressing gowns.

Valerie would have expected the Magpie's dressing gown to be plain and serviceable: white towelling, perhaps, or a matronly brushed cotton or winceyette. It was indeed white, and plain in design, but it was fashioned of slithery satin. Valerie couldn't help fingering it, then remembering to whom it belonged, drew her hand back as if she'd touched something contaminated.

The other dressing gown was made of a fine woollen, woven in rich dark colours. Hal's. Valerie touched it lovingly, running her fingers over the fabric. She buried her face in its folds and breathed in deeply, inhaling Hal's scent. It was enough to make her dizzy with desire.

After a moment of vivid fantasy Valerie turned her attention to the mirror-fronted cupboard above the vanity unit. She pulled its door open and surveyed the contents: a bottle of paracetamol, a packet of plasters and a tube of antiseptic cream, toothpaste, deodorants, and Hal's shaving tackle. She took his razor out and turned it over in her hand: no cheap and flimsy disposable razor for Hal, she noted with satisfaction. Nor was it a trendy high-tech affair, with double blades and lubricating strip and swivelling head. Hal's razor was solid and old-fashioned and uncompromising, the sort that took real razor blades. How, Valerie wondered suddenly and inconsequentially, did modern-day suicides manage to open their veins with disposable razors?

She caressed his razor, avoiding the lethal blade, then

returned it to its place in the cabinet and took out the bottle of aftershave: an expensive, exclusive brand, of course. She unscrewed the top and inhaled; it conjured up an instantaneous and dizzying vision of Hal. Valerie closed her eyes in ecstasy, then opened them and looked towards the bath. She could almost see him there in the shower, the water sluicing off his skin, his beautiful, perfect body . . .

Faint with the power of her imagination, Valerie none the less managed to restore the aftershave to the cupboard and close the door. It was time for the bedroom. Hal's bedroom.

Near the door was a dressing table, covered with various bottles and jars of lotions and potions. Moisturisers and dry-skin preparations, Valerie noted with scorn. What did the Magpie expect? She was old – of course she had dry skin. All of the lotions in the world weren't going to restore her youth, or Hal's love. Why didn't she just give up and admit defeat?

Valerie opened the wardrobe. On one side were the Magpie's clothes, just as she'd expected: dowdy black skirts and black clerical shirts, and a few casual things. Hal's clothes took up more than half of the wardrobe. There were several clean white overalls, a number of shirts, some casual chino trousers and a pair of jeans, smart woollen trousers, a navy blazer with brass buttons, a hemp-coloured linen jacket, and a couple of dark lounge suits. Collectively they gave off a whiff of Hal; his personal perfume assailed Valerie and she breathed it in deeply as she fingered the garments one by one.

Time was getting on, she realised suddenly. She was nearly done, but she should be making a move soon. Valerie proceeded to one of two chests of drawers. It was the Magpie's, she found as she pulled out the top drawer. Black tights, white slips. And knickers, both black and white. To her surprise and disgust, the knickers weren't the sort that middle-aged women should wear, practical and ugly and modest. No: they were sexy knickers, lacy wisps cut low in the front and high on the sides. The Magpie ought to be ashamed of herself, wearing things like that, Valerie thought with a disapproving frown as she examined a pair. Of course she shouldn't really blame her for trying to keep her husband's interest, but that was a lost cause. Poor pathetic Magpie – she could almost feel sorry for her.

The other chest of drawers, Valerie noticed suddenly, had an old-fashioned man's hairbrush set on the top. She dropped the Magpie's knickers, slammed the drawer shut, and hurried to examine her new find. Lovingly she picked up the silver-backed brush and extracted a few short honey-gold hairs from among its bristles. Fumbling in her pocket, she found a tissue and wrapped the hairs carefully, then tucked the precious tissue into her bra for safekeeping.

She pulled out the drawers one by one: Hal's socks, Hal's underwear. A stack of snowy white cotton boxer shorts, laundered and pressed. Valerie lifted out the top pair and buried her face in them. They smelled only of soap powder and fabric softener, not of Hal, but they were *his*, and precious to her. Surely, she thought, he wouldn't miss just one pair when he had so many. And it would mean so much to her to have them. She folded them and put them in her pocket, a talisman of Hal. She would sleep with them under her pillow, tonight and every night until Hal himself was hers.

With that thought, she turned to the bed. Hal's bed. Resisting an impulse to lie down on it and put her head on his pillow, she lifted the pillow nearest to her. There was a white nightdress under it, folded neatly; she pulled it out and held it up. This was no concealing Victorian garment, buttoned up to the neck. It was a confection of a nightdress, a froth of delicate lace and a wisp of gossamer silk. A hideously, obscenely expensive nightdress, the sort that a man buys for a woman.

And there were only two reasons why a man would buy a

nightdress like that for a woman, Valerie knew. Either he
loved her very much, or he was feeling enormously guilty.
She felt certain that the first was not true; Hal no longer loved
the Magpie, if indeed he ever had. She had probably trapped
him into marriage, seduced him and become pregnant, and
he had stayed with her for the sake of the child. There didn't
seem to have been any more children, which in itself said
something.

So it had to be the second reason. Valerie's heart sang, suddenly, as it came to her that Hal was feeling guilty over *her*,
because he'd fallen in love with her. Her atavistic impulse to
rend the nightdress, to tear it to shreds, faded with that smug
certainty. Let the Magpie keep her nightdress, Valerie thought
magnanimously, stuffing it back beneath the pillow. She didn't
have Hal's love, and never would, so let her keep the nightdress, her husband's guilt-offering. Hal was *hers*, or would be
as soon as the Magpie was out of the way.

Light-headed and light-hearted, Valerie retraced her steps
down the stairs, out of the window, and round the corner to
her car, bearing her two precious trophies.

As a working woman, Hazel Croom valued her weekends.
Saturdays were taken up with shopping and housework and
other necessary tasks, plus, of course, doing the church flowers most weeks, and thus were little more than another
working day. But her Sundays were precious to her.

They usually followed a pattern. She would be up early to
peel the potatoes and prepare the veg for Sunday lunch, then
off to St Mark's for Mass. As a proper Anglo-Catholic, Hazel
fasted before Mass; that meant no breakfast, and not even a
cup of tea. For one who believed in the importance of a good
nutritious breakfast to get the day off to a proper start, this
was quite a sacrifice, but that was what gave it value; if she'd
been one of those people – like many of those foolish girls at

her school, for instance – who normally skipped breakfast, or only had a piece of toast, fasting would have had no special meaning. Each Sunday morning, though, as she readied the joint and set the timer on the cooker, Hazel could look at the empty teapot and feel virtuous.

When she came home from Mass, of course, she could and did put the kettle on straightaway. No other cup of tea in the whole week tasted as good as that first one on a Sunday, and she savoured it accordingly. By then the joint would be cooking away, filling the house with the tantalising perfume of roasting meat, and all she would have to do was turn the heat on under the veg and pop the potatoes in to roast while the kettle boiled. Then she could retire to the sitting room to enjoy her tea, drunk out of Mother's best bone china, set out on a doily-covered tray that she would have prepared before she left for church.

Then came making the gravy and the other finishing touches: laying the dining room table with the good silver and the bone china dishes, and popping her plate into the warming oven so that it would be just the right temperature. Finally, she allowed herself a small glass of pale, dry sherry from the decanter in the sitting room. This is what happened on a Sunday, and always had.

It would never have occurred to Hazel Croom that this ritual was unnecessary, or might be changed. Now that her parents were dead and she was on her own, she could have opened a tin of soup for Sunday lunch, or even had one of those Marks and Spencer's chilled ready meals which always looked so appetising, and no one the wiser. But for Hazel any such radical thoughts were out of the question. Sunday was Sunday, and that was that.

So on this Sunday, like every other, she served up the oblig-atory four veg, in Mother's best china bowls, and carved her joint. It was the one meal of the week that was served and eaten in the dining room rather than the kitchen – never mind that the food got a bit cold in transit, that was the way it was done. This week it was a nice leg of spring lamb; Hazel cut off two thin slices and laid them carefully on the warm plate. The rest of the lamb would of course not go to waste; it would provide the foundation for her evening meals for the better part of the week. Sliced cold with a bit of salad on Monday, curried on Tuesday, and shepherd's pie on Wednesday. Lamb had been Mother's favourite, and though Hazel herself preferred a nice bit of beef, mad cows or no mad cows, she'd continued to serve lamb at least one Sunday a month.

The pudding would have been done the night before: a nice trifle, perhaps, which would also last for several days, or an apple tart. Today it was fruit salad. Hazel spooned some into a dish and poured on a bit of cream.

When the meal was finished, and coffee drunk from one of Mother's demitasse cups, Hazel cleared the table, carried the dishes through to the kitchen, and tackled the washing up. On weekdays she would leave the plates in the wooden rack to dry naturally. But Sundays were different; the bone china would be wiped carefully with a tea towel, and carried back to the dining room to be put away till the next week. Then Hazel was free to enjoy the rest of the day: reading the Sunday papers, later having tea with a slice of fruitcake, watching *Songs of Praise* on the television.

For years her Sunday routine had included, after her tea, returning to St Mark's for Evensong. Father Gervase had done Evensong so beautifully, even though at times Hazel was the only one in the congregation. Now, though, in the interregnum, Evensong had been discontinued; the priest who took Mass on a Sunday morning had his own parish elsewhere, and squeezed St Mark's in amongst his regular duties. It just wasn't the same.

It never would be the same again, Hazel acknowledged to herself. Not without Father Gervase.

Usually, later on Sunday evening, she would have to do some marking, and prepare for Monday's lessons. But on this particular Sunday, half-term week stretched ahead of Hazel: no marking, no lessons. So after *Songs of Praise* she set herself another useful task instead.

She had been carrying the same black leather handbag for as many years as she could remember: a hard-sided one with two handles, very much like the style favoured by the Queen. It was of good quality to begin with, of course, and she had taken good care of it. Once or twice she'd had to have the clasp mended, and the leather handles had been replaced, but it had served her well. Now, though, it finally did seem to have reached the end of its useful life. The clasp had gone again, and when she'd taken it into Long Haddon on Saturday to have it repaired, the man had looked at it and shaken his head. 'Why don't you just get a new one?' he'd said.

And so she had. This new one wasn't as well made – you just couldn't find the same sort of quality these days, Hazel knew – but with care it should last her for several years. Tonight she would transfer the contents of the old handbag into the new one.

It was a straightforward task, as she didn't believe in cluttering up her handbag with rubbish. A leather notecase, a small purse for coins, a cheque book, an engagement diary, an old-fashioned powder compact that Mother had given her on her twenty-first birthday, a comb, a lipstick, a pen, a set of keys, and a handkerchief. But at the bottom of the handbag was something else: a scrap of paper with some writing on it.

Hazel took it out and examined it: the paper appeared to be part of a page from a pocket diary, torn out neatly, and the writing proved to be a name and phone number. *Phyllis Endersby*, it said in a precise, upright hand.

Who was Phyllis Endersby? And why had she given her phone number to Hazel Croom? Was she a parent of one of the children at the school? Hazel couldn't remember an Endersby amongst the pupils, and it was a fairly distinctive name.

She sat for a moment with the scrap of paper in her hand, puzzling over it. And then it came back to her: Father Gervase's induction at his new church. She'd met Phyllis Endersby there; Father Gervase himself had introduced them, at the reception following the service. He'd made a point of it, saying that they must meet. Mrs Endersby was Hazel's counterpart at St Stephen's, Branlingham, Father Gervase had explained, the doyenne of the flower rota and every other rota that was going, the guiding light of the Mothers' Union.

They had chatted for quite some time, Hazel now remembered, and had indeed found that they had a great deal in common. Phyllis Endersby was a good ten years older than Hazel, of course, and a widow, but they saw the world in much the same way. When they'd parted, Mrs Endersby had written her name and number on a back page of her diary, torn it out with care, and presented it to Hazel. 'If you're ever this way,' she'd said, 'do come for a cup of tea.'

And why not? thought Hazel now, impulsively. For the next week she was a free agent. Why not have a little trip to Branlingham? It would do her good to get out and away from Letherfield for a day. She would enjoy a longer visit with Phyllis Endersby. And if she happened to be in Branlingham, of course it would be rude not to drop in and call on Father Gervase while she was there. Hazel nodded to herself and reached for the phone.

It had been quite a few months since Shaun Kelly had spent a Sunday afternoon at home, in his London flat. And if he had anything to say about it, he wouldn't be doing it again in the near future. Once he had finished reading the Sunday papers, there was nothing to do: he didn't enjoy watching sport on television, and a flick through the channels yielded nothing else worth watching.

None of the nice restaurants in the vicinity of the flat, the ones that he frequented during the week, were open on a Sunday, so he'd had to make do with a takeaway curry for his lunch. And though the licensing laws had changed so that many pubs were open in the afternoon, Sunday was the exception to that: there was a gap of several hours during which all of the pubs were shut.

And so Shaun slumped on his sofa, poured himself a stiff drink from a bottle of Bushmills, and gave himself over to self-pity.

Val had told him not to come this weekend. That hadn't come as a total surprise, after the way she'd been behaving lately, never returning his phone messages. And when he'd been down to Rose Cottage on Thursday for the *Hello!* photo shoot, she had been distant and detached, almost as if they were mere acquaintances rather than lovers. At the time he had tried to convince himself that she was just being cautious, with all of those strangers about. But he didn't believe it, not really.

Val was slipping away from him; he could feel it. There was no reason why this should have happened – they were so good together. Good in bed, and in every other way. There was only one explanation for it, as far as Shaun was concerned: she had met someone else. Some other bloke, perhaps someone local, had come into her life and was easing Shaun out.

She was the best thing that had ever happened to him, his ticket to the life he'd been born to live. He was *not* going to lose her.

★

Hal and Margaret had enjoyed a rare day together. After lunch they'd gone off to visit the garden of a stately home, open for viewing that day under the National Gardens Scheme, where by prior arrangement they'd met Alexander and his partner Luke. The rendezvous had been planned weeks in advance, at a place roughly equidistant between them, and factored into busy schedules. It had been a great success: the weather had been glorious, and they'd spent hours together exploring the extensive gardens. Then, eschewing the tables set up in the stable block, they'd taken their tea and cakes into the open air and sat on the grass, soaking up the warmth of the sun and delighting in one another's company until it was time to go their separate ways.

Refreshed and exhilarated, Margaret and Hal came home in the early evening. They watched a little television – in Margaret's case, at least, a rare treat – then, discovering that they were hungry again, repaired to the kitchen. Hal made sandwiches from the remains of the chicken, and they opened a bottle of wine. By the time they'd polished off the sandwiches and drunk half the bottle, they were both feeling relaxed and mellow.

'Busy week ahead?' Hal asked, refilling Margaret's glass.

'Mmm.' She grimaced. 'I don't want to think about that yet, but it looks to be pretty frightful – meetings every night, if I recall. Even Friday evening, when I should be allowed a rest, I have a big meeting for all of the clergy in the Archdeaconry, about church security.'

Hal shrugged philosophically. 'All part of the job, my dear.'

'Oh, I know that.' Her voice was light. 'I'm not complaining, really. I just feel a bit guilty, leaving you on your own so much.'

'I'm used to it by now.' Hal emptied the bottle into his own glass.

'And how about you? Still at Branlingham Vicarage this week?'

Hal nodded. 'And for several more weeks, by the look of it. It's quite a job.' He sipped the wine, savouring it on his tongue. 'I've finished the drawing room, and it looks stunning, if I say it myself. But there's much more to do.'

Margaret picked at the crumbs on her plate. 'What do you make of them?' she asked with idle curiosity. 'The Finches, I mean?'

'Oh, they're very nice.' He shrugged.

'I'm just always interested in what makes other people's marriages work,' confessed Margaret, 'and they seem rather an unusual couple, from what I've seen of them. He's quite a lot older than she is, I'd guess. And he does seem to have his head in the clouds a bit. She strikes me as the practical one.'

'He's been married before,' Hal said shortly, addressing one of the points she'd raised. 'His first wife died.'

'Oh, really? That's interesting.'

She wasn't just saying that; Margaret genuinely did find people interesting. Hal could see more questions coming, and he was even less inclined to talk about Rosemary Finch than he'd been earlier in the week. He changed the subject back to one that had occupied them for much of the evening, repeating a point that had already been made several times. 'Alexander looked well, didn't he?'

'Very well indeed,' she agreed, always willing to be deflected onto the subject of her son, no matter how repetitiously. 'He claims it's all down to Luke's cooking.'

After a few more minutes of rehashing the afternoon, Hal drained his glass with a last swig. 'I think I'd like an early night.'

'If that's an invitation,' said Margaret, following suit, 'I accept.'

She put their glasses and plates into the dishwasher while

Hal locked up, then they went upstairs together in companionable silence.

But when Margaret lifted her pillow to retrieve her nightdress, she stopped short. 'What have you done to my nightdress?' she queried.

Hal was on his way to the bathroom. 'What do you mean? I haven't touched it.'

'I always fold it up, but it's been just sort of stuffed under the pillow. You must have done something to it, Hal.'

He protested his innocence. 'I didn't. Why would I?'

Hal had no reason to lie, and Margaret knew him well enough to sense that he was telling the truth. The implications of that line of thought dawned fairly quickly. 'But if you didn't, Hal, someone else has,' she stated with certainty. 'Someone else has been in the house.'

'But that's ridiculous,' he countered. 'You were probably in a hurry this morning, and did it yourself.'

'No.' Driven by instinct, she went to her chest of drawers and pulled out the top drawer. 'Look,' she said, her voice beginning to shake. 'Someone has been in here, messing about with my knickers. I'm sure of it. I can feel it. Someone has been in our house.'

Hal, unable or unwilling to face the implications, still tried to deny it. 'There hasn't been a burglary, my love. The television, the video, the stereo – they're all still here. Nothing is missing or we would have noticed it by now. I think you're imagining things.'

'Someone has been in our house,' Margaret repeated adamantly, and the eyes she turned to her husband, pupils dilated, were enormous with fear.

Chapter 11

The following week was a fairly typical one for Gervase. As he became enmeshed in the affairs of his new parish, a sort of routine evolved. In the mornings he was usually shut in his study, either with a parishioner or with his books, writing sermons or fiddling with something for the parish magazine. He tried to have lunch with Rosemary before going out in the afternoons, making his round of parish and hospital visits. Evenings, unless he had a meeting, were spent at home. Each day was different, but most were similar.

For Rosemary, though, whose routine had more definable fixed points in it, mostly based on Daisy's schedule, that week was not to be typical. Half-term week meant that Daisy would be at home all of the time, and this was complicated by the fact that Hal had moved on, as promised, to paint Daisy's bedroom.

Daisy was of course excited by this development, and wanted to be there all of the time, watching Hal's progress and chattering to him. Rosemary, embarrassed by the intimate revelations she had shared with him, had pretty much avoided Hal for the last few days of the previous week; now she found herself spending a great deal of time with him and

Daisy. It was Daisy who did most of the talking, but Rosemary grew more and more comfortable in his company. The unease she'd felt the week before – that sensation of having exposed herself to him, making herself vulnerable – disappeared in the torrent of Daisy's chatter, and his easy response to it. Hal was so good with Daisy, Rosemary marvelled. There were very few people who were able to strike that perfect note, neither patronising nor ignoring her; Hal had from the very beginning seemed to know exactly how to treat her. Daisy, in return, adored him.

At various times Rosemary tried to suggest that perhaps he might be happier working alone, without the distraction of Daisy's chit-chat, but Hal was always adamant that Daisy's company was nothing but a pleasure.

On Hal's part, he *did* enjoy Daisy, for her own sake; there was a rapport between them that defied explanation. But he was beginning to admit to himself that much of the pleasure was a result of her mother's presence. Rosemary Finch fascinated him; the more he saw of her, the more he wanted to see of her. Even Daisy's constant flow of chatter couldn't get in the way of the growing understanding between them. They would look at each other over Daisy's head, and smile, each seeming to know what the other was thinking. At times he wished that he and Rosemary could talk, but he recognised that it wasn't really necessary: they understood each other without words.

The dynamic changed on Tuesday afternoon. Rosemary had a phone call from Annie Sawbridge, suggesting that the two of them might visit Kinderland. Annie needed to finalise the plans for Samantha's birthday party, less than a week hence, and wanted to make sure that Rosemary's fears for Daisy's safety were put to rest. Gervase was out; Hal offered to watch Daisy while her mother was away. 'Oh, I couldn't ask you to do that,' Rosemary demurred.

'You didn't ask me. I volunteered,' he reminded her.

So Rosemary went to Kinderland and returned, bemused by the experience, to find that the two of them had managed very satisfactorily without her. She wanted to tell Hal about it, but couldn't really do so with Daisy there. On Wednesday, though, the day that Hal would finish Daisy's room, the girl was invited to spend the day at Samantha's house. Daisy was torn between her desire to be at home with Hal and her eagerness to see her best friend after several days of separation; inevitably the latter won out, and Rosemary found herself alone with Hal.

There was no awkwardness between them, no reserve; Daisy had broken those barriers down, and for that Hal rejoiced.

The furniture had been moved into the centre of the room while Hal worked round the edges. Rosemary sat on Daisy's bed, her knees drawn up under her chin. 'It was quite extraordinary, this Kinderland,' she told him. 'Enormous. And each bit was decorated with painted backdrops to look like a different part of the UK – London with Tower Bridge and the Houses of Parliament cheek by jowl, Scotland with shaggy highland cattle standing next to Loch Ness, and so on.'

'But what exactly do they *do* there?' Hal queried.

'Well, that's what I wondered. But the answer is that they play, until they drop with exhaustion.' Rosemary smiled to herself at the memory of the frantic children she'd seen. 'They get all hyped up, and run about. They go up ladders, and come down slides into masses of multicoloured balls, and crawl through tubes, and climb on ropes.'

Hal frowned, thinking of Daisy. 'Sounds dangerous.'

'That's what I thought at first, as well, when Annie told me about it,' she admitted. 'But it's all constructed with safety in mind. Everything is padded, and well supervised. I don't think she could hurt herself.'

'So you're going to allow her to go.'

Rosemary nodded. 'She'll have a wonderful time, and I'm sure she won't come to any harm. At least that's what I keep telling myself. And she and Samantha would both be heart-broken if I didn't let her go.'

They talked on: about Daisy, about themselves. 'I don't think I've told you about the concert that Gervase and I are going to on Friday night,' Rosemary said. She explained to him about the programme, the performers and the venue. 'And Daisy is all set to spend the night with Samantha. She's never stayed away from home before, without me, so of course I'm a bit apprehensive about it. But Samantha's mum suggested that she sleep over tonight as a trial run, just to make sure it will be all right on Friday night.'

'It will be fine,' Hal said reassuringly. 'Daisy is tougher than you think, and she adores Samantha.'

'I hope so – I'd be so disappointed if I couldn't go,' Rosemary confessed. 'I've been looking forward to it for weeks. My birthday treat,' she added shyly.

'Oh, is it your birthday on Friday, then?'

'No, not till next week,' she admitted. 'It's an *early* birthday treat. But I am looking forward to it.' She knew that Hal shared her taste in music, and would appreciate her anticipation.

'It sounds splendid,' he said with sincerity.

'I'll tell you all about it next week,' she promised.

For a moment Hal paused in his rhythmic wielding of the paint roller. Friday – why did Friday ring a bell? There was something happening on Friday, but at the moment he couldn't recall what it might be.

Hazel Croom was enjoying her visit with Phyllis Endersby. When given the choice of dates and times, she had opted to go for morning coffee rather than afternoon tea. Knowing

Father Gervase's habits as she did, his unstinting giving of himself to his parish, she realised that he was likely to be away from the Vicarage in the afternoon, but he was almost always at home for lunch. If she were to drop in at the Vicarage at lunch-time, the chances were excellent that she might see him. And he would of course invite her in to join them; to do otherwise when she'd come such a long way would be rude, and Father Gervase was never rude. So she kept her eye on the clock as she drank Phyllis's coffee and nibbled the proffered shop-bought biscuits.

Phyllis Endersby's house was much as she had expected, a tidy bungalow with a neatly manicured front garden. Phyllis was a keen gardener; her herbaceous borders were the envy of Branlingham, she told Hazel with some pride. 'Just you come round in the summer,' she said, 'and you'll see. It looks nice now, with the tulips and the wallflowers. But come summer, with the marigolds and the alyssum and the busy Lizzies, there's nothing in Branlingham to touch my borders.'

Hazel enjoyed gardening as well, though her taste ran more to old-fashioned roses, so there was much to talk about. Father Gervase had been right: the two women had much in common.

In appearance they were very different. Hazel was tall, angular and spare; she knew, as one does know these things, that her shape had given rise to her nickname amongst the children at her school: 'Croom the Broom'. Phyllis, in contrast, was short and well padded – not fat by any means, but solid, as though the years had compacted her mass downwards. Phyllis was also some ten years older than Hazel. And they weren't quite from the same class; looking about at Phyllis's collection of china cat ornaments – they marched across the shelf above the electric fire and inhabited various other surfaces in the room that Phyllis called the lounge/diner – Hazel admitted to herself that her hostess was perhaps just a bit . . . *common*. But class didn't matter any more, she told herself, and when it came to the things that counted they were in agreement. Both had voted Conservative all of their lives, were great fans of Margaret Thatcher, and still felt aggrieved at her ouster. And both were passionately interested in the Church, not least in Father Gervase.

Fortunately for Hazel Croom, Phyllis Endersby also shared her taste for gossip. Once they had thoroughly explored the virtues of Father Gervase, they moved naturally on to the subject of Rosemary.

'Keeps herself to herself,' Phyllis stated, a note of disapproval in her voice. 'She hasn't been to a Mothers' Union meeting yet, though I've invited her personally – I'm Enrolling Member, you know. And with preparations well under way for the church fête, we've still yet to see much of her. She's agreed to take on the bookstall, but she hasn't turned up yet at a meeting. Of course,' she added in a more conciliatory tone, 'she *has* got her hands full, with the little Down's syndrome girl.'

Hazel sniffed, not afraid to be overtly disapproving. 'That's a fine excuse,' she said. 'You should see what she does all day long, when Father Gervase is out and Daisy is at school. She *reads*. Sits about on the sofa and reads novels! I can't tell you the number of times I've caught her at it when I've called round, stuffing some nasty-looking paperback under a cushion and hoping I wouldn't notice.'

'Oh?' Phyllis encouraged her to go on.

'And all round her, everything covered in dust. She's a shocking housekeeper.' Hazel knew that this charge would carry a great deal of weight with her hostess, an exemplary housekeeper herself. Not a speck of dust would find a home in Phyllis's bungalow, not even on the cat ornaments, and the immaculate surfaces exuded a faint perfume of Dettol.

Phyllis clicked her tongue against her teeth. 'Tsk, tsk. I had no idea. No wonder she doesn't let people in, or invite them round.'

'She's not much of a cook, either,' Hazel went on. 'Not from what I've seen, anyway.'

Phyllis was not much of a cook herself: she'd always preferred cleaning and gardening, though when her husband was alive, and the girls at home, she'd done her best. But now, as a woman on her own, she virtually lived off ready meals from the Marks and Spencer in Saxwell. So she kept quiet on this point and developed another line of attack, one on which she was herself on firmer ground. 'And what about her dress sense? She looks like she gets her clothes from church jumble sales!'

Hazel had already noted that Phyllis's wardrobe was vintage Marks and Sparks: a knife-pleated plaid skirt, knee length, and a lambswool jumper in a coordinating shade of green. 'I'm sure she *does*,' she stated. 'All of the parish cast-offs. Most of the things she wears I've seen on other people. I've even seen her in *my* old clothes!' Unconsciously she smoothed the sleeve of her dress; it had come not from Marks and Sparks but from the best dress shop in Long Haddon, the one that Mother had always patronised. The sight of Rosemary in one of her blouses – though she acknowledged to herself that the Vicar's wife probably had no idea of the provenance of the garment – had been such an affront that she'd begun giving her discarded clothes to a charity shop instead of donating them to the church jumble sale.

'I suppose she's a good mother,' Phyllis ventured, thinking that perhaps it was time to explore Rosemary's positive points.

'Humph.' Hazel raised her eyebrows; as far as she was concerned, Rosemary had no positive points, and motherhood was in fact yet another indictment against her. 'She's saddled poor Father Gervase with that handicapped child. And she wouldn't listen to advice. We all told her that for their own good, and the good of the child, they ought to put her in an institution – there are plenty of special places for children like that, where they're cared for properly. But she wouldn't hear of it.'

Phyllis picked up the theme. 'And they haven't had any other children,' she said significantly.

'Exactly. Though perhaps that's just as well, under the circumstances. And she was useless when it came to young Tom,' Hazel added.

'Tom?' Phyllis seized on the unfamiliar name. 'Who is Tom, then?'

'Oh, you don't know.' Hazel nodded sagely; she'd been enjoying herself, and the chance to tell this part of the story to a new audience was a huge bonus. 'You didn't know that Father Gervase had been married before, then?'

'Married before?' Phyllis's expression, wide-eyed, was gratifyingly avid.

'Her name was Laura, and she was . . .' Hazel stared off into the distance and sighed, then searched for the words to go on. 'Laura was marvellous. A paragon. She was everything that Rosemary is not. Beautiful, well dressed, a wonderful cook, an excellent housekeeper. A perfect wife for Father Gervase, and a perfect mother to little Tom.' She told the story of Laura's early death, her eyes filling with genuine tears.

'But how sad.'

'It was more than sad – it was tragic. Poor Father Gervase was absolutely devastated. And when he was at his lowest point, that woman came along and took advantage of him. She wormed her way into his life when he was defenceless and grief-stricken, and the first thing you know, she'd trapped him into marrying her.' Hazel had never quite forgiven herself for being the instrument of Rosemary's entrance into Father Gervase's life; she didn't mention her role in it to Phyllis. 'I suppose he thought that Tom needed a mother. There's no other explanation for it. But it was all a terrible mistake, their marriage. I mean, what does she possibly have to offer to Father Gervase?'

It was meant as a rhetorical question, but Phyllis had been a married woman, and she felt that gave her the right to answer. 'Perhaps she's . . . passionate,' she speculated, with euphemistic delicacy. 'You just don't know what goes on inside other people's bedrooms, do you?'

Hazel pressed her lips together primly. 'But that isn't relevant. Father Gervase is a *priest*,' she stated, brushing an invisible speck of dust from her sleeve so that she wouldn't have to make eye contact when such an embarrassing subject was being discussed.

Phyllis, with a bit more experience of the world than Hazel, had rather thought that priests were men as well, but she knew when to keep quiet. 'More coffee, Hazel?' she offered in a bright voice.

'Just a drop.' Extending her cup, Hazel glanced at the clock. It was just gone twelve; she didn't want to arrive at the Vicarage too early.

What appeared to be a large white fur muff on legs appeared through the half-opened door and sauntered across the patterned carpet of the sitting room, putting one delicate foot in front of another, and without being invited or encouraged, jumped onto Hazel Croom's lap.

'Oh, Queenie,' Phyllis clucked. 'You don't mind, do you, Hazel? Only you're sitting in Queenie's chair.'

Hazel Croom did not care for cats and avoided them whenever possible. She wasn't allergic; she just didn't like their sly ways. Dogs were different – forthright creatures, dogs, and you always knew where you stood with them. In fact she'd always thought that she'd rather like to have a dog, not a little yappy dog, but something substantial like a golden retriever or a springer spaniel. Of course, that had been out of the question when Mother was alive, and now she feared it was too late.

She regarded Queenie, now kneading her lap and purring, with distaste. Never had she seen such an enormous cat, or one with quite so much fur. How, she wondered, did Phyllis manage to keep all of that cat hair under control? And why was it that cats always seemed to have such an unerring ability to know who didn't like them, and make straight for that person? 'She's very . . . large,' Hazel remarked, trying hard to be polite.

Phyllis was oblivious to her discomfort. 'Oh, I'm afraid that I spoil her. Don't I, Queenie?' she added, her voice changing to a sort of coo.

Queenie didn't deign to look at her; by now her eyes were slits of contentment and she purred as loudly as a small lawn-mower motor.

'She does like her titbits,' Phyllis continued, addressing Hazel, though her attention was still on the cat. 'She's especially fond of sausages.' Then, in the cooing voice, 'Aren't you, precious?'

This was getting out of hand, Hazel decided. She focused on the framed photos that adorned the sideboard amongst the china cats. 'Are these photos of your family?' she asked.

'Yes, that's right.' Phyllis reached for the one nearest to hand, and for the next quarter of an hour – until she judged it was time to make a move – Hazel was treated to, and pro-fessed great interest in, a potted history of the Endersby family, from the late Leonard Endersby to the three daugh-ters and the seven grandchildren. It was at least preferable to cats.

*

Gervase had been out all morning. Rosemary was well into lunch preparations when the call came from him to say that he wouldn't be back home until much later in the afternoon. It was by no means the first time this had happened; Rosemary occasionally felt annoyed about it, especially when Gervase waited till the last minute to ring, but she knew that it would serve no purpose to get cross with him. It was all part of the job. 'Have you started making lunch, then?' he asked.

'It's nearly ready. I thought you'd be home at any minute.'

'Why don't you ask Hal Phillips to join you?' Gervase suggested.

This time Hal didn't demur. 'You're taking it very calmly,' he observed as he followed her to the kitchen.

Rosemary shrugged. 'It's only lunch. Happens all the time – you ought to know that.'

'Tell me about it,' he grinned, pulling out a chair and making himself comfortable. 'But you've been putting up with it a lot longer than I have.'

'I suppose that means I'm more used to it. And Gervase was a parish priest when I married him, so I've never known anything else,' she added thoughtfully. 'You've had to make a bigger adjustment.'

'It's a bit hard on Daisy, though,' Hal observed.

Rosemary put the toasted cheese sandwiches on plates and brought them to the table. 'Well, yes. But again, this is the norm for her – it's been like this all of her life. Just as it was for me, growing up with a parish priest for a father. She understands that when her daddy is needed elsewhere, we have to do without him.'

'She didn't seem to understand that last week, when he missed the picnic,' Hal pointed out astutely. 'She was pretty cut up about it, if I recall.'

'Hmm.' She nodded in acknowledgement, sitting down across from him.

Hal pursued his argument. 'I'm not really talking about Margaret and me here – I can take care of myself, and it doesn't bother me. But if we had a young family, I think I'd feel differently about it. I mean, I just don't understand why a priest's family should come *last*. Everyone else's needs are more important than the needs of his or her own family.'

'I've never really thought about it like that,' she admitted, frowning. 'The number of phone calls I've had that go something like, "Rosemary, I'm sorry, but so-and-so needs me . . ."'

'My point exactly.' Hal hadn't intended to upset her; sensing that he had done so, he changed the subject abruptly. 'Does he always call you "Rosemary", then?'

She looked across at him, puzzled. 'It's my name.'

'How about everyone else? Doesn't anyone ever call you "Rosie"?'

That took her back a few years; Rosemary smiled involuntarily. 'Not for a long time. My father used to call me Rosie, when I was very small. But when I started school, I insisted on being called by my full name. "Rosie" seemed babyish to me then, and it was time to "put away childish things".'

Having allowed his sandwich to cool sufficiently, Hal picked up half of it and took a bite. 'Rosemary is a lovely name, and it suits you,' he pronounced in a thoughtful voice, when he'd swallowed the mouthful of melting cheese. Both strong and soft at the same time, he added to himself, though he didn't dare to say it aloud. 'But I think that from now on I shall call you Rosie. If you don't mind, that is.'

Rosemary felt herself blushing. 'I don't mind,' she said. But she couldn't look him in the eye; instead she focused on his hands, holding the sandwich. They were strong, capable hands, square in shape and blunt-fingered, as different as could be imagined from Gervase's delicate hands with their long tapering fingers. She had studied Hal's hands before, while he'd been working; the contrast between the two men's hands fascinated her.

Interrupting her thoughts, the doorbell rang. She looked up, startled.

'Expecting anyone?' Hal queried.

'No.' She pushed her chair out and went to answer it.

Hazel Croom stood on the doorstep. 'Good afternoon, Rosemary,' she said with a fierce smile.

'Oh! Hello, Hazel.' She hoped she'd managed to keep the dismay out of her voice.

'I just happened to be in the neighbourhood, and thought I'd call,' Hazel explained smoothly.

'Come in,' Rosemary heard herself saying. 'Please do come in. We're just having lunch.'

'I wouldn't want to disturb your lunch,' Hazel protested, but she was already through the door, looking round her with avid curiosity as she followed Rosemary to the kitchen.

'I'm afraid that Gervase isn't here,' Rosemary explained belatedly at the kitchen door.

Hazel could see that. She could also see that another man – one wearing an overall – was sitting at the table. 'Hello,' said the man, looking up from his sandwich and rising to his feet.

Awkwardly, Rosemary made the introductions, her cheeks burning. 'This is Hal Phillips,' she said. 'He's decorating the house. And this is Hazel Croom, one of our former parishioners, from Letherfield.'

The visit had not been a success, Hazel reflected as she drove back to Letherfield. Father Gervase's absence had ensured that it was a disappointment, of course, but there was more to it than that.

Rosemary had been behaving in quite a peculiar way, she'd observed. Jittery, nervous. Guilty, even. Why was she having lunch with a tradesman? She'd explained that Father Gervase had been called away suddenly, but surely that was no reason to give the poor man's lunch to a *tradesman*? A polite and well-spoken tradesman, admittedly, but a tradesman just the same.

Was there something going on between those two? Hazel thought back over the stilted conversation. There did seem to be a certain familiarity between Rosemary and the decorator, or perhaps a certain ease would be a better way of describing it. Nothing overt, though of course they wouldn't be so foolish as to betray anything in front of her if there *were* something going on.

What should she do about it? Hazel wondered. Should she somehow contrive to mention it to Father Gervase? That might not be wise until she was in possession of a bit more information. She might be wrong, and in any case he might not thank her for it.

Perhaps she could enlist Phyllis Endersby to help in monitoring the situation, she thought, to keep a close eye on Rosemary Finch and the decorator. But to confide her suspicions to Phyllis would be to surrender control.

No, perhaps the best thing would be just to wait, and watch. Branlingham wasn't *that* far from Letherfield, and Phyllis *had* said that she should feel free to drop in at any time. If there was something going on, Hazel felt sure that she would be able to divine it in good time.

If. Probably there was nothing to it, she told herself. She'd never had a very high opinion of Rosemary Finch, but she didn't think that even Rosemary would stoop so low as to carry on with a tradesman, right under her husband's nose. And how could any woman, even Rosemary, prefer another man to Father Gervase? It was unthinkable.

Probably, she concluded, it was all very innocent, and just as Rosemary had said: Father Gervase had been called away, and she didn't want to waste food. Rosemary's nervousness, her blushes, could be attributed to Hazel's unexpected visit; she always *had* been clumsy in situations like that.

But it would bear watching, Hazel concluded. It would definitely bear watching.

'I'm sorry,' Rosemary said when Hazel had gone. 'I'm so sorry about that.'

'Sorry?' Hal shook his head. 'But why are you apologising, Rosie? You didn't invite the woman. You did your best to entertain her. She didn't come to see you, anyway – it was quite clear that she came to see Gervase. There's nothing to apologise for.'

'I'm sorry,' she repeated. 'Hazel just makes me feel . . . oh, I don't know how to explain it.' She put her hands to her flaming cheeks. 'I can't cope with her.'

'You did very well.' He wanted to take her hand and give it a reassuring squeeze, but instead he went back to work.

And instead of following Hal to continue their conversation, as she'd intended to do, Rosemary decided to make Gervase his favourite dinner. Steak and kidney pie tonight, she resolved.

Gervase wasn't very concerned about food, and would eat anything that was put in front of him, but he did have a weakness for steak and kidney pie. Rosemary didn't make it often – steak, even stewing steak, was expensive, and she hated the slimy, slippery feel of the kidneys. Besides, Daisy didn't like steak and kidney. But Daisy wouldn't be with them tonight, Rosemary recalled; she was going to stay at the Sawbridges'. She and Gervase would be on their own, a rare occasion. That was reason enough for a special dinner. So it would be steak and kidney, and Gervase's favourite pudding as well: syrup sponge pudding with custard. Comfort food. And after dinner, if he didn't have to go out . . .

Rosemary checked the store cupboard to make sure that she had enough flour and golden syrup, then fetched her handbag and set off for the butcher's.

On his way back to Saxwell that evening, Hal stopped at a filling station with pails of flowers in its forecourt and picked out a bunch of red roses. For Margaret.

Chapter 12

Valerie had abandoned all pretence of writing; she hadn't touched *The Path Not Chosen* in over a week, since the day she'd bought the car. For some time before that she'd at least gone through the motions, getting up early and sitting at her computer for the allotted time, tinkering with what she'd already written or simply staring at the screen, lost in her own thoughts. But breaking her immutable routine, just once, had shown it up for the flimsy construct it was. Now she couldn't be bothered. The convoluted story of people who didn't really exist no longer interested her; she was caught up in living her own life.

Her telephone was set permanently to voice-mail mode, so that she never had to pick up the phone. She rarely even listened to her messages, deleting unheard anything from Shaun or her editor, Warren. Shaun would be wanting to come to see her, and Warren would be expecting progress reports on the book. Valerie didn't feel guilty that she had nothing to say to either of them; she simply wasn't interested. They were remote, unconnected to her, like people she'd known in another life, or read about in a book.

Most mornings, breaking the habit of a lifetime, she'd

stayed in bed late. She wasn't sleeping well, but she felt tired all of the time and lacked the energy to get up.

On Thursday, though, she rose early, having set her alarm the night before. There was something she wanted – needed – to do.

Valerie had spent a fair amount of time following the Magpie round the countryside, from one remote church to another; the Magpie came and went from home at all times of the day. But she'd never been up early enough to follow Hal. She'd seen him come home in the evenings on several occasions, pulling the white van into the drive and disappearing into the house. Now, though, she wanted to follow him at the beginning of his day, to know where he was working.

Calculating from the time he'd usually arrived at Rose Cottage, she reckoned that he must have left home about half past eight. Of course he might now have farther to go, and would need to leave earlier, so she would have to allow plenty of time. It was tricky: she couldn't just wait in her car in the Bury Road, especially not during rush hour, but if she took up her position in the phone box, he could be gone long before she would have a chance to retrieve her car. And if she just drove round and round the block, as she sometimes did, she could easily miss him. So she pulled her car round the corner from The Archdeaconry and lurked there, with the car facing out into the Bury Road, engine idling. From there she could just see the end of the drive, and could move quickly when the time came.

It was very nearly half past eight when she spotted the blunt nose of the white van easing out of the drive. Valerie put her car into gear and waited to see which way Hal would turn. A right turn would mean that he – and she – would have to cross a lane of traffic, and it would put him into the midst of the rush hour traffic heading into Saxwell town centre. She was betting that he'd turn left instead, and she was right. This meant that he had to pass her.

There weren't many cars heading up the Bury Road; most people were going into Saxwell at that time of day, not leaving it. So Valerie had no trouble pulling out behind the white van. Very soon they were into the country, the white van taking a circuitous but obviously familiar route which was in effect bypassing Saxwell, emerging onto a B road south of the town. They were headed back towards Elmsford, Valerie realised. But the van passed the Elmsford turning and went on towards the next village, Branlingham. Here Hal turned off; Valerie followed him through the village, past the school and the George and Dragon pub, and saw him turn again into a lane called Church End. She had been down enough such lanes recently in pursuit of the Magpie to know that Church End was most unlikely to lead out into another road, and that this must be his final destination.

Valerie pulled her car over onto the verge near the village hall, locked it, and walked down Church End.

Beyond the church, and slightly behind it, was a house that must be the Vicarage. It was an extraordinary house, Valerie observed: enormous in size and built of red brick, it could almost serve as an exemplar of Gothic Revival style, with towering chimneys and ecclesiastical details such as incised crosses, stone dressings, and arched windows with leaded stained glass. The front door, set into a pointed stone arch with carved head stops on the hood moulding, was so massive and grand that it could almost have graced a mediaeval cathedral.

And in the drive at the front of the house was Hal's white van. Hal himself was taking things from the van and carrying them in through the front door. After three trips he shut and locked the van and disappeared into the house, closing the heavy wooden door behind him.

Valerie went into the south porch of the church; it afforded a good view of the Vicarage, and would provide her with privacy, shelter, and a place to sit. She settled down on the stone shelf. It was cold and uncomfortable, but such things didn't matter. She would wait, and watch, all day if necessary. Sooner or later someone would have to come or go from the house, and she intended to be there when they did.

Sybil Rashe enjoyed Thursday mornings, and looked forward to them almost as much as she did to Wednesday afternoons. She had no clients on a Thursday morning, and it was her custom to visit her oldest and dearest friend, Mildred Beazer, for a cup of coffee and a natter.

Sybil and Mildred, just a few weeks apart in age, had grown up together in Elmsford and had been best friends at school. Their lives had taken slightly different turns: while Sybil had settled down with Frank and had the children, Mildred had married and buried two husbands. Childless in both marriages, Mildred was now much more comfortably off than her friend. Both husbands had left her well provided for, and in addition she collected two widow's pensions. But their friendship had continued through the years in spite of the difference in their circumstances, Mildred taking quite an interest in the Rashe children.

Mildred Beazer lived in a cosy house called The Haven, courtesy of the late Mr Beazer. In spite of the fact that she quite liked living on her own, she was not averse to the idea of taking on a third husband. To that end, she kept herself up rather better than her old friend Sybil Rashe: Mildred dyed her hair a flaming shade of scarlet, as exotic as the plumage of some rare tropical bird, and was perpetually on a strict diet to maintain her figure. The numerous cigarettes that she smoked during the course of a day helped, of course; sometimes Sybil thought that Mildred must live on fags and black coffee.

On Thursday mornings, fresh from an afternoon at Rose Cottage, Sybil would be full of little titbits about Miss Valerie, and Mildred was a most satisfying person to share them with. Unlike Frank, who was indifferent to these things, Mildred encouraged her to tell all, and Sybil did so with relish.

This Thursday, then, was like many others. They sat in the sun room which the late Mr Beazer had had put up as an extension at the back of The Haven. South-facing, it got good light in both the morning and the afternoon, and Mildred spent much time there, wreathed in a cloud of smoke.

'Have a fag?' Mildred offered, shaking one from a pack and holding it out invitingly towards her friend.

Sybil looked at it with longing. 'No, I mustn't.'

'Oh, come on. Just the one,' Mildred urged. 'Keep me company.'

She succumbed to temptation. 'Well, just the one, then. No one will know.'

It was all part of a ritual. Sybil had once been a heavy smoker herself, back in the days when everyone smoked. But she'd given it up years before, to set a good example for the children. In this goal she'd had mixed success. Brenda was a confirmed and self-righteous non-smoker who had never even sneaked a furtive fag in the school bicycle shed. Terry she wasn't so sure about; he never smoked in front of his mother, or in the house, but once in a while Sybil thought she could smell stale smoke on his clothes or his breath. And in Kim she'd had a total failure: Sybil's younger daughter went through two packs a day in spite of, or perhaps because of, her mother's condemnation of her 'filthy habit'.

Apart from the nicotine kick, Sybil missed the lovely tarry taste of cigarettes, and the way they gave you something to do with your hands while you were drinking coffee. She knew – everyone knew these days – that cigarettes were bad for you. As long as Mildred twisted her arm, though, Sybil allowed herself to be talked into smoking just one. One fag a week wouldn't kill her.

Mildred didn't believe in filtered cigarettes, to Sybil's great joy; if she were going to transgress, she might as well do it properly. She flicked Mildred's lighter with her thumb and sucked in that first heady lungful of tar. It was bliss. She savoured it as long as possible, then slowly let the smoke out through her nose.

'So, Syb,' Mildred said, 'what's the latest? How are the kids?' This, too, was part of the Thursday ritual; she always asked about the children first, saving the subject of Miss Valerie until later.

Sybil pulled a face. 'That Kim. I swear she'll be the death of me yet, Milly. All this wedding palaver. I'm sure I don't know what that girl is up to, wanting to get married in church.'

'Will they be married at St Mary the Virgin in Elmsford, then?'

'No.' Sybil shook her head. 'I don't really understand all the fuss, but it's something about parish boundaries. The caravan is in Branlingham parish, apparently. So that's where they're getting married. St Somebody, Branlingham.'

Mildred, who had always been Church while Sybil was Chapel, was more *au fait* with ecclesiastical matters. 'That's right,' she nodded. 'St Stephen's.' She might have gone on in that vein, and tried to explain the parish system to her friend, but she knew that Sybil wasn't really interested.

'Mind you,' Sybil went on with a sniff, 'it's not as if I've seen Her Royal Highness this week. I've only spoken to her on the phone. She wanted me to give her some addresses for the wedding invitations. So I wrote them all down, like, and one night I dropped by the caravan, but they were out – down at the pub drinking away all their dole money, I don't doubt. And when I rang ahead the next night to say that I'd stop by with the list, Kim put me off. Said she'd come and collect it over the weekend, if you please.'

'I thought they weren't on the phone.'

'Oh,' Sybil said in the mincing tone that was reserved for the subject of Kim, or occasionally her daughter-in-law Delilah, 'they weren't. But they've got one of these fancy new mobile phones now, haven't they?'

Mildred knew that Sybil's grievances against her spoilt younger daughter could occupy them for the rest of the morning, and she judged that it was time to change the subject. 'How is Miss Valerie, then, Syb?'

Sybil had been waiting for this moment; she frowned. 'I don't mind telling you, Milly,' she said darkly. 'There's something Not Right with that girl.'

'What do you mean?' Mildred's eyes widened. 'Is she poorly? There's a bit of flu about, perhaps that's what it is.'

'Not flu,' stated Sybil. 'In my opinion, Milly, she's been sickening for something for weeks. Remember, I told you last week that she'd had a bad headache, the poor lamb.'

Mildred remembered. She nodded sagely.

'Well, she's ever so much worse. It's not a headache – I don't know what it is, to tell the truth. I don't mind telling you I was shocked when I went into that house. I've never seen the like, Milly.' Sybil drew on her cigarette, prolonging the suspense as long as possible.

She achieved the desired result; Mildred's curiosity was truly aroused by these tantalising hints. 'What was it, then?' she demanded.

'You would think to look at it,' said Sybil deliberately, 'that Rose Cottage was some sort of pigsty. I tell you no lies, Milly – that's what it looked like. Just like Frank's pigsty. As if I hadn't been there every Wednesday that ever was, tidying the place up and keeping it clean for Miss Valerie.'

Mildred's lively imagination came up with a vivid picture of squalor and filth. 'It must have been those magazine people,' she speculated. '*Hello!* magazine. They were there last week, weren't they, Syb? I've always heard that journalists were a dirty lot. Endless cups of coffee, and fag ends all over the place.'

This was not an inaccurate description of Mildred's own habits, but Sybil forbore to point this out. She shook her head. 'I don't think so. It's Miss Valerie that's changed, and I don't know how to explain it.'

'What do you mean, then?' Mildred reached for her ashtray, already overflowing with cigarette ends, and stubbed out the one she'd just finished. Immediately she lit another, then brushed some stray ash from her trouser leg. Mildred always wore trousers; her legs, though trim, were so badly afflicted with varicose veins that they resembled aged Stilton cheese. There were long waiting lists for varicose vein operations, and she had been waiting for a very long time. She could have afforded to go private, but it was a matter of principle with her: she would wait as long as necessary.

Sybil smoked in silence for a moment, trying to gather her thoughts into something coherent. 'Miss Valerie has always been house-proud,' she said. 'To tell the truth, she's always kept that house so tidy that sometimes I've felt like she doesn't really need me at all, though I'd never say as much to her. But now there's dust everywhere, and crockery in the sink. And stacks of post everywhere, all over the kitchen table and in other rooms as well, not even opened. And that computer of hers, that she spends so much time working at, stone cold.'

'But if Miss Valerie had the flu . . .' Mildred persisted.

'Oh, no. There's more to it than that, Milly.' Sybil tapped a long column of ash into the ashtray. 'She's not right in *herself*. She wouldn't even let me into her bedroom. When I told her I needed to get in to change the sheets, she told me to go away. Almost wild-eyed, she was. Don't you see what I'm trying to tell you?'

Mildred leaned forward. 'You mean . . .'

'There's none that thinks more highly of Miss Valerie than I do, Milly. You know that as well as me. I wouldn't say a word against her, and that's God's truth.' She paused and concentrated on her shrinking cigarette, wanting to make the most of what was left. 'But there's something Not Right. Up here.' She touched her own temple, and went on dramatically. 'If you ask me, Milly, Miss Valerie has gone doolally. Queer in the head.'

Mildred stared at her, open-mouthed, as Sybil pinched the last half-inch of her cigarette between thumb and forefinger and sucked it avidly, then, as it began to burn her fingers, dropped it into the ashtray with real regret. 'She hasn't got the flu,' Sybil stated gravely. 'What she wants is her head examining.'

After lunch Gervase headed for the church before he started on his afternoon round of calls; especially since the break-in, he stopped into St Stephen's frequently, just to make sure that all was well.

There was a woman sitting on the stone shelf which ran along the inside wall of the south porch – an attractive young woman. She was very still, almost trance-like in the quality of her stillness. She wasn't crying or visibly distressed, but Gervase sensed, with the instincts developed over long years in the priesthood, that she was troubled in some way. He hesitated; there was often a very fine line in dealing with people like this, who might want to talk or just as likely might not wish to be disturbed.

'Are you all right?' he said tentatively.

Valerie looked up at him, seeing a tall, middle-aged man with wavy grey hair and a gentle, elongated face. Slope-shouldered and slightly stooped, he was dressed in black: black trousers and a black shirt with a white dog collar. The Vicar. 'Yes, thank you,' she said. Her voice came out in a croak; she rarely spoke these days.

He wasn't convinced. 'If there is anything I can do for you . . . if you'd like to talk, I'm available.'

His words were soft, and he had a kind face, inviting trust and confidence. For one wild moment she was tempted by his offer. What a relief it would be to talk about it, to pour out the burden and the turmoil of her love for Hal, the pain of waiting for him to be hers at last.

But she mustn't, she told herself sternly. He was One of Them. A black-and-white priest, probably in league with the Magpie. And Hal was in this man's house at this very moment. She must be strong. Valerie shook her head. 'No, thank you.'

The priest smiled, and it transformed his rather serious face into a countenance of singular beauty. Perhaps he sensed her hesitation, for he said, 'If you change your mind, you know where to find me. I live over there.' He pointed to the Vicarage.

Her eyes followed the gesture, and stayed fixed there; immediately she forgot about the presence of the priest, tensing with excitement. The door was opening, and someone else was coming out. Not Hal; her shoulders slumped in disappointment. It was a woman. A woman, probably the Vicar's wife.

Valerie had a clear view of her. If she'd feared that the Vicar's wife was some siren who would try to steal Hal away from her, her fear had been misplaced, she saw with relief. Although the woman didn't appear to be as old as her husband, she was a frump in the time-honoured tradition of vicar's wives. Not ugly, Valerie admitted, but plain. A thin, pale face with oversized round spectacles. Limp, mousy hair in a plait down her back, and an untidy fringe that overlapped her glasses. And her clothes! Dowdy wasn't the word: the woman had no dress sense at all. The shapeless garments, oversized and ill-fitting, hung on a frame that could not be described as curvaceous by any stretch of the imagination.

Not a threat at all. Valerie almost laughed aloud at the thought of this drab woman as a rival for Hal's affections. It was ludicrous.

Rosemary walked to the Sawbridges' to collect Daisy. The overnight trial run had apparently gone very well; anxious for her daughter's well-being, she had rung several times to check on her and had been assured by Annie that Daisy was having a wonderful time with Samantha. But it wasn't until she saw Daisy for herself that she really believed it. No tears for her mother, no homesick tantrums. Daisy had truly had a wonderful time, it was clear. Parting from Samantha and returning home seemed to be more difficult for her than being away from her mother had been.

Only now could Rosemary admit to herself how traumatic the whole experience had been for *her*, if not for her daughter. The separation from Daisy – for the very first time – had elicited a complicated emotional response. Anxiety, love, protectiveness, guilt. Yes, guilt, she realised: guilt that perhaps in abandoning Daisy she was being selfish, putting her own needs above the needs of her child.

Rosemary really wanted to go to that concert on Friday night. She'd been telling herself that it might not work out, that she mustn't get too excited about it, but she hadn't been able to help looking forward to it for weeks, and wanting desperately to go. Now, for the first time, she began to believe that she *would* go. Daisy would be fine at Samantha's, would in fact be delighted to repeat the experience. She need not feel guilty about leaving her; she was free to go and enjoy herself. She and Gervase would have such a wonderful evening, a rare and marvellous treat. Just the two of them.

She began to think concretely about Friday evening. As long as she'd convinced herself that it wouldn't happen, she hadn't worried about any of the details. But what, Rosemary now asked herself, what was she going to wear?

Presumably, she thought, this would be a fairly posh occasion, and people would dress up for it. And it wasn't just the concert, either: Gervase had really splashed out and had bought tickets for the supper beforehand, salmon and strawberries in the marquee. She didn't have any salmon-and-strawberries clothes.

The problem exercised her mind as they walked back home, Daisy chattering on about Jack the kitten. 'Can't I have a kitten, Mummy?' she repeated for the umpteenth time. 'I want a kitten just like Jack. Black and white.'

'Perhaps one day,' Rosemary equivocated in automatic response, only half listening.

When they got home, there was the excitement of Daisy seeing her newly redecorated room in all its splendour. It was pink, just as she'd wanted and Hal had promised. Fresh pink paintwork, and as a surprise Hal had added a wide frieze halfway up the walls: black kittens with pink-and-white-striped ribbons round their necks. She squealed in delight, and for the rest of the afternoon was torn between playing in her resplendent room, and talking to Hal, who was now working in the entrance hall. Her mother was redundant.

Rosemary, meanwhile, went to her wardrobe in the vain hope that she would find a lovely frock lurking there, unremembered. There was nothing, she realised with growing gloom, that would do. She had clothes that were suitable for parish functions, but not good enough for this occasion. Perhaps, she thought, the dress she'd worn for Gervase's induction at St Stephen's might do, but on inspection it was far too heavy and dark for the warm spring temperatures that now prevailed.

Then Rosemary had a sudden inspiration. One of the empty bedrooms in the Vicarage had been put to use as a collecting point for bits and pieces for the next church fête. As and when people did their spring cleaning or had a general clear-out, they'd been bringing boxes and bags of their discards and depositing them at the Vicarage. There just might, thought Rosemary, be something in there.

She switched on the light and went in, carefully skirting boxes of books and heaps of miscellaneous rubbish. There were, if she recalled, several bin liners full of clothes. Locating them and dumping them out on the floor one by one, she sorted through the contents.

Perhaps this hadn't been such a great idea after all, she thought ruefully. Most of the garments had been discarded for good reason: they were well worn, or soiled, or singularly ugly to begin with. There were one or two things that weren't too hideous, but they proved not to be anything close to her size. Too short, too wide. Rosemary once again regretted the fact that she was not the stereotypical vicar's wife that her mother had been in that department, handy with a needle and able to transform the tattiest of parish cast-offs into something stylish and well fitting.

Just as she was about to give it up as a bad job, Rosemary spotted a large box in the corner. It had come, she remembered, from Branlingham Manor, where for centuries the local nobility had lived; a younger son of that family had been responsible for building the Vicarage in the last century. The family had gone some years since and the Manor had been sold for death duties; it was now owned and inhabited by the local MP. He and his wife were not church-goers, except just before a general election, but they followed the age-old tradition of salving their consciences by giving the church things they no longer wanted. Just after the Finches had arrived in Branlingham, this box had been delivered and had been stored unopened.

Rosemary opened it now. The MP's wife was noted locally for her exquisite taste in clothes; even her cast-offs were likely to be better than anything that Rosemary had ever owned.

Most of the things in the box proved to have belonged to the MP and not his wife: an old tweed jacket with a burn mark on the sleeve, several pairs of trousers that seemed to have been let out to their limit, a moth-riddled pullover. But near the bottom she found a dress. Perhaps, Rosemary told herself, it would be ripped or soiled. Carefully she lifted it out.

It was a beautiful dress, of a quality and workmanship that clearly had cost a great deal of money. The fabric felt wonderful to the touch, silky yet substantial. In style it was classic and simple, neither frilly nor too severe, with a straight skirt and a softly draping bodice, cut on the bias. The colour was dusty rose.

There didn't appear to be anything wrong with it; perhaps its previous owner had just grown tired of it, though Rosemary couldn't imagine why. It really was a wonderful dress. And it was her size.

She took it through to the bedroom and tried it on. Standing in front of the mirror, she admitted to herself that it was perfect: it fitted as though it had been made for her, the colour suited her, and the cut was flattering. Rosemary smiled at her image in the mirror. She would feel marvellous in this dress, and Gervase would be proud to be seen with her. She wouldn't tell him about it now, or show it to him; she'd leave it till tomorrow, as a surprise. Tomorrow night was going to be something special, a night to remember.

★

Margaret's long week was nearing the end, for which she was profoundly grateful. Her life was always busy, but this week had been even busier and more stressful than usual. She'd scarcely seen Hal; it wasn't fair to ask or expect him to stay up late at night when he had to get up and work in the mornings. His job might not be as stressful as hers, or demand such long hours, but it was physical work, and he needed his sleep.

It was nearly midnight, and Hal was already in bed. Margaret still had work to do, paperwork that had been squeezed out by the week's activities and could wait no longer.

She made herself a cup of coffee, then realised that the throbbing in her head was not the continuation of the vague unease that had hovered round her through the week, but an incipient headache. Margaret was prone to migraines; she hoped that she wasn't getting one now. She couldn't afford to, with one more day of this hellish week to be got through.

Quietly, lest she disturb her sleeping husband, Margaret went through the darkened bedroom into the ensuite bathroom and found the bottle of paracetamol. She took two, washing them down with black coffee.

Back downstairs in her study, she massaged her temples for a moment and tried to compose her mind to concentrate on the things that needed to be sorted out. On her desk was a vase of flowers: red roses, her favourites, bought and arranged by Hal and left there where she would find them the night before. It had been a thoughtful gesture, typical of Hal, and Margaret smiled fondly, feeling better already.

The papers before her related to Friday night's meeting, an important one which involved all of the clergy in her archdeaconry. The meeting was on the critical subject of security, arranged and set up some time ago but made all the more relevant – and urgent – by the recent spate of church break-ins within the archdeaconry. There had always been the odd isolated burglary, of course; open churches and visible treasures had forever been a temptation to the opportunistic thief. But what had been happening lately seemed more concentrated and planned, and the stakes were escalating. First it had been nicked candlesticks; now, just this week, two churches had suffered break-ins involving thefts of major quantities of silver from inadequately secured safes. Another had lost a valuable painting and a pair of Jacobean chairs, and a fourth had had its irreplaceable mediaeval eagle lectern stolen. Dealing with the immediate after-effects of these violations had further added to the stresses of Margaret's hectic week; it was even more important now that Friday night's meeting should be a success.

She had lined up various professional specialists to address the assembled clergy: a policeman, an insurance valuer, an antiques expert, and a man from a security firm. Many of the clergy, she knew from dealing with them in the wake of the break-ins, had no idea of the value of the things that filled their churches, let alone a grasp of sensible precautions. Church doors were left unlocked round the clock, valuable items were prominently displayed, and safes left ajar, or with the keys in plain sight.

What she *hadn't* done, and needed to do now, was to check through the list of clergy and see how many had returned their reply slips to say that they were coming. A few of them might need chasing up. She'd planned to do it earlier in the week, and would have done, but ironically she had been too busy dealing with the break-ins. It was important that as many of the clergy as possible should be there.

There were over a hundred and fifty churches in the archdeaconry, but in these days of combined benefices, only about half that many priests. It was still quite enough to keep track of: seventy-eight incumbents or priests-in-charge. Six women, seventy-two men. Margaret had on her computer a list of those who had replied in the affirmative that they were coming, and another list of those who had sent their apologies. Both lists needed to be checked against a master list to see who had slipped through the net. And there was a small pile of last-minute reply slips which she'd not yet had time to sort through.

This was the first such archdeaconry meeting she'd called, though she'd been to a few in her days as a parish priest. She had been rather terrified of her archdeacon, an imposing man with awesome eyebrows, and would not have dreamed of flouting a command from him to appear at an archdeaconry meeting; others must have felt the same way, as attendance had always been good. So she was surprised at how many negative reply slips she'd received, until one of her clergy had tipped her off: many were staying away in protest, because she was a woman. Naïvely, perhaps, she had never considered that possibility. It made it all the more important that those clergy who were not offended by her gender should attend.

By the time she'd entered the late reply slips onto the respective computer lists, and checked everything against the master list, almost everyone was accounted for. There were always a few, of course, who were chronically incapable of sending things back on time, or who had lost the relevant bit of paper. She would have to chase them up by phone tomorrow.

Seven delinquents, seven phone calls. One of them, she noted, was someone who had himself suffered a break-in at his church just over a week ago, and certainly ought to be there for the meeting: Gervase Finch.

Chapter 13

Rosemary hadn't heard a word from Christine in over a week. She half hoped, without really believing it, that her erstwhile friend had sensed Rosemary's discomfort at being forced to entertain her and her lover. Knowing Christine as she did, though, she was sure that she would hear from her eventually. And the next time she meant to be prepared, with a choice of excuses at the ready: she had the decorators in, Gervase was about the house, it was half-term week and Daisy was at home.

The call came on Friday morning, just after breakfast. Rosemary answered the phone, and decided to take the initiative before Christine had an opportunity to invite herself. 'I'm afraid this isn't a good day,' she said with a firmness that surprised her as much as it did Christine. 'Daisy is at home all day – it's half-term week. And—'

'Oh, good.' Christine cut Rosemary off, outmanoeuvring her. 'That's just what I was hoping, that you would be home with Daisy all day. And of course I know it's half-term week. That's why I'm ringing, actually.'

Rosemary was baffled. 'Yes?'

'I was hoping that I might bring Polly and Gemma over to

spend the day with Daisy,' she explained. 'I'm so glad it will be convenient.'

Of course, thought Rosemary. And she had walked straight into Christine's trap. 'Yes, all right,' she agreed; at least it was better than having to entertain Christine, with or without her lover.

'And I'm sure that Daisy misses Polly and Gemma,' Christine added. 'She'll be thrilled to see them, I know.'

They would be there in less than an hour; now she would have to break the news to Gervase. He was still at the kitchen table, having a quick look at the morning paper before he went off to his study.

'That was Christine,' Rosemary said in what she hoped was a neutral, if not cheery, tone.

'Oh, yes?' Gervase looked at her over the tops of his reading glasses and his voice held a cynicism that appeared only when Christine was mentioned. 'And what did she want?'

'She's suggested that she might bring her girls over to play with Daisy today,' Rosemary said with some understatement, trying not to sound defensive.

Gervase was not taken in. 'Suggested? I can imagine. What did you say?'

'I don't see the harm in it. And Daisy *is* fond of the girls.' Perhaps, she told herself, it *would* be good for Daisy.

Christine and her girls arrived, as expected, within the hour. 'I've time for a quick coffee before I have to shoot off,' Christine said, giving Rosemary no choice but to invite her in.

Settled at the kitchen table while Rosemary made the coffee, Christine spoke in a loud stage whisper. 'So – who is he, then?'

'Who?' Rosemary turned to look at her. 'What are you talking about?'

'That gorgeous man. Who is he?'

'Gorgeous man?' Rosemary echoed; she really had no idea what Christine was going on about.

'Oh, don't play coy with me, Rosemary.' Christine smirked at her. 'That gorgeous man in your entrance hall.'

'Hal?' She was still baffled. 'Are you talking about Hal? He's the decorator.'

'Who else would I be talking about?' Christine was growing impatient with Rosemary's evident obtuseness. 'I could *see* that he's the decorator. He was scraping wallpaper off the wall. But who *is* he? And why haven't you mentioned him to me before?'

'I did tell you that we were having the house decorated,' Rosemary defended herself.

'But you didn't tell me that your decorator was so . . .' she searched for a word, then fell back on 'gorgeous. You're a sly one, Rosemary. Keeping him all for yourself.'

'Don't be silly.' Rosemary felt herself blushing; she turned her back on Christine's leer and busied herself with the coffee. *Was* Hal gorgeous? She'd never really thought about him in those terms before. She knew that he had a nice smile, and was quite pleasant to look at. But gorgeous? In any case, that wasn't what was important about him.

Christine went on, unabashed. 'Isn't Gervase frightfully jealous that you're on a first-name basis with the dishy decorator? I'm surprised that he would leave you alone in the house with a man who looks like that.'

'Gervase has nothing to be jealous about,' Rosemary insisted.

Christine, observing the colour of her cheeks, wasn't so sure.

Rosemary was determined to change the subject. 'What time will you be collecting the girls?' she asked.

'Does it matter?' Christine poured a dollop of milk into her coffee.

'Well, it does, in fact.' Now Rosemary was smiling, her discomfiture forgotten. 'We're going out this evening, and will have to leave the house by a little after five.'

'Oh?' This aroused Christine's curiosity; as far as she knew, Rosemary and Gervase went out just about as often as she and Roger did, which was to say never. 'Where are you going, then?'

Rosemary explained about the concert. Christine, not musical herself, wasn't really interested in the details, but one question occurred to her; a calculating look crossed her face. 'What about Daisy? Are you getting a baby-sitter in?'

'She's going to stay overnight with a friend in the village,' Rosemary explained, for once one step ahead of her. Christine wouldn't have asked without an ulterior motive, and it wasn't difficult to figure out what that might be.

The long-case clock in the hall chimed; Christine looked at her watch with a philosophic shrug. 'Oh, I must love you and leave you. I'm supposed to be meeting Nick in a quarter of an hour. We're having a day out,' she went on with a self-satisfied smile. 'I'm not sure where – he says it's a surprise.'

'When will you be back to collect Polly and Gemma, then?' Rosemary prompted.

'Oh, say four o'clock, if that's all right with you. I'll tell you what,' Christine added impulsively. 'When I come back, I'll do your hair for you, as you're going out this evening. I could do it in a French plait – that would look smashing.' It would also give her an opportunity to tell Rosemary all about her day.

'Yes, all right.' Why not? thought Rosemary. She never bothered with things like that, but this was indeed a special occasion, and worth a bit of effort to look as nice as possible.

Just before lunchtime, Gervase was in his study working on his sermon for Sunday when he was interrupted by a phone call from the Archdeacon.

After a few mutual pleasantries, she got to the point, in a slightly roundabout way. 'First of all, I do hope that you and your wife will be able to come to the Archdeaconry garden party, Saturday week. I don't think I've had a reply from you about that,' she said diplomatically.

'Oh, I'm sorry,' Gervase apologised. 'I'm not very good about replying to invitations. But I'm sure we'll be there.' He couldn't remember receiving the invitation, let alone mentioning it to Rosemary; he would have to go through the papers on his desk one of these days soon and look for it. Very soon, in fact.

That gave the Archdeacon the opening she needed. 'And I haven't had a reply slip back, come to that, about tonight's meeting. Perhaps you're just not used to our customs in this archdeaconry,' she added in what she hoped was a tactful way. 'I'm a bit of a stickler for reply slips – I do find that they make everyone's life easier, mine in particular.'

'Tonight's meeting?' he echoed in confusion.

'The archdeaconry meeting on church security. Tonight, at Hardham Magna church hall.'

Gervase's mind was a complete blank. 'I'm afraid I don't know what you're talking about, Archdeacon. I don't know anything about this meeting.'

Still being diplomatic, she suggested, 'Perhaps the letter was lost in the post. But never mind.' Quickly she outlined the substance of the meeting and emphasised its importance for everyone in the archdeaconry. 'It's especially important for people like you, with a first-hand experience of a church break-in, to be there,' the Archdeacon concluded.

Gervase chewed on his lip. He could see the relevance and value of the meeting, but there was no way that he was going to disappoint Rosemary; she'd been looking forward to this night out for weeks. 'I'm really sorry, Archdeacon,' he said.

'But I won't be able to make it. I'm taking my wife to a concert tonight.'

There was a significant pause at the other end of the
phone. 'Perhaps I didn't make myself clear,' she said in a voice
that was gentle, yet underlaid with steel – a voice that demonstrated why Margaret Phillips had risen so quickly to the
office of Archdeacon. 'I consider this meeting to be a priority,
and I'll expect to see you there. I'm sorry,' she added, 'but
there will be other concerts.'

'Yes, all right,' Gervase capitulated, recognising that he had
little choice. He was, after all, under her authority, and she
had come as close as possible to issuing a direct command.

An impulse of empathy for Rosemary – after all, in the
past she had so often been on the receiving end of similar dis-
appointments herself – prompted Margaret to add, 'And do
tell your wife that I'm sorry about the concert.'

Not half as sorry as he was, Gervase reflected bitterly as
the Archdeacon rang off. He put his head in his hands and
sat for a very long time, gathering his thoughts and his
courage. How on earth was he going to break the news to
Rosemary?

There was no point in beating about the bush. 'I'm afraid I
have some bad news,' Gervase said immediately as he came
into the kitchen for his lunch.

Rosemary turned an alarmed face towards him, and a pre-
monition, or some instinct, told her straightaway the nature
of the news. 'You can't go tonight,' she said in a flat voice.

'Oh, my dear, I'm so sorry. The Archdeacon . . .'

'No, don't tell me. I don't need to know the details.' She
gave him a strained smile, blinking her eyes at the sudden
tears that threatened.

Her brave acceptance made it worse for Gervase. 'I'll
make it up to you, I promise,' he said. 'I know how much

you've been looking forward to it, my dear. But there's a meeting—'

'Don't.' Rosemary looked away from him. 'Just don't, Gervase. Don't say any more. I can't bear it.' She turned back to her lunch preparations, buttering bread for sandwiches.

He stood for a moment, watching her deliberate movements, then sat down at the table.

Rosemary went to the fridge and took out a packet of sliced ham and a tomato, then continued with her sandwich-making in silence. She found a knife and began slicing the tomato. Halfway through, perhaps not seeing as clearly as she pretended, she nicked her finger with the knife. It wasn't a bad cut, but it started bleeding almost immediately, the red of her blood mingling with the paler red of the tomato. 'Oh!' she cried.

The pain in her voice alarmed Gervase. 'What is it?' he demanded anxiously.

'I've cut myself.' Rosemary gulped as she dropped the knife. 'Don't worry – it's just a nick. I'm not going to bleed to death.' She grabbed a sheet of kitchen roll and wrapped it round her finger. But it was enough to destroy the barriers of her self-possession; her tears began to flow, and once she'd started crying she found that she couldn't stop.

'Don't cry,' Gervase begged her. 'Please don't cry, my dear.'

Rosemary sat down abruptly and buried her head in her hands. 'One night. One little concert,' she said through her tears. 'I should have known it was too much to ask, too good to be true.'

'The Archdeacon said to tell you that she was sorry.'

'She's sorry!' Rosemary said with uncharacteristic bitterness.

He was much moved by her pain, but felt that he needed to defend himself. 'I tried – truly I did.'

'I'm not blaming you,' she said, though a part of her couldn't help feeling betrayed. So many times she'd been let down, so many times she'd assured him that it didn't matter. It was the nature of Gervase's job; she'd accepted when she married him that it would have to come first. But this time it was different: this time it mattered. And Gervase knew it.

'I wish with all my heart that this hadn't happened,' he said helplessly. 'I wish there were some way . . .'

At that moment, as if on cue, Hal came into the kitchen to rinse out his coffee mug. He stopped. 'I'm sorry. Is this a bad time?'

Hal. Of course.

Gervase turned to Hal like a drowning man to a life preserver. 'Hal. Please, don't go.' He took a deep breath. 'Rosemary and I are meant to be going to a concert tonight.'

'Yes, I know.' Hal nodded.

'But there's some meeting. The Archdeacon rang . . .'

'Oh, yes,' he recalled. 'The one on church security. She mentioned it.'

'. . . and she's left me no choice,' Gervase went on. 'I can't miss it. So I wondered if you . . . I know it's asking a lot, but Rosemary is so disappointed. She's been looking forward to this a great deal, I think. If you should happen to be free this evening . . .'

'I don't know . . .' Hal hesitated.

Tired of being discussed as though she weren't present, Rosemary raised her head and looked at Hal, her eyes brimming with tears; she opened her mouth, but no words came out.

'Of course I'll go,' he said instantly, and was rewarded with a smile of radiant intensity.

Rosemary looked into the mirror, scarcely recognising herself. Christine, she admitted, had worked magic (at a cost, of course: she'd had to listen to the details of Christine's day out with Nick). Her hair, in an intricate French plait, gave her a look of sophistication which Christine had enhanced with some skilfully applied make-up. And the dress, that wonderful dress . . . It was even more flattering than it had been when she'd first tried it on, the colour bringing out the delicate pink flush of her cheeks. She felt like Daisy on her first day of school, and wanted to twirl round as Daisy had done, admiring herself from all angles.

It seemed wrong, she told herself to bring herself back down to earth, to be feeling so wonderful, so happy, when she was going without Gervase, when he would be stuck in some boring meeting while she enjoyed herself. It was something *he'd* planned, something they'd meant to be doing together as a rare treat. But she wasn't going to allow that to spoil her enjoyment, Rosemary resolved, looking herself in the eye in the mirror. Cinderella *would* go to the ball, and she wouldn't feel guilty about it.

Gervase wasn't even there to see her off; he'd taken Daisy to the Sawbridges', and planned to leave straight from there for the drive to Hardham Magna. That was a disappointment. She hoped that perhaps he would wait up for her; she was bound to be home later than he.

Since Gervase had taken the car, Hal had agreed to collect Rosemary and drive her to Dennington. She'd expected that they would go in his van, so was surprised when she looked out of the bedroom window and saw a small sporty green car pull up in front of the Vicarage. And the man who got out of the car was almost as unexpected: Hal was wearing a suit and tie. Of course he would be, she told herself, but she'd never before seen him in anything but an overall. It made him seem like a stranger – a handsome stranger, rather than the Hal she was so comfortable with – and, recalling what Christine had said about him, suddenly Rosemary felt shy. She took a few deep breaths as she went downstairs to open the door to him.

'I say, Rosie,' he exclaimed with frank admiration in his voice. 'You look smashing.'

Uncharacteristically, she believed him.

Valerie had also been surprised to see the sporty green car. It had been her good fortune to be approaching The Archdeaconry just as it pulled out of the drive into traffic, and she had recognised Hal at the wheel. Of course he would have a proper car, she realised, not just a van. It must have been concealed in the garage at the side of the house.

She hadn't even expected Hal to be home by now; it wasn't yet five o'clock. Where could he be going, all dressed up and driving his smart car, at this time on a Friday afternoon? There was no question but that she would follow him and find out.

Once again he took the road that led south from Saxwell towards Elmsford, and once again he passed the Elmsford turning and went into Branlingham. By now Valerie guessed that he might be going to the Vicarage. Perhaps, she theorised, he had left something behind when he'd finished work, and needed to retrieve it. She couldn't imagine that he would be calling there socially; it was too early for dinner or even drinks, and the Magpie was not with him.

She pulled the car over onto the verge, as before, and went down Church End on foot. As she reached the shelter of the church porch, she saw Hal – looking achingly handsome – waiting at the front door. Then the door opened; she couldn't quite see who was on the other side. Valerie expected Hal to disappear inside, at least for a moment, but to her surprise a woman came out, locking the door behind her. It must be that vicar's wife, Valerie realised, though she didn't look nearly as much of a fright as she had done yesterday. Hal opened the car door for her and helped her with her seatbelt before going round to the other side and getting in.

Where on earth was Hal taking that woman? That ugly,

frightful woman? Valerie waited till he'd driven past the church, then hurried back to her car, hoping to catch him up. But by the time she reached her car and drove out of Branlingham to the Saxwell road, the small green car was nowhere to be seen in any direction. Frustrated and angry, Valerie headed back home to Elmsford.

By the time they arrived at Dennington, just after six o'clock, the blue-and-white marquee was already filling up with those who had booked their salmon-and-strawberry suppers. Rosemary wasn't sure how the system worked; she handed their tickets to the woman on the door. 'What name is it booked under?' demanded the woman.

'Finch,' said Hal.

The woman consulted her seating plan, then led them to a table. 'This way, Mr and Mrs Finch.'

Hal didn't correct her, but smiled conspiratorially at Rosemary. 'Thank you,' he said to the woman with grave courtesy. He pulled Rosemary's chair out and sat down across from her. 'Well, Rosie. Would you like some champagne?' he suggested.

'Oh, that sounds awfully . . . decadent,' she protested; Gervase might have bought them each a glass of wine, but he certainly wouldn't have stretched to champagne.

Hal laughed, in a gentle rather than a mocking way. 'You sound just like a vicar's wife,' he teased.

Rosemary felt herself blushing. 'I *am* a vicar's wife.'

'I'm prepared to concede that you are, most of the time,' he said. 'But tonight doesn't count.'

In a funny way, she knew exactly what he meant. Tonight was something out of the time-and-space continuum of her life, a thing apart.

That feeling continued and intensified through the evening, as she felt more and more detached from the person who was

Rosemary Finch, wife to Gervase and mother to Daisy. The music – in the majestic mediaeval splendour of Dennington Church – was sublime, transporting her to another plane of existence. And it was wonderful beyond words to share the experience with someone who felt it as she did. Gervase, she knew, would have enjoyed the evening for her sake, taking pleasure in her joy, but he would have remained unmoved by the music; he probably would have been thinking about his sermon for Sunday, mentally rewriting it, instead of listening. But Hal was equally enraptured by it all. There was no need for him to tell her so; Rosemary could sense it. It was strange, the way that Rosemary could be so utterly absorbed in the music, and at the same time be so intensely aware of Hal beside her, his arm warm against hers.

During the interval they eschewed the noisy crush in the refreshment marquee and walked together in the churchyard. It was a perfect late spring evening, just a few weeks before midsummer, light still and balmy with the retained warmth of the day, yet shimmering with the magic of the anticipated night; insects whirred and birds made the sort of noises they make when preparing to settle down for the night. The gravestones cast long shadows in the grass. Rosemary spared a thought for those who slept beneath their feet, pitying them that they were beyond the disembodied joy she felt tonight, drunk more on music than on champagne.

After a few minutes of silence, she and Hal began sharing in words their wonder at the music they'd just heard. Their taste in music was more than similar; they spoke the same language.

'The Tallis,' she said. 'When that soprano went soaring up to the top note, I felt my hair stand on end.'

'I've never heard it done so well,' he agreed. 'I sang that solo once, when I was a chorister, and it's always been a favourite of mine.'

She stumbled slightly on an uneven bit of ground; he caught her by the elbow and felt her shiver. 'Are you cold?' he asked solicitously. 'Do you want to go back inside?'

'Oh, no.' Rosemary stopped by the boundary wall of the churchyard and leaned her elbows on it, gazing out over the surrounding fields. 'When we go back in, it will be that much closer to being over,' she said with a strange logic that he none the less understood. 'And I wish that this evening didn't have to end, ever,' she added, so softly that Hal sensed that the words were not intended for his ears.

Valerie was soaking in the bath when the doorbell rang. She was startled; Friday evening was not a time for unexpected callers. Whoever it was, if she ignored them they would go away. She sank back into the bath and tried to recapture the fantasy that had been occupying her mind before the interruption. Hal, of course, wearing a suit and looking incredibly handsome. He was escorting her to some high-powered literary function; all of the other women were staring at him, and envying Valerie. And at the end of the evening, they would go home, and—

The bell went again; Valerie frowned. Well, they could press the bell as many times as they liked. She was not going to answer it.

After a few minutes the intermittent sound of the bell turned into a constant noise, as her unwanted caller leaned on the buzzer, then began banging the knocker. They weren't going to go away, Valerie realised with annoyance. In any case, her bath – and her fantasy – had been spoiled.

She climbed out of the bath, towelled herself off, and took her time anointing herself with body lotion and scented powder, then slipped into a dressing gown. In the background the noise continued unabated. 'I'm coming,' Valerie muttered, wrapping her damp hair in a towel and finding her slippers. She went down the stairs and opened the door just a crack, prepared to tell off whomever had had the nerve to disturb her.

'Val, me darlin',' drawled Shaun. 'Sorry that I had to ring the bell, but I left me key at the office.'

Valerie tried to shut the door in his face, but he'd already inserted a foot in the door and was pushing his way in. 'But sure and I remembered the food, though,' he announced in his most pronounced stage Irish brogue, holding aloft two carrier bags.

'Food?' She looked at him blankly.

'Didn't I promise that I would bring along a Chinese take-away, to save you having to cook?'

'Did you?' Valerie hadn't seen Shaun since the day of the *Hello!* shoot, over a week before, nor had she spoken to him; his numerous messages on her voice mail had been deleted unheard.

He grinned at her. 'I left a message this morning. Two, in fact.'

'Oh.' She didn't know what to say to him.

Shaun noted her state of undress, and, in a state of heedless excitement, drew his own conclusions. 'But if you're not hungry, darling, then neither am I.' He dropped the carrier bags and slipped his hand inside her dressing gown, caressing her breast.

Valerie thought of fighting him off, but decided that, on the whole, going to bed with Shaun would be preferable to eating a meal with him and having to make conversation. This way she wouldn't have to talk to him, and she could always close her eyes and pretend that he was Hal. Docilely she allowed him to lead her up the stairs to the bedroom.

As Shaun pulled at the loosely tied sash of her dressing gown, Valerie drew away and said, 'Just a moment, Shaun. I have to dry my hair.'

'Never mind your hair, darling,' he groaned urgently. 'I want you – now. It seems like for ever since we've been together.'

'My hair is wet.' She eluded his grab in her direction and went to her dressing table.

Shaun took advantage of the temporary delay in the proceedings to undress himself and throw back the duvet on the bed. He stretched out full length, believing himself to look alluring, and waited for Valerie.

A few minutes later she approached the bed, her hair now dry; she found the sight of him not at all seductive. How, she wondered in a dispassionate way, had she ever thought him attractive? The pale elongated body with the sparse gingery chest hair now repelled her. But she would go through with it; she unfastened the sash and let her dressing gown slip into a silken pool at her feet as she moved slowly towards the bed. Gasping with desire, Shaun tensed, and his hand went under the pillow. He brought out a pair of white boxer shorts.

In his state of excitement, it took him a moment to register what it was he was holding. He looked at the boxer shorts, then at Valerie's shocked white face. Instantly he understood; all of his worst fears were confirmed by the expression on her face.

Rage overwhelmed him. Leaping up, he shook them at her. 'So *that's* what you've been up to, you cheating bitch!'

Valerie stopped short, recoiling from the anger in his voice. 'No, you don't understand.'

'I understand, all right.' Now his voice was controlled, but all the more frightening for that. 'Who is he, you whore?'

'No one. There's no one.'

'Lying bitch,' he spat, taking a step towards her.

She shrank back. 'No, Shaun.'

Deliberately, he held the boxer shorts between his hands and ripped them in two, then threw them onto the bed.

Smiling grimly, he advanced on her with equal strength of purpose and struck her full across the face.

'No, Shaun,' she cried in horror.

He hit her again. 'Lying, cheating whore,' he shouted.

When Hal and Rosemary came out of the church after the concert, the night was beginning to draw in, and the last of the light was fading rapidly in the west. They found the car where he'd parked it in the field, and once the traffic had cleared they were on their way.

'So,' Rosemary sighed; she felt as if she'd been holding her breath for quite a long time.

'Yes.'

'It was the best concert I've ever heard.' Her voice was reflective rather than enthusiastic; she was still floating in an altered state of consciousness.

'Yes.'

'The Gibbons,' she said. '"See, see the word is incarnate" must be the most perfect anthem ever written, at least in one sense.'

He followed her thought processes effortlessly. 'The whole Gospel story is there, in that one anthem.'

'When they sang "He is risen up in victory", I wanted to cry.'

'Yes.'

Off and on through the journey they talked, though they felt no pressure to do so. Ahead of them the sky was darkening, passing from a triumphant salmon to a deep violet. A few small clouds adorned the sky like scraps of purple velvet, and one by one the stars appeared.

The closer they drew to Branlingham, the longer were the periods of silence. The quality of the silence changed, as their thoughts progressed from their shared response to the music to matters more personal, inextricably bound up with the music but more difficult to talk about. They had developed the habit of honesty between them; now they were feeling their way through uncharted territory.

As the car approached the Branlingham turning, Rosemary said softly, 'Thank you so much, Hal. For . . . everything. Tonight has been wonderful.'

'Don't thank me.' All of Hal's half-formed feelings about Rosemary had coalesced that evening into a focused certainty. His hands clenched on the steering wheel. 'Listen, Rosie,' he said abruptly. 'I have to tell you something. I—'

'No.' Her voice was quiet but firm and she stared straight ahead out of the windscreen. 'No, you mustn't. Don't you see, Hal? Everything will be spoiled if you say it.' If you don't say it, she went on to herself, if we both pretend we don't know what's happening, we can go on as we are, for just a bit longer anyway.

Chapter 14

On Saturday morning, Valerie looked at her face in the mirror with clinical detachment. The bruises were severe, and would probably get worse before they got better, but eventually they would fade, and for the moment they could be concealed with make-up.

Although she regretted the bruises – and the pain that went with them – she did not really regret what had happened. It had achieved something that she could not have engineered in any other way: Shaun was now out of her life, for good. She'd told him to leave her house, and not to come back. He wouldn't dare to return, after what he'd done to her, and that made it all worthwhile. She would never have to see him again, never have to hear his odious voice, never have to endure his caresses or have him slavering over her in bed. She was done with him.

Now she could concentrate on the things that really mattered; now she could spend all of her energies on Hal.

Gervase was still feeling very guilty, in spite of the fact that Rosemary had not after all been deprived of going to the concert. He'd let her down, and he was acutely aware of that fact.

He had waited up for her, of course, wanting to hear all about it, but she had been rather subdued. She'd said that she had enjoyed the concert, and the supper beforehand as well, but she hadn't exactly been bubbling over with enthusiasm as he'd expected. Perhaps, in spite of her protestations to the contrary, she was still feeling betrayed by him.

He hadn't had a chance to thank Hal properly, either, for his generosity in stepping in at the last moment like that and saving the day. He'd expected that Hal might come in and have a cup of coffee with them, but he'd dropped Rosemary at the door and had gone straight off home without even seeing Gervase.

It weighed on his mind during the Morning Office, and dominated his prayers: he confessed that he had fallen short as a husband, and asked that God, as well as Rosemary, might forgive him, and that he might be given a chance to make amends to his wife.

When he got home he went straight to his study and wrote a letter to Hal, thanking him for his kindness. Then he sought out Rosemary in the kitchen and suggested that today they should have a family day out together, a day out at the seaside. Gervase tried to keep Saturday as a day off – his one day off in the week – but was rarely successful in avoiding some pressing matter of parish business; today he was determined to do so.

Rosemary, who was still rather subdued, agreed readily. She packed a picnic lunch, they collected Daisy from the Sawbridges' and set off for the seaside.

As it was a beautiful day, with the potential of being quite warm, and was in addition a Bank Holiday weekend at the end of half-term week, there were inevitably quite a number of other people with the same idea. Traffic was heavy, but Gervase knew the back roads, and knew a few less populated beaches as well from their years at Letherfield, when they'd lived not far from the coast.

So they ate their sandwiches on the beach, then Gervase watched as an ecstatic Daisy paddled at the edge of the water. Rosemary took off her shoes, hiked up her skirt, and went in the sea with her daughter, throwing off her introspective mood and seeming suddenly as giddy as a girl herself, laughing and splashing. Perhaps, thought Gervase as he looked on with delight, his prayers had been answered and he'd been forgiven.

Samantha Sawbridge's birthday party was scheduled for the Monday, which was the Bank Holiday and the girls' last day off school. Rosemary had consulted with Gervase on the logistics of getting Daisy to and from Kinderland in Saxwell; as it was the Bank Holiday, he foresaw little difficulty in driving her there himself, with or without Rosemary, and collecting her when the party had finished.

But on Sunday afternoon, when he at last got down to the long-delayed task of clearing the paperwork on his desk, he found quite a few things that had hitherto escaped his notice. One was the invitation to the garden party at The Archdeaconry, now less than a week away, and another was a piece of paper summoning him to a Deanery clergy chapter Quiet Day, led by the Archdeacon. On the Bank Holiday Monday. Lasting all day, in Eleigh Green, the opposite direction from Saxwell.

Gervase groaned aloud. He *couldn't* let Rosemary down again, so soon after the last time. He thought that she had forgiven him, but it wouldn't do to remind her. And she hadn't really been herself this weekend; she'd seemed to alternate between dreamy abstraction and ebullient high spirits in a quite unpredictable manner.

He sat for a moment, pondering the dilemma. There must be a way round the problem, without involving Rosemary in it. He would have to make alternative arrangements himself, and tell her later, when it was a *fait accompli.*

After some thought he picked up the phone and rang Hal Phillips. Hal had been so helpful before; Gervase hated to impose upon him again, but it was better than upsetting Rosemary.

In the late hours of Sunday night, as Gervase slept peacefully beside her, Rosemary lay awake, her heart pounding. She hadn't slept well all weekend, but tonight was the worst; tonight sleep seemed an impossible state to achieve.

She felt wretched, and could only hope that Gervase hadn't noticed anything and was unaware of her torment. Rather than counting sheep, Rosemary was thinking about various books she'd read, novels in which the heroine loved two men at the same time. She'd always been inclined to dismiss this as impossible, nothing more than a fictional conceit.

That had been before this weekend. Now she knew that it was possible.

She still loved Gervase, as she always had and felt sure that she always would; nothing had changed in her feelings towards him.

But now there was Hal. She could no longer deny to herself that she loved him. Her final defences against him and against the growing sense of attachment between them had been swept away on Friday night.

A part of her couldn't wait to see him again, to feel the warmth of his smile, but the more sensible side of Rosemary recognised that it was a good thing to have the weekend away from him. Two whole days since she'd seen him, and with the Bank Holiday she would have another day of breathing space, to steel herself for the shock of being with him again. She was determined that he should never know how she felt about him; she would have to be careful, and guard against any accidental slip that would betray her. Perhaps, if she handled things right, if she could pretend that Friday night had never happened, they would be able to go on as before – as friends.

And of course Gervase must never even suspect; that was the most important thing. Already she had done him a great wrong. Thinking about it now, tears welled in her eyes and slipped silently down her flushed cheeks to dampen her pillow.

She'd done something she'd never done before; something, indeed, that she'd read about in novels but never even contemplated as a possibility for a happily married woman such as she, and now she regretted it bitterly, and hated herself for having succumbed.

A few hours earlier, when Gervase had made love to her, Rosemary had closed her eyes and pretended to herself that he was Hal.

On Monday morning, while Gervase was in church, Rosemary determined to make him his favourite breakfast. She had some sausages and a bit of bacon in the freezer, and eggs on hand, so by the time he returned home the kitchen smelled tantalisingly of frying bacon.

'A fry-up, as a special treat,' Rosemary announced. 'After all, it's a Bank Holiday.'

He smiled appreciatively and kissed her cheek on his way to the table. 'How lovely.'

'It *is* lovely,' affirmed Daisy, who was already well into her own breakfast and had a smear of egg on her face in testimony to her enjoyment of it. 'Lovely, lovely, lovely,' she chanted.

'Someone's in a good mood today,' Gervase observed, smiling at his daughter.

Daisy shoved half a sausage in her mouth. 'Today is Samantha's birthday,' she reminded him, her mouth full of food. She swallowed it and went on. 'Samantha's party. Remember, Daddy? Samantha's birthday, Samantha's party.

I'm going to Samantha's party. How much longer till we go, Mummy?'

Rosemary sighed; the party didn't start until two, and it was going to be a long morning with Daisy as worked up as she was. At least Gervase would be about to help bear the brunt of Daisy's high spirits. 'It's half past eight now, darling, so we won't be leaving for another five hours. Isn't that right?' she added to Gervase as she set his plate down in front of him. 'Thirty minutes will be long enough to get there, won't it?'

'It should be.' Gervase picked up his knife and fork, then set them down again; he couldn't put this moment off any longer. On Sunday afternoon he'd told her about the Archdeaconry garden party, and she'd accepted that news with equanimity. But he'd decided to leave telling her about today's change of plans until this morning, thinking that perhaps he'd find an easy way to break it to her. That wasn't going to happen. 'I have something to tell you,' he began nervously.

She stopped in the process of filling her own plate, then turned and looked at him. 'Oh, Gervase, no.'

'It's not as bad as it might be,' he said in what he hoped was a reassuring tone, and rushed into an explanation. 'I have to go to Eleigh Green for a Deanery clergy chapter Quiet Day – I just found out about it. That is to say, I've only just found the bit of paper,' he added honestly. 'But don't worry, my dear. I've made other arrangements to get Daisy to the party, so you won't need the car.'

'Other arrangements?' she echoed, baffled.

'I've rung Hal Phillips. He's promised to collect the two of you at half past one.'

Rosemary struggled with hysteria; she must not let Gervase see how upset she was, so with some effort she kept her voice quiet and calm. 'You've done what?'

'I've arranged it all with him,' Gervase said smugly, pleased that Rosemary was taking it so well. 'He'll collect you and take you to Saxwell, then bring you both home after the party.'

'Oh, Gervase, how could you?' she said with such feeling that he dropped his half-eaten sausage on his plate and stared at her.

'I thought you'd be pleased that I'd fixed it up, without worrying you. And he didn't seem to mind at all. He's very fond of Daisy, you know. And you get on well with him, don't you, my dear?'

She took a deep breath and tried to give a rational explanation for her panic. 'But how could you take advantage of him like that? It's his day off – a Bank Holiday! How did you know that he didn't have plans to do something with his wife?'

'The Archdeacon is leading the Quiet Day,' he explained. 'So I knew he'd be on his own. If he didn't want to do it,' he added with unarguable logic, 'he could have said no.'

There was no point quarrelling about it; everything had been fixed. Rosemary was no longer hungry. She scraped the contents of her plate into the bin, untouched.

Excited as Daisy was about the party, she scarcely seemed to register the fact that her father would not in fact be taking her, and when the bell rang at half past one she ran shrieking to the door. 'I'll get it! I'll answer, Mummy! Let me!'

Rosemary was relieved to have an extra few seconds to compose herself, and to fix on a welcoming but neutral expression. She came into the hall as Hal tried to extricate himself from a fervent embrace. 'Whoa, Daisy,' he said, and smiled at Rosemary over her head.

He hadn't changed; he was the same Hal. Rosemary's reserve melted and she smiled back. As long as Daisy was there, at least, it would be all right. 'Hello, Hal.'

'Hello, Rosie. Are we all set to go?'

Daisy was ready. She had her present for Samantha – she'd chosen and wrapped it herself – and she was dressed for the occasion: not in a party frock, but in leggings, a long-sleeved polo neck, and trainers.

Hal had brought the green car; Rosemary tried to claim the back seat for herself, feeling that it would be better to let Daisy sit next to him and carry the conversation. But he pointed out that it was an extremely tiny and cramped back seat, not really intended for adult passengers, and she would not be comfortable there. Daisy was accordingly belted into the back, but that position did not prevent her from thoroughly dominating the threesome. From behind their heads she chattered all the way from Branlingham to Saxwell, explaining to Hal that the reason she was not wearing her best party frock was that there were rules at Kinderland. She hadn't been there herself, of course, but Samantha had, for the parties of various friends, and had told her all about it. Legs and arms had to be covered, she informed Hal, and everyone put their shoes into a big bin at the door while they played in their sock feet. This was going to be the best party ever in the whole world.

Perhaps because they were so focused on Daisy, while remaining so aware of each other, neither Hal nor Rosemary noticed the blue car which stayed behind them all the way to Kinderland.

Valerie had once again been fortunate in spotting Hal as he left. This time she'd been in her look-out position in the phone box, but she'd seen him coming out of the front door and so managed to get to her car before he'd taken his out of the garage, and she was ready to follow him as he drove out.

He was driving the sporty green car again, and was wearing an open-necked shirt with a pair of khaki trousers. If he hadn't looked so marvellous – manly, yet casual – she might not have followed him on this occasion. She was mourning the loss of her talisman, destroyed by Shaun, and had half hoped that Hal and the Magpie might be going out for the day and thus give her an opportunity to slip back into the house and take another pair of boxer shorts. But the Magpie had left the house on her own, early, and Valerie had just about given up hope of even seeing Hal that day. She didn't know how long he would be gone or indeed whether the Magpie might be back at any moment, so she decided to follow him rather than chance her luck.

Where could he be going, on his own, on a Bank Holiday? Before long she realised that he was taking the same familiar route over which she'd followed him twice before: the road to Branlingham.

Having learned her lesson on Friday night, this time she did not allow herself to be caught out. Either he was going to remain at the Vicarage, she reasoned, in which case there was no hurry to follow him there, or else he was collecting someone or something and would soon be coming back out via Church End. So she pulled her car round near the village hall and waited.

In a few minutes the green car emerged from Church End; as it passed her, Valerie could see that there was a woman in the passenger seat – that woman again – and there seemed to be someone else in the back seat. She tailed the car back through the village and onto the main road, heading once again towards Saxwell.

When they'd reached Saxwell, though, Hal didn't return to The Archdeaconry; he drove into the town centre and back out again a short way, pulling into a car park next to a large warehouse-like building that bore a sign proclaiming it to be Kinderland. Valerie had no idea what that might mean, but she followed him into the car park and stopped her car a few rows short of his.

Hal got out, went round and opened the door on the passenger side, and waited while the woman emerged. Then he flipped the seat forward and helped a little girl out of the back. She was, Valerie noted with surprise, what used to be called, in less politically correct times, a Mongoloid child, clutching a present to her chest and virtually dancing with excitement. The three of them disappeared through the front door of the building. Valerie settled back to wait; she'd grown expert at waiting.

They were among the first to arrive. Samantha was there, with her parents, and baby Jamie in his carry-cot, and there were two other little girls, shoeless and excited. Two large tubs stood in their midst, ready to collect shoes and presents respectively; Daisy deposited her present in the appropriate bin and struggled with her shoe-laces, while Rosemary explained Gervase's absence and introduced Hal to Annie and Colin Sawbridge. 'And this must be the famous Samantha Sawbridge,' Hal said with grave amusement. 'What a pleasure to meet you. And happy birthday to you.'

Rosemary announced her intention to remain during the party. 'That will be all right, won't it? Hal, you can go home if you like, and collect us when it's over at five o'clock.' That, it seemed to her, was by far the best way to handle the situation.

But Annie Sawbridge shook her head. 'No, Kinderland don't really like having all of the parents hanging about. Only two chaperones allowed. That's us – me and Colin. Don't you have somewhere you could go for three hours?'

'I'll take care of Rosemary,' Hal assured them.

Rosemary wasn't ready to succumb. 'But Daisy . . . what if something happens?' she protested. 'Can't I stay about, just in case she needs me?'

'She won't,' Annie declared. 'Wee Daisy will be fine, you'll see. You just go off with your friend.'

Colin, discerning Rosemary's unease, reached into his pocket. 'Here,' he said impulsively. 'Take my mobile phone. If anything goes wrong – which it won't – we can ring you on it. How about that?'

She couldn't very well refuse, any more than she could tell them the real reason that she wanted to stay: being alone with Hal for the next three hours seemed a recipe for disaster. 'All right,' she accepted, trying to sound gracious. 'And thank you.'

Daisy, now in her socks and arm-in-arm with Samantha, barely glanced in their direction as they left.

Back in the car, Rosemary looked at Hal nervously. 'Where shall we go?' she asked.

'We could go to my house,' Hal suggested. 'Have a drink or something. Or tea.'

'No.' That sounded extremely dangerous. 'Why don't you show me the sights of Saxwell?' she suggested in a bright voice.

He raised an amused eyebrow. 'Such as they are.'

'Only I've never really been here except to shop, and there must be some interesting things to see. Isn't there supposed to be a Saxon well?'

'Very well,' he agreed, putting the car into gear. 'I'll show you the Saxon well.'

That feature, which had given the town its name, turned out to be located within the precincts of a large Victorian park in the town centre. The Victorians, with their passion for romantic ruins, had made rather a fuss over what was after all little more than an old hole in the ground. With no regard for faithfulness to the well's ancient origins, they'd erected an elaborate Gothic stone canopy over it, dripping with gargoyles and leering faces and pious angels bearing heraldic shields. All of this was a surprise to Rosemary, who had expected it to be in a neglected corner of a churchyard. 'A bit of a dog's dinner,' Hal said. 'Looks rather like a miniature version of the Albert Memorial, don't you think?'

'It does, rather,' she admitted, trying not to giggle. 'Not quite how I'd pictured it.'

'Well, now you've seen the sights of Saxwell. We can go into the church, if you'd like, or we can walk about here in the park for a bit.'

Rosemary opted for the latter; somehow it seemed safer to be out in the open with Hal than in an enclosed space, even a church.

The Victorians of Saxwell had used their Gothic folly as the centrepiece for what was really a rather nice town park. Wide walks and herbaceous borders radiated out from it, with spacious landscaped lawns in between, and round the edges were less tamed areas where the trees had been allowed to remain. A great many people – those who hadn't the means or the desire to get to the seaside – were taking advantage of the seasonably warm Bank Holiday weather to enjoy the civic amenities which the latter-day town fathers had so thoughtfully provided for them in the form of the park. Young couples pushed prams, while gangs of boys rollerbladed or skateboarded along the wide pavements, terrorising the pedestrians. Older folks sat on wrought iron benches, rich with Victorian curlicues, and dozed in the afternoon sun; families walked dogs and bought ice creams from the vendor who was situated by the elaborate iron gates.

'Would you like an ice cream?' Hal offered.

'No, thanks. I'm not hungry.'

'Let's walk, then,' he said. 'Perhaps we might have some tea in a bit.'

Rosemary was glad of the crowds; she felt less vulnerable

surrounded by so many people. But Hal took the lead and started off towards one of the more sparsely populated sections of the park.

He was silent for a few moments, then said abruptly, 'Listen, Rosie, this is no good. We've got to talk.'

Walking along beside Hal, she looked straight ahead rather than at him. 'I'd really rather not,' she said.

'Haven't we always been honest with one another, Rosie?' he appealed to her.

That was the problem, she realised suddenly. Their relationship had been founded on honesty, on understanding. Her idea that they would be able to ignore what had happened on Friday night and pretend that it hadn't happened was just not going to work. It was a non-starter. 'Yes . . .' she conceded, overwhelmed with a sense of foreboding. 'Yes, Hal. We've always been honest with one another.'

'And from the beginning – from the day we met – we've understood each other, haven't we, Rosie?'

'Yes.'

'Then I think you know what I'm going to say to you.' He stopped, forcing her to stop as well, but still she kept her face turned away. 'Look at me, Rosie.'

Unwillingly, she obeyed.

Now that he'd got this far, he seemed unsure how to proceed. He searched her face for what he knew he would find there, then said, 'Rosie, you must know that I'm in love with you.'

She gulped, and said nothing, staring down at the ground.

'I didn't ask for this to happen – I didn't *want* it to happen,' he went on. 'But it *has* happened, and I think we need to get it out in the open. And I have an idea – a feeling – that you might love me as well.'

If he was waiting for confirmation, he wasn't going to get it. Still she didn't speak.

'I'm not suggesting that we *do* anything about it,' Hal added.

'Oh!' she gasped in relief.

Misunderstanding the gasp, he tried to explain. 'That's what makes this whole situation so damnably difficult. I'm not suggesting that we change the status quo. This may sound daft, but loving you doesn't mean that I don't still love Margaret.'

'And I still love Gervase,' Rosemary blurted.

'Then you *do* love me,' he said with quiet satisfaction.

It was too late to call the words back; she nodded dumbly.

He drew in a deep breath. 'So where do we go from here, Rosie?'

'You've just said it yourself, Hal,' she said, urgency loosening her tongue. 'We don't have to do *anything*. Can't we just go on being friends? Seeing each another once in a while, and talking? Then nothing has to change, and no one but us will have to know about it. Not Gervase, not Margaret – no one. It will be our secret.'

'Our secret.' He nodded thoughtfully in agreement.

'That's all right, then,' she breathed, believing it, both reassured and elated. Perhaps, after all, she *could* have her cake and eat it.

He seemed about to kiss her to seal the bargain, but evidently thought better of it, and instead put his hand out. She shook it gravely, and they continued walking.

Valerie was almost paralysed with the shock of it. Although she was far too distant from them to hear the words they exchanged, she was equipped with a pair of binoculars and had seen the expressions on their faces all too clearly. And their body language spoke volumes as well: that woman – that hideously dowdy woman – was in love with Hal. *Her* Hal. And much as she wanted to deny it to herself, it was clear that he was besotted with her as well.

A witch, she must be – that was the only explanation that made any sense. She had cast some spell over him, bewitched him, enchanted him. For otherwise what could he possibly see in a woman as unprepossessing as that vicar's wife? She wasn't even young; though she had about a ten-year advantage on the Magpie, she was still nearer forty than thirty.

Foolish, fickle Hal. Valerie couldn't hate him, she could only feel sorry for him, to be ensnared by the Witch like that. A vicar's wife, for God's sake – a goody-goody, butter-wouldn't-melt-in-her-mouth vicar's wife, and she'd managed to steal Hal away from Valerie, right under her nose.

And what about the Magpie? Valerie's hatred for her evaporated in an instant as she realised that the Magpie and she now had something in common: Hal had betrayed them both.

She followed them round the perimeter of Saxwell Park at a discreet distance, always keeping them in her sight. Anyone looking at them must be able to see that they were lovers; their bodies yearned towards each other, though they didn't touch. How did they dare to have the nerve to flaunt themselves and their illicit passion about in a public place like that?

Valerie was glad for the binoculars, but wished that she had a camera. A photo of the two of them together like that would be something worth having; she suspected that the Magpie might be interested in seeing such a thing as well.

Without a great deal of warning, the weather changed. One black cloud on the horizon became two, and scudded swiftly across the sky, and soon it began to rain: fat drops which almost immediately changed to lashing sheets. The ice cream eaters, the dog walkers and the bench sitters all scattered for cover. Hal and the Witch made a run for his car, with Valerie in unnoticed pursuit. It took her a bit longer to get to her car, but she thought she knew where they might be headed, and she caught them up quickly.

Up the Bury Road Hal drove, and into the drive of The Archdeaconry. Taking his mistress into his own house in broad daylight, Valerie said to herself in outraged horror.

'His mistress,' she repeated aloud, vengefully. His lover, his paramour, his floozie, his tart, his strumpet, his trollop, his harlot, his whore.

The shamelessness of it – whatever would the Magpie say, if she were to find out?

Hal opened the door with his key. 'Come into the drawing room. I'll put the fire on.'

'Oh, I'm sopping wet!' Rosemary tried ineffectually to shake the rain from her skirt. 'I don't want to drip all over everything. Let me stand in the hall till I dry off a bit.'

'I'll get some towels,' he offered, and took the stairs two at a time, coming back down with a stack of fluffy towels from the airing cupboard.

She accepted one with gratitude and rubbed the worst of the water from her dripping hair and face, then started on her clothes. He did the same. 'I've never seen a storm come up like that, from nowhere,' he said, towelling his hair.

Reasonably dry after a few minutes, they grinned at each other somewhat sheepishly; they'd been so involved in their conversation, and so wrapped up in each other, that the storm had caught them out completely.

Hal took the wet towel from Rosemary, then folded her in his arms, in what was intended to be a brotherly sort of hug, and his cheek brushed hers. Her cheek was soft and still damp, smelling faintly of soap.

The jolt of primal desire, strong as an electric shock, caught Hal completely unawares. Up till now he'd told himself – had genuinely believed – that his love for Rosemary was cerebral, emotional, spiritual. Never physical. Now, though, in an instant he knew that he'd been wrong. He wanted her. He wanted to take her upstairs, to his bed. He wanted to remove her damp clothes, to feel her skin against his. He wanted to make love to her endlessly, to merge himself with her in a unity of rapture.

'Rosie – oh, God, Rosie.' His voice, broken and guttural, sounded strange in his ears, as if it belonged to someone else. He found her mouth with his own, hungrily, and kissed her like a starving man. She didn't resist; she responded with an eagerness that would have surprised him, had he not been beyond rational thought by then.

Afterwards, neither of them was quite sure what might have happened if the mobile phone in her handbag hadn't rung just then.

Rosemary pulled away from him, gasping, and fumbled for the phone. It seemed to take her an age to work out which button to push to answer it; her hands shook. 'Hello?' she choked.

'Oh, Rosemary,' came the distraught voice of Annie Sawbridge. 'I'm so sorry to disturb you, but it's an emergency.'

'Daisy?' She was shrill with foreboding. 'Daisy's hurt herself?'

There was a minute, terrifying pause. 'She's missing, Rosemary. We can't find her anywhere.'

Chapter 15

Daisy still hadn't been found when Rosemary and Hal arrived back at Kinderland. In the reception area, Annie Sawbridge was weeping, baby Jamie screamed in his father's arms, and seven small girls – Samantha, Lucy, Charlotte, Rebecca, Jessica, and two Laurens – milled about disconsolately, aware that their party had been spoiled. By now they should have been in another room, eating their pizzas. That was, in fact, how Daisy's disappearance had come to light: when the time came for the girls to file into the small party room for their birthday tea, a head-count had revealed that they were one short.

One pair of shoes remained in the bin, unclaimed.

'But I don't understand,' Rosemary said, fighting hard to keep her hysteria under control. 'Where could she be? How could she have disappeared? Wasn't anyone watching her?'

Through her tears, Annie tried to explain. The girls had scattered in all directions to play as their fancy took them; it was impossible for her and Colin to watch all of them at once, though they did their best, and Annie had been specially keeping an eye on Daisy. Then Jamie's nappy had needed changing; at the same time one of the Laurens had been bitten by Jessica and was screaming bloody murder, while Rebecca had had a jealous tantrum because her birthday was some months away. In the confusion Annie had lost sight of Daisy, but assumed that Samantha was looking after her.

Samantha, also tearful, confessed that she'd had to go to the loo and had left Daisy in the care of Charlotte.

Charlotte, when questioned, admitted that Daisy had gone off on her own, or maybe with Lucy.

Lucy denied it, her dark eyes brimming with tears; she hadn't seen her.

No one had.

'But what is happening now? Isn't anyone looking for her?' demanded Rosemary.

Colin Sawbridge explained that all of the children had been turfed out of the play area and the staff were all in there, combing every inch of the place. 'They told us to stay out here,' he added. 'They said it's all under control, and we'd only get in the way.'

For Rosemary it was like a living nightmare. Daisy, so vulnerable and so afraid of the dark . . . it just didn't bear thinking about. 'I want to look for her as well,' she insisted. 'I'm going in there. She's my daughter. They can't keep me out.'

'And I'm coming with you,' stated Hal firmly.

In the end it was Hal who found her, curled up in a tight ball of misery inside one of the giant flexible tubes. She'd heard the others calling for her and had ignored their shouts, but at the sound of Hal's gentle voice she crawled out and wrapped her arms round his neck, crying bitterly.

'Daisy, Daisy,' he murmured, stroking her hair. 'Daisy, my little love. What's the matter?' Then he called to Rosemary, anxious to put her out of her anguish as soon as possible, 'Rosie, I've found her.'

With a fierce maternal cry, Rosemary ran over and reached out her arms to her daughter, but Daisy clung even more tightly to Hal.

He sat with the girl hanging limpet-like on his neck, and with infinite patience he coaxed the story out of her.

Samantha had indeed left her in the care of Charlotte for a few minutes. As soon as Samantha had gone, Charlotte, who evidently was jealous of Daisy's friendship with Samantha, had taunted Daisy, telling her that Samantha didn't really like her at all and was still Charlotte's best friend. Viciously, she'd even called her stupid, and said that Samantha would never have a stupid girl for a best friend. It was the nightmare days of the old school all over again, and Daisy had fled for cover like a wounded animal, deeply distressed and afraid that what Charlotte said was true.

Hal was splendid with her, soothing without being patronising, allowing her to tell the story her own way yet prompting her sympathetically so that nothing was left out. He even managed to reassure her that Samantha was still her best friend, no matter what Charlotte said, and finally he wheedled a watery smile out of her.

Rosemary sat and listened to her daughter's story, overwhelmed with conflicting emotions. The relief that Daisy was safe, and the anger at Charlotte's cruel treatment of defenceless and vulnerable Daisy were understandable and natural feelings under the circumstances. But Rosemary admitted to herself one other emotion which she knew did her no credit: jealousy. And she wasn't sure of whom she was more jealous: Hal, for being the one to whom her daughter – *her* daughter – had turned for comfort, or Daisy, who rested cosily and guilt-free in Hal's arms, her head on his shoulder.

Rosemary suffered another night of sleeplessness, this time with even greater cause. Coming out of it was the determination on her part to avoid Hal on Tuesday, and a plan to carry that out.

The success of her plan was predicated entirely on her ability to get in and out of the house without using the front door, as Hal was working in the entrance hall. Since they'd moved into the Vicarage, they'd always used the front door. But there was another door. The house had been built in the days when at least half a dozen servants would have lived and worked there and was, in fact, divided clearly into two sections: the front door opened into the family portion of the house, and the public rooms, but the area on the right side of the house – the kitchen, pantry, laundry room and so forth, and the bedrooms above them – had once been the domain of the servants, with its own servants' and tradesman's entrance. This door was on the side of the house, and opened from a small porch into the kitchen.

The trouble was that there was no known key to the servants' entrance. But there was, Rosemary remembered, an old cigar box full of keys left behind by the previous incumbent. She thought she'd last seen the box in the pantry.

In the early hours of the morning, Rosemary left her sleeping husband and crept downstairs to the pantry by the light of a torch. Yes, the cigar box was there, put on the top shelf of the pantry for safekeeping. She got it down, carried it through to the kitchen, and dumped its contents out on the kitchen table.

There were a great many keys, of all sorts. Yale keys, Chubb keys, old-fashioned iron mortice keys, and quite a few other assorted keys for padlocks, suitcases, trunks or other unidentifiable objects long since passed into oblivion. Approaching her task logically, Rosemary sorted them into types, then examined the door in question. At some point a Chubb lock had been fitted to it, superseding the old mortice lock, so it was quite straightforward from then on; she tried each Chubb key until she found the one that fitted. It was the second-to-last one in the pile, but it was there, and the door swung open with a squeak of old hinges. Rosemary smiled to herself in satisfaction and put the precious key in the pocket of her dressing gown.

She scooped the rest of the keys back into the box and replaced it on its shelf in the pantry, then retraced her steps up the stairs, pausing at the door of Daisy's bedroom as she usually did in passing.

Daisy was sleeping soundly, curled into a ball and clutching Barry the Bear to her chest. To her mother's practised eye she did not seem to have suffered any lasting effects from the day's trauma. Her face was a bit flushed, but she looked peaceful and serene in sleep.

Rosemary went quietly back to her own bedroom. Gervase was awake, blinking at her in the light of the torch. 'Rosemary?' he said groggily. 'Where have you been?'

She hated to lie to him, so she didn't. 'The kitchen.'

'Whatever for?'

Now a lie was necessary, though it sounded fairly feeble to her own ears. 'I thought I'd left the milk out of the fridge, and I didn't want it to go off.'

'Oh,' he said, accepting it. He stretched out his arms to her. 'Come here, then.'

Rosemary went, and held him fiercely.

First thing in the morning she carried out the next part of her plan. 'Are you going to be in this morning?' she asked Gervase as he dressed.

He found his diary and consulted it. 'Yes, I should be. I'm seeing a wedding couple at ten for a marriage preparation session. In my study. I have to go out in the afternoon, though. After lunch.'

'Then you won't need the car this morning,' she guessed.

'Not till after lunch. And then I'll collect Daisy from school, and we'll be a bit late home. We've some shopping to do,' he said mysteriously.

So he had remembered that her birthday was tomorrow, Rosemary surmised. Pretending that she didn't understand the hint, she explained her intentions to him: although she usually bought her groceries in the village, this morning she wanted to do a big shop at the Tesco outside Saxwell, to stock up on staples. And she wanted to get an early start; the day after the Bank Holiday was bound to be a busy one, so if he didn't mind, she would leave directly from taking Daisy to school and get it over with straightaway. It would mean, she reminded him, that he would have to let Hal in when he arrived, and perhaps give him a cup of coffee.

'I think I can manage that, my dear,' Gervase said with a faint smile. 'I know you think I'm helpless, but I do think that I can manage to do that.'

Gervase managed very well. He let Hal in, offered him a cup of coffee, and chatted to him for a few minutes while he drank it. 'I'm glad that I have a chance to see you,' he said. 'Our paths haven't really crossed all that much while you've been working here, and I did want to thank you for all you've done. You've been so kind, and I owe you an enormous debt of gratitude.'

Hal smiled. 'Not at all.'

'But I do,' Gervase insisted earnestly. 'You've been a good friend to Rosemary, I think, and she needs friends – she's always been a bit lonely. And you've been wonderful with Daisy, from what Rosemary tells me. I'll never be able to thank you enough for what you did yesterday.'

The smile didn't falter. 'You don't need to thank me.' Hal

wished he knew exactly what Rosemary *had* told him about yesterday. Evidently it wasn't the whole truth.

After the wedding couple had left, Gervase had a few minutes to spare, and decided to go across to the church as he often did when he had the odd moment. Rosemary had not yet returned, so he told Hal where he might be found in the event that Rosemary or anyone else were looking for him.

There was a woman sitting in the south porch, a young blond woman of around thirty, attractive, wearing jeans and a shapeless shirt. She was the same woman who had been there a few days previously, Gervase realised. He gave her an encouraging smile, in case she wanted to talk, and she rose.

'Hello . . . Vicar,' she said, in the manner of one unaccustomed to addressing clergy, and unsure of the proper title.

Gervase stopped and nodded to indicate that the form of address was acceptable. 'Yes, hello.'

'You said that I might talk to you.'

'Yes, of course.' He indicated the Vicarage with a sweep of his hand. 'We can go over and talk in my study, if you like. It would possibly be a bit more comfortable, and private.'

'No,' she said quickly. 'Not there. How about . . . in the church?'

'As you like.' He led the way into the church and they sat down in a pew near the back.

For a moment she sat awkwardly, twisting her hands together. Gervase was used to such behaviour, and tried to put her at her ease by relaxing himself, and appearing attentive but not pushy. 'Take your time,' he said gently, adding after a pause the suggestion, 'You have a problem you'd like to talk to me about?'

'I wondered,' she said abruptly, 'what you would think about two people who were having an affair.'

Gervase felt that he was on well-travelled ground here: people often confided their own problems to him in third-person terms, and he was used to dealing with that face-saving and embarrassment-sparing approach. 'That would depend,' he replied, 'on their situation. If they were both free agents, and committed to one another, I would be inclined to take a rather relaxed view.'

She looked at him, surprised, as those who asked Gervase's advice about such matters often were. That wedding couple this morning, for instance: they'd been reluctant to admit to him that they were living together, assuming that he would disapprove. But Gervase was all too well aware of his own weaknesses in that area, and felt that a liberal and humane approach was called for. These days so many young couples lived together; it was the norm, as he had discovered through preparing a great number of them for marriage. An engaged couple – or any two people with a strong and permanent commitment – could it be so wrong for them to express their love physically? At any rate, he didn't feel that it was up to him to judge.

'But what if they were both married?' the woman asked. 'The man and the woman, both married to other people?'

'Ah. That's different,' Gervase allowed. No wonder the woman was troubled; he must tread gently. He guessed that she was already embarked on this affair, and not just contemplating it, so it was too late to warn her off. Absently his eyes followed the stone tracery of the east window, and his fingers stroked the poppyhead on the pew end, as he formulated his next words. 'When other people are involved – the wife, and the husband, and possibly children – then you're entering another area entirely. The consequences could be very destructive. Breaking up marriages – it's a serious matter.'

She turned large blue eyes on him. 'If your wife were

having an affair, would you want to know about it?'

This was a radical departure from the script. Gervase blinked at her, startled. 'I'm sorry?'

'I asked,' she repeated patiently, 'if you would want to know, if your wife were having an affair.'

Gervase recovered, and gave the question his serious attention, contemplating his tented fingers. 'No,' he said in a thoughtful voice. 'No, on the whole I don't suppose that I would.'

'Well, then.' The woman got up. 'Thank you for your time, Vicar,' she said, and was gone.

He stared after her. What on earth, he wondered, had that been all about?

Rosemary's evasive tactics were successful for the first part of the day; using the side door, and the back stairs, she was able to stay out of the entrance hall altogether. But late in the afternoon, Gervase and Daisy still away on their mysterious errand, she was getting a few things ready in preparation for Daisy's tea when Hal came into the kitchen.

'Hello, Rosie,' he said.

She didn't want to look at him; instead she gazed out of the window into the garden. It was not a pretty sight. The previous incumbent had let it grow into a jungle-like tangle, and nothing had been done to remedy that. 'Hello.'

'Do I get the feeling that you're trying to avoid me?'

There was no point in denying it. 'Yes.'

Hal sat down at the kitchen table. 'Oh, come on, Rosie. You can't avoid me for ever. We've got to talk about this. We can't just pretend it didn't happen.'

'I don't see why not,' Rosemary said; after all, she had based her marriage on avoiding confrontation, and was a master at the art of not asking questions to which she didn't want to know the answer.

'Because,' he reminded her, 'we've always been honest with each other. Even when it's been difficult.'

Sighing, she gave up, folding her arms across her chest and leaning back against the kitchen units. 'Yes, all right. You go first.'

'Fair enough.' Hal tried to think where to begin. 'Well, I suppose I should start by saying that I never meant for that to happen.'

Rosemary nodded, believing him. 'I know that.'

'When I suggested that we should go on as friends, I really thought we could do it,' he stated.

'That didn't last very long, did it?' A small, rueful smile twisted the corner of her mouth.

'No. And now I realise that it won't work,' he admitted. 'We can't go back. We can't just be friends.'

'I see.' Her voice was bleak; the alternatives were not pleasant to contemplate. She had spent a sleepless night agonising about them, and they seemed to boil down to two equally undesirable options. 'So that means that we have to decide. We've only got two choices.'

'Go on, tell me.'

Rosemary turned and looked out of the window again, relieved that he seemed to be willing to discuss it rationally, and that he hadn't made any attempt to touch her. He was going to make her spell it out, but perhaps that was the best way, the only way. 'We could have an affair.'

'Yes . .'

'If we're being honest, it's probably what we both want to do,' she forced herself to say, swallowing hard. 'But that doesn't mean it's a good idea. In fact, it's quite a bad idea. A terrible idea. If Gervase found out . . . if Margaret found out . . . we would take the risk of breaking up two marriages, of hurting two people we love. And there's Daisy. And we would have to lie all of the time, and . . . oh, it's just too complicated.'

'And the second choice?' he prompted.

'We could agree not to see each other again,' she said with real pain in her voice.

'I wouldn't want that.'

She clenched her hands together. The thought of never seeing Hal again, now that he had become such a part of her, was akin to contemplating the amputation of a limb: it was something she would get over, eventually, but she would never really be the same, never be a whole person again. 'No, I wouldn't either,' she admitted.

'There is a third alternative,' Hal said.

'What's that, then?' Still she looked out of the window.

He got up and came to her, turning her round to face him and putting a finger under her chin so that she couldn't evade his eyes. 'You could marry me, Rosie.'

'Marry you!' she gasped, astonished.

'Don't say you haven't thought about it, Rosie. We love each other. We understand each other. We'd make a wonderful team.'

'Of course I haven't thought about it! Aren't you forgetting something?' she reminded him bitterly. 'Two things, in fact. My husband. Your wife. We're both already married, Hal. Or had that little fact slipped your mind?'

'Sarcasm doesn't become you,' he rebuked her in a gentle voice. 'Just hear me out, Rosie. You're not the only one who's been thinking about this every second since yesterday afternoon.'

Alarmed at his proximity, not trusting herself, she moved away. 'Go ahead, then.'

He didn't attempt to follow her. 'I want to take care of you,' he began. 'I want to cherish you, Rosie. For ever.'

Rosemary uttered one stark word. 'Margaret.'

'Margaret is strong,' he said. 'Self-sufficient. She doesn't need me – not the way you do.'

'But Gervase *does* need *me*,' Rosemary stated flatly.

'That's just it. He leans on you too much – he's never even tried to stand on his own two feet. If he had to cope, he'd manage,' Hal analysed. 'It would be good for him for a change. Leaving him might be the best thing you could do for him, in the long run.'

Rosemary wished she could believe it. She discovered, to her horror, that she *wanted* to believe it. For a fleeting moment she allowed herself to imagine what life would be like if she were married to Hal. He *would* take care of her, and cherish her: no worries about money ever again, no need to be the one who had to cope. And to be understood, to be loved . . . Hating herself for the disloyal thought, she took it out on Hal. 'You'd like to believe that,' she said coldly. 'It shows a rather extraordinary turn of mind, if you're able to justify taking a man's wife away from him on the grounds that he'd be better off in the long run. I don't imagine that Gervase would see it quite like that. And I think I know him better than you do.'

'But *do* you really know him?' Hal persisted. 'Can you really say that you understand what makes him tick? He certainly doesn't understand you, or make any attempt to do so. Even I can see that.'

She pressed her lips together and closed her eyes but made no reply.

Seeing that he'd struck a nerve, he played what he considered to be his ultimate card. 'And you've never really believed that Gervase loves you. Needs you – yes, perhaps – but that's not the same thing.'

Rosemary flinched, knowing that he'd read her thoughts; it was too close to the bone, touching on her greatest insecurity. 'Don't, Hal,' she said in a small voice. 'That's unfair.'

He changed the subject, but pressed his advantage. 'And you know how much I adore Daisy,' he said, his voice and his face softening. 'I was a terrible father to my own son. I'd love to have another chance at fatherhood, with Daisy. There are so many things I could do for her.'

'Gervase loves Daisy as well. And she's his daughter,' Rosemary stated unanswerably.

Hal backed off. 'I'm not asking you to make any decisions right now, Rosie,' he said. 'That wouldn't be fair. Take a few days and think it over.'

'You said that we couldn't go back.' She hugged herself, as if suddenly chilled, and her voice sounded wistful. 'I accept that. But can't we just stand still?'

'In limbo? That's where we are at the moment, neither one thing nor the other,' he analysed. 'More than friends, less than lovers. Sooner or later we've got to go forward, to choose one path or another.'

'Yes, but it's a decision we *both* have to make, together,' she insisted.

Hal went to the kitchen door. 'Think it over, Rosie. I have to get back to work now.'

The enormity of what had just taken place hit Rosemary a few minutes later, as the numbness wore off, and the tears began to trickle down her cheeks. Abruptly she sat down at the kitchen table, her legs wobbly, and held her head between her hands. She couldn't believe that she'd had such a conversation, calmly discussing the possibilities of adultery and divorce with Hal with little more heat than if they were trying to decide what colour to paint the kitchen.

The strangest thing about it, perhaps, was that in all of the clinical and rational summing up of their alternatives, neither one had mentioned that it was *wrong*. They'd managed to avoid using those bald, accusatory words – adultery and divorce – but that's what they'd been talking about all the same, and she and Hal both knew that they were contrary to everything they both believed in. Oddly, at the time that had seemed an irrelevant factor, or at least no more important than a dozen other considerations. Now it seemed highly significant. Sin, Rosemary realised, was an old-fashioned word, and an unfashionable concept, but she was the daughter of a vicar and the wife of a vicar, and such things went deep. Swamped by guilt, she found herself in floods of tears. She had cried more in the past week than she had in many years put together.

This time there was no question of having her cake and eating it. Rosemary knew that she had to make a decision – a choice. And no matter which choice she made, something precious would have to be forfeited. Bowing her head over the kitchen table, she wept in the heaviness of that knowledge, and for the loss of her innocence.

Chapter 16

Rosemary's birthday dawned wet and grey, a real change in the weather. But a radiance that put the sun to shame shone in Daisy's face as she bounced into her parents' bedroom at an early hour. 'Happy birthday, Mummy!' she cried, throwing herself on the bed.

'Ugh,' Rosemary groaned, having slept very little, and that only recently. For Daisy's sake, though, she struggled into a sitting position, arranged her face in a smile, and gathered her daughter into her arms. The feel of Daisy's warm cheek against hers brought her to life. 'Thank you, darling,' she said.

Daisy wriggled in excitement. 'When are you going to open your presents?' she demanded. 'Open my present first!'

'Let's ask Daddy,' she teased, turning to the other side of the bed. Gervase was not there.

As she registered his absence, he pushed the door open and came through with a tray. It was her best tea tray, laid with a cloth and bearing the elements of breakfast: a boiled egg, some accompanying toast soldiers – only slightly charred, a glass of orange juice, and a pot of tea. There was even a flower, a single pink-and-white-striped tulip, in another juice glass.

'We surprised her, Daddy,' Daisy exulted. 'I told you Mummy would be surprised.'

Rosemary was indeed surprised, never having been given breakfast in bed before. Her tears, never far beneath the surface these days, brimmed over and trickled down her cheeks. 'Oh, Gervase, you shouldn't have,' she gulped, touched. 'You'll spoil me.'

'Nonsense, my dear.' He planted a kiss on her forehead as he settled the tray on her lap. 'It's your birthday, and you must be spoiled.'

'I made the toast,' Daisy informed her with eager pride. 'And I picked the flower, but I couldn't find anything else to put it in,' she added. 'Daddy made the egg and the tea.'

The egg was a touch overdone, but Rosemary pronounced it perfect, along with the rest of the breakfast. Though she wasn't hungry, she ate every bite, watched by Daisy. 'It was wonderful,' she assured her, then smiled her approval at Gervase. 'Thank you both.'

'Presents now, Mummy?' Daisy urged.

'Whyever not?'

'Mine first,' she insisted, producing a small, crudely wrapped parcel. 'I chose it myself. And I wrapped it myself,' she added unnecessarily.

Rosemary took it from her and opened it to reveal a hideous china ornament. It was probably intended to represent a dog, though it was like no dog ever seen, and was a lurid shade of pink at that, painted all over with crude flowers. 'Why, how beautiful!' she enthused. 'Oh, Daisy, thank you so much!' She gave her daughter a huge hug and a kiss.

'I knew that you would love it, Mummy,' Daisy said smugly. 'I thought it was so beautiful. And Daddy said that you wouldn't like it, but I knew he was wrong. His name is Jack,' she added, 'like Samantha's kitten.'

'I tried to steer her towards a bottle of scent,' Gervase confirmed with a sheepish look.

'But Jack is *much* nicer,' stated Daisy.

Rosemary kissed her again. 'Indeed he is. I shall put Jack on the mantelpiece in the drawing room, where everyone can see and admire him.'

Daisy beamed her approval of this plan. 'Now Daddy's present,' she said.

Gervase's present proved to be in a very large, upright box; Rosemary couldn't imagine what it might be. She had to get out of bed to open it, though he hadn't made much of an effort to wrap it, merely tying a ribbon round the box and sticking a bow on top.

It was a brand new, state-of-the-art vacuum cleaner.

'Oh, Gervase,' she said, stunned. 'However can we afford it?'

He looked as smug as Daisy. 'I used the last of the money from the leaving present. With this much house to clean, I thought you could really use one of these. See,' he pointed out, 'it's a Dyson. It doesn't use bags. That's what the salesman told me.'

Rosemary closed her eyes. She knew that his gesture had been well meant, and with the rational part of her mind she appreciated the generosity behind it. But her overwhelming emotion, unworthy though she recognised it to be, was disappointment. Selfishly, she wished that if he were going to spend that much money, and go to all that trouble, he might have bought something else – something more personal, if not romantic. And he was so pleased with himself. Swallowing her irritation with him, she managed a smile. 'Thank you,' she said quietly. 'It's wonderful.'

Daisy was not impressed. 'Now this one,' she said impatiently, presenting her mother with a box that was wrapped with some care in a cheerful floral paper.

'Who is this from, then?'

'It's from Granny,' Daisy informed her. 'It came in the post.'

Her own dear mother, who could always be counted on to buy something for *her*. Rosemary unwrapped it and found, nestled in tissue paper, a pretty blue blouse, made of washable silk and sprigged with little yellow and pink flowers. And there was a card as well, containing a cheque.

'What a marvellous birthday I'm having,' Rosemary declared.

Gervase smiled. 'And tonight we're taking you out,' he informed her. 'It's a surprise,' he added, at her inquisitive look. 'But I'll give you a hint – it will be a real family occasion.'

'I know, I know,' Daisy chanted. 'I know, Mummy.'

'Oh, Gervase.'

He bent over to kiss her and said softly, for her ears alone, 'I told you I'd make it up to you, my dear.'

Margaret's day had started not so pleasantly. Once again she'd been summoned out of her bed to the scene of another disaster, and this one was the worst to date. This was no mere vandalism or theft: it was a fire. Someone had broken into a church, had presumably taken various valuables, then had heaped hymn books under the organ and set them alight. The old, dry wood of the organ pipes had provided perfect fodder, and the blaze had virtually gutted the interior of the church. Providentially, the rain had kept the roof from going up, and the mediaeval stone walls still stood, blackened with smoke, but restoration would cost a fortune, and the church was of course underinsured.

There was little that Margaret could do, other than try to comfort the distraught priest. He was not very receptive to her ministrations, being one of the clergy who objected to a woman in her office. The irony of the situation gave her a certain grim, if guilty, satisfaction; he had been one of the non-attenders at last week's meeting on church security. If he had come, this might not have happened. A speaker at the meeting had outlined and emphasised ways to prevent just such an occurrence: storing hymn books and candles and matches and greasy cleaning rags and even the odd tin of paraffin together in plain sight, and especially under the organ, was a certain invitation to disaster, he'd said, and had urged keeping candles and matches under lock and key. For one church, at least, it was too late.

At least no one had been hurt, and that was, Margaret supposed, a blessing. Sooner or later, she feared, someone *would* be hurt in these increasingly unpleasant episodes: a priest or a verger would surprise a thief in the act and get clouted with a candlestick, or someone would just happen to be in the wrong place at the wrong time. There was nothing she could do to prevent it, and that was frustrating. Margaret did not like feeling out of control.

On her way back home at the end of a very long morning, distressed, headachy and out of sorts, she spared a thought for Hal. He'd still been in bed when she left, and they'd barely exchanged a word. In fact, she'd seen very little of him over the last ten days or so. She was going through such a busy patch at the moment that often she'd leave the house before he was up, and return home so late that he'd be asleep already. During the brief times when their paths had crossed and they'd had a chance to talk for a few minutes, he'd seemed distracted and not at all his usual sanguine self. It was no wonder, she thought: she really *had* been neglecting him. She would have to do something about it.

This afternoon, barring unforeseen emergency, she was relatively free. She'd meant to make a few preparations for the garden party, but she still had a couple of days in hand before that would have to become a priority. In any case, the weather was the main thing, and that was truly out of her control; Margaret didn't believe in wasting God's time with prayers for fine weather.

Perhaps, then, she could surprise Hal. Margaret had never been much of a cook, but she had a few dishes in her repertoire that Hal had always liked, and after some thought she decided that she should have a meal waiting for him when he got home from work. Chicken breasts sautéed in olive oil, and some lovely fresh spring asparagus from the local farm shop. A rich chocolate mousse, a nice bottle of wine. And then an early night. Delighted with her plan, especially the last bit, Margaret smiled to herself; they could both do with an early night.

She remembered, then, that it was Wednesday and thus Hal's squash night. But perhaps, with sufficient incentive, he could be tempted away from going out to the gym. It was, Margaret decided, certainly worth a try.

Rosemary had realised that there was no point in trying to avoid Hal; if he wanted to find her, he would manage to track her down. Accordingly, she opened the door to him that morning with as natural a demeanour as she could manage.

'Happy birthday, Rosie,' he said. She'd wondered if he would remember; she should have known that he would. He patted the capacious pocket of his overall. 'I have something for you. Later.'

Oh, no, she thought, hoping it wouldn't be the sort of gift that would put her in a compromising position, or force her into some kind of decision about their future. She couldn't deal with that just now.

And so her stomach clenched in nervous anxiety when, as she was making lunch, the kitchen door swung open. But it wasn't Hal – it was Gervase.

He advanced towards her, carrying a small box. 'I didn't want to give you this earlier, when Daisy was about,' he said. 'I wanted to give it to you privately.'

Rosemary swallowed and took the box.

Inside was an exquisite antique silver locket on a chain, heart-shaped and chased with a fine design. With trembling fingers she opened it. There were two tiny photos inside: one of a heartbreakingly young and dashing Gervase in his days as a curate, and the other was Daisy's most recent school photo. 'Oh, Gervase,' was all she could say, overwhelmed with emotions too complex to think about, let alone articulate.

Gervase lifted it from the box and with his delicate fingers he undid the clasp and fastened it round her neck. 'There,' he said. 'It looks lovely. You like it, then?'

'Oh, Gervase,' she repeated, and once again the tears threatened.

Hal didn't appear with his gift until after lunch, when Gervase had gone out and Rosemary was just finishing the washing-up. She dried her hands hastily on a tea towel.

To her immense relief, the parcel he produced was of an easily identifiable shape: flat and some five inches square, it could be nothing but a compact disc. She removed the wrapping paper from it carefully to reveal the latest recording by the ensemble they'd heard on Friday night; several of the pieces, she saw at once, were in fact the same ones the group had performed in the concert. 'Oh, how wonderful,' she said spontaneously and sincerely. Then she made the mistake of looking into his face.

He was regarding her with tenderness and a sort of sad gravity. 'I wish I could give you something else, my darling Rosie,' he said in a gentle voice. 'Something more . . . personal. But I thought that this was the next best thing. So that, no matter what happens, you'll remember.'

Tears stung her eyes, and she swallowed hard. 'Oh, I'll remember,' she said softly. 'No matter what happens, Hal, I'll remember.'

The day's surprises were by no means over. Shortly after Rosemary collected Daisy from school, Gervase arrived home with a bakery-made birthday cake. 'We'll have it now, with a cup of tea,' he announced. 'If we wait till later, it will spoil our dinner.'

'Birthday cake!' Daisy crowed. 'Is it chocolate?'

'Isn't that what you ordered, young lady?' her father reminded her.

'Yes, yes, yes. Chocolate birthday cake.'

'Let's take it into the drawing room,' Gervase suggested. 'Make a real party out of it. And I'll help with the tea, my dear.'

While he put the kettle on, she got out the best cups and little bone china cake plates, all seldom-used wedding presents, and, on impulse, found the wedding cake knife where she'd put it for safekeeping. There was no point in saving it, all wrapped up as it was; this occasion was as good as any other to use it. Rosemary gave it a swift polish and put it on the tray with the tea things.

The drawing room was looking festive already. Jack the grotesque china dog had taken up residence on the mantelpiece as promised, and he was surrounded by birthday cards. A few had come in the morning post: one from her godmother, one from Gervase's brother and sister-in-law, and one from an old friend from university days whom she hadn't seen for years but was the sort of person who never forgot a birthday. Nothing from Christine – she was the sort of person who never *remembered* a birthday. Then there was the one from her mother, one that Daisy had made with a bit of help from Gervase, and one from him, straightforward and as unsentimental as the vacuum cleaner. Hal had not given her a card, for which she was profoundly grateful as well as disappointed. Rosemary brought the laden tea tray through, while Gervase carried the cake.

'I'll get Hal,' Daisy offered, having long since gone onto a Christian-name footing with him.

'Hal is working, darling,' Rosemary put in quickly. 'We don't want to bother him.'

Daisy's face crumpled. 'But I *do* want to bother him! I want him to come to the birthday party!'

'Of course he must come,' Gervase said.

With a whoop, Daisy went to look for him; he'd finished the entrance hall on the ground-floor level and was working his way up the stairs, all of which necessitated scaffolding. 'Hal!' she shouted, clomping up the stairs. 'It's Mummy's birthday party, and you must come! Daddy says so, and I say so.'

He clambered off the scaffolding and gave her a hug. 'Do you, indeed? And what does Mummy say?'

Daisy shrugged. 'Mummy says that we mustn't bother you, but I'm sure that she wants to you come, really. And it's chocolate cake,' she added.

'Chocolate cake! Well, then. I shall come.'

Valerie hadn't been to Saxwell that day. Instead she'd gone straight to Branlingham, early enough to see the Witch taking her Mongoloid girl to school. She knew that was where they'd gone because she'd followed them, on foot, from her sheltered vantage point in the church porch to the gates of Branlingham Primary School. The trouble was that she'd grown accustomed to fine weather and had not brought an umbrella, and by the time this trip to the school took place, it was fairly tipping down with rain. But it was too good an opportunity to pass up, so she went after them in spite of the

rain. In one way the rain did Valerie a favour: under her own
umbrella, the Witch was utterly unaware that someone was
walking very close behind her.

How she hated that woman, that Witch. Her former ani-
mosity towards the Magpie had evaporated and, in any case,
had been nothing to the utter detestation she now felt for the
Witch. A home-wrecker, a selfish slut. Valerie wanted her
dead, wanted to see her lifeless body and spit on it.

But first . . . perhaps there were other things she could do
to her first. She ought to be made to suffer.

Back in the church porch a short while later, Valerie
observed Hal's arrival, then had a long and uneventful morning sitting on the stone shelf. No one came or went from the
Vicarage; the Vicar didn't even come to the church. Perhaps
he suspected, after Valerie's hint, that it wasn't safe to leave his
whore of a wife alone in the house with Hal.

After a while the chill from the stone struck through her
wet clothes and Valerie began to shiver. Her teeth chattered;
she wrapped her arms round herself in a vain effort to get
warm. It was no good – she was chilled to the bone.

Remembering vaguely that it was Wednesday and Mrs
Rashe would be coming, she decided to go home.

Sybil Rashe was already at Rose Cottage, running the
Hoover round the front room. She stopped at the sound of
the car and opened the door to Valerie. 'Miss Valerie, whatever is the matter?'

Valerie shivered. 'I'm afraid I've caught a chill.'

'I should think you have, out in the rain without a brolly.'
Mrs Rashe clucked at her like a mother hen. 'Come on, then,
Miss Valerie. Off to bed with you.'

She seemed frozen to the spot. 'Do you think I should?'

'I think you want your head examining, if you even need to
ask,' grumbled Mrs Rashe, enjoying herself hugely as she
grabbed Valerie's arm and propelled her upstairs. 'You look all

done in, you do. Now, do you think you can get yourself undressed and tucked into bed, or do I need to do it for you?'

'I can manage,' said Valerie.

Sybil Rashe wasn't so sure. Having snooped at her leisure through Miss Valerie's drawers, she knew that her charge possessed no suitable nightgown – no brushed cotton or winceyette, just frilly bits of nothing and scraps of satin. At the risk of overstepping the boundaries that she'd always so carefully observed, she went to the chest of drawers and pulled out a clean track-suit bottom and matching sweatshirt. 'Put these on,' she ordered.

Valerie complied, showing no coyness or modesty as she stripped off her wet clothes and stepped out of her damp underwear, then pulled on the dry garments.

'Now – into bed with you,' commanded Mrs Rashe, turning back the duvet. 'I'll pop downstairs and make you a nice cup of tea. That will sort you out, Miss Valerie. That, and a nice little nap.' She stayed long enough to tuck the duvet round Valerie's shoulders.

Valerie closed her eyes, exhausted by the effort. 'Thank you, Mrs Rashe. What would I do without you?' she murmured.

It was a moment that would long live in Sybil Rashe's memory, cherished and retold in years to come with suitable embellishment. Now she could hardly wait till Thursday morning, when she could recount the tale to Milly Beazer. As she filled the kettle and settled it on top of the Aga, the episode was already, in Sybil's own mind, beginning to take on the status of a legend: 'The Day I Put Miss Valerie To Bed'.

It was all very mysterious, thought Rosemary as she dressed for the evening. All she knew was that they were going out for a meal, but Gervase had dropped enough hints that she realised there was more to it than that.

She put on her new blouse with an old favourite blue skirt, then fixed the locket round her neck. In spite of the fact that she hadn't been sleeping, Rosemary looked well: tonight the flush in her cheeks was becoming, and there was a sparkle in her eye.

'Come on, Mummy,' Daisy urged. 'It's time to go, or we'll be late.'

Rosemary took her daughter's hand and they went to the car.

Their destination turned out to be a country pub, one with a reputation for good food. As a bonus it was picturesque, timbered and vine-covered, settled cosily into the folds of the rolling mid-Suffolk countryside. They were eating early, because of Daisy, but already the car park was full; the up-market nature of many of the cars – Mercedes, BMWs, Jaguars – demonstrated that the pub's reputation stretched a great deal farther than the local population.

Gervase gave their name to the man at the door. 'We've booked,' he said.

'Ah, yes, sir. A table for four. And your other party has already arrived. Let me show you to your table.'

Someone else? Rosemary's mind wasn't working fast enough; it must be the lack of sleep.

'I told you it would be a real family occasion,' Gervase was saying.

The young man rose as they approached the table, dressed in an expensively cut suit. The cut of his dark hair was equally expensive; his looks combined Gervase's eyes and hair with the classic chilly beauty of Laura's features. 'Happy birthday, Stepmother,' he said in an ironic voice, raising his eyebrows.

Tom.

It was a nightmare of an evening. Tom was charming to his father and attentive to Daisy, who had always idolised him. Towards Rosemary he was outwardly polite – cordial, even –

but she was acutely aware of his underlying hatred. Though Tom had grown up, it was one thing that had not changed over the years. If anything, he had only become more adept at shredding her self-esteem while hiding it from Gervase. His every word was a two-edged barb, with a hidden meaning directed at Rosemary's vitals.

And he dropped even the veneer of politeness when, for a few excruciating moments, Rosemary was left alone at the table with him as Gervase went off to talk to the waiter in private – presumably about a birthday cake – and Daisy insisted on going with him. 'Why are you wearing my mother's locket?' Tom demanded.

Rosemary drew in a sharp breath. 'Your mother's?' she faltered. Of course. It would be. That photo of the young Gervase . . . Her stomach flip-flopped; she felt sick. 'Gervase gave it to me.'

'He had no right. *You* have no right,' he said, naked hatred in his eyes and his voice. 'It was *hers*. It should be mine. You've taken everything else that was hers. Why should you have that as well?'

'Oh, you're admiring the locket,' said Gervase as he returned to the table. 'Doesn't it look well on Rosemary?'

'It was Mother's,' Tom pointed out in a different, suddenly civilised, voice.

'Yes, of course it was. I thought it was time that it should be worn again – there's no point keeping something as lovely as that shut up in a drawer,' said Gervase.

Tom smiled and said gently, 'I'd rather thought it ought to come to me. For my wife.'

'Oh?' Gervase said, surprised. 'Is there something you want to tell us, then? Have you found someone special?' Tom was well known for his ability to keep several girl-friends on the go at once; with his looks, it was no wonder that women flocked to him.

Tom gave a light laugh. 'Not a chance. Not yet, anyway. You know me, the more the merrier. I've plenty of time before I need to think of settling down. Besides,' he added jokily, his smile belying the sting of his words, 'you, of all people, ought to know the truth of that old maxim: marry in haste, repent at leisure.'

'Oh, you should have seen her,' Sybil Rashe said to Mildred Beazer on Thursday morning. 'All done in, she was. Looked like a drowned cat, and that's no mistake.'

Mildred listened avidly. 'She got caught in the rain, then?'

'Stood out in it, more like,' Sybil speculated, drawing on her forbidden cigarette. 'That's how she looked, anyway. Drenched to the skin. And she'd gone all blue, with her teeth chattering. And shivering all over. I tell you, Milly, I've never seen the like.'

'So what did you do?' Mildred prompted.

'Why, just what you'd have done, if you'd been there instead of me,' Sybil said generously. 'I marched her right up the stairs to her bed. "No nonsense, now, Miss Valerie," I told her. "I'm going to take care of you." She went like a lamb, and let me put her to bed.' With relish she described the shedding of clothes, the tucking in, the final words of praise from Miss Valerie. '"You've saved my life, Mrs Rashe." That's what she said, her very words. "You've taken such wonderful care of me. However could I manage without you?" Well, Milly, you can imagine how I felt.'

Her friend nodded as she stubbed out one fag and lit another. 'Proud.'

'Proud is the word. Proud that I could be of service to my Miss Valerie. I tell you true, Milly, it was a moment I will never forget.'

'So what happened then?'

Sybil frowned at the necessity to descend to anticlimax.

'Why, I made her a cup of tea, just like I said I would. But by the time I took it up to her, she was already sound asleep.' She finished her cigarette, rallied, and went on, 'But I tell you true, Milly. She's caught a chill, and a bad one at that. In fact, I'd be surprised if she hasn't caught her death,' she said darkly. 'Double pneumonia, at the very least.'

There was one more nugget of information about Miss Valerie which she would have liked to have mentioned to Milly: those bruises. But she had always prided herself on being the soul of discretion.

By the next day, Rosemary had not even begun to recover from the battering she'd received at Tom's hands. She was stunned, numb. Tom didn't intrude on her life very often these days; he had a life of his own now, in London, where he was doing a pupillage at a prestigious barristers' chambers in the Temple. The legacy of insecurity about her marriage which he'd left behind was always there, of course, but it had never been so painfully reinforced as it had at her birthday dinner. It was almost as if he *knew* what a state she was in, and was doing it deliberately.

She needed to talk about it, to tell someone how Tom had hurt her. Not Gervase, of course; that was out of the ques-tion – and always had been. There was only one person to whom she had ever confided her feelings about Tom.

Hal.

As if to make up for his attention to her yesterday, Gervase went out early, after breakfast, and would be out for the rest of the day. Though she tried to hide it, Rosemary was relieved, and could barely wait for him to go. She needed to talk to Hal.

She had by no means made up her mind what to do about her dilemma, but over the past couple of days the balance had shifted back and forth. Yesterday it had tipped in Gervase's favour, as he had so touchingly attempted to make her birthday a memorable one, and had largely succeeded – until last night. Now, after the horror of that dinner, things were different. And how could he possibly have thought that she would appreciate being given a piece of jewellery that had belonged to Laura? That was far worse than the vacuum cleaner.

Hal would understand. He always understood.

He was working up on the scaffolding that morning, scraping off layers of the past: anaglypta, painted dark brown and rendered even darker by the passing years. It was a shame, he said, that they couldn't have retained and restored the old anaglypta, but it was too far gone, damaged and peeling away in places, and the plasterer had had to remove large chunks of it to repair the walls. Hal had carefully and sympathetically decorated the ground-floor entrance hall in keeping with the period feel of the house, and now would do the same on the stairs; unfortunately, that meant that the anaglypta had to go.

Rosemary sat on the steps, leaning against the wall and with her arms wrapped round her knees. She was a bit below him, so that he could see her face but she would have to look up to see his. It was easier to talk to him like this, contemplating her knees, while he continued his rhythmic scraping. 'I just couldn't believe it, when we walked into that pub and saw Tom,' she said. 'I know it sounds a cliché, but my heart sank to the floor.'

He listened as she told him everything: the constant and underhanded sniping, Tom's terrible beastliness about the locket, Gervase's naïve engineering of the 'surprise', and his complete unawareness of the evening's subtext and her discomfiture. Hal might have spoken up for Gervase, might have pointed out that he was not to know how she felt about Tom, since she'd never told him, and had, in fact, gone to great lengths over the years to conceal their mutual antipathy. He might have said that Gervase clearly meant well. At one time, earlier in their relationship, he might have said those things. But now it was not in his interest to do so.

Sympathy – empathy, even – and understanding were what she required from Hal, and those she got, in full measure. He made all of the right noises in the right places, drawing her out, encouraging her to vent her feelings. Eventually he climbed down from the scaffolding and sat next to her, careful not to touch her but available if she should want comfort of a more physical kind.

Hal felt, instinctively, that her need to be comforted was so great, and her sense of disappointment in Gervase's lack of understanding so acute, that if he tried to make love to her right now, she would not stop him. He wanted it, of course he did, and he sensed that she wanted it too. But he feared that it would backfire, and work against his long-term aims. If she went to bed with him that morning, would she feel that she had thereby committed herself to him, or would the guilt of it drive her straight back into Gervase's arms? On the whole, he decided it was too risky. He felt the shifting in the balance of her conflicted emotions, realising that if he played it cautiously, and didn't rush her, she would probably come to him of her own volition. He was winning. He could wait.

Even when the tears ran down her face, he held back from touching her. If he took her in his arms, even in the spirit of comfort, he wasn't sure that he would be able to stop at that.

'And I don't want to wear that locket ever again,' she said miserably, at the end of her catalogue of woes.

'Then don't.'

'But . . .'

'Listen, Rosie,' he said suddenly. 'There's something I need to tell you. Something I want you to know.'

She turned to look at him, jolted out of her introspection. 'What's that?'

'I want you to know that I've never been unfaithful to Margaret. I've never even wanted to, before now.' He didn't tell her how many opportunities he'd had, and passed up. 'In fact, Margaret was the very first for me. Do you understand what I'm saying?'

Rosemary understood: he was telling her that Margaret, his wife, was the only woman he'd ever slept with. And she understood why he had told her. 'The same here,' she admitted, not looking at him, certain that he knew the truth of it before she said it. 'Gervase is the only one.'

'I'm not just toying with your affections, Rosie, and I don't treat this lightly. I love you. I know that I'm asking you to take a big step, but if you say yes – not today, necessarily, but one day soon – then I want you to realise that I'll be taking a huge step myself, giving up something fine and good.'

She wished, with a part of her mind, that he would make the decision for them, would make love to her right now and take the decision out of her hands. But she knew that was cowardly, and no real solution. That wouldn't be the end of the uncertainty and the pain – it would be only the beginning.

Chapter 17

The weather changed by the weekend. On Friday the rain cleared, so by Saturday afternoon, the afternoon of the garden party, the lawn of The Archdeaconry was dry, and lush from the heavy rains of midweek.

Margaret was relieved; she hadn't relished the prospect of moving the party indoors. Even discounting the dissident clergy, who would not darken the notional door, or even lawn, of a woman archdeacon, there would be in excess of a hundred people in attendance, and even a large house like The Archdeaconry would be stretched to the limit with numbers like that. Hal had suggested hiring a marquee, but with the soggy ground conditions, even that would not have been practical if the rains had continued.

Fortunately, though, the weather was on Margaret's side. And so on Saturday morning the real work began, though most of it was being done by other people. The gardener arrived early for an intensive session of trimming the lawn and tidying up the herbaceous borders after the bad weather. The food was in the hands of caterers, who also dealt with the setting up of the tables and other logistical matters.

'So there's nothing for me to do,' Hal surmised over a breakfast of croissants and coffee.

His wife smiled. 'Not so fast, darling.' She poured herself another cup of coffee. 'What about the drinks?'

'Drinks? But aren't the caterers doing tea?'

'I told you this a few days ago,' she reminded him patiently. 'Weren't you listening?'

He had the grace to look embarrassed. 'Sorry. I must have forgotten.'

Margaret raised her eyebrows. 'Anyway, the tea will be served late in the afternoon. I want to serve Pimm's for the rest of the time, and of course fruit juice for the non-drinkers. You agreed,' she prompted him, 'to do the Pimm's.'

'Yes, of course.' Now he remembered the conversation.

'You're such an expert at it. A Pimm's concocted by Hal Phillips is a thing of beauty and a joy for ever.'

It was Hal's turn to raise his eyebrows. 'Flattery will get you everywhere, Madame Archdeacon. But aren't you over-stating things just a wee bit?'

'Seriously, Hal. If you wouldn't mind doing it, I'd be very grateful,' she said in a different tone of voice. 'The caterers would probably take it on board, if I asked them, but I'd rather leave it to you. Then I know it will be done properly.' In addition, she thought, it would give him something to do, a function to perform, so that he wouldn't be at a loose end at a gathering that was essentially her show.

'And it will have the added benefit of keeping me out of mischief,' he grinned, keeping his voice light.

Margaret returned his smile. 'Absolutely, darling.'

Rosemary did not want to go to the garden party. When Gervase had first mentioned it, a week ago, her mind had been on other things and she'd said yes without thinking. It had seemed remote, irrelevant. Now that it loomed on the immediate horizon, she felt panicky and trapped.

'But what about Daisy?' she said as Gervase ate his cornflakes.

'It's already arranged, my dear.' He looked up at her, puzzled. 'She's going to Samantha's for the afternoon.'

'Yes, yes, yes,' said Daisy. 'We're going to push Jack round
in Samantha's dolly's pram.'

'Oh, yes.' Rosemary remembered arranging it with Annie
earlier in the week. 'Yes, of course. But what if it rains,
Gervase?'

He turned to look out of the window at the brilliant sunshine. 'It's not going to rain. It wouldn't dare to rain on the
Archdeacon's party,' he said with a faint smile. 'She wouldn't
allow it. And even if it did rain, I'm sure that there's a contin-
gency plan. It's not our problem.'

'I don't really have anything proper to wear,' Rosemary
fretted. 'Don't people wear flowery frocks and big hats to
garden parties?'

'We're not talking about Buckingham Palace, my dear,' he
pointed out. 'How about that nice pink dress that you wore to
the concert?'

The rose silk dress: that would have to do. She didn't want
to wear it again – didn't want to be reminded of that night –
but it was the only thing in her wardrobe that was even
remotely suitable. 'It's easy for you,' she said tartly. 'You
have the choice of your black shirt, or your other black
shirt.'

Gervase smiled. 'I suspect that the party will be rather
awash with black shirts and white collars, a veritable sea of
them. I shall be lost in the crowd.'

'Like penguins,' said Rosemary.

Daisy seemed to find this image hilarious, and dissolved
into giggles.

★

Valerie had been very ill. Feverish sweats alternated with shivery chills, and she'd scarcely left her bed in two days. She didn't know how she would have managed without Mrs Rashe, who had been utterly splendid; she had insisted, over-ruling Valerie's weak protests, on coming in each day and looking after her. She'd prepared nourishing broths and cups of strong tea and had sat by the bed to make sure they were consumed. She'd bathed Valerie's face with cold compresses when the fever was upon her, and piled blankets on the bed when she shivered.

Valerie knew that from time to time over the past two days she had been delirious with fever; she had a vague recollection of tortured dreams of Hal, in the arms of that Witch, lost to her for ever. She hoped that it had all happened in her head and not come out as a vocal delirium. Mrs Rashe hadn't said anything about it, but that didn't mean she hadn't heard anything.

On Friday afternoon the fever had broken, and Valerie found suddenly that she was feeling much better. At Mrs Rashe's urging, and under her watchful eye, she'd eaten her first solid food, and had even managed a bath.

So by Saturday Valerie was feeling ready to get out of the house. She was aware that Mrs Rashe would take a very dim view of such things, but she'd been firm with her: the cleaning woman was not to come to Rose Cottage on Saturday. The weekends were Sybil Rashe's family time, and as Valerie was so very much better, she could manage on her own.

It seemed such a long time since she'd been to Saxwell. The car virtually headed there of its own volition, through the town and up the Bury Road.

Hal's car – the green one – was just pulling out of the drive.

Shaun woke on Saturday morning in a strange bed. Sleeping next to him was that girl from the typing pool – he couldn't even remember her name. Kirsty or Katy or Kerry or some such; it didn't really matter. She was not a very appealing sight, with lipstick smeared round her mouth; that mouth, which she'd scarcely closed while awake, gaped slackly open in sleep, and a gentle snore issued forth. And her bedsit, in the half-light that filtered through the flimsy window shade, was squalid. Clothes – and not just the ones they'd shed last night in their rapid progress towards the bed – were strewn about the room untidily; there was a lingering and unpleasant smell of stale cigarettes and cheap scent.

She'd thrown herself at him, of course. Or at least Shaun told himself that now. He couldn't possibly have fancied her. Yes, he allowed, she had decent legs, and nice tits, and wore the sort of clothes that showed both off to their best advantage.

But that inane giggle, and her incessant chatter – the girl hadn't a brain in her head. Not that he'd gone to bed with her for her brains, Shaun admitted to himself. But the rest hadn't been so special either. Full of sound and fury and signifying . . . nothing.

Not like Val. His Val, his beautiful Val. Brains and beauty and the most wonderful body in the world.

He had blown it with Val, Shaun admitted to himself. He should never have hit her. That was the trouble with his Irish temper; it was in his genes, beyond his control, and he couldn't help it. His mind flashed back, unbidden, to that long-forgotten terraced house in Luton, to the horrifying sight of his father smacking his mother across the face, to the sound of her crying for mercy.

But she had provoked him. Val had lied to him, and gone behind his back with some other man. He had the proof, and she lied; what else was he to do?

Perhaps he shouldn't have hit her.

She had thrown him out, told him never to come back.

But he could make her change her mind, make her see that she had asked for it. He would promise never to hit her again. She would forgive him.

He would have her back. He *would* have her back.

Margaret had sent Hal out to get the ingredients for the Pimm's cocktail: lemonade, oranges, lemons, apples, cucumbers, and, of course, bottles of the eponymous liquor. He went to the Tesco on the outskirts of Saxwell, where they were sure to have everything necessary, though fighting the Saturday morning crowds in the car park and the supermarket aisles was not his idea of fun.

He started in the produce aisle, loading his trolley with fruit and cucumbers, then went along to the drink section. As he hesitated, trying to calculate how many bottles of lemonade he'd be likely to need, and how many bottles of Pimm's, he became aware that someone was standing at the end of the aisle, staring at him. Turning, he looked into the wide blue eyes of Valerie Marler. She didn't appear well to him, but that was only an impression, something to do with the violet shadows under her eyes, almost like faint bruises. But perhaps he was imagining it; after all, he scarcely knew the woman.

'Hello, Hal,' she said, her voice hoarse with a head cold.

'Good morning, Miss Marler,' he replied, cautious yet polite.

There was a pause, which Hal rushed to fill. 'Lovely day, isn't it?'

'Yes.' She nodded.

'Quite a change from a few days ago.'

'Yes.'

It was a way of life, raised to an art form, for well-bred English people: when in doubt, talk about the weather. 'Though I suppose we needed the rain,' Hal went on. 'It had been dry for over a fortnight.'

Belatedly, she entered into the spirit of the conversation. 'The flowers needed it, certainly. And the lawns.'

'We don't want to get into another one of those drought situations like we've had the past few summers,' Hal said.

'Hose-pipe bans and all that – not very satisfactory.'

'Though of course Scotland has had quite a lot more rain this spring than we have. Funny how that works sometimes.'

'Last year I seem to remember that it was the other way round. We had plenty of rain in the spring, and Scotland had hardly any. But still they told us that there was a drought. I never understood that.'

Hal judged that the conversation had run its course, or at least had gone on long enough for him to escape from it gracefully. It was of course possible for him, as a well-bred Englishman, to stand in Tesco all day, discussing the weather, but he had better things to do. Margaret would be wondering where he'd got to. 'I hope you've been keeping well,' he said pleasantly, preparing his exit with one of those conversational gambits which don't expect or want a truthful answer.

She shrugged. 'A bit of a cold. Nothing serious. And you?'

'Fit as a fiddle,' he said in a hearty voice. 'Keeping busy.' That triggered another thought. 'That magazine shoot. You know, the reason why you got me in to decorate in the first place. *Hello!*, wasn't it? How did that go?'

'Oh, very well. I think it's meant to be in next week's issue, or perhaps the one after that.'

'I'll keep my eye out for it,' he said, adding jocularly, 'I might be able to use it as an advertisement for my own work.'

She smiled.

'Well, it's been nice seeing you, Miss Marler.' Hal piled a dozen bottles of Pimm's into his trolley. If he bought too much he could always bring it back, but it was time to make his escape. She showed no signs of moving; he was the one who would have to go. 'Take care of yourself.'

'And you,' she said, not attempting to follow him as he headed for the check-outs.

Standing in the queue, he reflected on the encounter. Once she'd seemed to have a bit of a thing for him, he knew, and had in fact pursued him. She'd even made a few phone calls to him at home, and on his mobile. He'd never told Margaret, and certainly not Rosie; it had been just a bit worrying, he now admitted to himself. Plenty of other women had made overtures to him, had let it be known that they were available, but none had ever taken it quite as far as she had. Perhaps that was all in the past now. She certainly seemed as if she'd calmed down, Hal thought with relief.

Valerie's calm was born of resolve. Seeing Hal like that, face to face, talking to him in a normal conversational way, had galvanised her. She would *not* give him up. She wouldn't waste her time mooning about and feeling sorry for herself because some other woman had succeeded where she had failed.

It wasn't over. She would fight for Hal. To the death, if necessary.

Hazel Croom had just had a most enjoyable lunch with her new friend Phyllis Endersby. The weather was so lovely that they'd been able to sit outside in Phyllis's garden, well out of the way of the objectionable Queenie; the cat was far too lazy and complacent to venture out of doors, even in pursuit of titbits from the table.

Their friendship had progressed apace, with several long phone conversations since their first coffee together during half-term week, and Phyllis had insisted that Hazel come to lunch on Saturday.

They explored and re-explored their favourite topic of Father Gervase, neither of them tiring of the subject even when repetition set in. Father Gervase's virtues, and his wife's shortcomings, were endlessly fascinating to both Hazel and Phyllis. It was a most satisfactory friendship, Hazel felt.

Still, though, Hazel hugged to herself the secret knowledge of Rosemary and her familiar behaviour with the decorator; she was loath to share it with Phyllis, not out of any sort of consideration for Rosemary, but because she felt that in sharing it she would relinquish some sort of ownership of the secret.

Neither did she tell Phyllis that on leaving she planned to call in at the Vicarage. It was Saturday, and Father Gervase's day off. She'd been disappointed the last time; this time perhaps he would be at home.

Gervase was at home, but only just. He answered the door himself, as Rosemary was still getting dressed for the garden party; she'd been running a bit behind, trying to get Daisy ready as well. They ought to be leaving soon, he knew, though perhaps it wouldn't matter if they arrived a few minutes late.

'Hello, Hazel,' he said with courtesy, hiding his surprise. 'How nice to see you.'

She clutched her handbag – the new one – more tightly. 'I hope it's not a bad time to call.'

'Well . . .' He hesitated. 'We're going out soon. But do come in. I'm sure there's time for a cup of tea.'

'I happened to be in the neighbourhood, and thought I'd call in,' she explained, following him to the kitchen. 'I shan't keep you.'

Gervase put the kettle on as Rosemary came in. 'Look who's here,' he said brightly. 'Isn't this a nice surprise?'

Everything was in readiness for the party. The tables were set up, the caterers were in the kitchen putting the finishing touches on the food, and the fruit for the Pimm's had been cut up while the lemonade chilled in the fridge. Expecting the inevitable early arrivals at any time, Margaret and Hal went upstairs to get dressed.

Margaret felt that it was important to wear her clericals, as a sign of her authority, but as a concession to fashion she had decided to mitigate the severity of the unrelieved black with a silk jacket. The loosely cut jacket bore an abstract print in shades of soft dove-grey and pale blue, complementing her colouring. She put it on and studied the effect in the mirror.

'It looks marvellous,' Hal assured her as he knotted his tie. 'Just right. Not too frivolous, and not too austere.'

Margaret turned and regarded him approvingly. 'You look rather smashing yourself.' He was wearing his natural-coloured linen suit; it showed up his tan to perfection, and emphasised his trim figure. She had always quite fancied him in that suit. 'All you need is a Panama hat.'

He tipped an imaginary hat to her, grinning. 'At your service, Madame Archdeacon. Your Venerableness. Or should it be Your Venerability?'

'Get stuffed,' Margaret said affectionately.

Kim Rashe and Kev Juby had gone to bed, in the caravan they shared, on Saturday afternoon. It was something they did most afternoons, not just Saturdays: an enjoyable way to pass the time till they could go down to the pub a bit later. The George and Dragon in Branlingham was their local; it wasn't one of those pubs that stayed open all afternoon. The Swan at Elmsford, which did, was avoided on principle: that was where Kim's dad and his dart-playing mates congregated. Kim and Kev liked a bit of life, and the George and Dragon attracted a younger sort of crowd.

Now Kev was snoring, as he usually did at such times, and

Kim was propped up beside him smoking the cliché post-coital cigarette, an ashtray on her knee.

Somewhere on the floor next to the bed, the mobile phone chirped; Kim could guess who it was. She scrabbled among the discarded clothes and located it. 'Hello, Mum,' she answered in a bored voice. 'What do you want?'

'Well, I must say,' Sybil Rashe huffed. 'That's a fine way to greet your mother.'

Kim rolled her eyes, though there was no one to appreciate the gesture. 'Well, what *do* you want?'

'A bit of common courtesy wouldn't come amiss. But I suppose that's asking too much.' Having had her say on the subject of politeness, and realising that an apology would not be forthcoming, Sybil went on. 'Something's come in the post for you, came here by mistake. I wondered if you'd like me to bring it over a bit later, when I'm out. I was just asking instead of dropping by,' she added sharply, 'since you seem to think that your own mum needs an engraved invitation to come by and see you. Just like Buckingham Palace, I reckon.'

'Ha bloody ha,' muttered Kim, drawing on her cigarette and blowing the smoke out through her mouth. When no one was looking, she liked to practise blowing smoke rings. So far she hadn't had much success.

'Well?'

'Well, what?'

'Shall I come by, then?'

Kim shook her head. 'No, Mum. Not today. Kev and I are coming to you for Sunday lunch tomorrow, remember? I'll collect it then.'

As she pushed the button to disconnect the call, and dropped the phone on the bed, Kev stirred. 'Who was that, then?'

'Mum, of course. She wanted to come round.'

'Stupid nosy old cow,' he grumbled, turning over. 'I hope you told her to sod off.'

Kim gave him a sharp clout between the shoulder blades. 'Hey, that's my mum you're talking about.'

He ignored the blow. 'You *did* tell her not to come, didn't you?'

'Course I did.'

'All we need is to have her snooping round the place,' he said belligerently.

'She *would* get a surprise, wouldn't she?' Kim smiled to herself at the thought of her mother's amazement if she somehow managed to gain entrance to the caravan. It would almost be worth getting caught, just to see the look on her mum's face.

Those who arrived at The Archdeaconry before or just at the time specified on the invitation were inevitably the hard-core clerical bores, those who had hoped to beat the others there and have a private word with the Archdeacon before she was nobbled by anyone else. Several of these pitched up simultaneously, and Margaret found herself surrounded straightaway by several men in dog collars with various axes to grind.

Hal felt very much on the outside amongst this crowd. A female archdeacon's husband wasn't of any more concern to the clerical bores than a male archdeacon's wife would have been; it was the Archdeacon herself they were there to see and be seen by. So Hal circulated about with a smile and a jug of Pimm's, as an interested yet detached observer of the rituals.

Many of the clergy, he noted, were marked out by their garb. Others seemed determined to treat it as a social occasion and were dressed accordingly in suits and ties, but were equally marked out by the fact that their 'off-duty' wardrobes were often a remnant of a long-ago life: ties and trousers of the wrong width were a dead give-away.

And clergy wives were no longer the homogeneous, identifiable breed they'd once been, Hal observed. Not like his
mother, who had been a typical clergy wife of her time, and
had never even dreamed of holding down a job. Many of
these women clearly had careers of their own, with incomes
to match, and were dressed far more smartly than the stereo-
type of the clergy wife would allow.

He noted, as well, an interesting new phenomenon. The
handful of female priests of the Archdeaconry blended seam-
lessly into the crowd, generally indistinguishable from the
clergy wives, save for the discreet dog collars they wore with
their pastel blouses. But their husbands were not at all integrated with anyone else; they congregated in a small knot to
one side of the garden, a breed apart.

Hal had been watching for Rosemary; the party was well
under way when she and Gervase arrived. He restrained himself from going straight to them, but after a few minutes he
appeared at Gervase's side with his jug of Pimm's. 'Good
afternoon,' he said. 'Can I offer you a refill?'

Gervase shook his head. 'No, thanks. I'm driving, so I'll
have to make this one last.'

'I'd like some more.' Rosemary had already drained her
glass; she held it out towards Hal, looking into his eyes then
glancing quickly away.

Dutch courage, Hal said to himself. Steady on, Rosie. She
seemed lovely to him, in the rose silk dress, lovely, and vulnerable. He wished there were something he could do. But
his duties as a host, as well as his common sense, dictated
that he spend only a token amount of time with the Finches
before moving on.

Margaret, who had perfected the art of talking to one
person and seeming attentive to their every word, while at the
same time remaining aware of other people and other conversations, witnessed this encounter. Even at a distance she

could tell that Rosemary seemed nervous, ill at ease. Of course, they'd been in the area less than two months and she wouldn't know many of the people present. And at their first and only meeting at Gervase's induction, Margaret had realised that Rosemary was shy by nature: such gatherings would always be an ordeal for her. As soon as possible she would go to her; for some reason Rosemary aroused her protective instincts.

But the curate who was so earnestly and at such great length detailing the problems he was having with his vicar was not easily shaken off. Margaret was tempted to tell him that she'd already heard the vicar's side of the story; he had been one of the early arrivals. Instead she listened, nodded, and watched Rosemary Finch.

Margaret soon observed that Rosemary's eyes seemed to be following Hal as he progressed round the garden performing his duties as a host. That in itself wasn't really surprising, as Hal was one of the few people there that Rosemary knew. But given Hal's history for attracting the attention of women, it crossed Margaret's mind that there might be more to it than that. Was it possible that Rosemary Finch had a soft spot for Hal?

If so, she certainly wouldn't be the first, but Margaret hoped that it wasn't true, for Rosemary's sake. Hal she wasn't worried about. He could take care of himself, as he had so amply demonstrated on many occasions over the past few years. After all, if he could extricate himself from the predatory clutches of glamorous females like Valerie Marler, side-stepping the unwelcome attentions of a shy and rather plain vicar's wife ought to be child's play.

After a few minutes Margaret disengaged herself gracefully from the whingeing curate and made her way to where Gervase and Rosemary stood. 'How nice that you could both make it,' she said.

'I'm sorry we're late,' Gervase began, feeling that some explanation was necessary. 'We were just about to leave when someone came to the door – a former parishioner. We couldn't very well just go off and leave her. You know how it is,' he appealed to the Archdeacon.

'Oh, yes.' She turned to Rosemary . 'I imagine *you* know how it is, as well.'

Rosemary flushed. 'Giving cups of tea to people whom one would rather not let past the front door is something I'm used to.' Her words came out sounding, even to her own ears, far more bitter than she'd intended.

Margaret saw that she'd struck a raw nerve, and grabbed Hal's arm as he skirted round them *en route* to the curate's empty glass. 'I hope that doesn't include my husband,' she said lightly. 'I trust he hasn't been too much of a nuisance. I find, myself, that he's rather well trained – he tends not to get under foot, and is quite good at cleaning up after himself.' She tucked her arm through his and smiled at him, counting on him to say the right thing.

'I hope that I haven't given Mrs Finch any cause for complaint,' Hal said with a grin. 'No dirty paint brushes left in the kitchen sink.'

'Oh, Hal has been splendid,' Gervase stated earnestly.

Hal winked at him. 'I have the Archdeacon to answer to, don't I? My wife would have my guts for garters if I didn't give satisfaction.'

Mrs Finch, Rosemary thought. Not Rosie, not even Rosemary. Mrs Finch. Again she held her glass out to Hal for a refill, and drank deeply of the sweet concoction. She let the other three talk, making no effort to join in the conversation. It was all so . . . dreadful, seeing Margaret with her arm tucked familiarly through Hal's. She'd never seen them together before, had never even been able to imagine them together, as a couple: the brisk, efficient Archdeacon and Hal.

Her Hal. No, *not* her Hal, Rosemary reminded herself with painful honesty – Margaret's Hal. They were very much a couple, she now realised: in an odd way, much more of a couple than she and Gervase had ever been. Established, at ease together, sharing a common language and a common life. Mr and Mrs Phillips.

It was hot, so hot. The mid-afternoon sun beat down relentlessly on the garden of The Archdeaconry. Her head hurt; she'd had too much to drink. She was surrounded by a babble of voices, but the only one she could hear was Hal's. She couldn't bear to look at him, though she thought he was saying something to her. Mrs Finch again. The glass slipped from her hand and shattered on the flagstones as Rosemary fainted.

Chapter 18

Valerie woke on Monday morning with a sense that this was going to be an important day. She'd shaken off the lethargy, the apathy, which seemed to have crept up on her of late. She couldn't blame her illness; she now realised that the passivity had begun long before that. Now she'd had enough of negative energy. From now on, and starting today, she was going to seize what she wanted from life.

As a matter of fact she had started yesterday. She had returned to Saxwell, had watched from the phone box as Hal and Margaret left The Archdeaconry, and had once again gained entrance to the house through the open window at the back. This time she had been quick about it, not lingering to examine anything. She'd gone straight to their bedroom and taken another pair of boxer shorts from Hal's chest of drawers. And she'd taken one other thing as well – something she'd seen on her first visit – which she hoped wouldn't be missed.

Today, though, was the real start. First she had an old score to settle. She picked up the phone and rang Warren, her editor at Robin's Egg. It had been weeks since they'd spoken; she hadn't been taking his calls or returning his messages.

But she wouldn't allow herself to be side-tracked down that road.

Valerie and Warren had a history, of course; they'd been lovers briefly, for a few weeks only, over two years ago, shortly after he'd become her editor. She'd found him a disappointment in bed and moved on to someone else, but he'd had no hard feelings; they'd remained friends and congenial colleagues.

'Warren,' she said briskly.

'Valerie! For God's sake, where have you been?'

'I don't have time to talk about that. I have a request, Warren.'

Everyone at Robin's Egg, conscious of the amount of money her sales had brought in over the past few years, knew that Valerie Marler's requests were not to be treated as optional. Warren sighed. 'What is it, then?'

She was blunt. 'I want Shaun sacked,' she said.

'Sacked?' he echoed, surprised. 'Jesus, Valerie, what do you mean?'

'Surely you are familiar with the word.' Her voice dripped acid. 'Made redundant, given the push. I want him out. Today.'

Warren hadn't been particularly happy with Shaun's performance of late, and had in fact been looking for an excuse to get rid of him. Doing as Valerie asked, and letting her think that the decision was hers, would be a graceful way out of his dilemma. In any case, he knew better than to argue, or to ask for her reasons. One way or another, if Valerie Marler wanted Shaun's head on a silver platter, she'd damn well get it. 'You're the boss,' he conceded wearily. 'But, Jesus, I hope you know what you're doing.'

'I do.'

'And what about—' Before he could ask about her manuscript, she put the phone down, cutting him off in mid-sentence.

Smiling, Valerie set about the next order of business. This one wasn't as much fun, but was equally necessary. She rang a florist in Saxwell and ordered an extravagant bouquet to be sent to Sybil Rashe, Grange Cottage, Elmsford. The message: 'Thank you so much for everything. I am much better. See you on Wednesday.' Valerie didn't want Mrs Rashe poking her nose into Rose Cottage at odd times; she needed to be free to move about without fear of observation.

Obtaining a camera was next on her mental list. She had an ordinary sort of camera, but Mrs Rashe, with her instant snaps of Frank's birthday, had given her a better idea. One of those instant cameras would provide more flexibility, more freedom; she wouldn't have to worry about having photos developed, under the perhaps nosy eye of some film technician. That way she could take photos of whatever she liked. Whomever she liked. If she could get one with a zoom lens, so much the better.

It meant another trip to Saxwell. There was a specialist camera shop there, but on reflection she decided to be cautious and opted to go instead to the photographic department of Boots; if anything *did* happen, she would be less likely to be remembered at a busy chain store like Boots. In fact, just to be on the safe side, she would go to Bury instead of Saxwell. The farther from home the better; she couldn't be too careful.

Margaret was thoughtful on Monday morning. The incident with Rosemary Finch had disturbed her deeply and she'd thought of little else. Though her fainting could be explained away as a natural outcome of too much sun and too much Pimm's, it was clear to Margaret, that on a deeper level, the episode taken as a whole was a cry for help.

Rosemary needed help, whether she was conscious of it or not. Margaret, with her own experiences to inform her reading of the situation, knew intuitively that Rosemary was feeling isolated and lonely. Her husband was immersed in his job and had little time for her; she was shy and found it difficult to make friends, as well as being tied down by a handicapped child.

And, Margaret realised with some guilt, she partially had herself to blame. She had been the one who had told Gervase that there would be other concerts. How could she have been so insensitive, so oblivious to Rosemary's feelings on that occasion? This failure in empathy shocked her; no matter what her other failings might be as a human being or as a priest, Margaret prided herself on her empathetic nature. And that thoughtless, callous comment from her might have long-lasting repercussions in Gervase Finch's treatment of his wife; he might feel that he'd been given official permission to neglect her as a matter of policy.

Perhaps it wasn't too late to do something, she decided. It wasn't really her business to interfere, but could she really sit back and take no action, when she was so much to blame? Could she live with that on her conscience?

Margaret picked up the phone in her study and rang Gervase Finch. Could he please come to see her that afternoon? He could, and would.

Mummy, can I wear my best dress?' Daisy requested.

'Yes, of course, darling.' Rosemary was abstracted as she went to the wardrobe and found the pink-and-white candy-striped dress.

Daisy put her arms up and her mother settled the dress over her head, then did up the buttons. 'Pink hair ribbons, too?' the girl asked.

'Let me plait your hair, then.' Rosemary sat on the end of Daisy's bed and took the girl on her lap. Daisy was all arms and legs in the manner of seven-year-old girls, growing so fast; ordinarily Rosemary would have been conscious of that,

and of the sweet weight in her arms. But her mind was elsewhere. She brushed her daughter's hair till it shone, parted it
down the centre, then divided one side into three sections
and began plaiting it. The task was soothing and repetitive,
requiring no thought. Her fingers were deft and practised:
right over centre, left over centre. Daisy chattered on, but
Rosemary wasn't listening.

There was a hollow feeling in the pit of her stomach; her
head hurt. Rosemary knew what she had to do.

Gervase's appointment with the Archdeacon was set for two
o'clock, so he headed to Saxwell just after lunch. Inevitably he
was a bit nervous at the Archdeacon's summons; he had no
idea what it was all about, and wasn't even prepared to hazard
a guess.

She met him at the door and ushered him into her study,
indicating one of the two easy chairs rather than the straight-
backed chair in front of the desk. 'Please, sit down.' He sat. 'Is
it all right if I call you Gervase, Father?' she asked courte-
ously.

'Yes, of course, Archdeacon.'

Rather than go behind her desk, she took the other easy
chair to signify the informal nature of the discussion, shifting
it round to face him. 'You may call me Margaret, if you like.'

He knew that he wouldn't dare.

'I suppose you're wondering what this is about,' she began,
feeling as nervous as he looked.

Gervase nodded. 'The thought had crossed my mind.'

'You may think that I'm speaking out of turn,' she said,
'and you must feel free to tell me to mind my own business.
But I assure you that what I'm going to say is out of concern
for you, as the one who has the responsibility for overseeing
your spiritual as well as your material well-being.'

It was sounding more ominous all the time; Gervase

noticed a small frayed spot on the cuff of his black shirt and touched it with his finger.

'Gervase, do you love your wife?' Margaret said abruptly.

He wasn't sure what he'd been expecting, but it wasn't this. Astonished, he stared at her. 'Love my wife? Of course I love Rosemary. With all my heart.'

'Have you told her so, lately?'

Gervase pressed his lips together. 'I suppose I have . . . I don't know. I don't need to tell her. Rosemary knows that I love her.'

Does she? thought Margaret. Presumably so, though not necessarily. That was one thing that she could say for Hal. Even during those years when he'd neglected her, working day and night, when she'd scarcely seen him from one day to the next, he had always told her – told her every day – that he loved her. It was tenuous, not really a substitute for his attention, but at least it was something to cling to during the rocky times they'd been through. She believed him; she wanted and needed to believe him, but if he hadn't said it so often their marriage might not have survived. All of this went through her mind in an instant, and she said, 'I'm sure she does know. But women do like to be told once in a while.'

He shrugged, seeming more baffled than resentful.

Margaret knew that she needed to tread carefully or the resentment would follow on. She smiled, to put him at his ease. 'I'm speaking as a woman here, not as your boss.' Leaning forward in her chair, she went on, 'There's something even more important than telling a woman that you love her – after all, to coin a cliché, words are cheap. You've got to show her as well.'

'I don't understand.'

She moistened her lips. 'Let me tell you something. I don't know how much you're aware of my history. I don't talk about it very often, but given the nature of this conversation,

I think you deserve to know.' Unconsciously she twisted her wedding ring as she maintained eye contact with Gervase. 'I've been on the other side of the fence, myself. For years Hal was all wrapped up in his work, in running his own company. He didn't have time for his family. I was . . . well, I was unhappy. Very unhappy,' she amended. 'It all seems a long time ago now. But I can't forget how destructive it was. For me, for our marriage.'

The import of her words seemed to sink in slowly. 'Are you saying that you think I neglect Rosemary?'

'Not neglect,' she assured him. 'Nothing as strong as that. But it's a question of priorities. Hal's business was his priority, not his marriage or his family. I've experienced for myself how destructive that sort of choice can be.' Seeing that he was about to speak, she held her hand up. 'I know what you're going to say. You're going to say that the priesthood is a call-ing, a vocation, and not just a job. You're going to say that it's God-given, not the same at all as Hal's situation.'

'Yes.' He nodded. 'That's exactly right.'

She spoke deliberately to emphasise her words. 'Yes, Gervase, I believe that your priesthood is God-given. I'm not questioning that, and from what I've seen and heard, you're a very fine priest. But God has given you your family as well. Rosemary, and Daisy. They're a gift, something very special. And along with that gift comes a responsibility towards them, to love them and cherish them. To look after them, and spend time with them. Even if it means, sometimes, neglecting other things. Important things, or things that seem impor-tant at the time.'

Now he really looked puzzled. 'But, Archdeacon, you said—'

Margaret had the grace to blush. 'Yes, I know. "There will be other concerts" is what I said to you. That was the Archdeacon speaking, and I regret it. I was wrong to tell you that. I should have said "There will be other meetings", and told you to enjoy the concert with your wife.'

'But I still don't understand,' Gervase appealed to her. 'Why are you telling me this? Has Rosemary said something to you?'

She answered the second question first, her voice gentle. 'Rosemary didn't have to say anything to me. I've been there myself – I understand how she feels. And I'm telling you this because I care about both of you, and about Daisy – because I don't want you to wake up one day and find that it's too late. Like it very nearly was, once, for Hal and me.'

Hal finished painting the stairs and landing early in the afternoon. He took his roller and tray through to the kitchen and washed them carefully in the sink, then disassembled the scaffolding, folded up his drop cloths, and took everything out to his van. Only then did he go looking for Rosemary; he found her in the drawing room, curled up on the shabby sofa with a book open on her lap. She looked up from it so quickly that he suspected she hadn't really been reading it.

'Rosie?'

'Yes, Hal.'

'I think we need to talk.'

'Yes.' She dropped the book and got up, feeling stifled by the elegant but dark splendour of the room. 'But not here. Let's go outside. I need some air.'

He followed her out of the Vicarage. Neither of them said anything, but by unspoken consent they walked towards the church and into the churchyard. The tree under which they had sat for their picnic was now in full leaf, and to that tree they went. It seemed fitting that they should return to where things had begun, what felt to both of them like almost a lifetime ago. Rosemary sat in the grass and wrapped her arms round her knees, while Hal leaned against the tree trunk.

The countryside was by no means silent: insects buzzed, chirped and whirred; birds warbled their distinctive songs, and out of sight but not out of hearing was the road to Saxwell, with its distant rumble of traffic. But those noises were a background to the profound silence that enveloped Rosemary and Hal.

Without turning her head, she surveyed the gently rolling folds of west Suffolk, hedgerows bisecting the golden fields under a cloudless East Anglian sky so blue that it hurt her eyes: a beauty too intense to take in, too intense to last. Spattered amongst the hedgerows like drops of fresh blood were small clumps of poppies, the flowers of death and remembrance. And in the churchyard they were surrounded by innumerable reminders of impermanence, the leaning headstones and towering monuments to people forgotten many years since. Rosemary meditated on the dead beneath her, imagining the bones of the long dead mingling with the dust of those even longer gone, and she drew strength from the notion that all of these people had once lived and loved, had once walked the earth and believed their own lives and concerns to be of paramount importance. Time had proven them wrong; time had reduced them all to bones and dust.

Still she didn't speak. It was Hal who finally broke the silence.

His voice was quiet, almost a sigh. 'It's not going to work, is it, Rosie?'

'No.'

He didn't move, didn't turn his head to look at her. 'I'm sorry.'

Rosemary gulped. She *would* not cry. She would *not*. She closed her eyes to stop the sting of tears, then said what she needed to say. 'I can't marry you, Hal. It was crazy even to consider it. You and Margaret – you belong together. I didn't realise, until Saturday . . .'

'Yes.'

'It sounds like such a cliché,' she went on reflectively. 'But the truth is that we could never be happy at the expense of others. Margaret, Gervase. Daisy. It's just not possible, no matter how much we might wish otherwise.'

'No.'

'And an affair.' Her voice was still soft, but there was nothing uncertain about it. 'That wouldn't work, either. We both know it's wrong. But apart from that, we'd never get away with it. I'm not a good liar, and I can't hide my feelings.'

Hal smiled. 'You're a bloody useless dissembler,' he agreed, the tone of his voice taking the sting from the words. 'On Saturday you might just as well have hung a sign round your neck.'

'Oh, Hal.' She laughed in spite of herself. 'I'm so sorry. It was awful, wasn't it?'

'I felt so helpless,' he confessed. 'There was nothing I could do to stop you self-destructing.'

Rosemary pleated her skirt between her fingers and didn't look at him as she asked the next question. 'What about Margaret? Did she say anything afterwards?'

'No. I think she accepted the explanation of the heat and all that.'

She sighed. 'Well, that's something to be thankful for, at least. And of course Gervase was terribly fussed, but it would never have occurred to him that there was anything else in it.'

Hal plucked a blade of grass and shredded it. 'So.'

'So.' After all, it was left for her to say it. 'So that leaves us with the third option.'

'Yes.' He became briskly practical, in what would have seemed to an eavesdropper an inexplicable change of subject, but which Rosemary comprehended perfectly. 'I've finished the hall, landing, and stairs. So that's all right.'

'What will you tell Margaret? Or I suppose I should say the Archdeacon?'

'I'll think of something.' Hal tried out a few possibilities. 'Perhaps that you've tired of having your house torn up and want to give it a rest for a bit. Or that Daisy is allergic to the smell of paint. Or even that some other important job has come along that I have to give priority to. I'll make sure that she sends someone else in to finish up the rest of the house, if you want me to.'

'Perhaps that would be the best.'

But they were not quite ready to let go. Paradoxically, now that the decision had been made and agreed upon, and the words had been said, it seemed safe – even necessary – that they should touch as they had not previously allowed themselves to do, perhaps to confirm each other's corporeal existence even as they renounced it. Rosemary stroked the hair at his temple, feeling the texture of it, then traced the line of his jaw with her finger. Hal captured her hand and examined it minutely as though he'd never seen it before, looking first at the back of her hand with its short nails and reddened knuckles, then turning it over and studying the palm like a map, following the creases with his finger. Finally he lifted it to his lips and kissed the palm; her fingers curled involuntarily and she reclaimed her hand.

He stood and reached down to help her to her feet, then cupped her face between his hands and kissed first her forehead then her mouth, a long yet chaste kiss, charged not with desire this time but with regret.

'If only things had been different,' he said, not caring that it was a cliché.

Rosemary closed her eyes. 'If things had been different, none of this might have happened,' she countered. 'You might not have loved me. I might not have loved you.'

'I don't believe that, Rosie. And neither do you.'

She couldn't lie to him, not even at the end. 'No.'

There was truly nothing more to be said. They walked back towards the Vicarage in silence, as they had come. Hal stopped by his van and watched as Rosemary went on to the front door. She didn't look back.

After they'd gone, Valerie remained in the copse of trees, motionless and breathing shallowly. They had not known she was there; they hadn't been aware of anything but each other. And the noises of insect and bird had effectively camouflaged the click and whirr of the camera.

Eventually her breathing returned to normal and she relaxed her tensed muscles. The photos, clutched in her hand, were developing slowly. Valerie crouched down and spread them on the ground, watching in fascination as the images emerged on the glossy squares of card. Three photos. Three pieces of unmistakable, incontrovertible evidence.

The first showed the Witch touching Hal's face; in the second he was bent over her hand. And the third: the third was the most damning of all.

A quarter of an hour later, Valerie was back home at Rose Cottage. She went through to her study and took an envelope from the rack on her desk. In careful block capitals she addressed it, with the form of address she had gleaned from *Crockford's Clerical Directory*: The Ven. Margaret Phillips, The Archdeaconry, Saxwell, Suffolk. Into the envelope went all three photos, and with solemn ceremony she stuck down the flap and affixed a first-class stamp. She could easily catch the last village post collection; by morning the Magpie would be looking at the photos.

Rosemary made herself a cup of tea and took it into the drawing room, shutting the door behind her, though she knew herself to be alone in the house. The book that she'd dropped was still on the floor; she picked it up and placed it carefully on the table. Sunlight streamed through the stained glass panels of the south-facing window, dappling the shabby sofa with colours of a richness it had never possessed, even in its long-ago unshabby youth. Rosemary drew the curtains, then put her birthday CD into the player and turned the volume up a notch. She took one sip of her tea, finding it unexpectedly bitter; abandoning it, she stretched out on the sofa and gave herself up, for what she told herself was the last time, to tears.

Shaun had been told he could take his time in cleaning out his desk, but there was no point in waiting. He scrounged a cardboard box from the store room, then filled it with his meagre effects; Shaun had always believed in travelling light through life, taking what presented itself to him as it came along.

Warren was relieved that Shaun seemed to be taking his dismissal in good part. 'Plenty of other jobs out there, mate,' he'd said cheerfully, and the generous settlement should keep him going till he found one. But Warren didn't know Shaun very well.

No one at Robin's Egg did, in fact – not even the girls in the typing pool. He always kept his private life private; he would not be particularly missed. But everyone felt a bit sorry for him as he filled the box that had once held photocopier paper with the things from his desk. It had all been so sudden.

Shaun kept a smile on his face as he prepared to leave Robin's Egg for the last time. Damn them all to hell, he thought.

In the top drawer of his desk he found the key to Rose Cottage, put there for safekeeping several weeks before. He polished it on his sleeve, held it up and regarded it with an enigmatic smile, then dropped it in his pocket.

*

The mothers gathered outside the gates of Branlingham Primary School just before the end of school at half past three. It was a daily ritual, unchanging; they'd all got to know each other, at least by sight, and various friendships had been forged in these surroundings.

Annie Sawbridge often talked to Rosemary Finch while they waited for their daughters to emerge. She was vaguely aware, that afternoon, that Rosemary had not yet arrived. But her mind was on other things: she was hoping that Samantha would be on time, and not dawdling behind, as she needed to take her into Saxwell for a four o'clock appointment at the dentist's. It had taken months to get this appointment; if they missed it, they would be facing an even longer wait.

Samantha, unaware of her mother's agenda, was indeed dawdling behind, along with Daisy and Charlotte. Annie checked her watch as the girls came towards her. If they left straightaway, and the traffic wasn't too bad, and she was able to find a space in the car park, they might just about make it. 'Hurry up, Samantha,' she said, more sharply than was her wont.

'Where is Mummy?' Daisy asked, looking about.

'Oh.' Annie scanned the few remaining mothers. 'She's not here.' She checked her watch again, weighing up her options. Could she really go off and leave Daisy on her own? Their teacher, Mrs Denton, was there watching out for her charges; Daisy would be fine. 'She's probably just been delayed for a few minutes. I'm sure she'll be along in a wee while, Daisy.'

'Mummy will be here soon,' affirmed Daisy with confidence.

But it was Charlotte's mother who arrived as the Sawbridges were leaving. 'I have to get Samantha to the dentist,' Annie explained, taking Samantha's hand. 'And if we're late . . .'

Charlotte's mother turned and fell into step beside her. 'Isn't it a bore?'

The two women chatted about the vagaries of dental appointments. Behind them through the gates trailed Charlotte and Daisy.

Charlotte could see that her mother was involved in conversation with Samantha's mother, and took the opportunity for another cheap shot at Daisy. 'Your mummy probably isn't coming, ever,' she whispered venomously before skipping ahead. 'She probably doesn't want you any more.'

Tears welled in Daisy's eyes; she gulped. What if Charlotte was right? What if Mummy never came? What if Mummy didn't want her? She stopped and watched as the others walked off, leaving her behind; she was trying hard not to be a cry-baby, not to make Mummy ashamed of her when she did come. *If* she did come.

Then, through her tears, she saw a woman watching her from a few feet away. A pretty lady, with pretty yellow hair like Samantha's. The woman came up to her and crouched down to her level. 'Hello,' said the woman.

Daisy wasn't alarmed; the yellow-haired lady looked nice. 'Mummy hasn't come,' she said.

'Your mummy asked me to come and collect you,' the woman explained. 'I'm going to take you to your mummy.'

That was all right, then. Mummy *did* still want her. Daisy put her hand up trustingly and the woman took it.

Chapter 19

The compact disc came to the end of its programme and faded into silence. Rosemary remained on the sofa for a moment, staring thoughtfully into nothingness, then shook herself, blotted her tears with a damp tissue, and got up. After wiping her smeary spectacles on her skirt, she looked at her watch.

'Oh, no,' she said aloud. 'Oh, no.'

It was well after half past three. Daisy's school had let out almost a quarter of an hour ago, and Rosemary was late.

She had never been late before; if anything, she was usually early, to make sure that she was there when Daisy arrived at the gates.

It would be all right, she told herself as she hurried through Branlingham, almost at a run. Other children would still be there. Mrs Denton would look after her. It would be all right.

Rosemary strained her eyes for a small figure in pink-and-white stripes as she neared the school gates. But there was no Daisy, and no one else either; the place was quite deserted. Her heart lurched and began thudding uncontrollably.

'Daisy!' Rosemary called, going through the gates.

*

It had all been so easy, Valerie exulted as she drove back towards Elmsford. She hadn't intended to take the little girl, whom she now knew to be called Daisy. She had merely thought she would conceal herself near the school gates and watch as the Witch arrived to collect her daughter.

But the Witch hadn't come, and the opportunity was just too good to pass up. The little girl, on her own, waiting for her mother . . .

The Witch didn't deserve to have a child, Valerie told herself censoriously. It didn't take much imagination to know what she was doing when she should have been collecting her little girl. Alone in the Vicarage with Hal . . .

And the girl had come with her quite happily. She'd allowed Valerie to belt her into the back seat, and chattered to her as they travelled the short distance to Elmsford, via the back roads, though it had taken Valerie a while to become accustomed to the little girl's speech.

Back at Rose Cottage, Valerie drove the car into the garage and unfastened Daisy's seat belt. 'Come on in, then,' she said, anxious to get her into the house without anyone seeing. Rose Cottage wasn't overlooked, but one never knew about nosy villagers passing by, hoping for a glimpse of Elmsford's celebrity resident.

Once again Daisy took her hand, and allowed herself to be taken into Rose Cottage. 'Where's Mummy?' she asked as soon as they were inside.

'She'll be here soon.'

'But I want Mummy!' Daisy cried. The unfamiliar house, no sign of her mother . . . Her small face crumpled in dismay and she began to howl. 'Mummy! Mummy!'

Surely Daisy must have gone back into the school; if no one was there to collect her, Mrs Denton would have taken her back in. Rosemary pressed her hands to her heart in a vain effort to still its frantic pounding as she ran through the deserted school yard, struggling with the unexpectedly heavy door. The corridors were as vacant as the school yard had been. She went straight to Daisy's classroom.

Mrs Denton was shovelling a pile of books into a canvas bag, preparing to go home herself. She looked up as Rosemary Finch burst into the room, gasping for breath, her cheeks blazing with colour.

'Daisy! Is Daisy here?'

'Why no, Mrs Finch.'

'Oh, God! Where could she be?'

'Calm down, Mrs Finch,' said the teacher in a soothing voice; she was, after all, used to dispensing comfort, and pouring balm on troubled waters. 'Here, why don't you sit down for a moment and tell me what the problem is?'

Rosemary wouldn't sit, but she tried to calm herself enough to explain. Quickly she told her the story of arriving late at the school gates to find no one there.

'I'm sure she's fine,' Mrs Denton said sensibly. 'I watched her leave with Samantha and Charlotte and their mothers. She's probably just gone home with Samantha.'

'Oh, yes!' Rosemary's face was transformed with relief. Of course, that was it. Annie would have taken Daisy home with them.

But Annie hadn't, she soon discovered. The Sawbridge house was empty: no car stood in the drive, and no one answered her frantic ringing of the bell.

Rosemary sat on the front step and wept tears of disappointment, frustration and fear. If Daisy wasn't here, where could she be? After a moment, though, she pulled herself together. Giving in to panic wasn't helping anything. She must keep a clear head, and apply logic to the situation.

Remembering, suddenly, Daisy's disappearance at Kinderland – the reason behind it, and the form it had taken –

she decided that a thorough search of the school would be the way to start. Daisy could have gone back into the school; she might be, probably was, hiding in a classroom, tucked into a corner somewhere.

Rosemary returned to Branlingham Primary. The caretaker was about to lock the school gates.

'You've got to let me in,' she explained urgently. 'My little girl must be in there somewhere.'

The caretaker, impatient as he was to lock up and get home, took pity on the distraught woman and accompanied her through the building, checking every room, every nook and cranny that could provide a hiding place for a small girl.

But Daisy was not to be found.

Late in the afternoon Shaun went home to his flat in Earl's Court. He dumped the box near the door and poured himself a Bushmills straightaway; the first one he knocked back, then sat down to savour a second.

Drink – especially when it was Irish whiskey – usually rendered Shaun maudlin, at least initially, and so it proved on this occasion. He felt mightily sorry for himself, cursing everyone at Robin's Egg and consigning them to eternal damnation for the part they had played, actively or passively, in his dismissal. He knew he hadn't been liked; they'd all had it in for him, because they were jealous of his talents and his successes. He, and he alone, had made Valerie Marler a superstar, a household name, and this was how he was repaid.

Later, though, the alcohol began to direct his mind down other channels, and an idea began to form.

Deciding against another drink, he went through to the bathroom, where he showered and shaved. He dressed in fresh clothes, but was careful to transfer the key to Rose Cottage to the pocket of his jacket.

*

Faced with Daisy's hysteria, Valerie's elation began to evaporate. She managed to calm the girl down, at least temporarily, by breaking out the packet of biscuits she kept on hand for Mrs Rashe.

Soon the girl would be wanting something more substantial to eat; she probably was accustomed to having her tea right after school. Valerie went through to the kitchen, trying to think what she might give her. What did little girls eat? Definitely not the same sorts of things that Valerie did, the light and dainty repasts with which she maintained her elfin figure. Sausages, beans, fish fingers, beefburgers, chips: none of these things were to be found at Rose Cottage. And she certainly couldn't pop down to the village shop to buy them without raising questions which she wouldn't be prepared to answer.

It was only now that she began to comprehend the enormity of what she'd done. She had taken the Witch's child – a fine revenge, and it was immensely pleasurable to contemplate what agonies the Witch must be suffering at this moment. But what was she to do with her now? She couldn't very well take the girl home and say that it had all been a big mistake. She was committed.

As Gervase drove home towards Branlingham he gave serious consideration to what the Archdeacon had said to him. Was it possible that she was right, that Rosemary might be feeling neglected and unloved? He determined to get to the bottom of it as soon as he got home. They could talk about it; he could assure her of his love with words and with actions, as the Archdeacon had suggested.

But as he pulled up in front of the Vicarage, the front door flew open and Rosemary ran out, flinging herself at him as he got out of the car. Her hair was coming loose from its plait and her face was red with crying. 'Oh, Gervase!' was all she could say.

'My dear! Whatever is the matter?'

'It's Daisy! She's missing.'

He guided her into the house and coaxed the story out of her. It was entirely her fault, Rosemary maintained: she'd been listening to music, had lost track of the time, and had been late. If only . . .

Gervase, whom many of his parishioners past and present knew to be splendid in times of crisis, steered her away from useless self-recrimination and guilt onto more practical matters. What efforts, he wanted to know, had been made to find Daisy?

She had explored the school thoroughly. She had visited the Sawbridges' house, she had rung Charlotte's mother and various other parents of Daisy's friends and schoolmates. Nothing had turned up a trace of Daisy or a clue to her whereabouts. No one had seen her, no one knew where she was.

'And I didn't know where *you* were,' she finished. 'Oh, I've been waiting for you to get home – I thought you'd never come.'

Gervase recalled, with some guilt himself, that he hadn't told her he was going to The Archdeaconry. She might have reached him there, if she'd known. 'Well, I'm here now,' he said. 'And I think it's time to ring the police.'

Sergeant Zoe Threadgold simmered with resentment as she sat in the passenger seat of the panda car, *en route* between Saxwell police headquarters and Branlingham. She allowed DI Pete Elliott to do all the talking; he'd already pulled rank on her and insisted on driving.

Zoe Threadgold hated being driven, and that factor added to her sense of umbrage. But the main source of her grievance at the moment was a central one to her life: she loathed being treated differently because she was a woman. And that accident of gender was the only reason that she was now on the way to Branlingham.

A little girl was missing. Whenever a child went missing, it was police policy to send a woman officer to stay with the family until the child turned up, alive or dead. A woman was meant to be a soothing and comforting presence, making cups of tea and reassuring noises.

Zoe didn't like making tea, and she certainly didn't like making reassuring noises. She was intelligent; she was ambitious. She knew the direction she wanted her career to take. Already she'd achieved the rank of sergeant, but she assuredly didn't intend to stop there, and above all she wanted to get out of uniform and into CID.

And that meant playing the game, following orders. Being the token woman, if necessary, much as she loathed it.

It also meant, as far as she was concerned, keeping her private life private. Ironically, her colleagues all assumed that she was a lesbian. It served her purposes to allow them to believe that, as it provided a useful cover for her affair with a married superior officer, DI Mike Odum. No one who knew Sgt Zoe Threadgold on the job would ever have imagined it.

She wore her frosted blond hair very short, and in uniform she was the picture of brusque efficiency, of don't-mess-with-me militant feminism. Her colleagues wouldn't have recognised her off duty, her hair spiked with hair gel and a diamond stud in her nose.

Mike Odum was off duty tonight, though he'd told his wife otherwise; he and Zoe had looked forward to the evening together. He would bring a bottle, she would provide the food. And together they would make their own entertainment.

But now there was this missing kid. And unless she turned up within the next few hours, the evening was off. It just wasn't fair that she should be stuck with this – and all because she was a woman. Zoe crossed her arms across her chest and fumed.

DI Pete Elliott, in full flow, was not aware that Zoe wasn't listening to him, nor of her bad mood. If he sensed it subconsciously, it made him talk all the more. Pete Elliott found Zoe Threadgold rather frightening, and words were the best way to deal with that: words in abundance, on any subject.

Now, though, the subject was the case upon which the two of them were embarked, as he filled her in on the situation. The local bobby had responded to a call from the missing girl's father, Elliott told her, and the case had rapidly been bumped up to CID. Ordinarily it might have taken a bit more time to reach that stage, but the circumstances were exceptional: the little girl was mentally handicapped, Down's syndrome, and only seven years old. All of the obvious first steps had been taken. The girl's friends had been contacted; the school – the last place she'd been seen – had been searched. Now would come the house-to-house enquiries in the village, to ascertain whether anyone had seen the child or anything significant, and the search of the surrounding countryside would begin. All of those things that they wouldn't tell the parents: the sniffer dogs in the undergrowth, the dragging of the river. Either the little girl was alive, and might be found safe at any time, or . . . she was not. Almost always it was the first of these possibilities, but you could never be sure. Time was of the essence, especially as evening drew in. 'We're assuming right now that she's just wandered off,' he said. 'No evidence of abduction, and the mother admits that she was late to collect her from school. But there's a large area to search, and even if she's perfectly okay, we may not find her before dark.'

In spite of herself, Zoe found herself listening to his summary of the case, and thinking that it might be an interesting one. But Zoe Threadgold would not be taking part in the investigation, nor in the search. She was there, she reminded herself bitterly, to baby-sit the parents. It just wasn't fair.

Shaun took his time driving to Elmsford; he didn't want to arrive too early. He stopped at a motorway service station for a cup of coffee, and as he got closer to Elmsford he decided to find a pub for a meal and a drink.

Branlingham was the village just before Elmsford, and Shaun took his chances on finding a decent pub there. The George and Dragon was easy enough to find, in the centre of the village; whether it was decent or not remained to be seen.

They had Guinness on draught; that was a promising sign. Shaun eased his way up to the bar and ordered a pint from a barman with flaming red hair. The barman pulled it expertly, allowing it to settle between pulls, and creating a perfect creamy head. So many publicans didn't have a clue how to pull a Guinness, Shaun knew, and was thankful that he'd found one who did. It was worthy of comment. 'A beautiful pint, me friend,' he said in his most pronounced brogue, putting his money down on the bar. 'If your steak and kidney's half as good, I'll be havin' some.'

Mindful of the compliment, the barman grinned. 'Do you want the truth?' Shaun nodded.

'The shepherd's pie is better.'

'Then I'll have the shepherd's pie. And chips. No hurry – I'm of a mind to enjoy me pint.'

Shaun decided to keep his spot at the bar for now and move to a table when his meal was up. He took a deep drink of his Guinness and sighed contentedly. For several minutes he communed with his pint in silence, concentrating on it, but after a while he became aware of the conversations round him. There were several of these, but they all seemed to centre on the same topic.

A little girl from the village was missing, he gathered.

Missing since that afternoon. The Vicar's little girl, and she had Down's syndrome. By now everyone in Branlingham knew about her disappearance; they'd known, in the mysterious way of villages, even before the house-to-house enquiries had begun. No one had seen her; the police didn't seem to have any clues.

Speculation was rife. Perhaps she'd wandered off into the woods, one man with a strong Suffolk accent opined. Or fallen in the river. Someone else suggested that she might have been kidnapped, though the Vicar wasn't a very good prospect for raising ransom. A third man added weight to a similar possibility, recalling that he'd seen a shady-looking stranger in Branlingham just the other day. Not kidnapping for ransom, then, but some sex pervert who preyed on helpless young girls.

There was a major stir when Terry Rashe came in for his evening pint. Everyone wanted to buy Terry a drink; everyone wanted to hear his story, straight from the horse's mouth, as it were.

Terry Rashe, as all the denizens of the George and Dragon knew, was the caretaker at Branlingham Primary School. It was Terry who, with the frantic mother, had searched the school from top to bottom. Apart from the mother, he'd been the first on the scene. And of course the police had interviewed him extensively. Had he seen the girl? He had not, most emphatically, though he of course knew her by sight: straight brown hair and the slanted eyes of a Mongoloid child. Had he seen anyone else lurking about, anyone or anything suspicious? Again, he had not, though he admitted this with regret.

Shaun listened to it all with a certain abstract interest. It would be something to tell Val about, anyway. He finished his pint and embarked on another before his meal arrived.

Eventually the food came. The shepherd's pie was adequate, not brilliant, but the Guinness was good enough to make up for any shortcomings in the food. A third Guinness, then, for the road; even though the place was undoubtedly crawling with peelers, they had more important things on their minds than catching someone who'd had one pint too many. Not that he had, mind you; he could hold his beer, but the peelers might take a different view. Anyway, Elmsford wasn't far, just a mile or two away.

As he settled up, the barman gave him a wistful grin. 'You don't fancy a kitten by any chance, do you, mate? I've a load of them to get rid of.'

A kitten? Shaun had been regretting the fact that he'd not thought of getting some sort of present to take to Val. Why not a kitten? he thought. It might amuse her. And if it didn't, he could always drown it. 'Why not?' he said breezily to his new-found friend. 'Why the hell not?'

Time had ceased to have any meaning for Rosemary. She was frozen in a nightmare that had only begun, that had lasted for ever.

After her initial hysteria, and after she had done all that she could do, she retreated into a state of numbness, of shock. She couldn't cry, she couldn't think. Nothing reached her, nothing had any meaning but that one hideous fact: Daisy was missing.

She sat in the drawing room on the shabby sofa, clutching in a cold hand the grotesque china dog ornament that had been Daisy's birthday present to her. Less than a week ago, more than a lifetime ago. Other people came and went, tried to talk to her, tried to do things for her. They flitted at the edge of her consciousness, irrelevant if not unwanted.

The policeman, DI Elliott, whom she remembered from his visit to the Vicarage a few weeks ago. He seemed a nice man, genuinely concerned. But he hadn't stayed long. The one who'd been left behind, the woman called Zoe. She was hard, cold. She'd brought endless mugs of tea, had tried to make her drink them. Rosemary didn't want tea. She wanted Daisy. The mugs collected on the coffee table, full of cold scummy liquid. The latest mug was still hot, but remained untouched.

Phyllis Endersby had come, as well as various other parishioners, concerned or merely curious. Rosemary ignored them all. Annie Sawbridge had come, frantic with apology. She should never have left without checking that Daisy would be looked after. Daisy had said she would be all right, Annie explained. She *had* been all right when she'd last seen her. It was her fault; she was so sorry. But Rosemary scarcely listened. She knew that it was no one's fault but her own. She had been in dereliction of her duty. She had abandoned her own daughter.

Even Gervase couldn't reach her, not even with his combined pastoral skills and love for her. He was suffering as well, of course. But he had managed to hold on to some semblance of reality, of connection to the world.

It was to Gervase that the police made their periodic reports. Everything was being done that could be done. They'd interviewed Annie Sawbridge, the last person known to have seen Daisy. Still ongoing were house-to-house enquiries, and a thorough search of the area. Fortunately, at a fortnight before midsummer, the light would last, and they wouldn't have to call off their search for the night until after nine, or nearly ten if they pushed it.

Gervase reported it all to an impassive Rosemary. But it was only this last fact that got through to her in the form of a vivid image: Daisy, somewhere out there, alone in the dark, terrified.

Rosemary clutched the china dog even more tightly as tears brimmed over and trickled down her cheeks. 'She's so afraid of the dark,' she whispered.

★

Shaun decided that an element of surprise was required; if Valerie were to hear his car, or see it through the window, she might refuse to let him in. So he pulled over onto the grass verge, a quarter of a mile from Rose Cottage, and walked the rest of the way. In one pocket of his jacket was the key; in the other was the kitten, a minute ball of yellow fluff which mewed plaintively.

He'd timed his arrival carefully. It was just beginning to get dark.

Valerie had managed to feed Daisy; she'd discovered a tin of baked beans which Mrs Rashe had brought to tempt her appetite last week when she was ill. The beans had, of course, done no such thing, but Mrs Rashe had left them behind just in case. Daisy had found them very much to her taste, and had eaten the whole tin, followed by the rest of the biscuits. That would hold her till tomorrow.

Keeping her entertained and distracted was Valerie's other concern. As long as the girl had something else to think about, like food, she seemed reasonably content, but when there was nothing else to do she soon reverted to crying for her mother. Valerie had no suitable books, no toys, at Rose Cottage. There was no television in the front room, only a small set in Valerie's bedroom that she sometimes watched before going to sleep.

The television seemed the best bet for long-term distraction. Whatever long-term meant; Valerie didn't want to think about that just yet. So she moved the set into the guest room and installed the girl there. The room could be locked with a key from the outside, which could prove to be useful when Valerie had to go out – as she surely would, if only to get food – but she didn't think it was necessary to invoke its use when she was in the house. The girl had cause enough for fear without being locked into a room by herself.

Apart from the television set, the room was fairly sterile: just a bed and a chest of drawers and a wardrobe. But the girl seemed content to stay there watching television. Her viewing at home was probably strictly regulated; Valerie didn't care what she watched, just so long as it kept her quiet.

Now, late in the evening, Valerie was in the kitchen, drinking black coffee and attempting to make a list of things she needed to buy, trying to get her rusty brain round practical matters. The girl had eventually drifted off to sleep, lying on the bed still fully clothed in her pink-striped dress, in the middle of some inane television programme; Valerie had switched off the television and the light and had shut, but not locked, the door.

'Hello, darlin',' came a soft voice from behind her.

Valerie jumped, all other emotion eclipsed by the sheer unexpectedness of being startled. 'Oh! Shaun! You frightened me!' she gasped.

Shaun smirked. 'I just wanted to surprise you, darlin'.'

Her anger at him flooded back, magnified by this latest iniquity. 'What the hell are you doing here?' she demanded. 'I told you I never wanted to see you here again. And what the hell business do you have sneaking in here, frightening the heart out of me?'

'Glad to see me then, are you?'

'Get out.' She glared at him and pointed to the door. 'Now.'

Shaun took a step towards her. 'You don't mean it, darlin',' he wheedled. 'Not after all we've meant to each other.'

Her voice was stony. 'You mean nothing to me. You never did. Now get out of my house. Give me my key, and get the hell out. Now.'

He reached into his pocket for the key and dangled it in front of her tantalisingly. 'Come and get it,' he said, while at the same time producing the kitten from the other pocket. It mewed feebly and blinked its eyes in the glare of the kitchen light. 'And I've brought you a present, Val me darlin'. Something to keep you nice and warm in bed when I'm not here to do it.'

Before she could react to this, the door opened, and Daisy stumbled in, crying. 'It's dark!' she howled on a shuddering sob. 'You left me in the dark! I want Mummy!'

Shaun looked at the girl, then at Valerie's frozen face, and back at the girl. Straight brown hair, and the slanted eyes of a Down's syndrome child. Through the haze of the beer, the penny dropped. 'Ah,' he said, consideringly.

At the same moment, Daisy spotted the kitten in Shaun's hand. Her tears stopped abruptly. 'Oh!' she breathed. 'A kitten! For me?'

He stretched out his hand and gave it to her. 'Sure and it's for you, little lady,' he said in an ingratiating voice.

Daisy buried her tear-stained face in the golden fur. 'Oh, thank you. I'll call her Samantha, because she has yellow hair.' She held the kitten up and looked into its tiny face.

Valerie spoke at last, in a voice that sounded odd to her own ears. 'Why don't you take it up to your room now?' she suggested.

'But it's dark!'

Shaun leapt at the chance. 'I'll come up with you and turn the light on,' he offered.

'No!' Valerie took Daisy's hand. 'I'll do it. That is, if you'll wait here until I get back,' she added to Shaun.

'Oh, I'll wait.' He flashed a knowing smile. 'I'm not goin' anywhere, Val me darlin'.'

When she returned from upstairs, Shaun was sitting at the kitchen table with a glass and a bottle of Bushmills, having helped himself to a drink. 'Oh, I can see that we have a lot to talk about, me darlin',' he said. 'You've been a naughty girl, haven't you?'

He couldn't possibly know; perhaps she could bluff it

out. 'She's my niece,' Valerie said coldly. 'Visiting from London.'

'Oh, Val, Val, Val.' He shook his head. 'You've never been a very good liar. I know who she is, all right. The Vicar's little girl. Don't you realise that the peelers are out looking for her? Beating the bushes? Perhaps I should give them a call, and save them a bit of worry.'

Valerie forced herself to breathe deeply; she stood very still, meeting Shaun's mocking eyes. 'What do you want from me?' she said quietly.

He turned back to the bottle of Bushmills and began to top up his drink, going on as if she hadn't spoken. 'Or maybe I ought to ring the parents. Don't you think they'd be grateful?' he said as the golden liquid splashed into his glass. 'I think it's about time for you to be nice to me, Val. I want you back – you know that.'

Valerie's gaze never left Shaun, but out of the corner of her eye she could see the silver letter knife on a pile of unopened correspondence. She reached for it, and before Shaun could lift the glass to his lips, or turn back to look at her, she drove the knife between his shoulder blades.

Pete Elliott waited until the last streaks of light faded from the sky before calling off the search. Even then he was reluctant to do so; he was sure that Daisy Finch must be out there somewhere. And the chances of finding her alive would be decreased dramatically by the morning.

He'd felt fairly confident at the beginning that she had just wandered off, and would be quickly found. That had not proved to be the case, and it was worrying. It was looking increasingly likely that if she had indeed wandered off, some ill had befallen he – that she'd fallen in the river, or injured herself in some other way. The other possibility didn't bear thinking about: that she'd encountered, either just beyond the school gates or in the countryside, someone who preyed on little girls.

When he'd started out for Branlingham that afternoon, he hadn't thought he'd care so much. But then he'd met the parents, and had seen the photo of Daisy that they'd given him. So defenceless, she seemed, with those big trusting eyes. And the glasses – that was what really got to him. Those spectacles, dwarfing her little face. That face was now imprinted on his brain, and spurred him on until there really was no point in continuing.

He went himself to tell the parents.

It was Gervase who answered the door, trying to school his face into some semblance of neutrality, not too hopeful or too despairing.

'Come in, Inspector,' he said calmly. He liked Inspector Elliott; the policeman had an air of old-fashioned courtesy which was all too rare these days in any profession.

They stood awkwardly in the entrance hall. 'I'm afraid there's no news, Vicar,' Elliott told him with genuine regret, then went on to explain that they would be out again at first light. In the morning, in addition to the sniffer dogs, they would be using a helicopter with heat-seeking equipment, and even more searchers would be called in.

He didn't tell him that they would also be dragging the river. That was now inevitable, though Elliott had put it off so far, hoping for positive results with the search.

'And just so you'll know, and will be expecting it,' he added, 'the local and national press will be notified. We'll give them Daisy's photo to run in the papers and on telly, just in case someone's seen her. And we'll try to see that they don't bother you and Mrs Finch.' This, too, was something that Elliott had put off as long as possible, knowing that once the media were involved, there would be no going back.

'Thank you for telling me.'

'And perhaps,' Elliot suggested, 'you might want to ring any members of your family and tell them, before it hits the press.'

'Yes.' Gervase smoothed his hair with his long fingers as he took the implications on board. 'Yes, I'll ring Rosemary's mother, and my son.'

Elliott was concerned about Rosemary, who didn't seem to be coping at all from what he'd seen of her earlier in the evening. 'Is there anything else I can do for you and Mrs Finch? Would you like me to ring your GP?' he offered.

'Whatever for?'

'I thought that perhaps Mrs Finch might need a sedative. To help her sleep.'

Gervase gave a grim smile. 'I don't imagine there will be much sleep here tonight. But thank you anyway.' Belatedly he realised that he was neglecting the duties of hospitality, and that they were still standing in the entrance hall. 'Can I offer you a cup of tea, Inspector? Or coffee?'

'No, thank you. But I'd like a word with Sgt Threadgold.'

'She's with my wife,' Gervase said. 'I'll fetch her.'

Zoe came quickly, hoping for good news; it still wasn't too late to salvage her evening with Mike Odum.

'You'll be staying here with the Finches tonight,' Pete Elliott told her. 'You know what to do.'

She pressed her lips together and spoke through clenched teeth. 'Yes, sir.'

For several minutes Valerie stood with the letter knife still in her hand. Shaun was slumped over the kitchen table; the blow had caught him just right, and there hadn't even been too much blood. He was most certainly dead.

She forced herself to unclench her fingers from the knife. Her brain went into overdrive, as all of the detective novels she'd read as a teenager – all of those Agatha Christies –

flooded back upon her. She would have to get rid of the body, and clean the kitchen.

To give herself a little time, she went upstairs to check on Daisy. The light in the guest room was blazing, but already the girl was sound asleep, still wearing her glasses, curled into a tight foetal ball with the sleeping kitten snuggled against her cheek. Satisfied, Valerie shut the door and locked it behind her; it wouldn't do for the girl to wake and reappear in the kitchen.

She took her time going back down, trying to think just how she was going to dispose of Shaun. It wasn't as easy as it sounded, she knew. Burying him in the garden was out of the question; she would never be able to wield a shovel, even if she knew where to find one. Rose Cottage wasn't possessed of a cellar, or a convenient coal-hole, to stash him in temporarily. She would have to get him out of the house, tonight, and as far away from Rose Cottage as possible.

His car, she thought suddenly. He must have come by car. She would have to get rid of the car in any case. He would have keys in his pocket, and if she could get him into the car, she could abandon it at some distance away. Even if he were found, as he certainly would be eventually, there would be nothing to trace him to her.

That was the beauty of it, she realised, smiling to herself in spite of the terribleness of it all. Shaun had always insisted on keeping their relationship a secret. No one would be looking for him here.

As long as she was careful, and didn't make any mistakes at this point.

Valerie paused at the door of the kitchen, her hand on the knob, before going in; not, as in novels, because she had any doubt about what she would find there, or had managed to convince herself that it hadn't really happened, but rather steeling herself for the sight of him, and for what she had to do.

No mistakes. That meant wearing gloves. Giving the table a wide berth, she went to the sink and found a pair of rubber washing-up gloves. Not elegant, but they would serve. She pulled them on, then turned to the thing that had once been Shaun. He – it – was slumped over the table, his face in a pool not of blood but of whiskey; he'd dropped his glass, and knocked over the bottle of Bushmills, as the blow was struck.

Her stomach turned over in revulsion, an instinctive reaction reflecting her deep-seated horror of death. Touching him was unthinkable, but it had to be done. The pockets first.

A few minutes later it was accomplished: she'd retrieved his wallet, his diary, a handful of loose change, the key to Rose Cottage, and his ring of keys. The wallet and the diary would be disposed of somehow, along with the lethal letter knife; the longer his body remained unidentified the better.

Now she would pull his car up as close as possible to the door, and somehow drag him into it.

But when she went out, keys in hand, to move the car, she was astonished to find that it was nowhere in sight. Not in her drive, nor in the road. Where the hell had he put it? How like Shaun that was, she realised belatedly, to try to surprise her, to sneak up on her.

Well, it couldn't be helped. She couldn't go about scouring the countryside for Shaun's car. With any luck he'd concealed it somewhere where no one would find it, or notice it, for some days. Or perhaps she'd be able to find it herself in the daylight.

But for now, she would have to use her own car instead. The blue one, of course, and she remembered with a shiver of excitement that the blue Metro was untraceable: she had never registered it. No one knew that it belonged to Valerie Marler.

Chapter 20

It was a supreme irony, though unappreciated by anyone, that the issue of *Hello!* magazine featuring Valerie Marler on the cover arrived at the news-stands the same day as the newspapers with their front-page stories about a missing Suffolk girl.

Early that morning, both were pored over avidly by Tracy, the heavy-faced girl at the newsagents just off the Bury Road in Saxwell. There was local interest in the story of the missing girl; she lived less than ten miles away. Most of the national papers had treated it as a lead story, since the child had Down's syndrome, and there was of course the added interest in the fact that her father was a vicar; scandals and potential tragedies involving the clergy always seemed to capture the public's imagination. All of the papers had run the same photo, a close-up of the girl's bespectacled face. Tracy examined the innocent face and clucked in sympathy.

But she was even more interested in the cover story on Valerie Marler. Tracy always enjoyed reading *Hello!* when things were slow in the shop and her mother wasn't there to badger her into restocking shelves instead; the homes and lives of the rich and famous fascinated her, and here again was the local interest angle to make it even more intriguing. She was studying the details of a photo of the famous author in her kitchen, supposedly in the act of whipping up a multi-course gourmet meal on the Aga, when her mother looked over her shoulder.

This time Tracy didn't bother to conceal what she was doing, so entranced was she. 'Look here, Mum,' she said. 'That Valerie Marler. Lives not far from here, just down the road at Elmsford. Our local celebrity, like. Isn't she pretty, then? And just look at her house.'

Her mother scowled. 'I thought I told you not to go putting your mucky fingerprints all over the merchandise,' she said. But she couldn't resist looking. It was the kitchen that interested her more than its inhabitant. 'Cor, what I wouldn't give for a kitchen like that,' she sighed. 'I've been telling your dad for years that I need a new kitchen. Course, I wouldn't want a great clunky thing like that old Aga – a nice shiny new cooker would be more like it. And a nice shiny vinyl floor, instead of them quarry tiles. Murder to keep clean, I shouldn't wonder.'

The quarry tiles were very clean indeed that morning, murder notwithstanding. Late the night before they had been scrubbed with a brush, and rinsed several times until the water ran clear. No one looking at them now would ever know that they had been stained with mingled blood and whiskey.

It had been a gruelling night for Valerie. There was the physical exhaustion of getting rid of the body: she had found it unexpectedly, unbelievably heavy and unwieldy, a dead weight. Hauling and shoving it into the back seat of the car had worn her out, even before the long walk home from the secluded spot in the woods where she'd abandoned both car and body. Then there was the clean-up waiting for her at home, the scrubbing of the floor and table, the disposal of

Shaun's effects and the knife and her own blood-spattered clothing. She'd put them all in a bin liner which she'd tied up securely and thrown in the large industrial-sized rubbish skip behind the Swan pub; their rubbish was collected every day, and with any luck the black bag would be in a landfill within a few hours.

But the real exhaustion was mental. Valerie was overwhelmed by the two earth-shattering events of her day: she had abducted a child, and she had committed murder to conceal it. The consequences of either act could change her life for ever. The murder she hoped had been dealt with, and could now be forgotten, but the other problem was as yet unsolved – what was she going to do with Daisy?

There had been no sleep for Valerie that night, and for the first time in many weeks, Hal was the farthest thing from her mind.

Margaret had no presentiment of disaster when, coming downstairs after her shower, she picked up the morning post from the mat. There was the usual assortment of advertising circulars and catalogues, mixed in with correspondence both personal and professional. The bulk of it was for Margaret rather than for Hal.

She sorted through it quickly, dropping the most obvious adverts into the bin unopened, and carrying those letters that were clearly professional into her study and dropping them on the desk, where she would deal with them later. Anything that appeared to be personal she often took through into the breakfast room to be looked at over her toast and coffee.

The envelope in question was one such. It had been addressed by hand, in block capitals, not recognisable as being from anyone in particular, and it felt stiff, as if it contained an invitation or a greetings card.

Hal was already in the breakfast room. He'd made the

coffee and the toast, and had laid the table. 'Busy day today?' he asked conversationally, pouring her a cup of coffee.

'Not too bad.' Margaret took her napkin from its silver ring, then helped herself to a triangle of toast. 'I've kept the morning free to deal with paperwork and correspondence, and I've a committee meeting in the afternoon. In Bury.'

Before buttering her toast, she used her bread knife to slit open the envelope. Three stiff squares of card fell out; Margaret looked at them one by one. Her eyes, her brain, refused to make any sense of what she saw, of the images on the cards. But her heart felt suddenly as if a giant hand were squeezing it, crushing it to pulp.

It was the quality of her stillness that captured Hal's attention as he applied marmalade to his toast. He looked at his wife; her face was white, whiter than he'd ever seen it, and not a muscle moved. 'Margaret? Are you all right, my love?'

Without a word she passed the three photos across to him.

'Oh,' said Hal.

Margaret waited.

'Listen, Margaret. It's not what you think.'

She tried to smile; her face felt frozen. 'And what, exactly, do I think?'

'Oh, I suppose what anyone would be bound to think, seeing these – that we're having an affair.'

Her voice sounded very calm, almost conversational. 'And are you?'

'No!' he said forcefully. 'You've got to believe me.'

She said nothing.

'I know what it looks like. But nothing happened between us. What can I tell you to make you believe me?'

Margaret regarded him levelly across the table. 'The truth. Tell me the truth. You owe me that, Hal.'

He took a deep breath and forced himself to meet her gaze. 'The truth, then.' His eyes shifted away, to the photos on the table. 'We fell in love, Rosemary Finch and I. We never meant for it to happen, or wanted it to happen. It just . . . happened. We couldn't help it. But I never stopped loving *you*, Margaret. Through it all. And she never stopped loving Gervase. And we never slept together – I swear it. What you're seeing in these photos is the end of something that never happened.' He gave a short, bitter laugh. 'That's the irony of it all, isn't it? That this is the end. Yesterday afternoon. We've decided not to see each other again. Not ever. Nothing happened, and now it's over.'

'Nothing?' she echoed. 'You call it nothing, that after twenty-five years of marriage, you've fallen in love with another woman?'

'But we didn't have an affair,' Hal insisted. 'I was never unfaithful to you. We never slept together, not once.'

'Once would have been all right, then?'

'You know what I mean. And surely the important thing is that I still love *you*. That our marriage has survived. That Rosie and I won't be seeing each other again.'

Rosie, thought Margaret, her heart contracting once more. 'You're still in love with *her*, though, as well,' she stated.

He picked up his bread knife and drew a pattern on the tablecloth with its tip. 'You can't just stop loving someone overnight, on command. Yes, I still love Rosie. But I've made my choice, and I've chosen *you*.'

'And you thought that I'd never have to know about your little . . . lapse. You weren't going to tell me.'

'No, of course not. I never wanted to hurt you, Margaret. Especially not now – now that it's all over.'

'You never wanted to hurt me.' She closed her eyes, then pushed herself up from the table. 'I'm going to my study, Hal. To think for a few moments, on my own.'

He made no attempt to follow her.

Margaret shut the door of her study behind her and sank

into the chair, leaning her elbows on her desk. Hal smiled at her from the photo, carefree and at his most charming. She had always loved that photo of her husband and her son. Now she couldn't bear to look at it; she placed it face down on the desk.

She couldn't take it in, couldn't make sense of it. Hal had fallen in love with another woman. After all these years, after all they'd been through.

He hadn't been unfaithful to her, he'd said. They'd never slept together. That was supposed to make it all right somehow, to excuse it as not being important.

How like a man to think that it was about sex. Sex had nothing, or virtually nothing, to do with it. Hal had not been the first man in Margaret's life; while at school she'd had a number of boyfriends, and had slept with several of them. It had meant nothing. But this, *this*. Hal, her husband, the love of her life, had fallen in love with another woman. That it was love and not just a form of lust she had no doubt; Rosemary Finch was not the sort of woman to inflame a man with desire. No, Hal had loved her. He *still* loved her. The emotional infidelity was a hundred, a thousand times worse than physical infidelity. How much better it would have been if he'd just fancied Rosemary Finch and gone to bed with her, or given in to any of the women who had thrown themselves at him over the past few years. That she could have dealt with. She would have been angry, yes, and hurt, but she could have coped with it, and forgiven him.

Forgiveness. She was a priest; forgiveness was her stock in trade. At every service she raised her arm, made the sign of the cross, and dispensed it freely. Absolution. 'Almighty God, who forgives all who truly repent, have mercy upon you, pardon and deliver you from all your sins, confirm and strengthen you in all goodness, and keep you in life eternal.'

God would forgive Hal, of course. But now, knowing what she knew, how could Margaret ever forgive him?

Daisy seemed like a different child on Tuesday morning, and it was all because of the kitten. She came downstairs smiling, looking a bit bedraggled now in her candy-striped dress and her hair coming out of its plaits, the kitten cradled in her arms. 'Can I really really keep her?' she asked Valerie, with an expression that showed she scarcely believed it might be true.

Anything that kept Daisy content, not asking for her mother, was fine with Valerie. 'Yes, of course.'

'Mummy says that maybe I can have a kitten one day. Maybe. Not for sure.'

The opportunity was too good to pass up. 'Well, as long as you're here, you can keep the kitten,' Valerie promised.

Daisy beamed. 'She's called Samantha.'

'Would you like some breakfast?'

'Have you got cornflakes? Can Samantha have some cornflakes as well?'

Valerie never ate cereal, but Shaun liked cornflakes. He *had* liked cornflakes, and she always kept a box on hand for him. He wouldn't be needing them now. Valerie shuddered involuntarily as she found the packet in the pantry.

Hal hadn't moved from the table when Margaret returned. He'd stayed in his chair, not eating; with his strong, blunt fingers he had turned a triangle of toast into crumbs, which he absently pushed round on the table.

To Margaret, who knew him so well, he looked worried, anxious. But he looked up as she came into the room and gave her his most dazzling, charming smile. That smile which had worked its wonders for years, not just on her but on virtually every woman with whom he'd ever come in contact.

Margaret was not in the mood for that smile; she was not in the mood to be beguiled by her husband.

It was almost as if she were seeing him for the first time. Why hadn't she ever realised how calculated that smile was? She knew that he was aware of his own charm, but she'd never before been conscious of him turning it on, using it for his own purposes.

'You do understand, don't you?' he said in a wheedling voice. Like a small child, she thought. Like Alexander, when he'd wanted to get round her, wanted some little treat that she'd not been prepared to give him.

She was not moved. 'Oh, I understand, all right. You've made it quite clear. You've hurt Rosemary Finch, and you've hurt me, and now you want me to forgive you, to say that everything is fine.'

'That's not fair. I didn't mean for you to find out – I didn't want you to be hurt.'

Her voice was bitter. 'And that makes it all right?'

'I don't see why we can't just forget it.'

'Forget that you've undermined our marriage, made a mockery of it?' Margaret shook her head vigorously. 'Hal, it doesn't work like that. Don't you see? Nothing will ever be the same again. I trusted you. I thought I knew you. I believed in our marriage. Now I don't know what to believe.'

'But I wasn't unfaithful to you,' he repeated.

She closed her eyes. 'You just don't have a clue, do you, Hal?'

'Listen, Meg.' It was an old nickname, from the early days of their marriage and long since fallen into disuse; he certainly hadn't called her anything so frivolous since she'd become the Venerable Margaret Phillips. He got up and started to move towards her, arms outstretched. 'I've chosen *you*, not her. I want to make our marriage work. Isn't that the important thing?'

Margaret, shaken by the use of the ancient nickname, took a step backwards and held out her palm. 'No. Don't come any closer. Don't try to touch me. Not now.'

'What do you want me to do?' He folded his arms defensively across his chest.

She took a deep breath, then expelled it. That was the question: what *did* she want him to do? 'I'm not sure,' she admitted. 'But for now, you can move into the spare room. And don't even think about coming near me.'

'But, Margaret, Meg—' The doorbell chimed, interrupting him.

'You can get that,' she said in the same quiet but authoritative voice in which she'd conducted the whole conversation.

He went. On the doorstep was the girl from the newsagents' shop round the corner, holding a newspaper. Out of habit, though it was the last thing on his mind, Hal flashed her his smile.

'Oh, Mr Phillips,' the girl simpered. 'Mrs Phillips hasn't been round to collect her paper this morning, and I thought you might like to have one. Seeing as the big news is local, like.'

'Thank you, that's very kind.' He took the paper from her, repeating the smile, and Tracy went away happy.

But his smile faded rapidly as he carried the newspaper back to the breakfast room. He waved it at Margaret, everything else forgotten for the moment, his face showing genuine distress and shock. 'Look! The most terrible thing has happened! Daisy is missing! Daisy Finch!'

'Oh, dear God.' Margaret snatched the paper from him and scanned it quickly. 'I'm going,' she said, heading for the front of the house.

'*Where* are you going?'

'To Branlingham, of course. Her parents will be in the most frightful state.'

Hal stood at the door and watched her go, his arms hanging helplessly at his sides.

'Samantha is hungry,' announced Daisy when she'd finished her own breakfast.

Valerie poured some milk in a saucer and put it down for the kitten, who lapped it greedily. 'I need to get some food for her, and for us,' Valerie told the little girl. 'Could you stay in your room with Samantha while I go? You can watch television, if you like.'

Daisy agreed readily. 'Mars bars,' she said as she trotted up the stairs. 'Can I have Mars bars? Mummy doesn't let me, usually.'

'You shall have Mars bars.' Valerie followed her up; she still felt it was a good idea to lock the bedroom door behind her. Just in case.

She went, in the Porsche for a change since she no longer had another car, to the Saxwell Tesco.

It had been years since she'd bought food for children; she should have asked Daisy what she would like to eat, apart from Mars bars. Up and down the aisles she went, filling her trolley with anything that looked as if it might appeal to a young palate. Tins of beans – they were a proven winner. A tin of hot dogs, and a packet of sausages. Small pizzas, some frozen beefburgers, and a large box of fish fingers. Oven chips. More cornflakes. A loaf of white bread, and a jar of strawberry jam. A large jug of milk, and a bottle of lemon squash. Biscuits, crisps, Mars bars. Then there were the things for the kitten: tins of cat food, some cat litter, and a litter tray.

Valerie visited the clothing department as well; Daisy needed something to wear besides her striped dress. She had to guess at the size, particularly when it came to knickers and socks; Daisy seemed small for her age. Beginning to enjoy herself, she chose several pairs of each, in various sizes, then picked out a pair of jeans, two pairs of leggings, three colourful T-shirts, and a sweet little denim dress with patch pockets and smocking on the bodice.

She pushed her laden trolley to the check-outs, which were not particularly overburdened on a Tuesday morning. But as so often happens, she chose the wrong queue: the woman in front of her had, without noticing, picked up a leaking carton of milk, and someone had to be dispatched to the very back of the store for a replacement. They took their time about it. Valerie might have moved to another check-out, but she had already unloaded half of her trolley onto the conveyor belt by then.

'Always the way, isn't it?' said the waiting woman conversationally. She was thin, with nicotine-stained fingers, and her hair was an improbable shade of red. 'Sorry about that, love. Didn't mean to hold you up.' She cast her eye over the items on the conveyor belt. 'What sort of cat have you got, then?'

Startled, Valerie looked away, but was too polite not to reply. 'Oh, just an ordinary cat.'

'I used to have a cat, myself. A big old tom. But he died, and I've never got another.'

That statement seemed to require no response, so Valerie just nodded in acknowledgement, still not making eye contact.

'Mind you, cats are less trouble than children.' The woman looked pointedly at the trolley full of food. 'Less expense, as well. Though I never had any myself.'

Why was it, Valerie wondered, that the average English person, who wouldn't dream of speaking to a stranger in a lift or on a train, seemed to feel that the normal rules didn't apply when standing in a supermarket queue?

'How old is your little girl, then?'

Valerie caught her breath in dismay. 'My niece,' she mumbled. 'Visiting.'

*

Gervase had been answering the door himself, until the press started ringing the bell. Now it was Zoe Threadgold's job to go to the door and dispatch anyone who, in her opinion, had no business in the house. Her standards for admission were much more stringent than Gervase's had been, and her manner far more brusque; she sent various members of the parish packing, along with numerous representatives of the press.

And so it was Zoe who opened the door to Margaret. 'Yes?' she said in an uninviting tone.

'I've come to see Father Finch and Mrs Finch,' Margaret informed her.

'I'm afraid they're not receiving visitors at the moment. *Any* visitors.'

But Zoe had met her match. 'I'm not a visitor, I'm the Archdeacon.' Margaret stared her down with a level gaze. 'Father Finch's boss,' she added for good measure. 'If you would care to check with Father Finch . . .'

Recognising authority when she saw it, albeit grudgingly, Zoe opened the door wide enough for Margaret to squeeze through.

At the sound of Margaret's voice, Gervase had come into the entrance hall. He looked haggard, years older than he had the day before. 'Archdeacon!' he said. 'How kind of you to come.'

It wasn't an occasion for small talk. 'Don't be silly – of course I had to come. No news, then?'

He shook his head. 'Nothing.'

'How is Rosemary?'

'She's not doing at all well.' Gervase gestured towards the drawing room. 'She hasn't moved from there since yesterday afternoon. She won't eat, she won't sleep. I just don't know how to reach her.'

Margaret didn't hesitate. Ignoring Zoe, who hovered near

the door in a proprietorial manner, she went into the drawing room. Rosemary sat huddled on one end of the sofa, still clutching the china dog; she didn't look up. Without a word, Margaret sat down close to her on the sofa and put her arms round the other woman.

Something in that embrace reached through the layers of shock that cocooned Rosemary from her surroundings. Instinctively she relaxed and allowed herself to be held. 'There, there,' murmured Margaret, stroking her hair. 'You don't have to keep it in any more, my dear. There's no need to be brave. Go ahead and cry. It will be good for you.'

With a great flood of tears, Rosemary obeyed the Archdeacon's orders.

Valerie unlocked the door to Daisy's room to find the girl in a state of some agitation, clutching the kitten and jumping up and down. 'On the telly!' Daisy cried. 'I was on the telly! My picture! They said that I was missing! Am I missing?'

Of course. Why, thought Valerie, had she not anticipated that? She cursed her own stupidity. She hadn't seen a news-paper, or listened to the radio or the television, but it was inevitable that Daisy's disappearance would be reported by now.

She went down on her knees, grasped Daisy by the shoul-ders, and looked into her face. 'Of course you're not missing,' she said firmly. 'You're right here, aren't you? I know where you are, and you know where you are, so how can you be missing?'

That logic seemed to satisfy Daisy. 'Oh,' she said thought-fully.

Valerie rushed on to distract her. 'And now how about some nice biscuits, and some squash? You can give Samantha some food. And then you can have a bath, and change your clothes.'

They went downstairs. Daisy fed the kitten, then ate biscuits while Valerie unpacked the rest of the shopping. 'Look, Daisy, I've bought you some nice new clothes.'

One of the T-shirts attracted her attention. 'It's pink! Pink is my favourite colour!'

'I thought it might be. Would you like to wear this?'

'Oh, yes.'

'A bath, then, first, since you didn't have one last night.' Back upstairs they went. Valerie's children had been much younger than Daisy – only babies, really – when she'd given them baths; she wasn't sure whether the girl could take one on her own, or would be upset if she tried to help her. But Daisy seemed to expect Valerie to come into the bathroom with her.

Valerie ran the bath, added some foaming oil, then helped Daisy out of her dress and into the bath. The girl was so trusting; her life was literally in Valerie's hands. How easy it would be to hold her little head under water until she stopped breathing. Valerie had committed one murder already; what difference would one more make? And a small girl's body would be so much easier to get rid of than that of a grown man. Water in the lungs, there would be. She could throw the body in the river and when the police found it they would think the girl had just tumbled in and drowned. It would solve the overwhelming problem of what to do with Daisy.

But Daisy giggled, Valerie hesitated, and the moment passed. Not today, then. Maybe tomorrow. She *could* do it.

After the bath she wrapped Daisy in a soft bath sheet and dried her off, then dressed her in the pink T-shirt and a pair of leggings; both fitted just right, and Daisy was delighted.

'Oh, thank you!' said Daisy, throwing her arms round Valerie's neck and planting a moist kiss on her cheek.

Valerie's heart turned over; it had been a long time since a little girl had kissed her, and she'd forgotten how nice it could be. Involuntarily her arms encircled Daisy and tightened in a hug. If she closed her eyes, she could almost pretend that it was her own Jenny, lost to her for such a long while now. She had tried so hard to blot memories and thoughts of Jenny and Ben out of her mind, and had been largely successful; there was no point dwelling on a painful past. But Daisy's spontaneous hug brought it all back: the mingled pain and pleasure of motherhood.

Jenny would be just about Daisy's age now. On whom was she bestowing her hugs and kisses?

Valerie gulped, blinking back tears. 'Let me brush your hair now,' she suggested, and fetched her own hair brush.

The girl's hair was soft and silky; the rhythm of brushing it was hypnotic. Daisy seemed to enjoy having her hair brushed, so the exercise continued for a while. Then Daisy climbed onto Valerie's lap and put her soft cheek against hers. 'Thank you,' she said. Then, 'What's your name?'

'Auntie,' Valerie whispered. 'You can call me Auntie.'

Pete Elliott was frustrated. Almost twenty-four hours since the little girl had disappeared, and there was nothing. Not a trace, not a clue; it was as though she had walked through the school gates and vanished into thin air. No one had seen her, no one had seen anything. No old men in dirty raincoats hanging round the school gates had been spotted, even by those with the most vivid imaginations. And there had been, not surprisingly, no demand for ransom.

The search of the woods and the open ground, the dragging of the river: all had been equally fruitless. The dogs hadn't been able to pick up her scent anywhere, and the helicopters with their heat-seeking equipment had found nothing. There was not a scrap of cloth or a hank of hair to indicate that Daisy Finch had ever been in the vicinity.

Sitting in his panda car eating a quick sandwich from the

village shop – he didn't even want to take the time for a pub lunch – Elliott closed his eyes and pictured the innocent face of Daisy Finch, imprinted on his mind from the photo. Where the hell could she be? And how much chance was there that she was still alive, wherever she was?

It made him uneasy, this lack of any clues. It started his mind working down a different track.

What if, he theorised, she had not in fact ever made it very far past those school gates, or at least not under her own steam?

The school caretaker, Terry Rashe. He could have seen her standing alone, could have lured her back into the school and hidden her somewhere, in some cupboard or little room known only to him, while he helped her mother search the building. Then later, at his leisure, he could have taken her somewhere else. For whatever reason, whatever purpose; it was best not to think about that.

There was no evidence for this, no reason to believe it other than the fact that it was the first scenario he'd come up with that made any sense at all.

It could have happened that way.

Terry Rashe would definitely bear watching. He would interview him again, ask a few more questions. It was too soon to bring him in to 'assist the police with their enquiries', but something might come out of another interview. And in any case, Elliott would make sure that they kept an eye on him. And he'd send a team of officers back into that school to go over it again, with a fine tooth-comb. Not looking for a child this time, but for any evidence at all that Daisy Finch had been held there.

It was a long shot, a hunch, but it was all he had. It was worth pursuing.

He finished his sandwich, compressing the clingfilm into a ball and tucking it neatly into his pocket. In just a few hours, at four o'clock, there would be a press conference. The press – the national papers, and the broadcast media – were taking a great interest in the case. This was more than just a local story: it was news.

And at the rate things were going, he would have nothing to tell them. Nothing. Nil. Zilch. Bugger all.

Rosemary had cried for what seemed like hours, letting out her pent-up emotions in a flood of tears. Margaret felt that was a good sign, but after the tears had been exhausted, Rosemary retreated back inside herself, like the terrapin that Alexander had once had as a pet. She would not talk, she would not sleep, she would not eat; she sat like a Patience on a monument, clutching the little pink dog. Eventually, by force of will, Margaret got her to drink some sweet tea, replenishing her lost fluids.

For Gervase, the tears had been worse than the withdrawn silence, agony for him to endure. But he had stayed with his wife, and when it was over, he sat beside her on the sofa, disengaging one of her hands from the china ornament and holding it, unresponsive, between his own.

All of this left Zoe Threadgold without much to do, apart from answering the telephone. But her time was pretty well occupied with that task, as the press had fastened onto the story with avid interest. She dealt with it all quite competently, until one particularly persistent caller refused to take no for an answer.

'Someone called Hazel Croom,' she told Gervase. 'She insists on speaking to you. When I put the phone down she rings straight back, and says that she won't stop ringing until she's talked to you.'

Margaret looked at him questioningly. 'I suppose I must speak to her, then,' he said.

'I'll deal with her,' the Archdeacon stated, overruling him.

In her best archdeaconly manner, she took care of Hazel Croom in short order, explaining that Father Gervase could not possibly come to the phone just then; he was with his wife, they were both greatly distressed. Perhaps later, she promised. For now she would personally convey Miss Croom's message of support; she was sure that Miss Croom would understand.

The press conference was carried live on Anglia television. Hal, who had stayed by the radio and the telephone all day, hoping for some news, watched it with a growing sense of despair. Though they masked it with typical verbosity, the police seemed to have no clue at all to Daisy's whereabouts. They had made no progress whatsoever; they were no nearer finding her than they had been twenty-four hours earlier.

Hal was a man in agony. He loved Margaret, but she had left him. He loved Rosie, but she was lost to him for ever. And now Daisy. Hal truly loved Daisy; the thought of never seeing her again had been a painful adjunct to losing Rosie, and almost as difficult for him. Now, though, that seemed a minor consideration.

Daisy was missing, gone. In mortal danger, perhaps, or even – God forbid – dead. And he could do nothing.

Never, even when he'd lain in a hospital bed near death, had Hal Phillips felt so helpless. After the press conference, he did the only thing he could think of: he picked up the phone and rang Branlingham Vicarage. Listening to the rings, he justified it to himself. He had only promised never to *see* Rosie again, not that he would never talk to her. And in any case these were extraordinary circumstances, calling for a bit of latitude. It was too much to hope for that Rosie would answer, but he would settle for Gervase.

It was an unfamiliar female voice at the other end, and an unfriendly one. 'Yes?' she snapped.

The police, he surmised. 'Could I possibly speak to Mrs Finch? Or Father Finch, if she's not available?'

'The Finches are not taking any calls right now,' she said inflexibly. 'Would you care to leave a message?'

There was one avenue open to him, one possibility. 'This is the Archdeacon's husband,' he said. 'Could I possibly speak to her?'

'Just a moment.' In a very short time she was back on the line. 'The Archdeacon says that she doesn't wish to talk to you,' she reported, 'and asks that you not tie up the phone by ringing again.'

Valerie listened to the press conference on the radio, and decided that allowing Daisy unlimited, unmonitored television was not a good idea. But Daisy didn't seem to mind at all, finding the kitten to be more than enough to amuse her for hours on end.

In the evening, though, as bedtime drew near, Daisy made a request. 'Would you read me a story, Auntie? Mummy always reads me stories before bed.'

There were no children's story-books at Rose Cottage. But Valerie was a writer, a spinner of tales. 'I'll do something even better,' she promised. 'I'll *tell* you a story, all your own.'

Daisy climbed up on her lap, her preferred position for stories.

'Once upon a time, there was a little girl called Daisy. She had a kitten called Samantha, and they lived in a house with her Auntie.' The story unfolded, but only half of Valerie's brain was engaged in creating it; on a parallel track her mind was furiously pursuing other matters, as it had been all day. And she recalled one thing which had so far slipped her mind: this was Tuesday, and Mrs Rashe would be coming tomorrow. She must ring her and put her off somehow.

★

Sybil Rashe put down the phone. 'I don't like it, Frank,' she announced to her husband.

But Frank wasn't listening. He was leaning forward in his chair, intent on the television news.

The fact of the missing girl didn't particularly interest him; sad as it was, it was something that happened more often than you liked to think about. What did interest him was the fact that the girl had disappeared not in Somerset or Yorkshire or somewhere equally remote, but in his own small corner of the world.

The talk down at the Swan had been of little else. Though most of the London journalists who had descended on Branlingham were drinking at the George and Dragon instead, a few had strayed as far afield as Elmsford and the Swan. There they'd been descended upon by the locals, eager to buy them drinks and get some sort of an inside perspective on the exciting events that had overtaken them, while the journalists were equally eager to pump the locals for background information for their stories. Frank had himself chatted with a young man from Anglia News, and hoped to get a glimpse of him on camera so that he could point him out to Sybil.

Sybil's own interest in the matter was intense, not just because it was local but because Terry was involved. Terry, she could hardly wait to tell Miss Valerie, had been a key witness for the police, interviewed not just once but several times. He had been the first one, apart from the mother, to know that the little girl was missing, and the police knew how important his testimony could be. Her boy, her Terry; Sybil was so proud.

But now she wouldn't have a chance to tell Miss Valerie, not this week anyway, and by next week it would be old news. By then the media's short attention span would have moved on to something quite different, and much farther away:

floods in Scotland, or some Tory MP caught in bed with his secretary.

'I don't like it one bit,' she repeated to Frank when the news had finished.

'What's that, Syb?'

'Miss Valerie.' She frowned. 'She doesn't want me to come tomorrow.'

'Why not, then?'

'That's just it. She was very vague about it. Just said that it wouldn't be convenient for me to come tomorrow, thank you very much, and she'd let me know about next week.' Sybil stared at the advert on the telly without seeing it. 'I don't like it, Frank. Not one bit. It's just not like Miss Valerie, and that's a fact. There's something wrong at Rose Cottage. You mark my words.'

Chapter 21

Margaret, always an early riser, woke early on Wednesday morning and before she opened her eyes reached reflexively for Hal.

Hal was not there, and she was not in her own bed – *their* own bed. The bed was narrow, and the room full of stuffed animals: Daisy's room. Margaret's eyes flew open as it all came flooding back upon her. Daisy. Rosemary. Hal.

Hal.

She had managed to deal with the issue of Hal by resolutely banishing him from her mind; she had yet to relive the pain of Tuesday morning's revelations or think through their implications. It had been cowardly of her to refuse to speak to him on the phone, but she knew that she couldn't cope with it just now. All through yesterday she had been too involved with the sorrows of others to think about her own. In any event, the sorrows of the Finch family made her conflicted feelings about Hal pale into insignificance.

Sooner or later she would have to think about him, to ponder their future. But not now. Not yet.

She had to save all of her energies – physical, emotional and spiritual – for Rosemary Finch. Rosemary needed her.

*

'Damn!' Pete Elliott, intent on his thoughts rather than what he was doing – shaving – had just nicked himself. He grabbed a tissue to stanch the trickle of blood.

The day was not beginning very auspiciously, and he had an unpleasant feeling that it would continue in the same vein.

As the search for Daisy Finch moved into its third day, the likelihood of finding the girl alive became more and more remote.

The only thing that was on their side, he reflected as he regarded his grim face in the mirror, was the weather. Yesterday had been fine; today was predicted to be even better, sunny and hot. If, by some slim chance, Daisy Finch were alive and hiding somewhere in the woods, at least the weather wouldn't kill her.

But by now Elliott had almost discounted the possibility that she had left the school under her own steam. Surely, if she had wandered off, they would have found *some* trace of her, however slight. But still there was nothing, and he felt by now that there never would be.

And that left Terry Rashe. Thus far his handling of Rashe had been gentle; he hadn't even suggested the possibility to the school caretaker that he might know more than he was telling about Daisy Finch's disappearance. Now the time had come to lean on him.

True, the search of the school by the trained scene-of-crime officers hadn't turned up any evidence that Daisy had been held there, either in the caretaker's office or anywhere else in the building. But that might just mean that Rashe was cleverer than he looked, that he'd used some other hiding place that they didn't know about and hadn't found yet.

He didn't like the looks of Rashe. The man had been pleasant enough, if none too bright, but there was something about him that Elliott found unsettling. Perhaps it was the fact that his eyes were just that tiny bit too close together. That feature reminded him rather too much of Superintendent Hardy, he reflected ruefully; he'd never got on very well with his superior.

This morning he would lean on Rashe. Elliott was conscious that time was running out for him; this afternoon, at the very latest, he would have to see the superintendent. And Superintendent Hardy was not going to be impressed that in three days of looking for a little girl who had disappeared in broad daylight, they had found not so much as a hair.

Between them, Gervase and Margaret had managed to get Rosemary to bed on Tuesday night. Exhaustion had worn her resistance down. And Margaret, sensibly, had rung the Finches' GP, who had prescribed a mild sedative for Rosemary. She hadn't even known she was taking it, in the warm milk that Margaret coaxed her into drinking.

The sedative had done its work well. When Gervase woke in the morning, after a night of broken sleep and troubled dreams, his wife slept on soundly beside him, seemingly peaceful for the first time since Daisy's disappearance.

He leaned over and kissed Rosemary's forehead, but she did not stir. Her face was so pale, he thought, and her closed eyes were still puffy with the tears of yesterday.

She was so precious to him; he loved her so much. Yet he could not reach her, could not go with her into whatever hell she was inhabiting. This event, this cataclysm that had overtaken them, should have brought them together, but instead it was like an invisible barrier between them, shutting her off in her own private world of grief. How long could it go on like this?

For a moment Gervase stroked her hair, tangled and uncombed. Then, assured that she would not soon wake, he slipped out of bed and dressed in his clericals. It was time for the Morning Office.

St Stephen's welcomed him as it did each morning, embracing and enveloping him in palpable peace and serenity as he entered its doors. He passed through the nave to the chancel, went to his stall and knelt there. The opening words of the Morning Office from the Prayer Book, so familiar to him, flowed effortlessly, though his eyes were closed.

He opened his eyes again to read the Psalms appointed for the day. Always the Psalms were meaningful to him, no matter how often he read them. But his breath caught in his throat and his voice faltered when he reached the verses, 'Our heart is not turned back: neither our steps going out of thy way; No, not when thou hast smitten us into the place of dragons: and covered us with the shadow of death.'

As he neared the end of Psalm 45, he sensed subconsciously that he was not alone in the church, and a voice joined in with his for the opening of Psalm 46, the last appointed for that morning. 'God is our hope and strength: a very present help in trouble. Therefore will we not fear, though the earth be moved: and though the hills be carried into the midst of the sea,' said the confident voice of the Archdeacon as she slipped into the adjoining stall.

Together, then, they recited the Canticles, the Creed, the Lesser Litany, the Collects. The familiarity of the words provided a sort of comfort, and conscious of Margaret's support almost as a palpable presence, Gervase rallied, his voice growing stronger, as they neared the end of the office, the prayer of St Chrysostom. 'Almighty God,' he and Margaret said in unison, 'Who has given us grace at this time with one accord to make our common supplications unto thee; and dost promise, that when two or three are gathered together in thy Name thou wilt grant their requests: Fulfil now, O Lord, the desires and petitions of thy servants, as may be most expedient for them; granting us in this world knowledge of thy truth, and in the world to come life everlasting. Amen.'

After the Grace, Gervase bent his head over his clasped hands, praying for his daughter and his wife; Margaret slipped away as silently as she had come, leaving him alone with God.

By Wednesday morning, Zoe Threadgold had had enough. She'd done her best, and as long as it was just the parents to contend with, she'd managed. But now that the Archdeacon had moved in, Zoe knew that she couldn't stand much more.

She had always been scrupulous about keeping her private life not only private, but separate from work. That meant not using her relationship with Mike Odum in any way to her professional benefit; apart from anything else, her pride would not allow it. What she achieved, she wanted to achieve on her own, without any help from her lover. But on this matter, desperate measures were called for. She'd tried talking to Pete Elliott; he didn't want to know.

Zoe locked herself in the bathroom and punched in Mike Odum's number on her mobile phone. He answered on the first ring. 'Odum.'

'Mike! It's Zoe. Can you talk?'

'I'm alone,' he said. 'And lonely. I've missed you.'

She ground her teeth. 'And I've missed you. But that's not why I'm ringing, Mike.'

'What's up, then?'

'Mike.' She took a deep breath, steeling herself. 'You've got to get me out of here. You know that I never ask you for favours, but I'm desperate.'

'I know that doing the domestic thing isn't exactly your cup of tea.' He chuckled at the other end of the phone.

'It's not funny.' Zoe scowled, then tried to explain. 'The parents are bad enough – wet, the both of them, and no wonder, I suppose. But there's this other woman here who's making my life hell. The Archdeacon, she calls herself – she says she's the Vicar's boss. And bossy is the word for her. She's a right bossyboots. She keeps ordering me about, sending me off to make tea.'

Mike Odum leaned back in his chair and closed his eyes, enjoying the mental picture. So Zoe, his little tiger, had finally met her match – the idea did not displease him. 'So what do you want me to do?' he asked; he would force her to beg.

'I told you. I want you to get me out,' she repeated with some reluctance; this was costing her dear. 'If you do, Mike, I . . . I'll owe you one.'

'And I'll take you up on that,' he chuckled. 'I'll see what I can do. But don't hold your breath.'

Pete Elliott was trying to hold his breath. He was particularly sensitive to cigarette smoke; it made his eyes water, and gave him headaches. This often proved to be a real problem round the police station, and when interviewing people; the nervousness that even the innocent felt when faced with the police usually doubled any smoker's cigarette consumption.

And Terry Rashe was no exception. The ashtray in front of him overflowed with ash and fag ends, and he was smoking one now. The small room that served as his office was stuffy and foetid at the best of times, but the combination of the day's heat and the cigarette smoke made it well nigh unbearable.

'Can't you open a window or something?' Elliott suggested, fanning the smoke away from his face.

'Sorry. Sorry.' Terry Rashe had to stand on a chair to reach the only window in the room, small and set high in the wall.

'Thanks.' Elliott smiled at him; he liked to put people at their ease, having found that they were usually inclined to be more cooperative. 'That's better. It's a nasty habit, you know,' he couldn't resist adding, still smiling.

'That's what my mum tells me. And that's why I don't smoke in front of her. She doesn't even know that I smoke.'

A forceful mother was something that Pete Elliott could

understand. 'Well, you can trust me. I won't tell her,' he grinned.

Rashe sat back down on the chair and retrieved his fag from the ashtray. 'Like I said, Inspector, I don't understand why you've come back. I've told you everything I know. Yesterday, and the day before that.'

'And I do appreciate it,' Elliott acknowledged. 'You've been very helpful, Terry.'

The sergeant in the corner, his notebook open and pencil poised, raised his eyebrows but said nothing. He didn't really approve of Elliott's methods, but he'd seen their effectiveness in the past, and knew better than to open his mouth.

'I'm just wondering, Terry, if there might be one or two things that you haven't told me,' Elliott went on. 'When was the last time that you saw Daisy Finch?'

'You've asked me that before,' Rashe reminded him patiently. 'Not Monday, at least not that I recall. Some time last week, I think.'

'You're sure about that?'

'No, not really. Not positive. I didn't think it was important, if you know what I mean.' He took a drag on his cigarette. 'I knew her by sight, but I didn't pay any particular attention to her, more than any of the others.'

'The others. Do you like little girls, Terry?' Elliott's voice was soft, and he made the question sound innocuous.

'Of course I do. I wouldn't work at a school if I didn't. I don't see what that—' He stopped abruptly as the significance of the question penetrated his brain; his jaw slackened and his face drained of colour. 'Christ! You're not suggesting— You don't think—'

'Steady on, Terry.' Elliott rose to his feet. 'I think that per-haps it's time for you to come down to the station with me. Would you like to ring your solicitor before we go?'

'But I don't need a solicitor! I'm telling you the truth – I never laid a finger on her!' A film of sweat had appeared on his ashen face.

Now we're getting somewhere, Elliott thought. 'I haven't suggested that you did,' he said with a smile. 'You're the one who said it. I just think that we need to talk about this a bit more.'

'Are you arresting me, then?'

'If that's the way you want to put it,' said the policeman amiably, heading for the door. 'I'd prefer to say that we're just asking you to assist us with our enquiries.'

Hal, too, had slept poorly the night before; apart from everything else, he was unused to being alone in bed. But unlike most of the others, who had at least had some function to fulfil, Hal had nothing to keep him busy. He couldn't throw himself into his work; he had no work to throw himself into. Up until the beginning of the week, he had expected to be at Branlingham Vicarage for quite some time to come, and he had not yet lined up his next job.

The first thing in the morning, he'd switched on the radio. There was no news of Daisy – nothing positive, at any rate. The search for the missing girl was continuing, they said; they didn't have to add that the longer the search went on, the less likely was a positive outcome. Hal got up, showered and shaved, then dressed and went round the corner to the newsagents to buy the newspapers. Daisy's face had moved off the front page of most of them, but he bought copies of them all, just in case one of them might have some little detail that the others had missed.

Going through all of the papers in detail took time; time was one thing he had to spare. He sat for several hours at the table in the breakfast room with a cup of coffee in front of him. After the first bitter sip, he allowed it to go cold, absorbed in the papers.

There was jolly little new information; most of it was a rehash of speculation and background details. Some intrepid reporter, frustrated at the inaccessibility of the parents, had managed to track down a relative for a comment: Thomas Finch, who declared himself devastated at his half-sister's disappearance. 'Perhaps this will be a lesson to all mothers everywhere to be vigilant where their children are concerned,' was the sanctimonious quote he had offered. 'I'm not saying that Daisy's mother was at fault, mind you, but perhaps if she had taken more care . . .'

Hal made a disgusted noise in the back of his throat. Poor Rosie, with the deliberate cruelty of her stepson to contend with, on top of everything else. Please God, though, she might not see the paper, might not know what Tom had said.

By the time Hal finished the papers, the morning had gone. He closed his eyes, remembering Daisy and the unselfconscious joy she took in every aspect of life: dancing up the stairs to summon him for chocolate cake, taking off her shoes at Kinderland, squealing with glee over the kitten frieze in her bedroom, sleeping after the picnic, her face sticky with ginger cake and orange squash.

Squash, he thought with a jolt. Today was Wednesday; tonight was squash night.

Mike Odum was bound to know things about the investigation that hadn't made it into the papers. If he was skilful in his questions, Hal might just be able to find out what was going on.

For the first time in days, Hal felt that he had something to look forward to.

They were on their way to an interview room – Elliott, the sergeant and Terry Rashe – when they were intercepted by Detective Superintendent Hardy. He wasn't a big man, but he managed somehow to convey the impression that he was, and looking at him as he bore down upon them, Elliott was reminded yet again why he distrusted men with their eyes too close together. 'Could I see you in my office, Inspector?'

Elliott was terrified of Superintendent Hardy, but he was also at that moment intent upon interviewing Terry Rashe; that determination gave him the courage to suggest, 'Could it wait a few minutes, sir?'

'Now,' Hardy said, investing that monosyllable with so much weight that Elliott was left in no doubt that he meant it.

Once in the superintendent's office, Hardy sat behind his desk, and allowed the inspector to stand. He got straight to the point. 'You haven't found the girl.'

'No, sir, but—'

'No buts. You haven't found her. And furthermore you have no clues, no leads. Nothing. Sweet FA.'

Elliott swallowed. 'With all due respect, sir, I think we're on the verge of a breakthrough. We're just about to interview a suspect – the school caretaker. He's denying any involvement, but I'm sure that if I lean on him a bit he'll crack.' He edged towards the door. 'So if you don't mind, sir, I'll just be getting back to—'

'Not so fast, Inspector,' Hardy rapped out. 'The sergeant can do it. As of this moment you're off the case.'

'But, sir—'

Hardy went on as though he hadn't spoken. 'We're damnably short-staffed. Half the bloody department are on holiday, and the other half are out beating the bushes for that girl. Let's face it, Inspector – you're three days into the search. She's not going to be found alive.'

Hearing the superintendent articulate his own fears, though it wasn't at all unexpected, gave Elliott a hollow feeling in the pit of his stomach, and he found himself wanting to argue. 'She could be, sir. If we manage to break the caretaker – he might have her hidden somewhere. Like that man in Belgium, who locked those girls in a cellar and kept them for months.'

'Fat bloody chance of that. If he's had his filthy mitts on her, she's dead by now,' Hardy stated brutally. 'And I'm not asking you, Inspector. I'm telling you. It's high time to scale down the search, and, in any case, there's something else that's come along. A real murder, with a real body. I want you to take over.'

'A murder?' Elliott's mind raced. 'Who? Where?'

'Some boys have just found a car in the woods between Elmsford and Branlingham. With a body in it. Stab wound, apparently,' he said tersely. 'A man's body, not a little girl's, before you ask. The call came through a few minutes ago. So stop trying to argue with me, and get your arse over there.'

'Who shall I take with me?'

'Damned if I know. See if you can find yourself a sergeant somewhere. I don't care who it is.'

DI Mike Odum, who had heard about the body and guessed what Hardy and Elliott were talking about, hovered outside Hardy's door and timed his entrance perfectly.

'Sir,' he said smoothly. 'If I could make a suggestion. Sergeant Threadgold has put her name forward for a CID traineeship. She's a good officer, sir. Bright, hard-working. This would be a good chance to see if she's got what it takes.'

'Throw her in at the deep end, eh?' Hardy ruminated. 'I like it.'

'But Sergeant Threadgold is at the Finches', sir,' Elliott pointed out. 'She's the officer detailed to stay with the parents.'

That was enough to make his mind up. 'I'm sick and tired of hearing about the bloody Finches! You can collect Sergeant Threadgold on your way to the crime scene, Inspector Elliott.' He glared at Elliott's retreating back, then added in a voice that dripped with sarcasm, 'And perhaps one day, Inspector, when you've got a few minutes spare, you might explain to me how all of those bloody officers who are out there looking for that girl happened to miss a car with an effing body in it.'

Mike had done it! Zoe wasn't sure how he'd managed it, but suddenly, miraculously, she was out of Branlingham Vicarage and on her way to a crime scene. She was going to take part in a murder investigation, as a CID trainee, Pete Elliott had informed her, and Zoe couldn't disguise her joy.

'Who's been murdered, then, sir?' she asked, knowing that he would tell her anyway.

But Pete Elliott wasn't as voluble as usual; he was still smarting after his interview with Superintendent Hardy, and upset at being removed from the Daisy Finch case. 'We'll soon find out. I'm not sure whether the body's been identified yet or not. All I know is that it's a man. Not a little girl. Not Daisy Finch.' That, at least, was a blessing, reflected Elliott; as long as there was no body, there was still a chance that Daisy Finch was alive.

'But surely,' Zoe thought aloud, 'there must be a connection. I mean, sir, Branlingham isn't that big a place. There probably hasn't been a major crime in Branlingham for years. And to have two, within three days – doesn't it seem odd to you?'

Elliott considered what she'd said, accepting without question by now that whatever had happened to Daisy Finch, a crime was involved. 'You've got something there, Sergeant,' he admitted. 'Though what the connection might be escapes me. Unless we're looking at a suicide rather than a murder. Say the man molests Daisy Finch, kills her, maybe accidentally, then kills himself in remorse. I suppose that's possible.'

But when they'd located the blue Metro in the woods, penetrated the blue-and-white scene-of-crime tapes that surrounded the car, and had their first glimpse of the body, that notion fled. 'No one stabs himself in the back, between the shoulder blades like that, not unless he's a contortionist,' he said to Zoe with mordant humour. Death sickened him; this was the way he dealt with it.

'And then somehow disposes of the knife before getting in the car to die,' she pointed out. 'Thoughtfully making sure not to bleed on the upholstery.'

'Yes.' She was right: there was no murder weapon, and no blood in the car. He looked at her with respect; she didn't miss much, it was clear, and he would ignore her, or underestimate her, at his peril. And she wasn't as used to seeing violent death as he was, presumably, yet she hadn't turned a hair.

So they knew two things, thanks to Zoe: that the man had been murdered, and that he had not been stabbed in the car.

There was very little else that they knew for sure, even after the medical examiner had certified death and the photographer and other scene-of-crime officers had finished their gruesome business. The body still had no identity: the man's pockets were empty, and there was nothing in the car to provide any hints. That, Zoe remarked, was one of the strange things about it all. Someone had gone to considerable lengths to remove everything from the car – not just fingerprints, which had indeed been carefully wiped from the steering wheel, the dashboard, the lid of the boot, and even the fuel cap, but also the entire contents of the glove box and the boot. Not even a stray sweet wrapper remained under the seat.

'Whoever killed this bloke didn't want us to know who he was,' Zoe said.

Elliott nodded. 'But we'll find out.' He pointed to the number plate. 'Ring the DVLC right now, on your mobile.'

She did; the DVLC provided her with the name and address of a man living in Bury St Edmunds, a Mr Gilmore. 'Think it's him, sir?' Zoe asked.

'One way to find out.' He went back to the panda car. 'Let's go.'

'We're going to Bury, then?'

'Why not? It's not far, and it will be the quickest way. I mean, if he's got a wife who's wringing her hands saying her husband hasn't come home, then we'll be well away.'

Zoe was silent, thinking, for a few moments as Elliott steered his way back to the main road. 'He's been dead a while, hasn't he, sir? How long, do you reckon?'

'We won't really know till the post mortem, of course, and the medical examiner was being as coy as ever – he hates to be caught out or proven wrong, you see,' Elliott explained to the CID newcomer. 'But at a guess I'd say at least a day or two.' He wrinkled his nose in distaste at the memory of the flies and the smell.

'Have there been any missing persons reported in the last few days?'

'Daisy Finch,' he reminded her. Superintendent Hardy and everyone else might want to forget about Daisy Finch, but Elliott knew that *he* couldn't. That little bespectacled face still haunted him.

She gave an impatient shrug. 'Apart from Daisy Finch.'

'Don't dismiss her like that,' he warned. 'You're the one who suggested that the two things might be connected.'

'That was before we saw him. Now that we have, I don't see how they could be connected.'

But Elliott wasn't convinced. He wouldn't say anything to Hardy, of course, but it wouldn't hurt to keep his options open. 'Ring through to headquarters,' he instructed Zoe. 'Ask them about any missing persons reports – not necessarily just within the past few days. He could have gone missing some time before he died. And,' he added on an impulse that he didn't even explain to her, 'ask forensics to take that blue Metro in and go over it with a fine tooth-comb. Whoever cleaned that car out was careful, but they couldn't have removed everything. Hairs, fibres – I want to know if they find *anything*.' As she punched in the number he went on, 'And I want it quickly.'

With Zoe gone, the Vicarage seemed to have settled down to a semblance of normality, though of course it was far from normal. Rosemary continued to sleep, which worried Gervase, but Margaret assured him that it was what her body needed, a useful defence mechanism to cope with the pain.

Margaret prepared sandwiches from remnants of the Sunday joint, augmented with bits and pieces she found in the fridge, and joined Gervase at the kitchen table to eat them. Neither had much of an appetite, though in his case, at least, it had been two full days since he'd eaten very much of anything.

'I do appreciate what you've been doing here for us,' Gervase said awkwardly, putting a sandwich on his plate. 'It's been wonderful to have your support, and I know that Rosemary would join me in saying that. But I'm very conscious of the fact that you have a job to do. I don't expect you to stay indefinitely.'

Margaret shook her head. 'This is part of my job, as well,' she stated. 'And I'll stay as long as you and Rosemary need me.'

'You're very kind.'

'No,' she demurred, feeling guilty to be taking credit for something that allowed her to put her own life on hold at just the right time. 'As I said, it's part of my job, and the most important part, at this moment. But I will need to make a few phone calls, and cancel some meetings,' she added.

Silently he inclined his head in assent. Perhaps, thought Margaret, he recognised, as she did, that they were somehow bound up together in this. What an irony it was, she reflected, that just two days ago they had been together, discussing the future of *his* marriage. And during that meeting, some unknown fate had befallen Daisy, as the girl seemingly disappeared into thin air. At the same time, his wife and her husband had been together as well, unbeknownst to Margaret and Gervase, deciding between the two of them the future of *all* of them.

She prayed that Gervase would never have to know about that. The burden of knowledge was difficult enough for her to bear; no matter what happened with Daisy, Gervase had enough on his plate without that burden.

There was no distraught woman wringing her hands over a missing husband at the Gilmore home; Mr Gilmore was there himself, in the flesh, alive and well, a retired gentleman of advanced years. He was baffled; he had sold the blue Metro on to a garage last month in part exchange for a newer model, he explained, and he couldn't understand why the new owner hadn't yet registered it.

Their next stop was, of course, the garage. It was a small operation, not a large dealership, and the man to whom they spoke remembered the blue Metro well. 'A nice clean car,' he told them. 'Not too many miles on her, either, though she was all of five years old. Got her from an old gent who kept her nice and tidy.'

Zoe couldn't stop herself from asking the next question, though she wasn't sure whether it was the done thing. 'And the person who bought it off you. Was it a youngish man with ginger hair?'

The man looked surprised. 'No. Nothing like that.'

'Then who?'

'I remember very well.' He nodded. 'It was a woman. Young. Blond hair, very attractive. She paid cash.'

'Cash?' Elliott echoed. 'That must not happen too often.'

'No, it doesn't. That's one reason I remember. Apart from the fact that she was a real looker,' he added with a wink at the policeman.

Zoe was disgusted. 'So you didn't get her name, then,' she suggested in a voice that didn't hide her contempt for the man or his pathetic attempts at male bonding.

'Of course I got her name,' he said coolly. '*And* her address. I keep my books nice and tidy, like.'

'I'm sure you do,' Elliott interposed. 'Could you give us that information?'

The man went to his tidy desk and sat down, opening the ledger book which sat foursquare in the middle of the blotter. He ran his finger down a page, then turned it over to the next page. 'Last month, wasn't it? Yes, here it is. The blue Metro was sold to a Miss Kim Rashe, Grange Cottage, Elmsford.'

Pete Elliott's heart was pumping, adrenaline coursing through his body, but it wasn't until they were back in the panda car that he displayed his elation, punching the air with his fist. 'Rashe!' he said. 'I knew it! I knew that little toe-rag was involved. And you were right, Sergeant. This murder *is* connected to Daisy Finch's disappearance. I'm not sure how yet, but we'll find out. It's just about time for another little chat with Terry Rashe, don't you think?'

'Terry Rashe?' she echoed, bewildered. 'Who is he, then?'

Zoe had so quickly become one of the team that he had forgotten how recent her elevation was; he realised with a shock that just a few hours ago she'd been sidelined out of the action, making cups of tea for Rosemary Finch. 'Oh, I'm sorry, Sergeant. You haven't had the pleasure of meeting Terry, have you?'

He filled her in as they drove out of Bury, back towards Saxwell. 'He's the school caretaker. Wimpy little bloke, weedy. Something a bit shifty about him. He doesn't have a record – I checked that straightaway. But he didn't half turn green when I asked him if he liked little girls.'

'You think he's a pervert, then?' she asked baldly.

'Put it this way, Sergeant – it wouldn't surprise me. I could just about imagine him hanging round the school yard, hoping for a glimpse of some little girl's frilly knickers.'

Ordinarily Zoe would have interpreted such a remark as a sexist jibe, and responded in kind, but she realised that Pete Elliott hadn't meant it like that; she contented herself with saying, mildly, 'Not many little girls wear frilly knickers these days, sir.'

'Whatever. You know what I mean.'

'So are you going to try to get a search warrant for his house, then?' Zoe asked, leaping ahead.

'No,' Elliott said. 'Not just yet, anyway. Believe it or not, and I find it a bit hard to believe myself, he's married, and has a kid.'

'That doesn't mean anything,' Zoe stated in a prim voice. 'Lots of married blokes have some pretty strange hang-ups.'

Elliott laughed, not unkindly. 'I'll take your word for it. But what I'm getting at, Sergeant, is that if Terry Rashe *did* take Daisy Finch, he isn't keeping her at his house. Not with a wife and kid there. And she's not at the school. So either he's got another hiding place,' he said, his voice suddenly bleak, 'or . . .'

'Or she's dead, sir.'

He nodded thoughtfully; there was a lump in his throat.

Zoe didn't seem to notice, or perhaps she was being tactful. 'Is Kim Rashe his wife, then?'

'No – she's bound to be related, but Terry lives in Branlingham, not Elmsford. And his wife has some strange name like Jezebel. And remember,' he added, 'the bloke at the garage called her "Miss".'

'So are we going to talk to Terry Rashe now?' she asked,

trying not to sound too eager. 'Before he gets the wind up and does a runner?'

Pete Elliott shook his head. 'Not now. Terry's not going anywhere, as a matter of fact. He's at the station – I took him in this morning. It won't hurt our Terry to cool his heels for an hour or two. And in the meantime . . .'

'We'll talk to Kim Rashe,' Zoe finished for him, reaching for her mobile.

'Whoever she is.'

Chapter 22

On a Wednesday afternoon there was usually no one at home at Grange Cottage. But Sybil Rashe was making the most of her unexpected afternoon off, cleaning her own house for a change.

She was surprised when the doorbell rang or, rather, chimed 'Greensleeves'. The bell had been a birthday present for Frank, last month; it played a choice of jaunty tunes in a tinny, mechanical tone. Pulling off her pinny and putting down her duster, Sybil went to the door.

Police: a young woman in uniform, and a tall man who wasn't wearing a uniform but was holding out a warrant card for her inspection. 'Detective Inspector Elliott,' he announced, 'and Sergeant Threadgold.'

Sybil Rashe had had very little contact with the police in her life, but she did like to watch *The Bill* and *Inspector Morse*, so their presence held no terrors for her. It probably had something to do with that business of the missing little girl, she told herself. Why, her Terry had been interviewed by them yesterday, and to hear him tell it he was their star witness so far. 'Hello,' she said, smiling to let them know that they could count on her to be cooperative.

'We are looking for a Miss Kim Rashe,' said the tall man, the inspector. 'And this is the address we were given. Are you Miss Rashe?'

Sybil's smile turned to a frown of puzzlement. 'I'm *Mrs* Rashe. Kim's my daughter. She doesn't live here, though – hasn't done for over a year.'

'Could you tell us where we might find her, then?' asked the man politely.

'The caravan park, between here and Branlingham, just off the Saxwell road,' Sybil told him. 'It's the pink caravan.'

'Thank you very much for your help.'

They were turning to go. Sybil couldn't bear it – to be so close to a police investigation, and then to be disappointed like this. 'What's our Kim done, then?' she asked.

The inspector turned back. 'Nothing, Mrs Rashe. We just need to ask her a few questions.'

Desperation made her brazen. 'Is it about the little girl, then? Kim doesn't know anything about that, I can tell you. Now, Terry – he's my son.' She smiled with maternal pride. 'Terry knows a thing or two. The police have talked to him several times. He's their star witness, he told me. Do you know my Terry, Inspector?'

'Yes, I've spoken to Terry,' he said with a straight face.

'Then you know how helpful he's been. He's always been such a good boy, my Terry.' She had a sudden inspiration. 'Listen, would you like to come in? I could make you a cup of tea. You look thirsty, the both of you. And it *is* teatime.'

Elliott hesitated for an instant. A cup of tea *would* be nice, and he had a feeling that the voluble Mrs Rashe could be a source of useful information. But now was not the time. 'I'm so sorry, Mrs Rashe,' he said with real regret. 'We've got to get on.' Once again he turned, and once again he turned back; he may as well make use of the woman's eagerness to help, he decided. 'Could you tell me, Mrs Rashe,' he asked ingenuously, 'does your daughter Kim drive a blue Metro?'

She stared at him. 'A blue Metro? I should say not, Inspector. Kim doesn't drive at all, and that's the truth. Never even took a lesson. Kev, her fiancé, he has a clapped-out Escort. Orange, not blue. Wherever did you get an idea like that about Kim?'

'Does any member of your family own a blue Metro?' he persisted. 'Terry, for instance?'

The question baffled her into an uncharacteristic monosyllable. 'No.'

The woman, the sergeant, spoke for the first time. 'You're sure about that?'

'I ought to know what cars my own family drive,' Sybil stated indignantly.

'Yes, of course.' Elliott gave her a soothing smile and fished a card out of his pocket. 'We've really got to be going, Mrs Rashe. But here is my card. If you think of anything that you'd like to tell us, you can ring the station and ask for me by name.'

She took the rectangle of card and looked at it thoughtfully, running her finger round the edge, as the police returned to their panda car and headed for the Saxwell road.

'So what did you make of her, sir?' Zoe asked when they were under way.

Pete Elliott grinned. 'Well, one thing for sure. She hasn't talked to her blue-eyed boy Terry recently. She's a bit behind the times. I wonder what she'd say if she knew he was down at the station, even as we speak?'

'She wouldn't believe it.'

'You're right,' he affirmed. 'She's the sort of mum who always insists that her son is a good boy, even when he's confessed to multiple murders. Terry can do no wrong, as far as his mum is concerned.'

'And do you think she was telling the truth about the car?'

'What do *you* think?' he challenged her.

Zoe pulled the antenna of her mobile phone up and down as she considered the question. 'Well, she did seem genuinely surprised when you asked about it. At this point, I don't suppose she would have any reason to lie.'

'Unless she knows that Terry is somehow involved in this murder, and is trying to protect him,' Elliott theorised. 'That would be a jolly good reason to lie.'

'But where does Kim come into all of this?' Zoe wondered.

'That, Sergeant, is what we're about to find out.' Elliott turned off the Saxwell road towards the caravan park.

'The pink one, she said.'

There was only one pink caravan: not a pale, retiring pink, or a dignified deep rose, but full-blown Suffolk pink, strawberry ice cream married to prawn cocktail. It clashed horribly with the old Escort parked next to it, a car that owed its orange colour as much to rust as to its long-ago paint job.

'It's showtime,' Elliott announced, getting out of the panda car and striding to the door of the caravan. There was no bell; he rapped on it several times with the flat of his hand.

'Bugger off!' came a masculine voice from inside.

He gave the door another hard smack.

'Bloody hell,' muttered a female voice. 'Is that you, Mum? I told you not to come!'

'Police,' he said firmly and loudly. 'Miss Rashe, we need to talk to you.'

A number of indescribable sounds followed: bedsprings creaking, alarmed whispers, rustling of clothing. Elliott waited patiently, knowing that there was no escape for the caravan's inhabitants.

Eventually the door cracked open a fraction of an inch and a nose poked out. 'What the hell do you want?' challenged the woman.

'We need to ask you a few questions, Miss Rashe,' Elliott repeated. 'You *are* Miss Rashe, I take it? Miss Kim Rashe?'

'That's me,' she admitted, squeezing her bulk through the door and shutting it behind her. Kim Rashe was wearing nothing but a dirty towelling dressing gown, too small to meet very satisfactorily round her waist; her mountainous breasts spilled out above the tied sash, and her feet were bare. 'You haven't come at a very good time,' she said, stating the obvious. 'So ask your questions and piss off.'

'Miss Rashe, do you own a blue Metro?'

Her astonishment was even greater than her mother's; whatever question she had been expecting, this was not it. But she recovered quickly. 'Bloody hell. No. I don't own a blue Metro, I don't own any car at all – I don't even drive. Anyone will tell you. Ask Kev. Ask my mum.'

Zoe had been looking behind Kim as she squeezed out of the door, hoping for a glimpse of Kev. She hadn't seen Kev, but what she had seen intrigued her. 'We'd *like* to ask Kev,' she said, with a sideways glance at Pete Elliott. 'Do you mind if we come in for just a minute?'

'No! I mean yes! Yes, I do mind!' she shouted as they moved towards the door.

Elliott pushed past her, turned the knob, and threw the door open.

'Bloody hell.' This time the voice was Zoe Threadgold's, and Pete Elliott followed it up with ' 'Strewth!'

The inside of the pink caravan was like some sort of ecclesiastical Aladdin's cave, stuffed with candlesticks, crosses, crucifixes, sanctuary lamps, and communion vessels. And in the middle stood a large brass eagle lectern behind which Kev cowered, sheltering his nakedness.

Pete Elliott couldn't help it; he burst out laughing.

★

He laughed all the way back to Saxwell. His laughter was contagious; after a moment Zoe joined him, in spite of her resolution not to do so.

The two in the back seat, hastily and scantily clad, weren't laughing.

Pete Elliott knew all about the church thefts; he had been called out to investigate the majority of them, and knew that in the files of his own unsolved cases were descriptions of most of the items in the pink caravan. It would give him great pleasure and satisfaction to return them to their rightful owners, to close a stack of cases in one fell swoop.

Elliott managed to control his mirth by the time they pulled up in front of the police station. He turned to the two in the back seat. 'Okay, tell me about it. Before we go in. Why did you do it?'

'That should be fairly bloody obvious,' Kev said scornfully. 'Money, of course. Some of that stuff is worth a bloody fortune.'

'Then why have you still got it all? If you don't mind my asking?'

Kim replied with a sullen scowl. 'We've been looking for someone to buy it off us.'

'We got quite a lot of cash as well,' Kev added, as a matter of pride. 'Out of boxes and such, and in one church they left the safe standing open with all these offering bags in it, stuffed with cash.'

'But we've spent it all, so there's no use trying to get it back,' Kim put in with a certain grim satisfaction.

Kev had decided, seemingly, that confession was good for the soul. 'We got the idea when we went to see the Vicar about getting married,' he said. 'I'd never been in a church before. He showed us round, showed us some of the stuff they'd got. He told us that the church was full of priceless treasures.'

'He was right,' Kim affirmed. 'But only if you know where to flog it.'

When Rosemary woke at last, late in the afternoon, Gervase was sitting beside the bed. Her eyes focused on him slowly, and he anticipated her question before it came. 'I'm sorry, my dear. There's no news. Nothing.'

She turned her head into the pillow, too exhausted for words. Thanks to the sedative, her sleep had been dreamless, but she had woken up into a nightmare that had not gone away. Gervase took her hand and held it, realising, painfully, that it made no difference to her whether he was there or not.

After a while, Margaret looked in on them. 'She's woken,' Gervase whispered.

'Then I think it's about time for her to have something to eat,' Margaret stated. She went off and returned a few minutes later with a plate of scrambled eggs. At the smell, Rosemary grimaced and turned her head away.

Margaret sat on the edge of the bed and put her arm round Rosemary's shoulders, lifting her to a sitting position. With the plate on her lap, she persevered until Rosemary accepted a forkful of the eggs.

Watching his wife being fed like a baby was too much for Gervase. 'Do you need my help?' he offered, hoping that the answer would be no.

'I'll manage better without you,' Margaret said with a smile. 'You look as if you could use some fresh air, Gervase. Why don't you go outside and take a bit of a walk?'

He obeyed with alacrity, heading for the sanctuary of St Stephen's.

The day before, the Vicarage had been besieged by journalists, all hoping that the distraught family would give them some usable quotes, expressions of grief or hope. But Zoe had sent them all packing, and after Margaret had arrived, they'd had even less chance of getting anything. So they had all cleared off for greener pastures.

All save one, who was examining the interior of St Stephen's, hoping that somehow he might be able to make a story out of that whilst waiting for bigger prey. 'Vicar!' he said, spotting Gervase before the latter had a chance to flee. 'Could I have a word, Vicar?'

It was all too clear who, or what, the man was. Cornered, Gervase fell back on the time-honoured statement. 'I have no comment.'

Having the Vicar on his own was too good an opportunity to pass up; the man ignored his demur. 'I wanted to ask you about your son, Vicar.'

'My son?' Startled, Gervase halted his retreat. 'Tom?'

The journalist followed up his advantage, drawing a folded newspaper from his pocket. 'Yes. Do you have anything to say about his statement in the *Daily Telegraph*, blaming your wife for Daisy's disappearance?' What an exclusive it would be, if he could uncover a family rift!

'What?' Gervase snatched the newspaper from the man and scanned the column of print.

'Do he and your wife not get on, then?' suggested the journalist. 'Wicked stepmother, and all that?'

Gervase had the good sense not to answer. Instead he appropriated the newspaper, turned on his heel, and went back into the house to the telephone.

It took him a few minutes to locate the phone number for Tom's chambers and have the call put through. 'Tom?' he said when his son came on the line.

'They've found her, then?' Tom asked eagerly.

It was a moment before Gervase, intent on his own agenda, realised what Tom's natural assumption about the call might be. 'Daisy? No, I'm afraid she hasn't been found yet.'

'Then what is it?'

Gervase took a deep breath. 'I'd like to know the meaning of this quote in the newspaper, Tom. "I'm not saying that Daisy's mother was at fault", but that's exactly what you *are* saying.'

There was a short pause. 'Well, she was, wasn't she?' Tom said defensively. 'She was late to collect Daisy after school, or it wouldn't have happened. That's what you told me.'

Feeling as though he'd just been punched in the stomach, Gervase sought to control his voice. 'But what on earth were you thinking of, Tom, to say such a thing about your mother to a reporter? You must have known how it would come across!'

'My mother?' Tom said in a voice that was suddenly cold. 'She is *not* my mother. I wouldn't have thought that you'd need reminding of that.'

For Gervase, it was as if his world had suddenly turned upside-down yet again, for the second time in nearly that many days. 'And I wouldn't have thought that you'd need reminding that she *is* my wife,' he said, equally cold.

'I'm hardly likely to forget *that*.'

Gervase closed his eyes and took another deep breath. 'You owe Rosemary an apology.'

There was a pause at the other end of the phone. 'Not until she apologises to *me* for trying to usurp my mother's place. Not that she could ever succeed at it,' he added snidely. 'We both know that she's a pretty poor substitute. And we both know why you married her.'

'What do you mean?' Gervase asked, his voice deadly calm, each word distinct.

'You needed someone to look after you,' Tom pointed out in a patient, patronising tone. 'And she was the first one to come along.'

Gervase was silent for so long that Tom thought perhaps

he'd put the phone down. But when he spoke, it was with a strength and a fury in his voice that Tom had never before heard. 'That,' he said, 'is an utter and ridiculous lie. And until you are prepared to apologise for it to both me and my wife, you are not welcome in this house.' Only then did he put the phone down.

Pete Elliott had more pressing things on his plate than conducting the formal interview with the two hapless thieves, so he turned them over to someone else and went to his office to check on his phone messages. There was an envelope in the middle of his desk, marked 'Urgent'.

He opened it and unfolded the papers inside as the forensic pathologist put his head round the door. 'Oh, there you are, Inspector. I've just delivered a copy of that to the superintendent. I rushed the p.m. through, as you requested.'

'I haven't got time to read through the whole thing,' Elliott admitted. 'Can you tell me what it says, in fifty words or less?'

'Only if you'll do the counting,' the pathologist grinned. 'White male, about thirty. Died of a single stab wound to—'

Elliott turned his hand round in circles. 'Don't get all technical on me. Just hit the high spots.'

'Okay, okay. Just the one stab wound. He was struck from above and behind, which would suggest that he was sitting down when it happened. No other wounds or injuries, no signs that he defended himself, no scars or distinguishing marks. And as you guessed, he didn't die in that car. He was put there after death.'

'When did he die?'

The pathologist gave the expected answer. 'I can't tell you that, exactly. Not today, not yesterday. Probably some time the day before. What I *can* tell you, though, Inspector, is that very shortly before he died, he had a meal. We're talking less than an hour before. Shepherd's pie, chips, a bit of salad. And a fairly large quantity of beer. Guinness, at a guess.'

'Very interesting.' Elliott nodded thoughtfully. 'Very interesting indeed.'

He'd sent Zoe Threadgold back to her flat to freshen up, and to change out of her uniform. She returned promptly, dressed in a sober, almost prim, skirt and blouse.

Now she sat on a hard chair in his office and regarded Pete Elliott across the desk.

'I've had the p.m. report,' he told her.

'That was quick.'

'I asked him to speed it up. I reckoned it might help us to identify the bloke.' Elliott picked up the papers from his desk and waved them at her.

'And?'

He admired her terseness, her way of getting to the heart of a matter without messing about. But it was not his way, and he answered her question obliquely. 'Tell me what this says to you, Sergeant: shepherd's pie, chips, a bit of salad, a lot of beer.'

She looked puzzled at the seeming irrelevance, but replied, 'A pub meal.'

Elliott slapped his palm down on the desk and grinned at her. 'Got it in one! Well done! That's my feeling exactly.'

'I don't understand.'

'Our man's last meal, less than an hour before he died.' Again he waved the papers at her. 'It's all here, in the p.m. report.'

'I see.' She *did* see. 'So you're thinking, sir, that he ate in a pub just before he died. Which was . . . does it say?'

'He won't commit himself,' Elliott admitted. 'Probably some time on Monday. But if we work on this assumption –

and we haven't got a better one, Sergeant – then it was either just after lunch or just after dinner on Monday.'

'Lots of pubs are open all day now, sir,' she pointed out. 'He might have been eating in the middle of the after-noon.'

'Yes, and he could have eaten the meal at home – his own or someone else's – of course, or he could have been killed a long way from where he was found. But let's start with this. Let's just say that he ate a pub meal some time on Monday, and was murdered not long thereafter.' He turned to the map of the district on the wall behind his desk and put his finger down somewhere close to where the body had been found, deep in the woods near Branlingham. 'What I suggest is that we work out from here. Talk to the people in the pubs, the regulars, the publicans. If he *did* eat at a pub, someone will remember him.'

'Do we have a photo that we can show round?'

'He wasn't very pretty when we found him,' he reminded her. 'But they've done a photofit drawing for us.' He pulled it out of an envelope and passed it across to her. 'This will have to do. You keep it.'

She examined it and nodded, taking possession.

Elliott looked at his watch. 'It's nearly six o'clock – the pubs will soon be in full swing. So let's get going, Sergeant.'

'What about Terry Rashe?'

'Terry can wait,' he stated. 'We can hold him till tomorrow morning, if necessary. And the night is yet young.'

Before they could get out of the building, though, they encountered Superintendent Hardy in the corridor. He stopped and regarded them with disfavour. 'Do we know who our body is yet, then?'

'No, sir,' Elliott admitted. 'We're following up on a lead right now.'

'Good.' He wasn't convinced. 'But if I hear you're out there asking questions about Daisy Finch, Inspector, I will not be amused. Do you understand me?'

'Yes, sir.'

They started in Elmsford, simply because it was on the way to Branlingham. The Swan, a rather shabby pub near the centre, stayed open all afternoon and seemed to attract a fairly sedate crowd of middle-aged locals; darts appeared to be a big feature, along with the local beer. Hot bar meals were not on offer, only bags of crisps and peanuts and a few indifferent sandwiches.

No one in the Swan recalled having seen the mysterious man. Elliott was not surprised.

Next they tried the George and Dragon in Branlingham. Although it had only opened its doors at six, already it seemed much livelier than the Swan, with a young crowd well into their drinks, and availing themselves of the noisy electronic fruit machines. Elliott realised with a sinking feeling that there were a fair number of journalists there, in addition to the locals; they'd been drawn to Branlingham by the story of the missing girl, and had stayed on, unable to believe their luck, when an unidentified dead body had turned up as a bonus. But the journalists were easy to spot, if potentially difficult to avoid, and Elliott decided to begin with the publican.

With Zoe behind him, he approached the bar; it was tended by a young man sporting hair the colour of Kev's car. Discreetly he flashed his warrant card. 'I know you're busy, but could you spare me just a moment of your time?'

'Sure, mate. If you make it quick.'

'We're trying to trace the movements of a certain man, and wondered if by any chance you might have seen him. Say, on Monday?' Elliott nodded at Zoe, who produced the photofit.

'Ginger-haired,' Zoe added.

The barman didn't even have to examine it. 'If you call that ginger-haired.' He patted his own flaming thatch with a grin. 'That's what they call me, as a matter of fact – Ginger.'

'So you *have* seen him?' Elliott prompted.

'Yes, he was here, all right,' he confirmed. 'Monday night, it was. I remember, because it was the day that little girl went missing, and everyone was talking about it. He was a stranger, and we don't get many of those. That is, we *didn't*,' he added, with an amused inclination of his head towards a knot of journalists at a nearby table. 'But this lot only arrived yesterday.'

'He ate a meal?' Elliott suggested, trying not to sound too excited.

The barman grinned. 'He asked about the steak and kidney, and I tipped him off that the shepherd's pie was better. Not that my wife would appreciate me saying so. But I felt like I owed him one, after he told me that I knew how to pull a pint of Guinness. There's not many in this part of the world who appreciate the fine art of pulling Guinness.'

'And he wasn't from round here,' Zoe put in.

'Didn't I say? Guinness. He was a real son of the Ould Sod. As Irish as they come, with a brogue you could cut with a knife. Though,' the man called Ginger added, 'I had the feeling it was a bit put on, if you know what I mean.'

Elliott absorbed this information silently, while Zoe pressed on. 'And you'd never seen him before?'

'Never.'

'What time was this on Monday?' Elliott asked. 'Do you have any idea what time it was when he left?'

Ginger rubbed his chin thoughtfully. 'Oh, half past eight, I suppose. Quarter to nine, maybe? Something like that.'

'Hey, Ginger!' shouted someone from the other end of the bar. 'Aren't you interested in selling me a drink?'

'Keep your hair on, mate,' he chaffed. But he glanced

towards his waiting customers anxiously. 'Was there anything else you wanted to know?' he asked the police officers.

'Not for now.' Elliott slid one of his cards onto the bar with an unobtrusive motion. 'You've been very helpful. But if you remember anything else about this man, please do get in touch with me.'

'Will do, mate.' He moved down the bar, as they turned to go.

But at the last minute, Zoe turned back. 'I've just thought of one more question,' she said. 'Was Terry Rashe in here on Monday night?'

Before Ginger could answer, one of the denizens of the bar took it upon himself to reply in tones only slightly slurred by drink. 'Terry? Terry never had it so good as he did on Monday. Everyone was buying Terry drinks that night, trying to get the inside story on that little girl. I bought him a drink myself.'

Ginger nodded in confirmation. 'That's too right, mate. Terry was the most popular man in Branlingham on Monday night.'

'So he was here until late,' Elliott surmised, hiding his disappointment.

'Oh, no.' Ginger gave him a wink. 'No, Terry was out of here by nine o'clock, as per usual. A bit henpecked, our Terry is – he knows that Delilah would have his guts for garters if he wasn't home by nine. Lord knows, I wouldn't want to cross Delilah.'

Elliott didn't speak till they were almost at the car, but his grin was ecstatic. 'Good work, Sergeant,' he said warmly. 'Good work.'

Zoe bent her head and fumbled with the car door so that he wouldn't see her blush of pleasure; that sort of thing would do her street cred no good at all.

*

Hal was waiting when Mike Odum arrived at the squash court. He had abandoned any idea of the subtle approach, and in fact knew that he would have to get in first to avoid Mike's teasing queries about why he had cancelled last week's match at the last minute. His night in with Margaret; that seemed so long ago, and so irrelevant, and he didn't think that he could endure being chaffed about his uxorious behaviour right now, with the way things stood.

'I see that your friend DI Elliott is in charge of the Daisy Finch case,' he said to the policeman straightaway.

Mike looked surprised. '*Was* in charge. That's ancient history, mate.'

'What do you mean?'

'He was pulled off this afternoon.' Mike attended to his racquet as he spoke. 'We've got a murder on our hands, in case you hadn't heard. A bloke's body found in a car. He's been put onto that. Along with my little tiger,' he added, grinning at the memory of how that had come about. 'Rough or smooth?'

'Rough,' said Hal.

The spin of the racquet went his way, but on his first serve he hit the tin, losing his serve. He played badly, losing the game in short order.

As they came off the court between games, Mike's elation at the one-sided win translated into chattiness. 'But I'll tell you something about Daisy Finch, mate,' he said confidentially, as though a squash game had not intervened in their conversation. 'Something that even Pete Elliott may not know yet. I ran into the forensics chap in the corridor before I left the station.'

'Yes?' Hal prompted eagerly.

'And he's linked the two crimes. The car where the dead bloke was found – when they ran their tests, they found three lots of hair in it.'

Hal held his breath.

'The dead bloke's, of course. And some unidentified blond hairs. But the third ones . . .'

'Daisy Finch.'

'You've got it in one, mate,' Mike grinned. 'A perfect match with the hair samples we've had from Daisy Finch's hairbrush. It looks as if the kid was definitely in that car.'

Hal went on to win the next three games.

'Terry Rashe *could* have done it, sir,' she said as he drove back towards Saxwell. 'He could have killed him. The timing fits.'

Elliott, much as he wanted to believe that Rashe was single-handedly responsible for Branlingham's crime wave, knew better than to get carried away by wishful thinking. And it wasn't doing Zoe Threadgold any favours to let her fall into that trap, either. She was bright; she was keen as mustard. But if she wanted to make it in the CID, she needed to learn – and sooner rather than later – that being a good detective involved more than inspired hunches, clever guesswork and leaps of logic. He was there to teach her; it was up to him to play devil's advocate. 'But we have no reason to think that he did. No evidence at all, and no motive.'

'There's the car.'

'We still don't know who that car belongs to,' he reminded her. 'Kim Rashe swears that it's not her car, and there isn't anything to link it to Terry either.'

'But if the murder somehow has to do with Daisy Finch's disappearance . . .'

'We don't know that, either,' he said flatly. 'That was just a guess. At this point there is nothing at all to tie the two together. And we still don't even know that Terry Rashe has anything whatsoever to do with Daisy Finch's disappearance.'

'Don't you think we need to talk to him, sir?'

'That's why we're going back to the police station.'

Zoe subsided into sulky silence, her recent warm glow forgotten.

It had seemed a very long day to Gervase and Margaret. Rosemary, though she'd eaten the scrambled eggs and drunk some tea, had continued to be unresponsive, detached; it was as if the only way she could cope with what had happened was by a total withdrawal from her surroundings. Eventually they had given her another sedative and tucked her into bed.

Now the two of them sat at the kitchen table, drinking yet more tea. They made an odd pair: opposites in many ways, temperamentally as different as could be, and with the additional barrier of their roles of Archdeacon and subordinate parish priest to come between them. Yet they were growing easier in each other's company; the barriers had come down to an extent through their shared experiences of the past days.

Though he had tried to put it out of his mind, Gervase was still badly shaken by his verbal confrontation with his son, and he found that he wanted to tell Margaret about it. He showed her the newspaper article, then explained what had happened.

'But that's appalling!' she said.

'And now I wonder . . .' He stopped; his thoughts were too monstrous to voice aloud.

'You wonder whether Rosemary might have known all along how Tom felt about her, even if you didn't,' Margaret guessed.

He bowed his head. 'Yes. I've been . . . stupid. Blind.'

'Don't be so hard on yourself.'

'And you were right, of course,' he went on softly. 'When we talked, the other day. It's wrong for me to assume that Rosemary knows how I feel. I've never been good at telling her. And now . . .' Gervase sighed and shook his head. 'And now, just like you said, I might have left it too late.'

'It's not too late.'

He raised his head and looked at her, his eyes filled with tears. 'But I can't reach her. She's . . . gone. Daisy's gone, and Rosemary has gone with her.'

Margaret knew that it was true, and wished that she had words of comfort for him. But before she could formulate something to say, the phone rang. She got up and went to answer it.

'Hazel Croom again,' she said, coming back into the kitchen. 'She's being quite insistent. Do you want to speak to her?'

Gervase shook his head wordlessly.

Margaret returned to the phone. 'He's not able to come to the phone just now,' she said firmly. 'But I'll be happy to pass along a message.'

Valerie stood for a very long time beside the bed, gazing down at the recumbent child. Daisy lay on her side, her knees pulled up almost to her chin. Her dark hair was fanned out over the pillow, and her cheek was flushed a delicate shade of pink. The kitten, as always, was curled beside her, as still as the child.

It had been a wonderful day: the problem of Daisy had been superseded by, subsumed into, the joy of Daisy.

What a loving, what a delightful child she was, with her sunny personality and her unconditional giving of herself. The difficulties posed by her handicap seemed to matter not at all.

They had spent the whole day together, and it had sped by. Playing with the kitten had taken up a great deal of the time, of course, and there had been the stories as well; Daisy seemed to be enchanted by the tales that Valerie spun for her, and never tired of listening to the same ones over and over. And they'd spent some time in the kitchen, Daisy assisting

Valerie with the meal preparation. The girl hadn't been allowed near the Aga, of course, but she had been delighted to lay the oven chips out on a baking tray, one by one, while Valerie cooked the sausages. They'd eaten the fruits of their labours together, and Valerie had been astonished at how much she enjoyed the sausages and chips. It had been years since she'd consumed such a meal; in company with Daisy she found it delicious.

And at the end of the day, after Daisy's bath, she had tucked the girl into bed with tenderness. Daisy had put her arms round her neck and kissed her with her soft, warm mouth, and had been happy to receive kisses in return. 'I love you, Auntie,' she'd said as she drifted off to sleep.

Altogether a perfect day, Valerie reflected as her eyes devoured the sleeping child, yearning to touch her but afraid to disturb her slumber. At last she gave in and stroked the flushed cheek lightly; Daisy didn't stir.

The television had been moved back to Valerie's room, for safety's sake, and though she could have stood all night watching Daisy sleep, eventually she forced herself to go to her own room, telling herself that tomorrow would be another day just like today, and there would be many more to follow it, stretching out into the future.

She slipped into her nightdress, then into bed, and switched the television on with the remote.

The news was on, and after a moment of fighting in some remote country in Africa – of no interest to Valerie – the scene shifted to Suffolk. She sat up in bed and watched with fascination.

'Here in the sleepy Suffolk village of Branlingham,' said the voice-over, as the camera panned round the village green, 'where little Daisy Finch disappeared over two days ago, another drama is unfolding. The body of an unidentified man has been discovered nearby, hidden in the woods. A police spokesman emphasises that they do not believe that the two incidents are connected. Meanwhile, Daisy Finch's whereabouts are still unknown, though it is believed that a local man is assisting police with their enquiries.

'The dead man appears to have been the victim of foul play.' A photofit picture flashed on the screen; it wasn't terribly like Shaun, Valerie thought dispassionately. 'Police are anxious to establish his identity, so if you recognise this man, please ring the number on your screen.'

Valerie punched the remote and Shaun's image disappeared. It was all right; her efforts had paid off. They didn't know who Shaun was, and weren't likely to find out, and as long as they didn't know, she was safe. There was nothing, nothing whatever, to connect her to the dead man.

And Daisy was hers.

Chapter 23

As long as the police questioned Terry Rashe, he continued to protest his innocence. He went so far as to ask for a solicitor, though even on the solicitor's advice he didn't decline to answer their questions. But the answers were always the same: he knew nothing about Daisy Finch's disappearance, he had never laid a finger on her, and he didn't know the ginger-haired Irishman. He hadn't even noticed him in the pub that night, much less spoken to him, and he certainly hadn't killed him.

Late on Wednesday evening Pete Elliott and Zoe Threadgold went to their respective homes to try for a bit of sleep. Terry would remain in police custody overnight, in the hopes that by morning he might decide to change his story.

It wasn't much of a hope, and time was running out; they were entitled to hold him for twenty-four hours without charging him, but after that he had to be released unless they had an overwhelmingly convincing reason to keep him.

And in the morning, if anything he was even more intransigent. He smoked incessantly, which did Pete Elliott no good, and his replies became more and more terse. No. Nothing. Never.

Eventually Elliott, who had not slept well and by now was feeling quite ill from the smoke, suggested that they take a break. Fresh air was what he needed. Zoe followed him out into the station car park and watched as he breathed in great gulps of air. On market day in Saxwell, virtually bumper-to-bumper with traffic, this was not exactly the purest of country air, but exhaust fumes were preferable to tar and nicotine.

Elliott looked at his watch. 'We haven't got long, Sergeant. Do you still think he's involved, or do you believe him?'

'Well, sir.' She gave the question her considered attention. 'I don't think he's going to change his story, whether we believe him or not. But I still don't believe it's a coincidence that the car was bought by someone calling herself Kim Rashe. It might not have been Kim, but it was someone who knew her, or else why would they have given her name and address?'

He rubbed his pounding temples with both hands. 'At the moment that car is the only evidence we've got, full stop. It ties Daisy Finch in with the dead man, but apart from Kim Rashe's name, there is nothing to link it – or them – to Terry. The dead man's hair, Daisy's hair, but not Terry's hair.'

'But there *was* a third person's hair,' Zoe reminded him.

'Yes, blond hair. Long blond hair. Definitely not Terry's. In case you hadn't noticed.'

She ignored the sarcasm. 'But what about Terry's wife, sir?'

'Terry's wife.' Elliott stopped rubbing his temples and looked at her. 'Delilah, isn't it? Are you suggesting that she might be involved? In abducting a child, in murder?' In spite of all he'd seen in his years as a police officer, he persisted in maintaining a romantic view of women.

'Well, sir. It's not impossible, is it? What about Cromwell Street?'

'Indeed.' He considered the implications; up till now it had never crossed his mind that more than one person, let alone a husband and wife, might be involved. But it *was* possible.

Again he looked at his watch and made a quick decision. 'I'd like you to go to Branlingham and talk to her.'

'On my own?' She'd been waiting for this moment, but eagerness was unexpectedly mingled with apprehension.

'You can handle it, Sergeant. While I have one last go at Terry. And you know what you're looking for.'

Hazel Croom had never been sick a day in her life, had never missed a day of teaching on account of illness. She considered illness a form of weakness, akin to moral laxity, and was certain that it could be conquered by force of will. 'It's all in your head,' was her favourite reprimand to the girls at school when they were silly enough to complain to her about cramps, colds, flu, or any other ailment.

Mother had been the same; strong as a horse she'd been, up until the day when, at 84, she had sat down in her chair to listen to the wireless and had died quietly and without fuss during the shipping forecast. She'd been a great example to Hazel, who hoped to follow in her footsteps.

None the less, Thursday morning found Hazel Croom at home rather than at school. Unaccustomed as she was to illness, she scarcely knew how to describe the pain that beset her. It wasn't concentrated in her head, though her head throbbed. No, it was a general sort of lassitude, an awareness that all was not well.

It had started, really, on Tuesday, when she'd come home from school, turned on the wireless, and heard the news about Daisy Finch's disappearance. How her heart had ached for Father Gervase, though she acknowledged to herself that perhaps it was all for the best; the girl would have been a great trial to Father Gervase as she grew older.

She had tried to ring Father Gervase, repeatedly, over the

past two days, but some snippy policewoman and that woman archdeacon had refused to put any of her calls through.

Hazel needed, badly, to speak to Father Gervase. Not only did she need to proffer her sympathy, but also she felt that it was time for him to be put into the picture about his wife and that decorator. Obviously Rosemary was at fault in Daisy's disappearance: if she'd been on time to collect Daisy at the school gates, none of this would have happened. Even young Tom had said so, in the *Daily Telegraph*, and Hazel believed everything that was printed in that venerable Tory organ. She thought that she knew why Rosemary had been late, and reckoned that Father Gervase ought to be told.

Elliott was taking another break from the smoke, this time in the corridor, when Zoe returned. She shook her head as she approached.

He felt a stab of disappointment. 'No good?'

'No good, sir.'

'What was she like, then?'

Zoe smiled grimly. 'A real bitch. Quite capable of murder, if you ask me. But her hair is black.'

'Damn.' He shook his head. 'Well, it was worth a try.'

'She wasn't very happy that we'd kept her husband in overnight,' Zoe added.

He sighed as he looked at his watch. 'Well, she'll soon have him back again.'

Sybil Rashe paid her usual Thursday morning visit to The Haven and Mildred Beazer. It seemed an age since she'd seen Milly; so much had happened since last week. There was the little girl's disappearance, and Terry's involvement as a star witness for the police. There was that murdered man. There was Kim's arrest, though Sybil was so deeply ashamed of her younger daughter that she didn't want to talk about that. (Kim's dad had always spoiled her, that was the trouble. Then that no-good Kev had come along, and this was the result.) There was Miss Valerie, who had so mysteriously asked her not to come yesterday. And there was the long-awaited issue of *Hello!* magazine, which had been almost forgotten amongst the other excitements of the past few days.

But at The Haven everything was reassuringly routine, business as usual. Coffee was laid out in the sun porch, and they settled down for the first part of the ritual.

Mildred held out the pack of cigarettes. 'Have one?'

'No, thanks. I shouldn't.'

'Oh, go on, Syb. One fag won't kill you.'

'All right, then. Just one.'

Sybil lit up and inhaled that first blissful hit of nicotine while she considered where to begin. Terry, she decided; that would be a good start, but she would have to work up to it a bit, lay the groundwork. 'Shame about that little girl that's gone missing,' she remarked. 'Poor little scrap, is what I say.'

'Dreadful, that.' Milly shook her head lugubriously, and shrugged her shoulders in a world-weary gesture which was intended to convey her conviction that, sad as it was, it was all part of the miserable world they now lived in. 'Still, there you are.'

Sybil tried to keep her tone casual. 'I suppose you know that our Terry has been right there at the centre of it all. The police's star witness, he is.'

'Is that a fact?'

'I can't tell you the half of it,' Sybil said. 'Why, they've come to the school to talk to him several times. He was the very first one on the scene, you know. Just like in *Inspector Morse.* They reckon he might have seen something significant.' Her imagination got the better of her and she began to embroider wildly. 'Why, he might have seen some nasty old man in a dirty raincoat, hanging round the school gates for the past week.'

Mildred wasn't really indifferent; she just didn't care to have Terry as the main topic of conversation for the morning. She had watched all of the news reports about Daisy Finch, and this was the first she'd heard about a man in a dirty raincoat. 'Did he, then? They haven't said anything about that on the news.'

'Well, no,' Sybil admitted. 'I didn't say he *did* see that. But he *might* have, if you know what I mean.'

'What *did* he see, then?'

'That's between him and the police,' Sybil stated self-right-eously. 'And I haven't asked. It wouldn't be right, would it, him leaking official-type information, like, to anyone else? Even his mum, when he knows that I would keep as silent as the grave. But mark my words, Milly. There's more to this than meets the eye.' She tapped the side of her nose.

Mildred allowed her friend to rattle along in this vein for a few minutes, singing the praises of her son while she savoured her fag. She was biding her time, waiting for an opening. Eventually one came, as Sybil concentrated on fin- ishing her cigarette, making the most of the last few precious puffs.

'I saw your Miss Valerie the other day,' Mildred announced.

'Did you, now?' That was not exactly earth-shattering news, in Sybil's book. After all, she saw Miss Valerie every week. And Miss Valerie *did* live locally, so there was every probability that she would be seen now and then, out and about.

'At the Tesco. Behind me in the check-out queue. She was buying . . .' And here Mildred paused and prolonged the sus- pense by lighting up a fresh fag. 'She was buying the sort of food that kiddies eat.'

Sybil frowned. 'Miss Valerie? You must be mistaken, Milly. She doesn't have kiddies – you know that.'

'Well, that's what I thought at first. I thought it must just be someone who *looked* like Miss Valerie.'

'Well, there, then,' she nodded. 'You've never seen Miss Valerie before. You could easily make a mistake like that.'

Mildred ignored this judgement. 'And she was buying some clothes, for a little girl.'

'Then it certainly wasn't Miss Valerie!'

'She said it was for her niece, who was visiting. Has Miss Valerie ever mentioned a niece to you, Syb?'

'No,' she stated baldly. 'You must be mistaken, Milly. It was just someone who looked a bit like Miss Valerie.'

'It was Miss Valerie, all right.' Mildred scrabbled among the things on the coffee table and came up with what she was looking for – the latest issue of *Hello!* magazine. 'I'd just about convinced myself that I was wrong. And then I saw this.' She pointed to the picture on the cover: Valerie Marler standing in front of Rose Cottage, with the Porsche in the drive. 'This was the woman I saw in Tesco, all right. I'm sure of it. And I had to stop at the kiosk to buy some fags and a lottery ticket, so I was still in the car park when she came out. This is the car she got into. There's no mistake, Syb.' She held the packet of cigarettes out to her friend. 'Have another?'

Sybil took one without a quibble or a word of thanks, and her fingers shook slightly as she lit it. 'Then I must be wrong,' she said in a tone that combined bravado with humility. 'She must have a niece, after all.'

Pete Elliott was called to the phone as he was winding up his final interview with Terry Rashe. Time had run out, and there was certainly no basis for charging Terry with any crime. So the interruption was a relief.

He went to his office to take the call. 'Inspector Elliott,' he said into the phone.

'Inspector? This is Ginger, from the George and Dragon. You gave me your card. You said to ring if I thought of anything else.'

'Yes?' he said with quickening interest.

'Only I thought of something else, Inspector. I should have remembered it last night, but things were a bit busy. And you caught me by surprise.'

'Yes?'

'That bloke, the one who came in on Monday night. The one you were asking me about. The thing is, Inspector, he paid by credit card.'

'He what?' Elliott expostulated. Zoe came into his office to see a slow grin spreading across his face as the implications sank in.

'He paid by credit card. I've found the voucher, and I can give you his name.'

Elliott reached for a pen and a bit of paper. 'Go ahead.'

'It's a company credit card, issued to GlobeSpan Publishing Limited. And the name on the card is Mr S Kelly. I thought you might like to know that,' he added. 'I thought it might help.'

'Oh, it will help, all right,' Elliott assured him. 'Thank you, Ginger. Thank you so much.'

He put the phone down and grinned jubilantly at Zoe, waving the scrap of paper.

Zoe made the next phone call, to the offices of GlobeSpan, and reported her findings to the inspector, her smile matching his. 'Shaun Kelly is his name,' she said. '*Was* his name. I talked to his boss.'

'His boss? Did he explain why the bloke hadn't been missed in the last few days? I mean, you would have thought—'

'The thing is, sir, he was sacked. On Monday. His boss wasn't half furious that he'd used the company credit card after that.'

'I suppose that explains why he wasn't missed. Did they say why he was sacked?'

She shook her head. 'Not really. Seems he was the publicist for Valerie Marler, and they weren't happy with his work. That's all he would say.'

'Valerie Marler. Should I know that name?'

Zoe smiled. 'Probably not, sir. She writes books mostly for women. Not really my cup of tea either, if you want to know the truth.'

'Well, well, well.' Elliott sat behind his desk and leaned back in the chair, grinning idiotically. His exhaustion of the last days, of the last hours, had evaporated. Thanks to Ginger, he could finally see a way forward. 'We can start tracing his background, of course. Talk to his work colleagues, his friends, his family.'

'He wasn't married, the boss said. His only family is in Ireland, or so he told everyone, and he kept himself to himself at work.'

This didn't dent Elliott's new-found enthusiasm; it merely channelled it in a different direction. 'We'll call a news conference,' he decided. 'Later this morning, as soon as we can arrange it. We'll announce that we've got a name for our dead bloke, and see if that brings in any more information. It's bound to, you know. And,' he added, as an afterthought, 'we may as well kill two birds with one stone, so to speak. While we've got the press here, we'll get the Finches out to do the grieving parent bit, and make a plea for the return of their daughter. Tug at the heart-strings of the public. It's shameless, I know, but it can't hurt. And it might help.'

'Superintendent Hardy won't like it,' Zoe predicted.

His reply was succinct; his smile never faltered. Pete Elliott was not a man given to vulgarity, which made it all the more effective on the rare occasions when he succumbed. 'Bugger Superintendent Hardy,' he said pleasantly.

On Thursday morning Valerie decided that she needed to go out. The idea of leaving Daisy behind, letting her out of her sight, even for an hour our two, was painful to her, but she accepted the necessity for it. Her previous shopping expedition had only been intended to get them through a day or two; now that Daisy was going to be here for good, there were many more things that she would have to buy. More food, more clothes, perhaps a few toys and books. She would probably need to go into Bury, rather than Saxwell.

Daisy's face crumpled when she told her. 'Can't I come with you, Auntie?' the girl begged.

'No, darling. No, you can't. And Samantha would be very lonely if you left her by herself.'

'But can't Samantha come too?'

'I'm afraid not.' It was going to have to be the television again, she realised. But it should be safe now. Daisy Finch's disappearance was old news. She carried the set through to Daisy's room, and got her settled watching the children's programmes. It was a wrench to leave her; Valerie stood for a long moment by the door, finally forcing herself to go. Just to be on the safe side, she locked the bedroom door behind her.

Sybil Rashe, for once, couldn't wait to leave The Haven. There were too many questions that needed answers, too many things that she didn't want Milly to speculate about.

Miss Valerie. Miss Valerie – and Milly had been sure, positive, that it *was* Miss Valerie – had been buying clothes for a little girl.

There had to be an answer, a simple explanation of what seemed an inexplicable fact. Though she'd said to Milly that perhaps Miss Valerie *did* have a niece, she was positive that it wasn't so; Miss Valerie was an only child. No brothers, no sisters. Therefore no nieces.

A godchild, then? Perhaps Milly had just misheard her. There had to be an explanation. Dear God, thought Sybil Rashe, though she was not well known for invoking the aid of the Almighty, please let there be an explanation.

When she got home she turned on the telly, thinking that there might be something on the noontime news about the missing girl.

In the event she got more than she'd bargained for. The news conference at the Saxwell police headquarters was being carried live on the local channel.

It was that nice policeman, the inspector, who had been here yesterday, Sybil recognised. He read out a prepared statement, not about the little girl but about some body that had been found in the woods. 'The body, which was found yesterday in a blue Metro, near Branlingham, has been identified as that of thirty-two-year-old Shaun Kelly, a London resident. Will anyone who has any information about or knowledge of Mr Kelly or the vehicle please contact us. Your call will be treated in strictest confidence.' An 0800 number flashed up on the screen, along with a shot of the car in question and the photofit drawing of Shaun Kelly.

The policeman went on to say that a connection had been established between the deceased Mr Kelly and the missing Daisy Finch, and the public's help was once again asked for. Then the camera panned from the podium to two people sitting behind an adjacent table.

It was the parents. Sybil's heart went out to them, the woman dry-eyed but with evidence of much crying in her puffy eyes and flushed cheeks, the man looking grave and sorrowful and dignified. The Vicar, he was, dressed in black with a dog collar round his neck. On the top of the table he held his wife's hand tightly in his own. The woman licked her lips, swallowed, and spoke into the microphone in a voice raw with weeping. 'Please. Please. If anyone knows anything about our little girl, please help us to get her back again. Our little Daisy.' She said a few more words, and the Vicar added a few as well, but Sybil couldn't bear to listen. She was overwhelmed with empathy for the parents; what if it had been her Terry who was missing? How could she bear it?

And there was something more, as well, at the back of her mind. She couldn't allow herself to think about it, but it wouldn't go away.

A few miles away, in Saxwell, Hal Phillips sat in front of the television set. He scarcely heard what DI Elliott said, so fixated was he on Rosie. She looked so sad; if only he could be there with her, if only he could comfort her.

If only, if only.

Mike Odum had been right: there was a connection between Daisy and the dead man. But what could the connection be? Had the man taken Daisy, killed her, then killed himself? It didn't bear thinking about. He hoped, fervently, that Rosie was not asking herself the same question, and coming up with the same answer.

Farther away still, in Letherfield, Hazel Croom watched the news, tucked up on the sofa. She didn't feel like reading, so she was occupying herself by watching, with horrid fascination, what passed for daytime entertainment on television. Mindless game shows, embarrassing talk shows, soap operas featuring banal dialogue spoken in impenetrable accents. And snippets of news, like oases in the desert.

It was Father Gervase who commanded her attention, of course. He looked so noble, so brave in his sorrow, just as she would have expected. His shoulders sloped pronouncedly, and his face was etched with new lines, but that only made him the dearer to her. Dear Father Gervase. How dreadful that he should be put through an ordeal like this.

The girl was probably dead by now, reasoned Hazel. Father Gervase would be devastated. But perhaps, she told herself yet again, it was for the best. What kind of a life could a mentally handicapped child like that look forward to?

But Daisy, very much alive, was also watching television. She was annoyed when the news came on, and got up to switch the channel.

Before she reached the set, though, her attention was riveted to the screen. Mummy and Daddy!

Mummy looked like she'd been crying. Daisy moved up close to the television, nearly pressing her face against her mother's flat image. Mummy was asking about her, saying how much they missed her and wanted her back home. And Daddy too.

Daisy's eyes filled with tears as the faces faded from the screen. 'Mummy!' she howled. 'I want Mummy!'

Sybil switched off the telly and went to her tiny kitchen, on such a different scale than the one at Rose Cottage, to make herself a bit of lunch. The unease that she'd felt earlier had not faded; it had, if anything, become stronger and more focused. Now there was more to fuel it than just the matter of the child.

Two other things that the nice policeman had said on the telly had struck a chord with her, and she could no longer deny to herself that there was cause for alarm. First was the matter of the dead man's name: Shaun Kelly, the policeman had said. Sybil didn't know anyone called Shaun, but she knew for a fact that Miss Valerie did. Once or twice she had answered the phone at Rose Cottage when Miss Valerie wasn't there, and it had been a man called Shaun with an Irish voice. 'Just tell Val that Shaun rang,' he'd said.

And when Miss Valerie had been so ill, just the other week, she had said things in delirium. Much of it had been unintelligible, but several times she'd called out in a frightened voice, 'No, Shaun! No! Don't hurt me!'

Those bruises, vivid purple on her face and body – the bruises that Sybil hadn't mentioned to a soul, not even to Milly.

Miss Valerie had known this Shaun, all right.

The other thing that worried her also dated back to Miss Valerie's illness. Miss Valerie had come in out of the rain, literally, and Sybil had sent her straight to bed. Later she'd worried about Miss Valerie's car; since she'd come home in such a state, perhaps she'd not put it away properly, in the garage. But the Porsche wasn't in the drive, so Sybil took it upon herself to check the garage.

The Porsche was in the double garage, without a drop of water on it. And next to it was a car that Sybil had never seen before, still wet with rain: a blue Metro.

Sybil didn't know what to do. It was unthinkable that Miss Valerie was involved in anything criminal, anything wrong. There must be an explanation. And yet . . .

She made a quick decision. Abandoning her half-eaten lunch – she wasn't hungry, anyway – Sybil set off for Rose Cottage.

There was no car in the drive, Sybil noted: either Miss Valerie was out or, more likely, the Porsche was in the garage, where Miss Valerie liked to keep it, safe from the weather or passing vandals.

The garage had windows to the side. Walking quickly and confidently, as though she had every right in the world to do so, Sybil went to the garage and peered into the window, cupping her hands on the glass to afford her a better view of the dim interior.

Dim as it was, there was no mistaking what was inside: nothing. Not a red Porsche, nor a blue Metro. Nothing at all.

Sybil went round the back of the garage to the back of Rose Cottage. She tapped on the back door; not surprisingly there was no reply. She got her key out and began to put it in the lock, then was paralysed by an attack of conscience. Whatever would Miss Valerie say if she knew she was snooping about, checking up on her? It was monstrous, outrageous. She could well lose her job over it. And yet . . . Still she hesitated; as she stood there, immobilised with indecision, she heard it. Faint but unmistakable – the sound of crying. Heartbroken crying, interspersed with shouted words. 'Mummy!' the voice howled. 'Mummy!'

She couldn't bear it – the poor little scrap. No matter what, she had to rescue her. Sybil slipped her key into the lock and turned the handle, but as she pushed the door in, there was yet another unmistakable sound: a car in the drive. In a panic, she pulled the door to, resecured the lock, and scuttled off behind the garage, where she stayed until she was sure that Miss Valerie had gone into the house.

Valerie's shopping had taken longer than she'd expected; she had so enjoyed choosing toys for Daisy, and buying pretty dresses, that she'd lost track of the time. Daisy would be getting hungry for some lunch, she thought, and drove a bit faster.

She heard the cries as she opened the door of Rose Cottage. The hairs at the back of her neck prickled; she ran up the stairs and unlocked the door of Daisy's room.

Daisy was on the bed, screaming. Valerie went to her and gathered her in her arms. The girl didn't resist, but her howls were unabated. 'Daisy, Daisy, darling,' Valerie crooned. 'Whatever is the matter, my darling?'

'Mummy!' Daisy shrieked. 'I want Mummy!'

Valerie's stomach knotted. 'But darling, you've got Auntie. Auntie will take care of you.'

'Mummy!'

Gradually, through the girl's tears, the story emerged: she had seen Mummy on television. Mummy missed her, Mummy wanted her back. And she wanted Mummy.

Her palms clammy, her heart pounding, Valerie hugged Daisy to her. She sat on the bed and held her, kissing the top of the girl's head and stroking the damp cheek. Still Daisy cried, still she sobbed for her mother.

Valerie took deep breaths. She had no choice; there was only one thing she could do now. It was the last thing she wanted to do, but she had no choice.

'Come on, then, Daisy,' she said tenderly, hiding her own deep sorrow. 'Let's go.'

Sybil made herself a cup of strong sweet tea and sat staring at it as it grew cold.

That girl, little Daisy Finch, was inside Rose Cottage. Sybil was certain of it. Miss Valerie had taken her, though it was beyond Sybil to understand why.

The real issue, though, was what she was going to do with this terrible knowledge. Sybil held the card that the policeman had given her and stared at it, running her finger round the edge. He had asked her to ring if she knew anything. She knew something, all right. But she couldn't possibly ring him.

She couldn't shop Miss Valerie to the police – she just couldn't. Miss Valerie trusted her. She couldn't betray that trust.

But the little girl . . .

If it had just been the dead man, that Shaun, it wouldn't have been a problem. Miss Valerie had known him; she might even have killed him. But Sybil had seen the bruises. She knew that he deserved what he'd got, that death was probably too good for him, and that the world was better off without him. There was no temptation to help the police to solve his murder.

The little girl was a different matter. She was still alive. She was wanting her mummy. And oh, the heart-wrenching appeal that her mother had made! If anyone can help, she'd said. Sybil knew that she could help, that she had it within her power to restore Daisy Finch to her parents.

But it meant shopping Miss Valerie, betraying someone who had never shown her anything but kindness. Her Miss Valerie. She just couldn't. And surely the girl wasn't in danger. Miss Valerie wouldn't hurt her.

If only she could ask someone's advice, someone who knew what was at stake.

Terry, Sybil thought suddenly. She would ask Terry. He would know what to do; he was in on the police investigation, the police trusted him and had probably told him things about the case that the general public didn't know. Why, they might be on the brink of finding Daisy Finch without any help from her or from anyone else. Terry would be able to set her mind at rest.

She would ask Terry.

Hazel Croom had made up her mind: she was going to Branlingham. Painful as it would be for Father Gervase to hear the truth about that woman he'd married, it would be best for him in the long run, and it should be put off no longer.

But she couldn't very well go empty-handed. Father Gervase had always liked her sponge cakes, had often complimented her on the lightness of them. Rosemary's sponge cakes were like rock in comparison, and the gift of a sponge cake would be useful in pointing up Rosemary's deficiency in that area, as in so many other things.

There wasn't really time to make one from scratch, but Hazel's freezer was well stocked against such eventualities. She selected one and removed it; by the time she got to Branlingham, it would be thawed out.

Sybil didn't want to wait until Terry got home from work to talk to him, and she always preferred to avoid Delilah anyway. She picked up the phone, dialled the number for Branlingham Primary School, and asked for her son.

The secretary who answered was cool and distinctly unhelpful. Mr Rashe was not there. He had not reported to work that morning, he had not rung to say that he was ill. She did not, in fact, know where he was.

Baffled, Sybil knew that she now had no choice but to ring his home, and talk to Delilah if needs be.

There had never been any love lost between the two Mrs Rashes, Sybil and her daughter-in-law. Sybil had from the beginning felt that Delilah was unworthy of her son, that she had lured him away from his family with her siren call and got her claws stuck into him well and truly, and made him miserable ever since. She was a sluttish housekeeper; she was no better than she should be. Delilah, for her part, found Sybil Rashe's meddling and interfering in her family's lives to be insupportable. Most of the time they just avoided and ignored each other. Occasionally they could not avert contact, and the resulting confrontations were not a pretty sight.

Sybil rang the number, and Delilah answered. 'Is Terry there?' the elder Mrs Rashe demanded.

Delilah's voice was scornful. 'He's here, all right, but I'm not calling him to the phone.'

'But I need to talk to him. It's important.'

They went back and forth in this vein for several moments, Sybil insisting and Delilah refusing. They were a match for each other, but in the end Sybil prevailed, at least to the extent of prying loose some further information.

'If you must know,' Delilah said at last, 'he's in bed. Asleep.'

'Is he ill, then?'

'No, he's not ill. He just had a long night at the police station, is all. He only just came back from there this morning.'

Sybil's chest swelled with pride: her Terry, so conscientiously helping the police that he gave up a night of sleep in his own bed to do so. 'Well, you ought to be proud of him, like I am,' she lectured. 'Being the police's star witness, and all. He's doing his civic duty, just like I brought him up to do.'

'Civic duty!' Delilah snorted in derision. 'Is that what you think?' Her voice changed as she let loose. 'Listen, you stupid old cow. Your precious son isn't their star witness – he's their chief suspect. The police think that Terry took that little girl, then killed her, and they're not going to let go until they force a confession out of him. *That's* what your precious son has been up to, so I hope you're happy!'

The phone went dead as Delilah slammed it down; Sybil stared at the silent instrument in her hand with unseeing eyes.

The police thought that Terry had killed Daisy Finch. But that was absurd, impossible. Terry wouldn't, *couldn't* do such a thing. And besides, Daisy Finch was still alive; Sybil knew it for a fact.

No longer was Miss Valerie an issue; she was irrelevant. And the safety of Daisy Finch, the importance of restoring her to her sorrowing parents, was a mere detail. Terry was everything. The maternal instinct in Sybil, always strong, swelled to a magnificent crescendo. She was a mother lion, protecting her cub from marauding beasts. She was a mother bird, defending her chick with fearless bravery, confronting and vanquishing those who would harm him.

Terry, her son, her boy, had been unjustly accused. And she alone could save him.

The card the policeman had given her was still on her lap; once again she picked up the phone. Her hands trembled as she dialled the number, but inwardly she was calm, almost exaltant. She was going to save Terry.

It was market day in Saxwell. Even by mid afternoon it was still crowded, bustling with shoppers and congested with traffic. Everyone was intent on their own errands; no one's head turned to look at the red Porsche as it inched through the traffic into the town centre.

Daisy, dressed once again in her pink-and-white-striped dress, squeezed the yellow kitten tightly in her arms in the passenger seat. Bewildered by the rapid turn of events, she had stopped crying and watched out of the window.

In the driver's seat, Valerie kept her emotions under control by force of will. She concentrated on driving, on the traffic, and would not allow herself to think about Daisy. Neither of them spoke.

There was a double yellow line in front of the police station. Valerie pulled the Porsche up to the kerb, unfastened Daisy's seat belt, then leaned across the girl and opened the door. 'Go inside,' she said in a calm voice. 'Tell them who you are.'

Now that it had come to this, Daisy hesitated; she turned to Valerie. 'Auntie . . .'

'Go. Just go.' Valerie gave her a little shove.

Daisy got out of the car, still clutching the kitten, and stood uncertainly on the kerb, watching as Valerie shut the car door and pulled the Porsche out into traffic.

Valerie didn't look back.

Chapter 24

Learning the identity of the body was the first big hurdle in the murder investigation. Now the detectives could get on with the business of tracking down the killer of the man they knew to have been Shaun Kelly.

This, inevitably, was going to involve going to London to interview his associates there – work colleagues, neighbours, friends – as well as searching his flat in Earl's Court for any clues that might be found there. Pete Elliott was not looking forward to going to London; the capital city made him nervous, and being off his own patch was always an unsettling experience for him. Zoe Threadgold, on the other hand, could hardly wait.

But Pete Elliott, not Zoe, was in charge of the investigation, so things would be done in his time and at his pace. They would go to London, but not just yet. There were still loose ends to be tied up here in Saxwell.

Not least among those loose ends was the connection between the dead man and the missing child, that tenuous link of the hairs in the blue Metro. Daisy Finch still obsessed Elliott in a way that Shaun Kelly never had, and he was loath to leave Saxwell until he had some clue about what had happened to her, Superintendent Hardy notwithstanding.

The parents' emotional plea at the news conference had elicited a flurry of phone calls to the special number, many of them reporting sightings of the girl. As the first order of business Elliott was determined to work his way through the slips of paper on which these calls had been recorded.

He and Zoe, who was rather successfully curbing her impatience to get to London, sat in his office sorting through the slips; they could not afford to ignore them out of hand, or treat them as jokes. There were, however, quite a number of them that could go straight into the bin; Elliott was amazed at how many people had claimed to have seen Daisy Finch with the ginger-haired Irishman on Tuesday, by which time the police, if not the public, knew he was already dead. According to the slips of paper, the two of them had been seen on a ferry to Ireland, in a departure lounge at Heathrow airport, visiting the Tower of London, staying at a bed-and-breakfast in the Highlands of Scotland, and on the big wheel at Blackpool, as well as a number of more prosaic locations.

And there were an equal number of reported sightings of Daisy on her own. Elliott and Zoe sat on opposite sides of his desk and read them out to each other: she'd been seen eating candyfloss on Brighton pier and ice cream on the beach at Skegness; she'd been in Harrods' toy department and in Newcastle Cathedral. These could not be so easily ignored, though none of them sounded very promising.

'To tell you the truth, Sergeant,' Elliott admitted after they'd been through the lot, 'I don't think that Daisy Finch ever left Suffolk. She probably never got any further than Branlingham.'

'Are you saying, sir, that you think she's dead?'

He rubbed bleary eyes and sighed. 'I don't want to believe it. There's always a chance that she's still alive.'

'But where, sir?'

'Damned if I know. And with Terry Rashe such a wash-out, I don't know who can tell us,' Elliott confessed. 'I suspect that Shaun Kelly could have told us, but it's a bit late for that.'

Zoe was more interested in the dead man than she was in Daisy Finch, and she welcomed the shift of subject. She leaned across the desk. 'Listen, sir. We've been wondering about what Shaun Kelly was doing in Branlingham, eating at the George and Dragon and getting himself killed somewhere in the vicinity, when he lived and worked in London.'

'Yes?'

'I've been thinking about that,' she said. 'And I've remembered something. That bloke at GlobeSpan, his boss, said that he was the publicist for Valerie Marler.'

'Yes, that's right,' Elliott agreed. 'And you said that she writes women's books.'

'Well, sir, I think that she lives somewhere round here.'

'Ah.' He looked interested. 'Who would know about that, then?'

'Becky, who answers the phones,' was the prompt reply. 'She's always reading Valerie Marler's books, and trying to get me to read them. I'm sure she mentioned that she lives round here.'

Elliott sat up in his chair. 'Go and ask her, then. And ask her,' he added as a sudden inspiration, 'if Valerie Marler has blond hair.'

While she was gone he tidied the slips of paper on his desk into neat piles as his mind leapt ahead to the possibilities. If Shaun Kelly had been in the area to visit Valerie Marler . . .

Zoe was back in a few minutes, waving a magazine, her face alight with excitement. 'Look at this, sir!' She plopped it down on his desk in front of him. 'Becky had this with her – Valerie Marler at home, in Rose Cottage, Elmsford.'

The cover of *Hello!* magazine stared up at him; he stated the obvious. 'And she's blonde, all right.'

She folded her arms across her chest and waited. But Elliott seemed transfixed, staring at the photo. 'What is it, sir? Do you know her?'

Elliott exhaled on a long breath and said softly, 'No, but I wish I did. I think I'm in love. Don't you think she's the most beautiful thing you've ever seen?' He remembered, then, that Zoe was rumoured to be a lesbian, and what was meant as a rhetorical question took on new meaning; he blushed in chagrin at his *faux pas*.

Zoe chose to ignore his embarrassment as well as his question. 'Well, sir. Don't you think we should go and talk with her?'

He grinned and recovered himself. 'Definitely, Sergeant. As they say in the old movies, "There's not a moment to lose." Let's go.'

But as he rose from his desk the phone rang. He picked it up. 'Inspector Elliott.'

Zoe waited while he conducted a cryptic conversation with the person on the other end. It was a short conversation; as he put the phone down he looked up at her with his eyebrows raised.

'I'm afraid that the delectable Miss Marler will have to wait for a few more minutes,' he announced regretfully. 'That was Mrs Rashe – Terry's mum.'

'You gave her your card,' Zoe recalled. 'What did she want?'

'She wants me to come and see her. Says she's got some important information that she couldn't tell me over the phone.'

Zoe looked sceptical. 'It's probably nothing, sir.'

'Probably,' he agreed. 'But we can't afford to ignore her, whatever it is. And besides, she lives in Elmsford as well, so we can kill two birds with one stone. After we see her, we can call on Valerie Marler.'

He was already on his way out of the door; Zoe followed.

In the corridor, intent on the matter at hand, they walked right past the little girl. But the girl called after them. 'Hello,' she said.

Elliott turned and looked at her. His head was filled with visions of blond loveliness, and it took him a moment to focus on the small bespectacled face, the dark hair in plaits, the candy-striped dress.

'Hello,' the little girl repeated. 'I'm Daisy Finch.'

'Of course you are!' Elliott went down on his knees to embrace her, and was surprised to discover that he was crying.

At Branlingham Vicarage, Margaret was wondering how long this stasis could continue.

On Thursday afternoon, after the flurry of activity surrounding the morning's news conference had subsided, there was time for reflection. Rosemary, exhausted beyond exhaustion by the trauma of the news conference, had fallen into a troubled doze on the sofa, and Gervase was asleep in the chair. Margaret sat beside Rosemary, and at last allowed herself to think about the strange twist of fate that had brought her here. She was not unconscious of the irony of the situation – the fact that it was Rosemary Finch to whom she was devoting her attention. Even in Rosemary's fragile state, Margaret sensed a strength in her that was admirable and attractive, a core of integrity, and found herself wishing that they could have been spending time together under different circumstances. They might even be friends, she thought. She had always liked Rosemary Finch, from their first meeting; now she began to understand what Hal had seen to love in this outwardly unprepossessing woman.

That didn't excuse him, of course. When at last she allowed Hal to creep into her thoughts, like a finger probing an unhealed wound, it was still with extreme bitterness. Oddly, perhaps, she blamed Rosemary not at all for what had happened. She was just as much a victim of Hal as Margaret herself was, and that created a bond between them, even if Rosemary was unaware of it.

And Gervase. She and Gervase were alike in many ways, Margaret reflected. Or at least they had something in common: they had both thought that they understood what their marriages were about, and they had both been proven painfully wrong. They'd both imagined themselves to be walking on solid ground, only to find themselves struggling in quicksand.

For Gervase, with any luck, it might not be too late.

For her, and Hal, she wasn't sure.

How much longer could she avoid thinking about Hal? How much . . .

The doorbell rang.

Rosemary stirred and opened reddened eyes in which hope mingled with fear; it was the same each time the phone or the doorbell went. Gervase woke as well.

'I'll answer it,' said Margaret, and went into the hall. She returned just a moment later. 'It's Miss Croom,' she said, watching Rosemary's face fall. 'She's brought a cake, and she insists on seeing Gervase – she says that she won't go till she's seen him.'

Gervase sighed heavily and got to his feet. 'I'd better see her, then.'

Hazel was standing in the entrance hall, looking about her at the transformation the decorator had wrought. She smiled at the sight of Gervase coming towards her. 'Father Gervase!'

'Hazel. How kind of you to come,' he said with every evidence of sincerity.

'I've brought you a cake. One of my sponges – I know how you've always enjoyed them.' She proffered the plate.

'Doubly kind.' He hesitated for a moment, then gestured towards the kitchen. 'Shall we take it through? And I'll put the kettle on.'

Triumphantly she followed him; it was all going according to plan.

In the kitchen, he filled the kettle, switched it on, then took the cake from her and transferred it to one of their plates.

'First of all,' Hazel said, beginning a speech she'd been rehearsing in the car all the way from Letherfield, 'I want to tell you, Father Gervase, how sorry I am about poor Daisy.'

He inclined his head. 'Thank you. The waiting, and the not knowing, have been very difficult.'

'But perhaps, in time, you will be able to accept that it's all for the best,' Hazel continued. '"God moves in a mysterious way, his wonders to perform."'

'I don't know what you mean,' said Gervase.

'Oh, you know. Daisy being handicapped,' she floundered. 'She would never have had any sort of a normal life.'

Gervase was very still. 'You are assuming that Daisy is dead?'

'Well, she must be, mustn't she? It's all very sad, of course, and as you say, the not knowing . . .'

He suppressed an urge to grab the woman by the scruff of her neck and toss her out of his house, but he masked his anger by turning and fiddling with the tea things. He was not – had never been – a man given to violent impulses; the urge he had to pick up the silver cake knife and assault her with it shocked him, almost as much as it would have shocked Hazel had he given in to it.

Faced with Father Gervase's back, Hazel gained courage and went on with her speech. 'And if this has shown you one thing, Father, it must be that Rosemary was totally unsuitable as a mother. She should never have had a child.'

Gervase spun round, startling her with the intensity of his

expression and his voice. 'What an outrageous thing to say!'

Hazel quailed, but told herself that she hadn't really expected him to take it well. When he'd heard all she had to say, and had time to think about it, of course, things would be different. 'It *was* her fault that Daisy went missing,' she pointed out.

'And who told you that?' he challenged.

'It was in the papers. Even Tom said it, in the *Daily Telegraph*.'

Distantly, Gervase heard the phone ringing, or perhaps it was just in his head. His voice took on the same note of cold, implacable fury as when he'd spoken to Tom. 'That is my wife you are talking about,' he said. 'If you have come into my home to insult her, you can leave right now.'

'I'm only doing my duty,' Hazel said, standing her ground. 'You need to be told, if you can't see it for yourself, just what sort of woman you've married.'

The kitchen door burst open and Rosemary flew in, her face alight. 'They've found Daisy!' she cried, and the expression on her face prefigured the rest of the story. 'She's alive, she's well! And she's on her way home right now!'

'Thank God,' said Gervase quietly, as ten years dropped from his face. For him, the words were not just a figure of speech.

Hazel was forgotten; they were not even aware that she was still there. Her moment had come and passed, and she had not accomplished her mission. She was surplus to requirements; as an ecstatic Rosemary and Gervase embraced in the middle of the kitchen, she retraced her steps to the front door and back to her car.

'How did they find her? Where has she been?' Gervase wanted to know, leading Rosemary by the hand to the front of the house to wait for her.

'They didn't say.' Rosemary stood on tiptoe, straining for a glimpse of the police car. 'Just that she was alive and unharmed. I always knew she was still alive,' she added, her eyes behind her spectacles damp with excitement. 'I'm her mother – I would have known if she was dead.' She spotted the police car as it came up Church End and sped towards the front door.

They were both in the drive as the car door opened and Daisy emerged. The girl was cradling a small ball of yellow fluff. 'Her name is Samantha,' said Daisy. 'Can I keep her, Mummy?'

'Oh, my darling,' Rosemary cried, gathering child and kitten into her arms in a fierce, joyful hug. 'Oh, Daisy, of course you can keep her.'

She was no longer needed at Branlingham Vicarage, Margaret realised. Daisy was back, the police had departed, the family was whole again, and it was time for her to go home.

Time to face Hal.

She turned her thoughts towards him, painfully, as she drove back towards Saxwell. How could she face him? How could she bear it?

What if, she asked herself suddenly, it had not been Hal but some other man who had come to her in her role as a priest, in the confessional perhaps, and told her the story that Hal had told? How would she have reacted; what would she have said?

That cast a different light on matters, Margaret admitted to herself.

'You can't help the way you feel. You can only help what you do about it.' She had used words very like those when counselling troubled parishioners, and they applied in this situation. Painful as it was to contemplate, Hal couldn't help loving Rosemary Finch. And what he had done about it . . .

He had done nothing dishonourable. The opportunity had been there, presumably, and he had not availed himself of it.

He had been faced with a choice, and he had made the right choice. Done the right thing, the decent thing. And he had not told his wife, because he didn't want to hurt her. Because what had happened was now irrelevant, and he knew it would cause her pain.

If it had been any man but Hal, she would have reacted quite differently.

That gave her pause, and so did her next thought.

Was she completely blameless in what had happened? Had she been guilty of neglecting Hal, just as she had suggested that Gervase neglected Rosemary? In the past few weeks, perhaps so. Perhaps she had taken him for granted. Or, far worse, failed to take him seriously. Just as, during those first years of their marriage, he had failed to take *her* seriously. The tables had been turned comprehensively; she could now treat him as a decorative appendage to her life, as he had previously done to her. In her mind, and in the way she treated him, she had trivialised him, domesticated him. Good in the kitchen, even better in the bedroom: 'Every arch-deacon should have a wife.'

And Hal's newly revealed manipulativeness, the way he used his smile and his good looks: surely she had been complicit in that as well, encouraging him because she enjoyed having a husband whom other women lusted after?

But this thing with Rosemary Finch hadn't been about sex. As Margaret had apprehended from the beginning, it was much more serious than that. What had Rosemary offered him, on an emotional level, that she had not? Had *she* taken him seriously? There was no peace, no comfort, in thoughts like that.

'If we say that we have no sin, we deceive ourselves, and the truth is not in us.'

No, Margaret was by no means without blame, and the truth of that hurt her almost as much as the knowledge of Hal's emotional infidelity.

But she was too tired to think about it all just yet. Exhaustion, kept at bay till now by the necessity to be strong, hit her as she neared Saxwell. By the time she reached The Archdeaconry, she wanted nothing but her bed, and oblivion.

Hal had heard the car in the drive, and was waiting as she came through the front door.

'Daisy is safe,' she said before he could speak. 'She's home now. She's absolutely fine.'

His body sagged and he covered his face with his hands. 'Oh, thank God.'

Margaret regarded him in a detached sort of way, almost as if she were meeting him for the first time. A handsome man, yes, but one with far more complexity to him than that. Not trivial. 'You really care about Daisy, don't you?'

'Yes. Oh, yes.' It was obviously sincere and heartfelt, but he couldn't resist adding, with a sidelong look at his wife as he dropped his hands, 'Does that make things any better?'

She started up the stairs. 'No, I don't think so,' she said in a considered tone. 'On the whole, I think it makes things rather worse.'

He followed her to the top of the stairs, to the door of the bedroom.

'I'm going to bed,' Margaret stated.

'Meg . . .' he said, stretching out his hand. 'Listen . . .'

She hesitated for only an instant, a single heartbeat; caught unawares, he had insufficient time to press his advantage.

'No.' With that terse syllable she closed the door in his face. Not now. Not yet.

Sybil had nearly given up hope that the police would come. She waited at the door as they drove up, and there was no question of them having to wheedle any information out of her; she was bursting to tell them.

Terry was innocent. She was sure of that, she could prove it.

They let her have her say, not bothering to tell her that as far as they were concerned, Terry as a suspect was ancient history.

First she told them of her visit to Rose Cottage, leaving out the reasons why she had suspected Miss Valerie in the first place so as not to give Milly any of the credit. She had heard a child crying, she said, crying for its mother. If they cared to go along to Rose Cottage, Sybil was sure that they would find Daisy Finch there.

There was more. That Shaun Kelly, she said. She was positive that Miss Valerie had known him. She'd never *seen* him at Rose Cottage, admittedly, but she had her reasons for thinking that he'd been there.

And Miss Valerie had had a blue Metro, hidden in her garage. That was one thing Sybil *had* seen, and could swear to.

They thanked her as they left.

'And you won't be bothering Terry any more?' she demanded.

Elliott reassured her with a straight face. 'No, we won't be bothering Terry.'

Sybil nodded, satisfied.

As a substitute for thirty pieces of silver, it had not cost the police very dear.

Elliott was excited by what Sybil Rashe had told them. It fitted in perfectly with Daisy's story, coaxed out of her in the car on the way between Saxwell and Branlingham. She had been staying with Auntie, she said. Auntie was a pretty lady with yellow hair. Auntie had collected her from school that day –

she wasn't sure which day, she'd long since lost track of time. Auntie had taken her to her house in a blue car. Auntie had been kind to her, had let her keep Samantha and had told her stories. Auntie hadn't hurt her, not at all, and she hadn't been out of Auntie's house. She didn't know where Auntie's house was. She had seen Mummy and Daddy on the telly, and told Auntie that she wanted to go home. That was when Auntie had taken her to the police station, in a red car.

'I reckon we ought to go by Rose Cottage right now, and see what Miss Valerie Marler has to say for herself,' he suggested with an ironic wink. 'Since we're in the neighbourhood.'

Elliott had of course seen photos of Valerie Marler, but no photograph could have prepared him for the impact of her in person as she opened the door to them. The cloud of fair hair, the lustrous blue eyes; he was dazzled, almost befuddled, by her beauty.

Showing his warrant card, he identified himself and asked if they might come in and ask her a few questions.

'Yes, of course,' she said pleasantly.

She led them through to her sitting room. Valerie had already swept away every trace of Daisy from Rose Cottage, just as she had once swept every trace of Ben and Jenny from her life. Clothes, toys, books, food, even the cat tray and cat food: all had been bundled into bin-liners and taken to the nearest tip. Zoe's head swivelled round as she searched for evidence that the girl had been at Rose Cottage; there was nothing.

The questions were indeed few. 'I believe,' said Elliott, 'that you have been acquainted with a Mr Shaun Kelly.'

'He's my publicist. Or at least he *was*. I understand that he's been sacked.'

'And when did you last see Mr Kelly?'

She wrinkled her brow, as if trying hard to remember.

'Several weeks ago, it must have been. The day that *Hello!* magazine came for a photo shoot. Mr Kelly came along as well, to supervise.'

'You didn't see him this week, Miss Marler? Say, on Monday?'

Again she creased her brow, and shook her head. 'No. Certainly not.'

'What was your relationship with Mr Kelly?' Zoe interposed, ignoring Elliott's frown in her direction.

'I told you. He was my publicist.'

'Are you aware that Shaun Kelly is dead?' Zoe asked bluntly.

Valerie Marler's brows shot up. 'Oh, no. I hadn't heard. Poor Shaun. Did he kill himself, then? He must have been very upset about getting the sack – his job meant a great deal to him.'

'He was murdered,' Zoe told her.

'Oh, dear.'

Elliott looked daggers at his sergeant. 'Thank you, Miss Marler, for your time,' he said, getting up to go. 'You've been most helpful.'

'Not at all, Inspector.' She inclined her head serenely, and favoured him with a smile.

But Zoe couldn't resist asking another question. 'Miss Marler, do you own a dark blue Metro?'

Valerie's eyes widened. 'Why, no. My car is a Porsche. Red. You can look in the garage, if you like.'

'Thank you,' Elliott reiterated. 'That won't be necessary.'

She had done it. She had killed him. Elliott was convinced of that, in spite of the performance she was putting on for their benefit. And the red Porsche – that thought led straight to Daisy. 'What can you tell us about Daisy Finch?' he asked with what seemed an abrupt change of subject.

There was a fraction of a pause. 'Daisy Finch? Isn't she the little girl who's been missing?'

She was as cool as ever, but there was something indefinably different in her manner. Elliott looked at her intently, saying nothing, and after a moment she raised her eyes to meet his. What he saw, in the split second before she dropped them again, shocked him, and moved him.

Behind those beautiful blue eyes, he apprehended in an instant of shattering empathy, was someone who was frightened and needy. A lost child. Bereft, grieving. She had taken Daisy Finch, and she had given her up. She had loved Daisy – he was as sure of that, somehow, as he was sure that she had taken her. What had it cost her to surrender her?

All of this flashed through his mind in an instant, as he weighed up what to do about it, what to say next.

Zoe spoke first, aggressively. 'You know very well who Daisy Finch is.'

'Perhaps, Miss Marler,' said Elliott, 'you would be good enough to come to the station with us.'

She raised her chin to a defiant angle and looked at him challengingly; still he saw only the lost child behind her eyes, and it wrenched him far more than her unattainable beauty had done. 'Are you arresting me, then?'

Elliott chose his words carefully. 'No, I'm asking you to come in and answer a few questions.'

'I don't have to come, then,' she stated.

He might have expected that she would know that; she was an intelligent and educated woman. Fortunately for the police, few people ever realise that, unless arrested, they cannot be compelled to accompany the police. 'No, you don't have to come,' he acknowledged.

The look that Zoe fixed on him indicated very clearly that she wanted him to arrest Valerie Marler. He could have done so, but something held him back. He tried to explain it to himself: they had no evidence to tie her, definitively, to the murder. At this point it was all circumstantial. She *had* done it – the murder, and the abduction of Daisy Finch. Of that Elliott was sure. But he was still very far from being able to prove it, and she certainly wasn't about to confess. There was no point in rushing things, just for the sake of making a quick arrest. Valerie Marler was not a common or garden criminal, a menace to society at large; they could afford to wait and take it slowly.

'We will be back,' he promised. 'With a search warrant, and rather more questions. Unless . . .'

'Yes.' She looked at him levelly, without flinching; he forced himself to turn and go to the door.

Zoe followed him to the car, scowling. 'Why didn't you arrest her?' she demanded as soon as they were in the car. 'We know she took Daisy Finch. And she probably murdered that bloke as well. Why were you so easy on her?'

Because of that lost child he'd seen behind her eyes, he acknowledged to himself. But he knew that wouldn't cut much ice with Zoe. 'There's plenty of time for all of that,' he said. 'I prefer to take it slowly – get a search warrant, go over the house, find some hard forensic evidence. We can't just drag her off to gaol. Can't you see that she's not the sort of woman who can be easily intimidated? She's no Terry Rashe. She's intelligent, articulate—'

'And drop-dead gorgeous,' Zoe added cynically. God, what a pillock he is, she said to herself. I hope he knows what he's doing.

Thinking again about what he'd seen in that last level gaze, Elliott wasn't so sure that he did know what he was doing. He could get into a great deal of hot water with Superintendent Hardy over the decision he'd just taken. But right or wrong, he wasn't sorry; in some obscure way, he felt that he owed it to her. Because, whatever else she had done, Valerie Marler had loved Daisy Finch.

★

It wasn't until much later, after Daisy had been tucked into bed at last, that Gervase and Rosemary had an opportunity to talk. They sat at the kitchen table with cups of cocoa, until he screwed up his courage to say to her what he needed to say.

'I've had a lot of time to think about things, over the past few days,' he began. 'And I owe you such an enormous apology, my dear.'

Rosemary blinked at him, uncomprehending.

'It's not easy for me to say this,' he went on. 'But I'm afraid that I've been awfully stupid. I've taken you for granted, and put other things – other unimportant things – ahead of you. The Church is important, of course, but you and Daisy mean everything to me. I realised, too, that I'm not very good at telling you how much I love you. And this week, when Daisy was gone and you seemed so far away from me as well, when I thought that I would never be able to tell you, I couldn't bear it.'

'But what about Laura?' Rosemary said.

'Laura?' he echoed blankly. 'What about her?'

'You loved her so much. She was so beautiful. You were so happy together. And when she died, the grief almost killed you as well.'

Gervase stared at his wife. 'Is that what you think?' he said slowly.

'Of course. Hazel told me. Everyone knows how you felt about Laura.'

'You're wrong. Hazel is wrong. Everyone is wrong, if that's what they think.' He told her the truth, then: that it was guilt, not grief, that had assailed him at Laura's death. That Laura's outward beauty had masked a heart as cold as ice. That he and Laura had never been happy. That Rosemary's arrival in his life had been like a burst of sunshine, the best thing that had ever happened to him. That he could not imagine his life without her.

By now she was crying. 'But why didn't you ever tell me?'

'I thought you knew. Why didn't you ever ask?' he countered.

'I didn't want to upset you by reminding you about her. And I didn't want to hear you compare me to her, to force you to admit that you didn't really love me, that you only married me because you needed a wife.'

He was crying, too, and laughing at the same time. 'Oh, Rosemary. Is that really what you've thought all these years?'

She nodded.

'Then you've been very silly,' he declared. 'We've *both* been very silly, Rosie.'

'Thank God,' she said quietly, squeezing his hand, 'it's not too late.'